Ocean of Fear
Faith in the Parks, Book 3

J. Carol Nemeth

Sign up for my newsletter at www.jcarolnemeth.com/ and receive a free short story.

Dedication

I would like to dedicate this book to the memory of my father, the Rev. James W. Pruitt and to my mother, Mary Sue Amick Pruitt. My parents instilled in my siblings and me the love of camping and the outdoors at an early age. I still remember our first camping trip in an old canvas army tent that closed by tying long strings at the door, and it had no floor. We slept on old army cots. I must have been three or four years old. We soon graduated to one with a floor and a zippered door where creepy crawlies were encouraged to stay out. My parents introduced us to the national parks and monuments as well as state parks, and we traveled from the mountains to the coast as often as we could. We climbed lighthouses, descended into caves, swam in the ocean, visited presidents (homes), and saw where man took flight to name only a few places. Thank you, Mama and Daddy, for spreading our wings and giving us the love of travel!

Acknowledgements

Just as in my novella A Beacon of Love: Prequel to Ocean of Fear, I did a lot of research for this novel, Ocean of Fear, Faith in the Parks, Book 3. While doing that research my husband, Mark, and I drove down to Cape Hatteras and checked out various museums, libraries, bait shops, books stores, wherever anyone sent us to ask questions. A few of the helpful folks we met in our journey along Cape Hatteras were Helen Hudson and Sherry Hesse, both librarians at the Hatteras Branch of the Dare County Library in Hatteras Village, NC as well as Tama Creef and Stewart Parks at the Outer Banks History Center in Manteo, NC. Thanks to each of you for your time and for your help. I came away with more information than I could use in both books, but I had what I needed. Thanks again. Who knows when the rest may come in handy?

I would also like to express my gratitude to Jamie McDavid, the young woman on the cover of this book. She makes an excellent Ruth Campbell. Jamie and her husband are friends of my daughter, Jennifer, and son-in-law, Flint. She serves in the West Virginia Air National Guard. Thank you for your service to our country, Jamie.

To my publisher, Cynthia Hickey, thank you for another beautiful cover. Spot on with the tension, and it goes so well with the title. Perfect for a romantic suspense!

And last but never least, my gratitude and my heart belong to my husband. Mark drove me to Cape Hatteras September before last in the RV, and an hour from Oregon Inlet Bridge we were waylaid by Hurricane Maria. We had to wait it out in Washington, N.C. while she battered the coast. When she finally scooted out to sea, we headed to the Cape where operation cleanup was in progress. Mark took me everywhere I wanted to go to research. We parked the RV in a campground and drove the car for miles up and down the coastline to libraries, a history center, book stores, museums and bait shops. Anywhere folks sent us for information, Mark drove me. Thank you, sweetheart, for your giving heart and for your patience. We had a lot of fun, didn't we!

Psalm 56:11

In God have I put my trust: I will not be afraid what man can do unto me.

Somewhere off the coast of Cape Hatteras, NC
August 10, 1990

Prologue

P retty exciting, isn't it, Mr. Amato?" Tom Barnett, the head of the salvage operation halted beside the elderly man on the boat deck. He removed his hard hat, swiped the sweat from his forehead then replaced it. "Surely they've found something this time."

Howard Amato, his thick white hair blowing in the strong ocean wind, watched as the yellow two-man submersible surfaced in the choppy Atlantic waters. He watched as the crane operator expertly guided the long hydraulic arm across the heaving deck of the salvage ship. He was paying the man a lot of money to perform his duty. As a matter of fact, he was paying an astronomical amount of money for this whole infernal expedition. He just hoped that the men in the submersible had found something this time. At the age of seventy-nine, he didn't have too many more years to devote to the search for the one thing that had consumed him his whole life.

"You'd better hope so." Howard's voice was gruff as his gaze swept the dark clouds swirling just to the south. "This expedition is done for. They didn't find anything on the first two dives. This is the last chance. We're about to get socked in with a major storm, and we have to head into shore."

"I'm sure it's *The Satisfaction*, Mr. Amato. It has to be. All the other expeditions you've pursued throughout the years haven't even produced a boat. We at least have a boat that fits the description of your uncle's rum-runner."

Howard turned to face Tom squarely in the eye, his own

1

narrowed, a sneer on his lips. Tom took a step back, fear written on his features.

"Mr. Barnett, I may have plenty of money to pursue other expeditions, but I'm not a young man, and I'm running out of time. If you can't get this job done, I'll find someone who can. And you won't live to tell the tale. Do I make myself clear?"

Tom's Adam's apple bobbed in his throat. "Yes, Mr. Amato. Very clear."

"Good."

The submersible was lifted from the choppy waves and moved to its resting place onboard *The Lucky Find,* water streaming from its smooth, round surface.

"Now let's see what the divers found. They'll have to go into the compression chamber for a time, but I want to know what they found first. Understood?'

"Yes, sir." Tom glanced in the direction of the submersible. "The divers are climbing out so let's quickly check with them before they head into the chamber."

With a cane to steady him on the heaving deck, Howard made his way to the divers followed by Tom Barnett.

"Report," Howard demanded in a sharp but course voice, leaning heavily on his cane.

Before either diver could speak, a man of about fifty walked up and placed an arm around Howard's shoulders giving him a gentle squeeze then kissed his wrinkled temple.

"What's up, Pops? Any news?"

Howard cuffed the man's cheek with affection. "Hush, Sabastian. We're just about to find out. Please, gentlemen. Tell me what you found."

One of the divers walked around to a basket attached to the side of the submersible near the robotic arms used in their search for artifacts. He retrieved a large, flat, square item and handed it to Howard.

"Mr. Amato, this is what we found. It's the name plate for a boat named *Caper's Run.* There are a couple other smaller items. A glass bottle that I would date around 1900 and a few pieces of broken ceramic ware. That's it. Nothing more."

Howard's face acquired a red tinge, his nostrils flared as his features pinched in anger. Tom Barnett swallowed, his face turning pale. The crew glanced at one another, unsure what to expect from the billionaire. Shuffling uneasily, all eyes turned toward Howard Amato.

The wind whipped around the ship even as the first fine raindrops began to spit, leaving tiny wet marks on the wooden deck. The ocean waves lifted the ship, then dropped it again, indicating the wind was growing stronger and the need to head for land was imminent.

"So, what you're telling me is the boat we've just spent the last three days diving on is not *The Satisfaction?*" Howard's hoarse voice raised, anger oozing from every pore.

The diver swallowed hard, his Adam's apple an obvious sign of his distress. When he spoke, his voice broke, causing him to have to start over again. "N...no sir. It's not. It's not *The Satisfaction.*"

Howard's chin raised high, a glare in his eyes as his gaze took in first the divers, then Tom Barnett. Then it swung around to the crew that stood stock-still as if hoping he wouldn't notice them. Not a chance. He made eye contact with each and every member. Howard raised the *Caper's Run* name plate in the air and slammed it to the deck. With the help of his cane and Sabastian's arm, he made his way toward his cabin.

"Make them disappear, Sebastiano," Howard ordered his son in soft but raspy tones. "See that it's done. All of them, so no one's the wiser. You know how to take care of things."

Sabastian gently squeezed his father's shoulders. "Sure, I do, Pops. Just leave it to me. I'll take care of everything."

Cape Hatteras, NC
Present Day

Chapter One

"Now, look at *that* guy," Bethany Rogers elbowed Ruth Campbell lightly on the hip as Ruth stood beside the younger girl's high stool. "He's just flat drop-dead gorgeous."

Ruth bent over and glanced out the tiny ticket window as a tall young man walked past, hands loosely tucked into the pockets of his blue jeans. A shabby denim ball cap covered his dark brown hair but it couldn't hide his ruggedly handsome features. His navy blue hoodie jacket only enhanced his physic and certainly did nothing to cover it up. Ruth dropped her gaze back to the cash drawer and slammed it shut.

"You are incorrigible, Beth," she sighed. "Is that all you ever think about? Guys?"

"Well, yeah. And food." The eighteen-year-old volunteer shoved her long brown hair behind her ears and turned a cheeky smile on Ruth. "He was pretty good looking, huh? Even *you* have to admit that."

"No, I don't. I barely saw him." Ok, so maybe that wasn't a hundred percent accurate, but it didn't really matter. He was a tourist and would be vacating the premises shortly. A quick tour of the lighthouse and the keeper's quarters. A stroll around the grounds. Then voila'. He'd be on his way. No more tourist. And certainly no one to turn her head about.

Beth scrunched her nose and furrowed her brow. "Ruth, you're such a spoil sport, you know that?"

Ruth chuckled and put on her NPS "Smokey-Bear" hat. "Sorry. Anyway, I have to head up to the gift shop to drop off the cash bag. Then I'm heading out to make my rounds."

"Searching for nests already? But it's late April."

"That's right, sweetie. It's perfect piping plover nesting time," Ruth laughed. "Now say that three times fast."

Beth rolled her eyes and shook her head with a touch of disgust. "Biologists."

Ruth laughed again and opened the door on the side of the little ticket building. "I'll see you later, Beth. Stay out of trouble, okay. I know that's a challenge for you but at least try."

"Hey, what's life without a little fun?" At Ruth's stern look, the younger woman lifted her hands in defense. "Okay, okay. I'll stay out of trouble, but I won't stop trying to get you to have some fun."

Ruth closed the door on Beth's words, ignoring them. Or attempting to. Beth was always telling her she was a boring person and needed to lighten up. The younger woman told her she lived the life of a nerd and that she needed to have some fun every now and then, but Ruth preferred to let things stay as they were. She loved her job as biologist and natural history interpreter. Sharing her love of nature with visitors to Cape Hatteras Lighthouse and Cape Hatteras National Seashore was the dream of a lifetime. What more could she want?

She walked up the path to the gift shop and through the double glass doors.

"Hi, Naysa." Ruth greeted the sixtyish woman in a volunteer uniform behind the cash register. "Here's the cash bag from the ticket booth. Not many visitors this afternoon. But then, I guess that's to be expected. It is late April."

"Oh, sure." Naysa Withem shoved her glasses up and waved a hand in dismissal. "Things won't really pick up until mid-May. Not till the kids start getting out of school anyway. Maybe even into June, you know."

Ruth nodded, her honey-colored ponytail bouncing beneath the back brim of her hat. "Yeah, I know. I'll see you later, Naysa. I'm heading home after my rounds. You have a good evening. Tell Mike I said hi, will you?"

"Sure will. Checking on your nests?"

"Yeah. I hope to find at least a couple being built. They're getting harder to spot, I'm afraid."

Naysa cast a sympathetic gaze as she leaned on the counter. "Well, be careful out there, sweetie, and have yourself a good evening."

Ruth stepped outside the gift shop and tucked her head, zipping up her uniform jacket. As she looked up and took a step, she slammed right into someone, jamming her "Smokey-Bear" hat down over her eyes.

Hands clasped her upper arms and held her away, then lifted the brim of her hat. A pair of concerned steel-blue eyes gazed down at her from a ruggedly handsome face beneath a shabby denim ball cap that covered dark brown hair. It was Beth's drop-dead gorgeous guy.

Ruth gasped and stepped back

"Are you okay?" the guy's deep voice rumbled. His gaze roved over her face then settled between her eyes. "Looks like your hat left a mark on the bridge of your nose. Mostly just a scratch, I think."

Ruth removed her hat and ran her finger across the bridge of her nose. It stung a little but she didn't really feel anything there. She placed the hat back on her head, and barely met his gaze as she spoke. "Thanks. Sorry, I...I wasn't looking where I was going. Have a good day."

She ducked her head and started to walk away.

The man caught her arm. "Hey, no it was my fault. Can I buy you a cup of coffee to say I'm sorry?"

Ruth jerked her arm away and stepped back, panic squeezing her insides. No, now was not the time. He was just a park visitor. Nothing more. He didn't mean anything by it. She attempted to tamp down the feelings that threatened to wash over her and plastered as close to a smile as she could muster onto her face.

"Thanks, but no, I have to get back to work." She tossed a stilted wave and hurried away before he could stop her again.

~

For such a beautiful woman, she sure was acting strangely. Gage Hampton watched as the woman's honey-blond ponytail swung back and forth as she hurried away. Hurried? She was almost running away. Was it something he'd said? Thinking back over their brief conversation, he couldn't think of a thing that should have made her wary of him. She was wearing the National

Park Service uniform so he'd be working with her come Monday morning. Interesting.

Gage strolled toward his car, climbed in and drove to the beach parking lot. He'd been in Buxton for a few days and had settled into a townhouse on the beach. Today he'd driven over to the lighthouse to walk around before starting work on Monday. He'd walk up the spiral painted beacon another day. For now, he just wanted to get a feel for the grounds and the lay of the land.

He parked his car in the beach parking lot and strolled over the sand toward the ocean. Wow, what a view. He watched as the white-capped waves rolled toward the shore. As the new NPS park police officer on Hatteras Island, he had a lot to learn, especially after his last job. This was quite a contrast from the Grand Canyon where he'd worked as a park police officer.

Ramming his hands into his jean pockets, he shook his head. This would take some getting used to. From dry desert canyons to the Atlantic Ocean? Oh yeah.

~

Ruth strolled slowly down the beach, her binoculars hanging from her neck and her clipboard under her arm. She tried to get the face of the young man at the gift shop out of her mind. He'd raised a profusion of feelings within her. Panic, fear, wariness, attraction. Attraction? Nope. That was impossible.

Yanking up her binoculars, she scanned the sandy beach along the vegetation line then several feet out. Time to focus on what she was here to do. Find nests of the piping plovers, those sweet little light-sand-plumed birds with bright orange legs that dashed about the beaches. At least when you could spot them. It was becoming harder and harder to find them.

Standing still she scanned down the south side, then turning, scanned the north end of the beach. Wait. Ahh, yes. Success. She spotted a pair of orange legs moving near the vegetation. Marking it with a landmark, she moved slowly in that direction. When she was about thirty feet away, she zeroed in with her binoculars again and watched as not only one, but a pair of piping plovers worked in unison to build a nest.

Excitement stirred in Ruth's middle. She would do everything she could to see that this couple were undisturbed and the family grew to maturity.

"Finding anything interesting in your sights?" a male voice spoke from a few feet behind her.

Ruth's heart leapt into her throat even as butterflies took flight in her stomach. Without turning around, she knew it was the man from the gift shop. Had he followed her here on purpose? Panic threatened to overwhelm her. No, just stop and turn around. Face him and see what he wants. He's a visitor who has every right to be on this beach.

Swallowing hard, Ruth dropped the binoculars to her chest and slowly turned. As much as she didn't want to meet his gaze she had to in order to assess the situation.

His steel-blue eyes held a benign smile, his lips curved in a grin. "Did you find something interesting? You were searching for quite a while there."

Ruth glanced back up the beach toward the plover nest. "Umm, actually, yes. I'm doing a study on the piping plovers on Cape Hatteras National Seashore, and I spotted a pair."

The man's eyebrows rose quizzically. "Really? And is that unusual? The tone of your voice sort of indicates it might be."

Ruth nodded. "Unfortunately, it is. The piping plover is a threatened species."

"Threatened?" His brow furrowed.

"Yes. All along the Atlantic coastline of the US and Canada. They're not quite endangered but heading in that direction."

The man's face twisted into a thoughtful expression, his hands propping on his hips. "What would cause that?"

"Oh, a variety of reasons, people being at the top of the list." Ruth reached up to adjust her hat as a gust of ocean wind threatened to unseat it. "Nests get accidentally stepped on or crushed by people or vehicles on the beach. The very presence of people can cause the birds to desert their nests, then predators or the hot sun take a toll on eggs or chicks. Then there are various recreational, residential and commercial developments that contribute to their endangerment. I could go on. Their numbers will continue to dwindle if we don't do something about it."

"I see. And that's what you're doing?" He tilted his head in her direction.

"Well, I'm trying to do my part."

"So, what is your job here?"

8

Ruth clasped her clipboard to her chest like a barrier between them. "I'm a biologist and one of the natural history interpreters here at the seashore. But I really should be going now."

Giving him a wide berth, she hurried around him.

"I know, you have to get back to work, right?"

Ruth heard a note of humor in the man's voice and without understanding why, she stopped and turned back to him, so out of character for her. "Yes, actually, I do. But…I hope you enjoy your stay here at Cape Hatteras."

The man looked out at the ocean with a thoughtful expression then he turned his gaze back to Ruth. A grin lit his handsome face. "Thank you. I believe I will."

Chapter Two

Ruth climbed the spiral staircase to the top of Cape Hatteras Lighthouse Monday morning, opening all the windows in the window alcoves as she climbed. It was imperative to get a flow of fresh air moving through the enormous tower before visitors arrived. Even in the early spring morning, climbing two hundred fifty-seven steps could raise a sweat. Someone back in the day when they planned and built this monstrosity had considered the need for rest breaks and had built landings with windows. How considerate.

When she reached the top, Ruth removed her "Smokey-Bear" hat and laid it on the old oil reservoir, opened the door and propped it open then stepped out onto the cast-iron balcony. The chilly morning sea breeze whipped her ponytail into her face, and she grabbed it and held on. Zipping her jacket to her chin, she stepped to the balcony rail, leaned her elbows onto the smooth, rounded surface and stared at the bright morning horizon. The eastern sky was lit with a golden sun split by gold-rimmed clouds. It held the promise of a gorgeous day. *Thank You, Lord. What a beautiful day You've given us. Whatever You've got in store, help me to be faithful to You.*

Ruth's eyes moved inland across the white-capped waves as they washed ashore with the low tide. As was her habit, her eyes swept the beach. She was always looking for wildlife such as egrets and cranes. Occasionally a beached whale or porpoise would appear. Even old ships and naval equipment of all types showed up along the shoreline sometimes. That's what made beach combing so interesting. You just never knew what would show up.

Her eyes settled on a dark object that hadn't been there yesterday when she'd walked the beach after church. What was that? It must've come in on last night's high tide. She hadn't brought her binoculars with her this morning, and she snapped her fingers in frustration. Curiosity piqued, Ruth hurried down the stairs and out to her car. She drove toward the beach parking lot, then hurried down the beach to where she'd spotted the object.

Ruth's heart froze in her chest as she gasped in horror. It wasn't just an object. It was a man. He lay face down in the sand, but from the decomposition of his hands and the back of his neck, she was glad he was. A rope was tied around the man's feet, a long, frayed, length trailing away from the body. Bile rose in her throat and she stepped backward several feet as she tugged her cell phone from her pocket. Swallowing hard, she turned away, glancing around to see if anyone else was on the beach.

Ruth hit speed dial for the NPS park police dispatcher.

"Hi, Liz. Yeah, it's Ruth Campbell."

"Oh, hi Ruthie. What's up?" the perky voice on the other end of the line asked.

"Liz, I found a dead body on the beach just south of the lighthouse."

"What? A dead body? Seriously?"

"Yeah. Seriously."

"Oh, Ruthie. Ok, I'll send somebody out there ASAP. Hey, be careful, okay? The perp might still be lurking around, ya know."

"No, no. I don't think so, Liz."

"What do ya mean?"

"This guy washed ashore, and it looks like he was underwater for a while."

"Oh, my goodness. One of those. Okay. Ruthie. Hang tight. Help is on the way."

"Thanks, Liz." Ruth clicked the button and hung up the call.

As a biologist she'd done her fair share of dissections and studied various mammals and sea life. She drew the line at humans. She was not nor ever would be a medical examiner. Humans were not her area of expertise.

Ruth tugged her jacket collar up and stuffed her hands in her pockets. She paced the beach while waiting for the park police officers to arrive. Staring off at the ocean, she listened to its calming low-tide growl, attempting to ignore the only other occupant of the beach. Why did *she* have to be the one to find the body? She shook her head and heaved a sigh.

There was no telling who he was, where he'd come from or how long he'd been under water, but the fact his feet were tied was not a good thing. She knew enough about biology and decomposition to know that he'd been down there for a couple of weeks at least. Ruth's stomach roiled at the thought. How was it that she could study all manner of mammals but when it came to humans, she did not have the stomach for it?

She risked a glance in the direction of the body, then quickly looked away. Nope. No way.

"Good morning," a now familiar voice spoke from a few feet behind her. Ruth spun around to find the man from the gift shop from last Friday afternoon standing there. Only this time there was no grin on his face. And that wasn't all. He was in full NPS park police uniform, his "Smokey-Bear" hat tilted forward on his head. His jacket was zipped halfway up his chest, revealing his gray uniform shirt beneath, his badge peeking out.

Ruth swallowed her shock. "Good morning. Why didn't you tell me you worked for the park service?"

He had the grace to look a little ashamed. But only a little. He shrugged. "You seemed to be in an all fired hurry to get away and get back to work both times I spoke to you. Didn't seem to be an urgent thing to bring up."

Warmth surged into Ruth's cheeks. "Well...I...um...I was up in the lighthouse opening up this morning, and I spotted this object on the beach down this way. It wasn't here when I came for a walk yesterday after church, so I thought I'd come see what it was. All kinds of things wash ashore along the beach. You just never know what you'll find."

"So I see," he tilted his head in the direction of the body. "But before we begin with all that, maybe we should start over. My name's Gage Hampton. I just arrived last week, and today's my first day on the job. Here, that is. I've been park police for several years."

"I'm Ruth Campbell. As you already know, I'm a biologist and one of the natural history interpreters."

Gage held out his hand. "It's a pleasure to meet you, Ruth."

Ruth eyed his hand for a few seconds before slowly placing hers into it, then with a quick shake she released it and yanked her hand back.

"I may be a biologist, but this isn't my area of expertise." Without looking at it, she waved a hand in the direction of the body.

Gage chuckled. "No, I imagine not. Wayne Mitchell's on the way. He'll help me process the scene. I'm pretty sure he's already called a medical examiner, although I have no idea who that would be. At least not yet. But I can go ahead and start by taking your statement."

~

Gage jotted down notes as Ruth Campbell told her story. He could listen to her talk all day long. Her voice had such a lilting musical quality, very restful and calming. She avoided looking at the soggy corpse lying on the sand and chose instead to gaze out at the waves as she spoke.

Between taking down notes, Gage observed her. He'd noticed she didn't have her uniform hat with her this morning. Perhaps she'd left it in the lighthouse where she'd been when she'd spotted the body. He certainly didn't mind. The first time he'd seen her, her honey-colored hair had been pulled back in a ponytail, but her hat had covered the majority of it. This morning without the hat the wind tossed it over her shoulder and whipped fine tendrils freely around her face. Nice. And her almond-shaped hazel eyes were beautiful.

"So, you see, I called Liz as soon as I arrived and realized it was a man. A dead man." Those troubled, beautiful eyes turned on Gage, reminding him that he was supposed to be conducting an investigation here, not girl watching.

Heat rolled up his neck into his face and he dropped his head as he gazed at his notepad, hoping his wide-brimmed hat covered any telltale signs of redness. What in the world was he thinking? Had he even gotten everything she'd said? Probably not. What kind of professional was he?

"Okay, so let me see now." Gage glanced back over what he had written looking for gaps in his notes. Oh yeah. "So...um...can you go back over the part where..." and he had her retell the rest of her experience, only this time he kept his eyes on the notepad and listened carefully.

As Ruth finished her tale for the second time, another NPS

13

park police officer walked across the sandy beach to meet them, sand kicking up from his shoes as he walked. Average height and stocky build, he sported a military high and tight haircut, his "Smokey-Bear" hat in his hand. When he'd introduced himself to Gage last week, Wayne had told him he was proud first and foremost of his former Marine military service, but he put everything he had into his park police work. Gage suspected he was good at his job. He'd soon find out what kind of park policeman he was.

He tipped his head toward Ruth. "Morning, Ruthie. Not the best way to start your day. Sorry it had to be you."

Ruth tucked her hands into her jacket pockets and shrugged her shoulders. "Good morning, Wayne. I guess it's better me than a seashore visitor. That would leave a lasting vacation memory, wouldn't it?"

Wayne rumbled a humorless chuckle. "That it would."

He turned to Gage. "Morning, Hampton. You getting settled into life here at the seashore? A little different from the Grand Canyon, huh?'

Gage nodded, one side of his lips lifting in a grin. "A little bit. Yeah, I'm getting settling in. I've never worked anywhere like this before, so I'm…intrigued."

Wayne slapped him on the shoulder. "Well, that's good, because it's a whole different way of life out here. I hope you like seafood."

"I love it. Can't say I get much of it out west. More buffalo and elk there."

Wayne laughed. "Nothing wrong with those either."

He glanced toward the corpse lying on the sand and walked over.

Following him, Gage noticed Ruth stayed right where she was, barely turning her head to follow their movements.

Wayne knelt beside the body. "Obviously the ME's going to be more educated than me, but I'd say he's been underwater a couple of weeks. Pretty eaten up by sea life. That rope around his ankles tells me he didn't just fall off a boat and drown."

"Nope," Gage agreed. "And I doubt whoever dropped him overboard intended for him to ever be found. Sheer bad luck on their part. Look at the end of the rope. It looks like it rubbed against something over a period of time and was slowly cut through. It's not a clean cut; very ragged and frayed."

"Yep, I agree. Probably landed on one of the old WWII vessels out there and rubbed against a sharp piece of metal." Wayne raised his voice. "Sure you don't want to check this out, Ruthie? It's fascinating. Should be right up your alley with all the biology stuff and all."

"Nope. I'm good."

"There's probably some sea life in here somewhere."

Ruth's face paled, and her hand flew to her mouth as her eyes squeezed shut.

Gage rushed to her side but didn't touch her. "You going to be okay?"

She nodded but didn't open her eyes.

Gage turned a furrowed brow toward Wayne. "Not cool, man."

Wayne stood and walked over, patting Ruth on the shoulder. "Sorry, Ruthie. Guess I pushed that a little too far."

Ruth swallowed and opened her eyes. She gave him a tight smile. "You're forgiven, Wayne. Jesus said forgive seventy times seven, right? That's four hundred and ninety. What are you up to? Four hundred and eighty?"

Wayne had the grace to look sheepish. "I just like picking on you, girl. My granny always said 'the birds pick on the sweetest cherries'. You're just a sweetheart, is all."

"Well, don't do me any favors. You're getting perilously close to the end of your forgiveness limit." Ruth chuckled and punched him on the bicep. "No, you know I'll keep forgiving you."

"I know it." Wayne squeezed her shoulder in a fatherly manner.

Gage was so new to this place and these two had worked together for a while. He was eager to find out more about Ruth. Where was she from? Did she have family? Did Wayne look out for her? What was her background? Why was she so standoffish? Questions ran like a list through his mind.

Wayne glanced at his wristwatch. "I called the medical examiner over in Raleigh. That's in Wake County. It's a four-hour drive for him. The tide will be at its lowest at nine-thirty, in half an hour, and the body is lying within the tidal area. He won't get here until after one-thirty. They're rebuilding the new Oregon Inlet bridge and only have one lane open at a time. That'll delay him for a while. That would leave him very little time to examine the body before high-tide and water would already be up around the body before then."

"So, what's going to happen?" Ruth asked.

"He's being flown out by chopper, and he's bringing along a couple of team members to expedite things. There's no time to waste on this one. Thank goodness the first high tide came in around three this morning."

"What do you mean?" Gage shifted his feet in the sand.

"Well, I don't expect you canyon dwellers to understand," Wayne teased with a wink. "Naw, it's okay. You'll get used to the tides after you've been here a while. Every day the tide times move up anywhere from twenty minutes to an hour or so. If he'd washed ashore at nine o'clock last night, we'd be looking at a high tide coming in anytime now. Processing a crime scene on such short notice with an ME hours away can mean lost evidence."

"Gotcha," Gage nodded. "Anything we can do to start the process before they get here?"

"Yeah. I have some barriers in the back of my SUV. Let's get them set up before a crowd shows up. It'll be easier for the ME to do his job without gawking onlookers. Ruthie, mind standing here and keeping folks away if they come by?"

Gage saw the expression of distaste flash across Ruth's face, but she held her chin up and nodded. "Sure, I can do that. Nothing to see here, folks. Just keep moving along. No dead bodies here. Lots of beautiful ocean to view out there."

Wayne shook his head and chuckled as he walked away. "You crack me up, Ruthie."

Gage caught Ruth's gaze and grinned. "That spiel ought to work. Just smile. That'll be a sure-fire distraction."

Chapter Three

Ruth hung around the crime scene long enough to watch Gage and Wayne erect a canvas barrier around the corpse on the beach and to watch the arrival of the helicopter bearing the medical examination team. It landed in the parking lot next to the beach then Wayne went to accompany the team to the crime scene. A few spectators had arrived after the barrier was set up, but Ruth was able to persuade them to keep moving along. Gage used stakes and yellow police tape to cordon off the area.

When the ME team proceeded inside the canvas enclosure, Ruth decided it was time to go. She'd done her duty and she needed to get back to work. Her uniform hat sat on the oil reservoir at the top of the lighthouse. Because of her over exuberance to get to the beach and discover what the unknown object was, she now had to climb all the way back up and retrieve it. Oh well. It wasn't the first time she'd climbed that staircase more than once in a day.

She'd always admired the picture of Captain Unaka Benjamin Jennette, the last lighthouse keeper that was on display in the lighthouse keeper's museum near the lighthouse. Referred to affectionately as Capt. Naka by locals, it wasn't unusual for him to climb the lighthouse staircase several times a day, most of the time hauling oil for the lantern that lit the old Fresnel lens.

Ruth turned away from the scene and headed for her car.

"Hey, wait up," Gage called after her. "Where're you going?"

Ruth turned back, her feet slipping in the sand. "I've played out here on the beach long enough. I need to get to work. Besides, I left my hat up there." She pointed at the peak of the lighthouse.

"I came down in such a hurry to discover what that was," she indicated the canvas enclosure, "I left my hat up top. I took it off before I went out on the balcony so it wouldn't blow away."

"I see. Makes sense." Gage smiled and his eyes swept her face. "You know, the other day I asked if you'd like to grab a coffee. The offer still stands. Not now, obviously, but when we're both off and have some time. That is if you like coffee."

Panic stirred in Ruth, her heart racing in her chest. She tried to swallow but it took a couple times to actually succeed. She shook her head. It felt like a block of wood on a swivel.

"Oh…um…thanks…but…no. I don't…um…no…I don't think so. I'm…um…pretty busy right now writing a paper for my PhD class. But thanks anyway."

She turned and fled. Jogging across the parking lot, she pulled out her keys, climbed into her car and drove away. The further away she got, the panic eased, but a new question filled her mind. Gage Hampton wasn't the visitor she'd thought he was. She had to work with this man. And for a short time, she'd found herself relaxing in his presence. Until he'd asked her out for coffee, and that hadn't been completely unpleasant. Not at all. Was the panic she felt because of the past or because she'd been drawn to his invitation? She wasn't about to delve into that question. The past was better left alone, and she wasn't going to accept his invitation so why consider it? Best to just leave things as they are.

~

As Gage stared after Ruth, he tilted his head and scratched his chin. What was that all about? She'd actually seemed to be warming up to him the last couple of hours and then when he'd mentioned grabbing a coffee with her sometime, she'd gone into a panic of some sort. Then he remembered how earlier that morning when he'd introduced himself and shook her hand how she'd quickly snatched it away.

Gage ran his hand around the back of his neck then shook his head. Ruth Campbell was an enigma. She was the most beautiful woman he'd ever seen, and he'd met a pretty fascinating one in Kate Fleming at the Grand Canyon. But Ruth? Ruth was beautiful with the voice of an angel. However, there was something mysterious about this woman. One minute she would almost warm up to him then the next she'd panic and flee. She intrigued him and he wanted to discover more about her.

Why? What did he have to offer a woman. He didn't know what was in her past but he sure knew what was in his.

"Hey, Hampton." Wayne's voice pulled him back to the crime scene.

Gage turned to see Wayne waving him over. He glanced back the way Ruth had driven away. His heart said pursue her, that she seemed to be worth it. But his head told him he wasn't and that his past would only bring her heartache.

~

Ruth beat feet up the lighthouse to retrieve her hat then attempted to hurry back down so she could get back to work, but she was waylaid by visitors trekking upward. They had questions for her about the lighthouse, so she was more than willing to impart her knowledge. She loved interacting with seashore visitors and talking about the history of the lighthouse, its past keepers or the natural history of Hatteras Island. It was what her job was all about.

When their questions were answered, she directed them to continue climbing. If they needed further assistance, one of the lighthouse volunteers awaited at the top to help them. Ruth excused herself, continuing down the lighthouse staircase.

Skipping down the final cement steps outside the lighthouse, Ruth hurried across the path to the primary lighthouse keeper's quarters which was used for office space. It stood a short distance from the duplex lighthouse keeper's quarters which now housed a museum. Pulling out her keys, she unlocked the front door into the office space and stepped inside. It seemed no one else was in right now. Good. She could work on her natural history interpretive program for Friday night without interruption.

Climbing the stairs to the second floor, she was once again thankful her office was in the back. It afforded her privacy and usually no one bothered her.

This had been the home of the last lighthouse keeper, Unaka Benjamin Jennette, his wife Sudie and their seven children. Sometimes Ruth could imagine hearing the voices of the children as they ran around the house or as Sudie called them all to supper. Unaka, or Capt. Naka as he was regularly called, had been dedicated to the lighthouse. What must he have seen from the top of the beacon? What storms must they have weathered on this island?

Ruth removed her hat and hung it on a hook on the wall by the door then settled at her computer. Time to get to work. The morning distraction of finding a body had really put her behind. She shivered at the thought. How horrible it had been. Whoever that man was, he hadn't deserved to be murdered. Hopefully Wayne and Gage could get to the bottom of the case and figure out who had killed him and why. Unable to get the image out of her thoughts, she attempted to think of something more pleasant instead.

As she waited for her computer to boot up, a pair of steel-blue eyes above a quirky grin took shape in her mind. Ruth closed her eyes and shook her head but the image was still there. No, that's not the pleasant something she had in mind. Although it wasn't unpleasant, puppies, horses on the beach, piping plovers, those were more in line with what she had in mind. Gage Hampton was *not* where she wanted her mind to trail toward.

With her computer booted, she pulled up the program she'd started a couple days before and continued working on it. However, the image of Gage Hampton kept inserting itself in her thoughts.

This just wouldn't do. She turned on her MP3 player, and put on some instrumental gospel music trying to distract herself as she pulled up data to add to her interpretive program. She managed to finish it then pull up the paper she was working on for her PhD. It was on her research of the piping plovers and would benefit the national seashore as well as help toward her PhD, but Gage's steel-blue gaze remained with her as she worked.

Ruth found Gage was hard to ignore. *Lord, I have a job to do, and You know I don't trust men. Please take this…this…whatever this is away. It's making me quite uncomfortable. I just want to do my job and earn my PhD. Isn't that what You have planned for me?*

~

Ruth stood at the foot of Cape Hatteras Lighthouse just before eight o'clock Friday night, flashlight in hand, as a small group of visitors gathered around her. She greeted each of them as they walked up, asking how their day had been, where they were from, what they'd seen on Hatteras Island so far; just chatting with them as they waited for everyone to arrive.

Right at eight, Ruth spotted a young man in a faded, denim

ball cap walk up and stand at the rear of the group. When her eyes met his, he grinned then dropped an eyelid in a wink.

Warmth surged through Ruth and upward, fanning over her cheeks. She forced her gaze away. Great. Gage Hampton was here. She hadn't seen him all week. Not since she'd left him on the beach with the medical examiners and the dead body she'd found. *Lord, help me get through this. There's no reason why I should feel pressure, but I do. I've never felt this before. Why now? Why did he* have *to come? I'll just avoid those eyes. Yep. That's what I'll do.*

With a deep breath and a lift of her chin, Ruth began.

"Well, folks, let's get started. Welcome to our Friday evening interpretive program. I notice many of you have flashlights. That's great. You'll need them to follow along as we walk to the various sites we'll be checking out tonight. I just ask that you keep the beams aimed at the ground and not in your neighbor's face. I'm sure they'll appreciate that too.

"Although the sun has gone down now, you may have noticed the sky was a pinkish-red this evening. Have you ever heard the saying 'red sky at night, sailor's delight'?"

Several hands in the group raised, heads nodded and grunts rumbled through the group.

"Do you know where that saying came from?"

One gentleman raised his hand.

"Sir." Ruth pointed to him.

"From when the sailors used the sky to navigate on the ocean back before they had electronic instruments."

"That's correct," Ruth replied. "They actually had another saying as well. 'Red sky in the morning, sailors take warning.' So, by the sign of the sky this evening I'd say we should have a great day tomorrow. I hope you enjoy it."

A chuckle skittered through the crowd.

Ruth pointed up at the towering lighthouse above them. "Cape Hatteras Lighthouse stands one hundred ninety-eight and a half feet tall, and is the tallest lighthouse in North America. She cuts an impressive silhouette against the night sky, but we're a little too close to tell that here. As we walk around, you'll be able to get a better look. You'll also see the beacon better as well. The beacon reaches out twenty-four nautical miles and flashes every 7.5

seconds."

Ruth continued to talk about the impressive history of the black and white spiral-painted tower, eliciting interested nods from the group.

"If you'll follow me, we'll walk over to the side of the duplex lighthouse keeper's house where there's a wonderful view of an egret's nest. They've just built it up in a tree between the house and the beach. They haven't yet laid the eggs. Tomorrow I'll climb up there to install a camera so we can watch the progress of the young egrets. We'll see as the eggs are laid then hatched, and as the young mature. Then we'll see them become fledglings and watch as they strike out on their own. It'll be a fascinating study. We'll post the video on our NPS website so you're welcome to watch along with us."

Ruth ignored Gage as he stayed at the back of the group. She got into her program with the delight she always received when sharing the knowledge she loved to share with seashore visitors. The group asked lots of questions as they followed her from site to site.

At the end of the program, Ruth led the group to the entrance near the parking lot and thanked them for coming. Many of them came to her and told her how much they appreciated her program and the time she took in taking them around.

When the last visitor had gone, Ruth glanced over to find that Gage stood to the side leaning against the Cape Hatteras welcome sign.

Oh boy. She'd hoped he'd melted away with the rest of the group. It had been a long day and she was ready to go home, kick off her walking shoes and be done.

Gage straightened from the sign, hands in his jean pockets, and strolled over.

"You're one very knowledgeable lady, you know that?"

Ruth buried her hands in the pockets of her jacket, then glancing down, kicked a toe of her shoe against the surface of the sidewalk. "Thanks. I've been known to be called a nerd on occasion. On several actually."

"If that's the case, then you're the most beautiful nerd I've ever seen."

Ruth's breath hitched in her throat. She waited for the panic that usually followed when she found herself alone with a man, but it didn't come. Strange. She searched his face in the glow from the light illuminating the welcome sign. He looked sincere. No guile there at all. Even the first couple times in his presence she felt the stirrings of panic, but now? Nothing. She wondered what had made the difference.

The ocean breeze banged the weight on the flagpole behind the sign, pealing a hollow, metallic sound. Ruth drew in a deep breath, unsure of what to think of this lack of panic. No, she couldn't trust it, or him. She didn't know him at all. She'd only met him a couple of times, and even if she'd be working with him, she still needed proof that he could be trusted.

"Thanks. No one's ever told me that before. Just that I'm a nerd. A full-fledged nerd, through and through."

"Why, because you've found something you love to do? Something that interests you?"

Ruth shrugged her shoulders.

"It's because it's something they don't understand why you would love it." Gage shifted his hands out of his pockets and crossed his arms over his chest, his feet spread shoulder's width. "I enjoy law enforcement. I love my job. I'm not particularly fond of situations like what we dealt with on Monday morning, but I deal with it because it's part of the job, but that's just a small part of it. I love investigating, and I love helping people."

"Why?"

"What do you mean, why?" Gage asked

"Why do you love helping people? What got you started in law enforcement?"

Gage's brow furrowed and his eyes shifted off to his right toward the parking lot, then after a moment returned it back to Ruth. "Just…some things I saw in my youth. I thought I could make a difference."

Ruth gave a faint smile. "That's a worthy goal, and a great reason to love your job. And you're not a nerd."

Gage's lips turned up in a grin. "Nothing wrong with being a nerd, lady. Especially a beautiful nerd."

A sliver of pleasure slipped beneath the armor of Ruth's doubts and concerns. She quickly tried to erect her battlements back up again, but she feared it was too late and that Gage

Hampton may have already infiltrated where no one had been able to before. Could she shove him out and do a patch job? *Oh Lord, help me. I can't afford to let a man in. It's just too painful.*

Chapter Four

Boss," Lennie Campo knocked on the cabin door, "Boss, I got news for ya."

"Stop your pounding and come in here, Lennie," called a voice from within.

Lennie turned the door knob and entered the beautifully appointed room. A white Berber carpet covered the floor silencing his steps as he approached the mahogany desk where Antonio Amato leaned back in his cordovan leather desk chair, his feet propped on the edge of his desk. Fine blue drapes bracketed the large portholes that ushered in the morning sunlight and sea breeze along the right wall above the brown cordovan leather couch. Matching armchairs were positioned opposite with an Italian painting of the city of Pompeii and Mt. Vesuvius above them. On the back wall a wet bar stood with another Italian painting of a vineyard on the wall behind it.

In his mid-fifties with silver-edged black hair, Antonio swiped a hand across his handsome face then eyed the man standing in front of his brightly polished desk with his usual lazy, hooded gaze. His underlings knew not to trust the casualness of that expression, however. It could turn deadly in an instant. "So, what's this news you come busting in here to tell me?"

Lennie spread his feet wider to support himself as the boat rocked. Excitement filled his voice as he spoke, his hands lifting in animated accompaniment. "Boss, he floated up, then he washed ashore. They found him."

Antonio's brow furrowed as he raised a hand in the air. "Woah, woah now. Who? What are you talking about, Lennie? Make sense here. Start over and make sense."

Lennie sighed heavily and his shoulders drooped then he

began again. "Joe Pachino, Boss. He floated and washed ashore yesterday. The seashore park cops found him."

Antonio dropped his feet to the floor and leaned forward. He clasped his hands together, his arms on his desk. "What do you mean he floated? You and the guys were supposed to see that he didn't ever see the light of day again."

"Boss, we tied a sack of cinderblocks to his feet. There should a been no way he'd a come back up."

Antonio stood and leaned his hands on the surface of his desk, his hooded gaze not so casual anymore. "A sack of cinderblocks? Why didn't you idiots encase his feet in concrete? There wouldn't have been a rope to come loose."

Lennie shrank back, then stepped back a pace, wisely keeping silent. Antonio came out from behind his desk and walked to stand in front of the couch, peering out the porthole.

"How did you find out about it?"

"One o' the guys who lives in Manteo and keeps a watch on stuff for us just happened to be passin' through Buxton and heard someone talkin' about it."

Antonio turned to look at Lennie. "How did he know it was Joe?"

"Who else have we knocked off in the last couple o' weeks, Boss?"

"Where did the cops take him?"

"Don't know. They flew him off in a chopper, Boss. It could be anywhere."

Antonio turned back to the porthole. "They're going to have their medical examiner check him out. I just don't know where that would be. Get on it and find out."

"Sure thing, Boss."

"And take Harland with you. Now get going."

~

Ruth held on for dear life as she strapped the camera to the branch of the tree. Yes, she had a safety harness, but did she trust it? Not really. This was not something she'd looked forward to doing. She didn't have a real fear of heights or she'd never climb the lighthouse but climbing this tree to position the camera above the egret's nest was a whole different matter. If she fell from the tree, she could be maimed for life.

Just concentrate on the job and get done, Ruth Campbell. There. It was as secure as it was going to be. She angled it and checked her cell phone screen. Perfect. It was a great angle. They should get some awesome views of the young egrets when they hatched. Excitement shot through her in anticipation of the coming experiment and how the whole world could join in.

Ruth pocketed her phone and began her decent. She'd climbed up when the egret parents had left, and she wanted to hurry down before they returned.

At the bottom of the tree, she slogged through the brackish water that nearly reached her knees and clawed through the undergrowth back to the open yard near the end of the duplex lighthouse keeper's house. Ruth had used fishing waders to keep herself dry. It had been quite a challenge climbing the tree but she'd managed.

"What in the world are you doing?" a familiar voice she hadn't heard in a while called from across the yard.

Ruth glanced up to see her cousin, Margaret Lawrence, headed towards her looking none too happy. Beside her strolled none other than Gage Hampton, a wide grin splitting his handsome face.

"Maggie?" Ruth's voice squeaked in astonishment at the sight of her cousin. "What are you doing here?"

"I asked you first." Maggie stopped in front of Ruth and pointed up at the tree with the large nest. "What were you doing up there? Besides putting yourself in grave danger."

Ruth smiled. "It's great to see you, Maggie."

"Don't change the subject. Why didn't you have a spotter out here. I suspect there's an OSHA regulation about that somewhere."

Maggie turned to Gage. "Wouldn't you think so?"

Hands on his hips, Gage shrugged his shoulders but before he could respond, Maggie turned back to Ruth. "Ruthie, you're going to get yourself killed one of these days."

"Maggie, I was just putting a camera above the nest so the whole world can see when Mr. and Mrs. Egret hatch their family. They've just built the nest and the blessed event shouldn't be too much longer now. I had to get it up there while they were away."

"And it had to be you? And what about a spotter?"

"Yes, it had to be me." Ruth propped her hands on her hips. "So maybe I wasn't thinking when it came to a spotter, but I didn't do a free climb, okay? I had a safety harness. Does that make you happy, Mother?"

Ruth smiled then broke into a laugh.

~

Gage watched as Maggie grabbed her cousin in a hug, both woman laughing. He enjoyed their banter and for the first time he saw Ruth truly relaxed. With the smiles and laughter, she was stunning, nearly stealing his breath away. Then he sobered. She'd forgotten he was present. Perhaps he should just back away and let the cousins enjoy their time together. He seemed to put a damper on her life. Far be it for him to understand why, but it seemed to be so.

He took a few steps back, then turned to walk way.

"Where are you going, copper?" Maggie's voice called. "We're not finished yet."

Gage stopped and turned a quarter round. "Yeah? You said you were looking for your cousin. I helped you find her. My job here is finished."

He tipped his hat. "You ladies have a great day."

He spotted a question in Ruth's gaze, but it was best if he turned and walked away. At least for now.

"What's your name, copper?" Maggie asked.

"Hampton. Gage Hampton."

"Well, Gage Hampton. Thanks for helping me find my Ruthie. I owe you one." Maggie winked. "And I always pay back what I owe."

Gage waved a hand. "Not necessary. Have a good day. See you around, Ruth."

She lifted a hand in a small wave and sent him a faint smile. Hmmm. That was an improvement. Perhaps there was hope.

~

"I have to get back to my house and shower, Maggie." Ruth removed her waders and slipped her feet into a pair of clogs then headed toward her car. "I'm sure I've picked up every tick on the island, and I want to scrub before they attach. Want to come home with me? Where are you staying? And you never did tell me why you're here."

"I've come to do a photo shoot, and I was hoping I could stay with you. My car's in the parking lot so I'll follow you home. I'll tell you the rest at your house."

"There's more?"

"Oh, yes." Maggie stopped by Ruth's car. "I'm parked over there. I'll see you at your place."

Maggie followed Ruth to her little two-bedroom cottage built on Pamlico Sound just south of Buxton. The house was painted bright yellow with white trim, and a small covered stoop welcomed visitors to the front door. Around the back, a covered porch sported an old-fashioned wooden porch swing where Ruth loved to spend her evenings reading and studying. The view of the sound was mostly unobstructed and Ruth was blessed with gorgeous sunsets. The sound gave her plenty of sea life study material, and she windsurfed right from her backyard.

As they climbed out of their cars, Maggie assessed the little house. "This is quant and adorable, cuz, and so you."

"Thanks. It's not the grand New York City apartment you're used to, but I love it. And it is me."

"Hey, nothing wrong with that." Maggie gently touched Ruth's arm. "As long as you love it and you're comfortable in your own skin, that's all that matters, Ruthie. Don't ever let anyone tell you different."

Ruth gave Maggie a hug. "I love you, Maggie. You're always so good for my ego."

"That's because I believe in you when sometimes I don't think you believe in yourself, sweetie."

Ruth stepped back and took Maggie's hand. "Sometimes I don't know what to believe."

"I know you don't. Come on. Show me this little castle. Is it yours?"

"No. I rent. But it's a nice rental."

Ruth led Maggie through the sage and cream living room, then showed her the seafoam blue bedroom and the peach bedroom. The kitchen, though modern, was decorated like a 1930's depression era kitchen as was the two small bathrooms. Black and white checkered tile on the floors, a clawfoot tub with a large shower head in both bathrooms as well as pedestal sinks. Modern toilets prevailed, however.

"This is adorable, Ruthie." Maggie peeked at her reflection in the old-fashioned bathroom mirror. "Did you decorate this?"

"Well, the landlord did the hardwired stuff and appliances, but the decor is mine. He also allowed me to paint."

Maggie walked from room to room. "I love it. If I can't have my high-rise apartment, I'd take this any day. I love the touch of sea-theme you have going on with the light seafoam blue and sage. You have quite the eye for color."

"Thanks, Mags. Hey, sorry to cut it short. But I'm itchy and feel creepy crawly. I'm going to hit the shower. Make yourself at home, then you can tell me what else is going on."

While Ruth showered, Maggie found her stash of herbal teas and boiled water in the electric teapot on the counter. She poured the steaming water over two teabags in a couple of mugs she found in the cabinets. When Ruth emerged in a fresh uniform and her damp hair spread over a towel across her shoulders, her eyebrows lifted in appreciation.

"Sweet. I was just thinking how a mug of tea would be nice. Glad you made yourself at home."

"It's easy to do when the home is so homey." Maggie spread her arms wide and glanced around the kitchen. She scooted a mug of tea across the small butcher block island in the middle of the room and placed a clear-lidded glass container of honey with a dipper toward Ruth. "Here you go."

"Thanks." Ruth sat on the metal-legged bar stool at the island and doctored her tea, then took a sip. "Mmmm. Delicious. Thanks. So, spill. What's the more you had to tell me?"

"Dad's coming to town too. He should be arriving soon."

"What? Uncle Owen's coming too? That's great. But why's he coming? Not for your photo shoot, I'm sure." Ruth used the towel over her shoulders to towel dry her hair.

"Nope, not for my photo shoot. He's actually on the search for an artifact. You know he lives in Florida these days, but he's been in Jamaica recently looking for some artifact or other. I can't keep up. He can tell you more when he gets here."

"Will he be staying here as well?" Ruth didn't think her little house had room for all three of them. With no sofa bed, how would she accommodate everyone. There were only two beds in two small bedrooms. Perhaps she and Maggie could share....

"Don't worry, sweetie. He'll be staying somewhere in town. He told me he's already made arrangements." Maggie walked around the small kitchen opening cabinets. "What do you have that we could cook up for supper tonight?"

"There's some red drum in the freezer. If you set it out to thaw, we can make some delicious fillets with a salad. I also have some red potatoes we can slice, season, and fry up if you like."

"Sounds yummy. Well, now that supper's planned, what's next?" Maggie leaned her elbows on the island surface, her chin in her palms.

Ruth stood from the stool, and ran her hand through her hair, tossing the towel over her shoulder. "I don't know about you, but I have to get back to work. When do you begin your photo shoot? What's it about? And where's it going to be?"

"Whoa, whoa, whoa." Maggie laughed, holding up her hands. "One question at a time."

"Well, you haven't said anything about it." Ruth walked over to the back door and picked up her work oxfords from the floor. She took a seat at the kitchen table to put them and a pair of socks on. "Tell me about it."

Maggie leaned a hip against the counter and crossed her arms over her middle. A smile lit her face as she spoke. "Ruthie, I'm so excited about this shoot. I've been hired by a company whose developing some old property along the beach just north of the lighthouse. It's been sitting unused for years and the owner is redeveloping it. He wants to make it into a classy restaurant. He's also bought the hotel across the road and has refurbished it into a new upscale hotel. Most of the work is already done on the hotel, so he wants me to come in and do the photography for the advertisements. They haven't begun on the restaurant yet."

Ruth stood up and reached for the uniform jacket she'd tossed on the kitchen chair when she'd come in. "You know, I've seen them working up there. The hotel really looks amazing on the outside. Nothing like what it used to look like. The building where the restaurant will be has sat empty for decades. Nearly a century, actually. Mary Kelly, the librarian at the Hatteras Village library told me it was used as a speakeasy in the late 1920's during prohibition. As a matter of fact, her grandfather and grandmother helped put them out of business. Her grandfather was a Bureau of Prohibition agent."

"Really? That's interesting." Maggie tapped her forefinger on her chin. "It would've been great to see it in its heyday, huh? I'd love to get a look on the inside of that building. Especially if it's been sitting for nearly a century."

"Yeah. How unsafe must that be?" Ruth reached for her hat. "Gotta go. Make yourself at home. I'll be back later. Love you, Mags, and I'm glad you're here."

"Me, too, Ruthie. Love you."

Chapter Five

Antonio Amato sat at a table under the awning on the sky deck of his 187-foot yacht at the exclusive Diamond Sands Yacht Club. His hooded gaze was fixed out to sea even as his fingers gently circled the top edge of his iced drink glass. Condensation rolled down the sides, and he mindlessly stroked the damp surface, wetting his fingers, then returned to the top and circled the top edge again.

Joe Pachino had failed him and he'd had to be dealt with. Now he was back. But there was no way the cops could link the low-life to him, an upstanding business man. Why couldn't his underlings have just done the job right?

Lennie had reported that Joe's body had been flown to Raleigh and had been examined by the state ME. That meant a report had already been filed. Lennie and Harland hadn't been able to get into the secured facility to get a copy of that report. Without it, Antonio had no way of knowing what the feds knew concerning Joe. And most likely, it had already been filed with the authorities. Had they been able to identify him?

Had they been able to link Joe Pachino to him? Surely not. Maybe they had the means to identify him physically but there was nothing to link him to Antonio. His gut told him he was safe. And if they tried, he'd worm his way out somehow. He'd been taught by the best.

Shaking his head, he released a heavy sigh. Pops had taught him to run the family business with an iron fist, and Gramps before him. During the late 1920's Gramps' Uncle Tony Amato had been one of the biggest names in the mafia business in Chicago during Prohibition. Right up there with Al Capone and Lucky Luciano. He'd run liquor from Jamaica on a rum-runner boat up the east coast and had a restaurant right here in Buxton with a speakeasy in the back. That is until that rotten Bureau of Prohibition Agent, Mike Kelly, took him out. Antonio had heard the story since he was knee-high to a grasshopper. He was even named after Antonio Amato. His Gramps, Howie Amato, had told him how Mike Kelly had sunk his Uncle Tony's rum-runner boat, *The Satisfaction*, with Tony on-board. But that wasn't all that had gone down with the boat.

Antonio stood suddenly and reaching into his pocket, pulled out a freshly laundered, monogrammed handkerchief, and wiped his damp fingers on it. Tucking the linen square back into his pocket, he stepped inside the yacht and down the companionway to his office. His footfalls were muffled by the Berber carpet as he walked. Once inside, he closed the door behind him. He'd left his cell phone on his desk when he'd gone on deck. Snatching up the device, he hit a speed dial button and settled into his leather chair behind the desk, propping his feet on the smooth, shining mahogany surface.

After a couple of seconds, he heard a deep rumble of a voice. "Hello?"

"Hey, Pops. How are you?"

"Antonio? Is that you?"

"Yeah, Pops, it's me."

"Where ya at, Antonio? I ain't heard from you in a while. What's goin' on?" The rumble took on an accusing tone.

"Yeah, I know, Pops. I've been busy with the hotel in Buxton. You know. We're doing the big remodel, and we're about finished with it. We're about to start on the advertising. The photographer should be here soon to begin."

"Oh, well that's good. And what about great-Uncle Tony's restaurant? When ya startin' on that?"

"Soon, Pops. Soon. Hey, listen. I have a question for you. Do you remember the journal that Grampa Howie kept?"

"Yeah, what about it?"

"Where is it?"

There was silence on the line for a few moments, then, "Hmmm, I ain't seen it in a long time."

Antonio released a heavy sigh and rubbed his forehead. He loved his Pops, Sebastiano Amato, with all his heart, but as a man of seventy-eight, he was forgetting more and more.

"Pops, could it be in the bank safe deposit box?"

"Oh, I don't know, Antonio. I don't know where that old thing is. Why you want it?"

"Pops, do you remember Grampa Howie talking about the treasure that his uncle Big Tony brought back from Jamaica? And what he did with it?"

"Treasure?" A moment of silence prevailed as Sebastiano thought about Antonio's question. "Yeah, Tony brought back a treasure, but I never saw it. None of us did. It went down with the rum-runner. Those feds sunk Tony's boat, and he went down with *The Satisfaction*. Sad really. But I don't know what happened to the journal."

"Yea, that's what I remember, too, Pops. I need that journal. I'm going to fly one of my guys up to Chicago. Go with him to the bank and check the safe deposit box. See if it's there. If so, give it to him so he can bring it to me. Okay?"

"Yeah, yeah, sure. I can do that, son."

"Thanks, Pops. I'd come myself, but I've got this hotel renovation I'm overseeing. Just give it to Lennie. You can trust him."

"Sure. Lennie. Just like the old chauffer I used to have when ya was growing up."

"Yeah, just like that. I have to go. I love you, Pops."

"I love ya, son. Come see me."

"I will, Pops. Soon. I promise"

Antonio clicked off the call then pushed another speed dial button, calling Lennie. He wanted him on the next flight to Chicago. He wanted that journal, ASAP.

~

Gage had just returned from a routine patrol up Route 12 to the Oregon Inlet Bridge and was about to head south when he spotted Ruth Campbell standing in her waders in the brackish water near the turn to the lighthouse. Rather than continuing down Route 12, he made the turn and pulled over just past her position, parked behind her car and climbed out of his park police SUV.

As he approached, he noticed she scanned the treetops, seemingly oblivious to his footfalls on the pavement. Tipping his head back, he searched for whatever might have grabbed her full attention but he failed to spot anything.

"So, what has your…"

"Shhhhh," Ruth hushed him without turning around, her arm swinging around, one finger held aloft behind her and pointed in his direction. The other arm slowly raised, a finger pointed toward the top of a tall loblolly pine.

Gage stopped in his tracks at the edge of the marsh and followed her pointing finger. It was hard for his gaze to penetrate beneath the green needles surrounding the brown trunk of the tree, but then his eyes lit on a huge white bird perched on one of the branches.

"Wow," his awed whispered word slipped out as he dared not move. "I see it."

In the lower part of his vision he spotted Ruth's head nod. They stood there for several more minutes while she slowly snapped pictures with her digital camera, careful not to make sudden movements as she worked.

When Ruth seemed satisfied with what she had, she turned and gingerly made her way out of the murky water then walked toward the grassy area where Gage stood and headed past him toward her car.

"Hey wait up." Gage's voice was soft, still not willing to disturb the bird.

Ruth continued on but slowed her pace a smidge.

Gage matched his stride to hers. "So, what was that anyway? I mean, I know it was a bird, but it was one heck of a huge one."

Ruth opened the hatch of her SUV and laid her camera inside, not once glancing at Gage. "It's a whooping crane, and that one's likely about five feet tall. They're an endangered species and they haven't been seen in these parts in nearly seventy years."

"Really? And you don't find that just a little exciting? You know, being a biologist and all?"

Ruth finally looked at Gage, excitement spilling from her eyes and a smile trying to tilt up the corners of her lips, but she was holding it in. Why, for goodness sakes? Because of him? His heart clenched in frustration. What was it about him that made her want to withdraw?

"Okay, I get it." He held up his hands defensively and took a step back from her. He held his frustration in check as he spoke.

Whatever held her back, he wasn't going to lash out. "I don't know what it is about me that makes you want to hold back but it's okay. We don't have to be friends. We do, however, have to work together sometimes. I'll keep my distance because I, for whatever reason, make you uncomfortable. I'm sorry for that. I truly am."

Gage turned to walk away. "Have a great day, Ruth."

~

As Gage walked away and climbed into his patrol car and drove away, a swirl of emotions invaded Ruth's heart. Shame, gladness, frustration, sadness, interest. How could that be? Gage Hampton was a man and men spelled trouble. If an emotion should be present, it should be fear but it wasn't. Yet she'd driven him away, hence the shame.

Ruth shook her head and turned back to remove her waders and dropped them into the plastic tote that waited in the back of her SUV. Even as she chided herself for her poor behavior, she didn't have time to analyze her emotions right now. She had work to do. A new bird species had made a reappearance to the cape and she intended to catalog and keep an eye on it. If a mate appeared and they bred a family in this area, she wanted to know about it. This was an amazing find, and she'd do everything she could to protect the fledgling family if there was one.

The image of Gage's sad face refused to leave her as she snapped the lid on the wader tote and secured her camera. As she attempted to concentrate on her work, he just wouldn't go away as he'd physically done. She slammed the hatch lid and hurried around to the driver's door, yanked it open and climbed in. Gage Hampton was too ruggedly handsome and appealing for his own good. It was time to stick her nose into a good biology book and forget about the man. She had Friday night's evening nature walk to prepare for and she'd better get started.

~

"So, did you find the journal?" Antonio asked without preamble as Lennie walked into the office onboard the yacht. "Don't dare tell me Pops didn't get it for you."

"Oh no, Boss. He got it. It was in the safe deposit box, just like ya thought." Lennie placed a leather briefcase on the smooth surface of the mahogany desk and released the catches, flipping open the lid. "Just as pretty as ya please, there it was. At first, I didn't think he was gonna let me bring it, but when I told him how much ya needed it, he relented and sent it on. I told him ya'd return it. Don't know if ya will or not, but that's how I got him ta let it go."

Antonio reached into the leather case and removed a brown leather-bound book. Howard Amato's journal. He opened it and carefully thumbed through the yellowed pages, gazing on the handwritten words. Gramps Howie had watched as his uncle Tony's rum-runner had been sunk by the feds in an explosion. His uncle had gone down with the boat. Grampa Howie had funded several salvage dives over the years searching for that boat but had never found it. There was more on that boat, and he, Antonio, intended to search and find it. It had been Howie's dream and now it was his.

~

Maggie parked her Lexus in the nearly empty parking lot and, tossing her camera bag over her shoulder, hurried into the newly refurbished luxurious building. A fifteen storied steel and glass affair, The Brigand's Cove Hotel sat on the west side of Hatteras Island just north of Cape Hatteras Lighthouse overlooking Pamlico Sound yet the upper floors had a full view of the Atlantic Ocean.

A brass-trimmed glass revolving door spun smoothly as Maggie gave it a push, allowing her entry to a magnificently appointed lobby. Decorated in the art deco period of the 1920's, shining brass trimmed everything. Teal, burgundy and black adorned the thick carpet on the floor while art deco wall sconces lent light to the room. Matching art deco chandeliers hung from the high ceiling. Brass elevators were built in the art deco style and gleamed in the light from the chandeliers. A long reception desk of Italian marble would greet guests on the right while a large fireplace of matching Italian marble on the left was surrounded by Italian leather couches and chairs.

A thrill ran through Maggie. She almost wished she could just check in and stay awhile but taking photos for this luxurious resort hotel was nearly as good. She couldn't wait to see the rooms, the pool and the spa. There was also an on-site restaurant featuring a Chef de cuisine. This was in addition to the restaurant that would eventually be across the street in the old building.

"Miss Lawrence?" a voice coming from behind Maggie

caused her to spin around. A tall, dark man in his fifties, silver edging his black hair, held out his hand as he approached. His hooded dark eyes were a bit chilly, but his lips held a smile. "I'm Antonio Amato. How do you do?"

Hmmm. Definitely a businessman. "Yes, I'm Maggie Lawrence. It's a pleasure to meet you at last."

Maggie shook his hand then pulled hers back. She never encouraged long handshakes with anyone. Ever.

"Welcome to our fair shores. So, you're from New York, right?"

"Yes, that's right." Maggie swiped a swath of her long auburn hair behind her ear.

"Well, that's alright. I'm from Chicago, but I won't hold it against you." He chuckled. "You come with great credentials. I hope you'll do very well for us and take some amazing pictures of our hotel."

"Well, thank you. I enjoy what I do, Mr. Amato. I love taking pictures. Perhaps you'd like to show me what you're looking for in your advertising and I'll get started. I can get your thoughts and ideas, then I'll take the pictures. Afterward, I'll go over them with you. If there's something else you'd like, then we can go back, I'll take more or redo something you'd like done differently. Once things are the way you want them, I'll send them to your advertiser. I'll be staying in the area for a while, working on some other projects. If your advertiser needs something redone, I'll be here and I can take care of it."

Mr. Amato nodded, his lips pursing in thought. "I like that plan. Let's get started. I actually have an appointment in a while, but I'll go over some things with you first, then I have an assistant who will join us and she'll finish up with you."

Maggie nodded, pulling the strap of her camera bag further up on her shoulder. "Sounds great. I'll follow you."

~

Three hours later, Maggie shook the hand of Antonio Amato's assistant, Jane Williams, tugged her camera bag strap onto her shoulder and pushed the revolving door open. She stepped out into the late afternoon sunlight and welcomed the light ocean breeze. Breathing deeply, she walked to her car and climbed in, opening all the windows. Even for mid-April, it was warm out, hinting at a promise of the summer that was right around the corner. The hotel had actually been rather stuffy since there were no guests, and they weren't using the heat or the AC.

As she pulled her car to the edge of the parking lot and waited for a couple of cars before pulling out, she looked over at the old building that had once been a restaurant a long time ago. A sign still hung above the door but it was barely legible after the battering of decades of storms and the fading of the sun. What did it say? The Rus-- --ok. Wow. She had no idea what that could mean. She only knew it was a restaurant because Ruthie had told her it once was.

Curiosity was getting to her. Maggie wanted so badly to see what was behind those doors, but they called that trespassing. Hmmm.

Glancing left then right, she realized traffic had long since cleared up and she could go. She glanced at her wristwatch. Ruthie would still be in her office. Yep. She would pay her a visit.

~

Ruth was almost finished with Friday night's program when a tap sounded on her office door.

"Come in." she called, her eyes never leaving the screen.

"Hi, Ruthie, what are you doing?"

At the sound of her cousin's voice, Ruth swung her desk chair around. "Mag's, what are you doing here?"

"We both seem to have the deplorable habit of asking one another that question and then not answering, don't we, cuz?" Maggie dropped onto the corner of Ruth's desk and, reaching a hand across, she patted Ruth's shoulder. "But if you recall, I asked first."

Ruth smiled and shook her head. "I'm working on Friday night's nature walk program. You?"

"I just came from taking pictures at The Brigand's Cove Hotel for Mr. Amato."

Ruth sat up a little straighter and smiled brighter. "Oh, and how did that go?"

"Pretty good, actually, but he's your typical business man who wants it done his way with very little negotiating even if, I the photographer, have a better eye for something. But I think if I tell the advertiser I think something else might work better, they may request a different shot. I told him I'd be here for a while, and I can re-shoot whatever the advertiser needs."

"Wow, that's great. I can't wait to see your photos. Can you show them to me? I doubt I'll ever get inside that hotel, so your pics are probably the closest I'll ever come to seeing inside."

"Sure, I'd be happy to." Maggie shrugged her shoulders. "Think you can do me a favor?"

"If I can. What's up?"

"Remember when we were talking the other day about the old restaurant across the street from the hotel that Mr. Amato is going to refurbish and remodel?"

Ruth nodded. "Yeah. What about it?"

"Didn't you say that one of the local librarians is a descendant of somebody from back then?"

Ruth nodded again and leaned her elbow on her desk. "Yep. That would be Mary Kelly at the Hatteras Village Library. Her great-grandparents were pivotal in taking down the mafia rum-runners here at Hatteras. The mob boss Big Tony Amato had a restaurant and speakeasy there. It was called The Rusty Hook."

Maggie snapped her fingers. "Those are the missing letters. I was trying to read the sign above the door, but it's so old and faded I couldn't read it. The Rusty Hook."

The words tripped from her tongue softly as she thought it over. "It's a cool name, Ruthie."

Maggie stopped and turned back to her cousin. "Wait a minute. What did you say? What was the mob boss's name?"

Ruth shrugged her shoulders. "Big Tony Amato. Same as your new boss."

"Yeah, that's what I thought you said. Antonio Amato and Tony Amato." Maggie crossed her arms and lifted a finger to her chin, tapping it thoughtfully. "Come with me and let's go talk to Mary Kelly. I need to know more. I want to go inside that place. And I mean before it's renovated."

"What?" Concern filled Ruth's voice. "Mags, that's called trespassing. I'm sure there's even a sign or two or a dozen posted around that property. You could end up in jail. Or worse."

Maggie lifted her chin, a grin tilting the corners of her full lips. "Oh, I wouldn't be going alone, Ruthie."

A bad feeling stirred in Ruth's gut as the hair began to stand on the back of her neck. She had a feeling she knew where Mags was going with this and she didn't like it. Not at all.

"Mags," she started shaking her head.

"What can it hurt to go talk to your friend the librarian?" Maggie stood from the corner of the desk and grasped Ruth's hand. "Come on. It's almost four o'clock. She's sure to be there for a while yet. Let's just go talk to her and find out more about the building and what happened to the mob guy and her great-grandparents. She sounds like a well of information."

With a sense of dread, Ruth picked up her "Smokey-Bear" hat and placed it on her head, following Maggie to the stairs. As she recalled, it had been Maggie that had gotten them into scrapes when they were kids, not the other way around. And somehow, she had a feeling they were heading into something that didn't compare with anything they'd ever done before.

Chapter Six

T he Hatteras Village Library was a small building on the east side of the village and Maggie parked her Lexus in one of the few spots reserved for patrons. Almost dragging Ruth behind her, Maggie hurried to the front desk.

The sixtyish librarian sitting behind a computer glanced up over her wire-rimmed glasses and recognized Ruth, a smile instantly brightening her face.

"Ruth Campbell, as I live and breathe. What brings you to the library today? Researching piping plovers and those egrets nesting by the lighthouse keeper's quarters?"

Ruth sighed heavily. "Well, not exactly, Mary. This is my cousin, Maggie Lawrence, and she has some questions for you concerning your great-grandparents and the mob boss that went down with his rum-runner in 1928."

Mary's eyes shifted to Maggie and she smiled at the island newcomer. "Oh well, I don't know a single thing about piping plovers, but I know a lot about Mike and Ava Kelly and Big Tony Amato. That's a huge story in these parts. Right up there with Blackbeard and his evil pirates, you know. How do you do, Maggie? Welcome to Cape Hatteras."

"Thanks, Mary. It's a pleasure to meet you." Maggie tossed her long auburn hair over her shoulder and set her purse on the counter. "I'd love to hear all about your great-grandparents and the rum-runner they put out of commission."

"Oh, that they did, Maggie," Mary nodded as she stood and walked from behind her computer. "Follow me."

Grabbing her purse, Maggie followed the older woman and Ruth followed Maggie. Mary took them back to a display along the back wall of the library where two enlarged portraits hung above an open book in a plexiglass display case.

Mary stopped beside the display and turned to Maggie and Ruth. She pointed at the two sepia-colored portraits, one of a beautiful, young light-haired woman and the other of a handsome dark-haired young man. "These are the portraits of my great-grandparents, Michael Kelly and Ava Sinclair Kelly. Aren't they a handsome couple? Oh my, they were so in love. Mike was a Bureau of Prohibition Agent who came here in 1928 to put a stop to the rum-runner who was bringing alcohol into the US through North Carolina as well as moving it on up the east coast and inland further north. He had no idea who that was at first, then he discovered it was none other than the mob boss Big Tony Amato."

Mary clasped her hands and paused for a dramatic moment. "My great-grandmother Ava Sinclair was the first librarian on the island. Big Tony Amato kidnapped her and nearly spirited her away to Chicago, but Mike Kelly rescued her. He fell in love with her and married her. He also helped her start the first book mobile system on the island. Ava had a brother, Martin Sinclair, who was the sheriff, and the three of them, along with the help of the captain of the Coast Guard station, put Big Tony Amato out of business. For good."

"Amato. That's the same name as the man who's remodeling The Brigand's Cove Hotel and the old Rusty Hook restaurant." Maggie's brows furrowed. "Could they be related?"

"Yes, it's the same family," Mary said, nonplused. "They've owned land on this island since prohibition days. When Big Tony died, his nephew Howard inherited everything."

"What happened to Howard?" Ruth asked.

"He died in 2005. He was ninety-four years old. He searched for *The Satisfaction*, his uncle's rum-runner, for most of his life but he never found it. Rumor has it, his uncle had a treasure he brought up from Jamaica that went down with the boat, but who knows."

"Wow, that's fascinating," Maggie shoved her hair behind her ear. "What an amazing story. And Howard's uncle ran The Rusty Hook restaurant, right?"

"That's right," Mary nodded. "He had a speakeasy in the back of the restaurant."

Turning, she pointed at the open book inside the plexiglass case. "This is the book that my great-grandmother Ava Kelly wrote about the rum-runner and how he was taken down. It's hand written by Ava herself."

Ruth stepped closer to the case. "She must've been quite an amazing woman."

"She certainly was," Mary said, her soft tone filled with awe.

"Has anyone been inside that building since it was abandoned so many years ago, Mary?" Maggie turned her attention directly on the older woman.

Mary furrowed her brow as she crossed her arms over her ample breast and lifted a hand thoughtfully to her chin. "According to Ava's records, once Howard returned to Chicago, no one returned there for many, many years. It fell into terrible disrepair. I would imagine that if the current Mr. Amato is planning to remodel it, he must have been there recently. Why would he want to make such plans if he hadn't been there?"

"That's true, Mary," Ruth nodded, turning a dark gaze on Maggie. "Nothing to see there, I'm sure. Just an old dusty, and most likely, very dangerous building."

Much to Ruth's chagrin, Maggie cast a wink and pert grin in her direction. "Hmmm. You never know."

"Well, I'm pretty sure that property is posted No Trespassing," Mary said, "You could get into a lot of trouble going in there."

Ruth snapped her fingers. "Yep. Not to mention you could die just trying to get in. You know, rotten boards and such."

"Where's your sense of adventure, ladies? Life's too short not to take a chance now and again."

Ruth and Mary exchanged concerned looks.

"Don't let her talk you into doing anything stupid, Ruth Campbell." Mary warned.

"Not a chance." Ruth shook her head adamantly, her arms crossed over her chest in defiance. "She won't talk me into going into that old building."

~

"I can't believe I let you talk me into this," Ruth whispered as she and Maggie shuffled along the wooden walkway in the darkness beside the old abandoned Rusty Hook restaurant. With dark hoodies covering their heads, they stuck to the shadows as they moved toward the back of the building built right onto the old pier. Waves crashed against the pilings, sending a shiver through the rickety structure.

"How did you learn to pick locks anyway? You picked the lock on that chain link gate like it was nothing." Ruth followed Maggie as they rounded the back corner of the building and stopped to catch their breath.

So far, no boards had given way beneath their feet, but they creaked loudly with every step they took. Would the ancient wooden beams give away their position? Her gut churned at the thought. Every second she was out here she regretted more and more giving in to her cousin's ridiculously dangerous plan. Her whole career weighed in the balance of their actions tonight. How could she have been so stupid? She'd let Mags talk her into some hairbrained plans during their childhood and youth, but this? This was the crowning glory scheme of schemes. If she got out of this unscathed....

Maggie turned a grin on her cousin as she leaned against the sun and wind battered boards. "You don't want to know."

Ruth rolled her eyes. "No, I probably don't. Now what? It looks like there's a door over there, but it's hard to see out here. I'm afraid to turn on a flashlight."

"Come on. Position your body so you block the light then I'll block it from the other side. I need to get a look at the lock."

They stepped over to the door and when they were in position, Maggie turned on her small flashlight. After a quick perusal, she picked the antique lock and pulled on the door. It wouldn't open at first, but after yanking on it, she was able to persuade it to open. It squeaked loudly, curdling Ruth's blood. Stepping inside they pulled the door nearly closed behind them, leaving it slightly cracked. Turning, they perused the room in their flashlight beams.

"Wow, would you look at that." Ruth swung her beam around the room. "Mary once told me how there was a gun fight in the speakeasy between Mike Kelly, Sheriff Sinclair and Big Tony and his men. There you have it. The tables are shot up as well as broken glass on the bar and the floor."

A stage was built on the right side of the room with a dais in the corner beside it, long unused musical instruments sat covered with nearly a century of dust. A bar ran along the left side, behind it dust-covered liquor bottles of every variety lining a mirror-decorated wall. Many bottles were broken, as was the mirror.

Tables were turned over and displayed splintered bullet holes. The walls were covered with cobweb and dust lined heavy drapes.

"I bet they covered the walls with those drapes to keep the cops out, huh?" Maggie grinned, her eyes lit with excitement.

"No doubt." Ruth nodded, eyeing her cousin. "You know, you're excited about this, aren't you?"

"You think? Come on." Maggie led the way through the room and to a doorway. "There's a hallway through here. Let's see where it leads."

They searched through several rooms, closets, and an office decorated in Chinese red and mahogany that looked like it could've been the boss's office. Could this have been Big Tony Amato's sanctum?

Maggie riffled through the desk searching for...well for anything that looked interesting.

"Here, Ruthie. Take a look at these."

She handed Ruth a pile of papers, and Ruth thumbed through them. "Wow, this is pretty interesting, Mags. Take a look at this. These are Big Tony's receipts for his liquor purchases in Jamaica."

She thumbed through more papers. "These are all receipts, Mags. Nothing more."

Maggie nodded and added them to the pile she had thumbed through. "Yeah. Same here."

She stuffed them back in the drawer then pulled another drawer open. Pulling out more papers she handed them to Ruth. "You know, these are mostly receipts. You'd think he would've kept a ledger of some kind. Think it went down with the boat?"

"Probably. After all, he was on the rum-runner when it went down. It went back and forth and he probably kept better records as he traveled."

They looked through what they pulled out. Then stuffed them back in the drawer.

"Nothing more to see here," said Maggie.

"Then we should get out of here." Ruth stood and headed for the door. "We came, we saw, we found nothing. Let's go."

Maggie stood a little slower. "Yeah, you're probably right. Unfortunately, it all probably went down with the rum-runner."

She turned but found she was alone. Ruth was gone.

~

"Ruth?" Maggie retraced her steps to the speakeasy. "Ruth? Where are you? Ruthie?"

Turning the corner from the hallway into the speakeasy she found her cousin standing by the door out to the pier, gazing out into the night.

"Ruth? What are you doing?"

"I'm waiting on you but I'm not waiting much longer. I'm ready to get out of here."

Maggie hurried across the room, relief filling her, and hooked her arm through her cousin's. "Alright. Let's go. I owe you one, cuz. Thanks for coming with me. You stepped out of your comfort zone, and I appreciate it. More than you know."

"You're welcome, but just get me home before the police come and haul us off to jail for trespassing. I enjoy my day job and somehow I don't think they'll let me keep it if they find out about this."

"No, I suppose not."

Maggie locked the door behind them and they started to move back around the building, but Maggie caught Ruth's arm. She pointed toward the end of the pier.

"Do you think that's where they used to bring in the booze?" she whispered. "It looks like the remnants of a ladder and an old block and tackle setup. I imagine that's what they would've used back in the late 1920's."

Ruth shrugged, glancing in that direction, then around the corner of the building toward the front. "I don't know. Probably, seeing as how they were sneaking it into the speakeasy. Didn't Mary say they brought it inland through here as well? It wouldn't be difficult to imagine them bringing it up here then across the road to Pamlico Sound where they would transport it across the water inland for distribution. That's what they did during Prohibition after all."

"Yeah. Big Tony Amato must've been making a mint from rum-running," Maggie said with a gleeful whisper.

"If I didn't know better, I'd say you were enjoying this just a little too much." Ruth grabbed Maggie's hoodie sleeve. "Come on. Let's get out of here."

Sticking to the shadows, they hurried along the side of the building back to the chain link gate that blocked the entrance to the walkway along the side of the building. After quickly exiting, Maggie relocked the padlock, but before they could turn and walk away, a set of headlights fixed on them.

Turning, both women found they were facing a patrol car. Maggie's heart sank. What had she gotten Ruth into?

~

Ruth's heart sank clear to her stomach as she turned to face the headlights fixed square on her and Maggie. In its place she felt a lump similar to a rock take shape. The car in front of her was a patrol car. Her worst nightmare had materialized. The police had arrived, and now her career was over. All she could do was shake her head and wonder why she'd let Maggie talk her into doing this.

"Ruth? Maggie? What in the world are you doing here?" A familiar voice spoke from beyond the headlights as a car door slammed shut. Then the darkened shape of Gage Hampton walked toward them from the driver's side of the patrol car.

Ruth wasn't sure if things had just gotten better or worse. She didn't know how to react to this turn of events, but she was thankful it wasn't the local police.

"Gage!" Maggie exclaimed. "Thank goodness!"

Gage stopped in front of the two women, a flabbergasted expression on his face. "What's going on? Please tell me you didn't do what I think I just saw you doing?"

Ruth refused to open her mouth and decided it was only fair to let Maggie deal with it.

Nonplused, Maggie shoved her hoodie from her head and smiled at Gage. "Well, that depends on what you *think* you saw."

Gage propped his hands on his hips. "What I *think* I saw? I saw you either unlocking or locking the gate to that chain link fence that is posted with a No Trespassing sign on it. Is that what *you* think I saw?"

Maggie's grin was sheepish. "I can neither confirm nor deny."

Gage tossed his hands in the air and rolled his eyes. "You've got to be kidding me. What in the world would possess you two to go in there, especially when it's posted?"

He turned his eyes on Ruth, but she kept her gaze lowered. "Ruth, talk to me. Do you know how much trouble you two could be in?"

"Yes." Ruth swallowed hard keeping her gaze on the ground.

If she didn't look at him maybe he'd return his attention back to Maggie. Let *her* answer his questions. It was *her* idea after all.

Gage paced the old restaurant parking lot a couple of times then returned to stand in front of the women.

"I can't interrogate you two here on the roadside." He swiped off his uniform hat and ran his hand through his hair then settled it back on his head. "I don't want one of the local cops to stop and ask what's going on. Ruth, can we go to your place? It gets you two back home and you can explain what the heck you were doing."

"Or you could just walk away, Gage." Maggie shrugged.

He took a step closer and looked her in the eye. "That's not happening. I'll follow you home. Where's your car?"

Maggie released an irritated sigh. "Across the road in the hotel parking lot."

"Fine. Be careful crossing the road." He climbed into his patrol car and slammed the door. He backed the car around and followed them as they ran across the road to Maggie's car, then followed as Maggie drove away, leading the way to Ruth's cottage.

Ruth sat fuming as Maggie drove south. The gamut of emotions she'd been through tonight had left her exhausted, but at the moment she was just plain furious. Maggie had talked her into this hairbrained scheme and they so easily could've been caught by local police. Instead it had been Gage on patrol. There was no guarantee he still wouldn't turn them in. Was he a by-the-book kind of guy? Would he see it as his duty to turn them over to the police? It wasn't his jurisdiction but he could certainly hand them over.

"Well, it could certainly have been worse," Maggie chuckled. "Thank goodness it was Gage who came by and not a local yocal."

Ruth shook her head. "Everything's a joke to you, isn't it, Mags. What if it had been a 'local yocal?' It's my career on the line. You can just go on as before. You're a freelancer. No big deal. I can't do that. My career could be over. Do you understand that? Over. Zilch. Nada. But in reality, it's not your fault. It's mine, because once again, I let you talk me into it. I never could say no to you."

Ruth felt tears clog her throat and seep into the corners of her eyes. She shook her head. Maggie reached over and squeezed her hand.

"I'm sorry, Ruthie. I never should have pushed you. I knew you didn't want to go, but I pushed anyway. I'm really sorry."

Maggie stopped the car in Ruth's driveway and turned off the engine.

"That's just it, Mags. You're always sorry. *After* the fact. And we're not kids anymore."

Ruth climbed out of the car and stormed up the front steps to unlock the front door. Without waiting for the others, she went inside and put on a pot of coffee. She was slicing coffeecake she'd baked the evening before. Anything to keep busy.

"Come on in, Gage," Maggie was saying as she opened the front door. "Oh look, Ruth's already got coffee brewing."

Ruth glanced up from the coffeecake, her gaze slamming into Gage's. Her heart tripped up and took off at a breakneck speed. Swallowing hard, she lowered hers back to the coffeecake. The tension in the room sparked liked electric arcs from a loose electrical wire.

"You have a nice place here, Ruth." Gage's voice was tight as he laid his hat on the end of the counter.

"Thanks. Have a seat at the table and I'll bring the coffee and the coffeecake."

Maggie reached into the cabinet for the glass honey pot. "I've got the sweetener and the mugs. Just make yourself at home, Gage."

When they were settled around the table and Gage was eating coffeecake, the tension in the room eased a bit. Ruth nibbled at hers and sipped her coffee while Maggie ran a running commentary about her job. If she thought that would keep Gage from asking questions about their earlier activities, Ruth knew that wasn't going to happen. When she hazarded an occasional glance in his direction, she could see he was biding his time.

When Gage's coffeecake was finished and he leaned his elbows on the table to sip his coffee, he pinned both Maggie and Ruth with a hardened gaze.

"So now that the niceties are out of the way, would you two like to tell me what you were doing at The Rusty Hook tonight? From your attire of black sweatpants and hoodies, I'd say you were up to no good. Explain."

His gaze floated between them as he waited for one or the other to begin. Then pinning Ruth with a steady gaze, he gentled his voice and asked, "Ruth, would you please tell me what was going on?"

Ruth took a deep breath and lifted her gaze to meet his. She opened her mouth to speak but before she could utter a word, Maggie held up a hand.

"No, it's not Ruth's fault. Yes, she went with me, but under a lot of protest. And I mean, a lot. She didn't want to go. I talked her into it."

Maggie got up from her chair at the table and paced the room a couple of times, then came to halt in front of Gage. Crossing her arms over her middle, she looked him in the eye.

"Ever since I heard the story of Big Tony Amato and how the Kelly's took him down, I've wanted to see inside The Rusty Hook. I suppose I romanticized about it. Maybe even thought I'd find something from that era. All we found were old liquor purchase receipts from Big Tony's runs to Jamaica. Nothing more."

"You mean to tell me you snuck into a posted property on the chance of finding something and found nothing?" Gage lifted a questioning hand and shrugged his shoulder.

"Yep, that about sums it up," Ruth's voice was soft as she nodded.

"Do you have any idea what was at stake here?" Gage pointed the remark at Ruth.

Ruth lifted her gaze to his, her voice strengthening. "I thought about it every second I was in there, believe me."

Maggie kicked his foot half playfully. "So what are you going to do, copper? You going to turn us in like the good cop you are? Or are you going to let us go like the friend I hope you are?"

Gage scrubbed a hand down his face in frustration and let his gaze roam around the room as he thought about her words. He propped a hand on his thigh and returned his gaze to the two women.

Heaving a deep sigh, he shook his head. "You've put me in a bad position, but not intentionally. You didn't know I'd be passing by there on patrol at the very moment you were coming out of The Rusty Hook and relocking the gate."

He held up a hand. "I don't even want to know about how you

know how to unlock and relock locks. That's called breaking and entering. Generally, a felony offence, by the way."

His gaze swung back to Ruth and her heart rate picked up. Why did it have to do that?

"I can't be responsible for ruining your career. You're far too necessary to the needs of this seashore and the park service. Just do me a favor. Don't listen to your cousin when she asks you to follow her on any more hairbrained schemes. Okay?"

Ruth found her head nodding before she could stop it. But he was right. She had gone on more than her fair share of idiotic adventures with her cousin and she needed to steer clear.

"Hey, not all my plans are hairbrained," Maggie said. "I've had some great ideas too. Right, Ruthie?"

Ruth thought for a moment then nodded. "Yeah. Some. Like the time you started an aluminum can drive to raise money for old Mr. Williams when he needed heart surgery. She was only thirteen years old, and she raised enough money to have the surgery done."

"Hmmm. I'd forgotten about that one." Maggie's brow furrowed.

Gage stood. "All right. I'll let it slide. This time. Just stay out of trouble, ladies. Please. I suspect that the current owner of The Rusty Hook isn't someone to contend with. That property isn't posted for nothing. It's likely not very safe."

"It seemed pretty shaky," Ruth said. "Every time the waves hit the pilings the whole place would shake."

Maggie nodded. "Yeah, it did. If Mr. Amato does decide to remodel that place into a restaurant, it's going to take some major overhauling of the pilings."

Gage reached for his hat and placed it on his head. "I need to get back out on patrol. Promise me you'll stay away from that place. Both of you."

"I promise," Ruth held up her right hand.

Maggie heaved a sigh, nodded and held up her hand. "I promise."

"Good." He turned his gaze on Ruth. "Thanks for the coffee and the coffee cake. Did you make the cake?"

She nodded.

A grin lifted one corner of Gage's handsome lips. "It was delicious. A nice break from my evening patrol."

Warmth flowed through Ruth but she refused to drop her gaze, meeting his head on. He had no right to be so handsome. And why did she care anyway? She wasn't interested, right? Men were only trouble. "Thanks. How much longer before your shift ends?"

He glanced at his wristwatch, his grin growing. "Half an hour."

"Well, you timed that well, didn't you, copper?" Maggie gave him a light punch on the bicep. "Hey, looks like I owe you twice now, huh? Thanks, Gage."

He gave her a rueful glance. "Yep. I'd say so. And you're welcome. Goodnight, ladies."

Chapter Seven

That Spanish mackerel was delicious, Ruthie." Maggie wiped the dishes as Ruth washed them. "Where in the world did you learn to cook like that? I know I didn't teach you, and Dad, well, you know Dad. He's not much of a cook."

"I've just learned to read a cookbook, Mags." Ruth placed the baking dish in the drainboard. "It's not that hard. I really enjoy cooking."

"Hmmm. Well, you've made some tasty dishes since I've been here. I'm impressed."

A strange and very loud noise in front of the house caused both women to stop what they were doing and stare at each other.

"What's that?" Maggie dropped the dish towel on the counter.

"I have no idea. I've never heard it before." Ruth ran her hands under the water to get the soap off and grabbed the dish towel as Maggie headed for the front door. She followed close behind, taking the towel with her.

Maggie reached for the doorknob and both young women stepped out on the front stoop. There, just a few feet from them, a huge RV had stopped in front of the house, its diesel engine growling in idle.

"What in the world...?" Maggie began as the door of the RV swung open and a set of automatic steps slid out and down. A man in his early sixties descended the steps and walked toward the women.

"Dad?" Maggie called.

"Hi, Maggie. Hi, Ruthie." He waved a hand above his head.

Maggie skipped down the front steps and gave her father a hug. "Dad? What in the world? I thought you were staying in a hotel in town."

"Nope, I never said that. I said I'd made arrangements, honey. Hi Ruthie, sweetheart. How are you doing?"

Ruthie laughed and ran to give her uncle a hug. "Uncle Owen. Oh, my goodness. It's so good to see you. But we certainly weren't expecting to see you arrive in…well, in something like that."

Uncle Owen released Ruth and stepping back, laughed heartily. "Well, I've been taking my time coming up from Florida. You know, stopping along the way. An RV's great for that. Don't need a hotel. Got my own."

Ruth eyed her uncle. It had been a couple of years since she'd seen him. As a professor at the University of North Carolina, he taught history, but Maggie had told her he was on a sabbatical doing research. His black hair was now more salt than pepper as was the bushy mustache that he'd always sported. Maggie had gotten her auburn hair from her mother who had been a beauty just like her daughter. Uncle Owen wore tortoiseshell rimmed glasses, and his skin was tanned. Much of his research took him to outside digs and historical areas as much as libraries and museums.

"So where do you plan to park that thing, Dad?" Maggie linked her arm through his. "You're going to give us a tour, right?"

"Why of course. I've got reservations at a local campground just south of here. It's on Pamlico Sound. I should get in some good fishing while I'm here, don't you think?"

"I'm sure you will, Dad. I'm sure you will." Maggie patted his arm as she and Ruth followed him into the RV.

~

"You told me you were coming here to do research on an artifact, Dad." Maggie placed a heated-up plate of Spanish mackerel, red beans and rice, coleslaw and hush puppies in front of her father as he settled at the kitchen table. "That's all you said. Tell us more."

Ruth placed a glass of lemonade in front of him then she and Maggie took chairs at the table.

Uncle Owen bowed his head and said a quick prayer before lifting his fork and filling it. "Mind if I eat first, sweetheart. I'm starved. And this looks amazing. Who cooked?"

"Your favorite niece, of course. I don't cook, you know. But who knows. Maybe one day I'll pick up a cookbook and give it a try. That's how Ruthie learned."

"I'd say she learned well." Uncle Owen refilled his fork. "This is delicious, Ruthie."

"Thanks, Uncle Owen. Now, please tell us about this artifact you're looking for. What gives?"

Owen took a sip of his lemonade and wiped his mouth on his napkin. "Well, a couple of years ago I was reading an article written by a local librarian about the history of the prohibition story that her great-grandmother Ava Sinclair Kelly had written. I was compelled to search for the treasure that Big Tony Amato had pilfered from Jamaica. I don't know if it's still here on the island or if it went down with him on his rum-runner. I suppose there's a fifty-fifty chance of either one, but I had to go to Jamaica to research and discover what the treasure actually was."

He took a bite of his now cooling food, then he took two more before he continued his story.

"Apparently Big Tony Amato stole a Spanish cross named *La Cruz de San Mateo* from a museum in Kingston. Saint Matthew's Cross is a golden cross with a ruby heart in the center. It's approximately eight inches long by six inches wide and, except for the ruby heart, it's made of solid gold. It was brought over to Jamaica by the Spaniards sometime in the 1500's. I haven't been able to narrow that down yet."

Ruth and Maggie exchanged astonished glances.

"So that's what Mary was talking about," Ruth said. "The treasure that is believed to have gone down with the rum-runner."

Owen's fork stopped halfway to his mouth. "You've heard of it?"

"Oh, yeah, Dad. We've heard of it. Mary Kelly, the librarian in Hatteras Village is the great-granddaughter of the prohibition agent that sent Big Tony to his watery grave. It's believed around here that the treasure went down with him. No one knows what the treasure is though."

Owen chewed and swallowed his bite thoughtfully. "Well, it is a possibility. I was hoping it was still here on the island."

Ruth snapped her fingers. "I wonder if Mary would let you get a look at her great-grandmother's book. Could she have mentioned where the rum-runner went down?"

"Surely everyone who's read it has tried to dive on it," Maggie waved aside her words. "Wouldn't you think?"

Ruth shrugged. "Wouldn't hurt to ask for Uncle Owen's sake."

Owen stroked his mustache. "I'd like to meet this Mary Kelly. Sounds like she's the same librarian who wrote the article I read?"

"She's the only local librarian who's a direct descendant of the Kelly's." Ruth placed another serving of Spanish mackerel on Owen's plate.

"Then I need to meet this lady." Owen dove into the tender fish.

"Yep," Maggie nodded. "She's right up your alley, Dad."

~

After parking in the beach parking lot, Ruth strolled north of the lighthouse along the beach looking for late piping plover nests, loggerhead turtles heading inland to lay eggs, anything out of the ordinary. She checked on her piping plover nest that she'd camouflaged with vegetation after she'd found the parents building it. The chicks had long since hatched and had begun to stray from the nest.

When she'd gone quite a way and didn't find anything more, she headed south, passed the lighthouse and continued down the beach. She hadn't gone far when she spotted something that filled her with delight and trepidation at the same time.

A female loggerhead turtle had left the surf and was making her way across the sand to the dunes. Keeping her distance, but following nonetheless, Ruth watched as the slow marine reptile made her way to the soft sand of the dune area.

"Hey what's up?" Ruth turned to see Gage jogging toward her. Dressed in jogging shorts, a knit hoodie and running shoes, he stopped beside her, panting. "Find something interesting?"

"Oh, yes." She couldn't have prevented the excitement in her voice if her life had depended on it. She pointed toward the loggerhead. "Look at that."

Gage's gaze swept from her to the huge turtle climbing the dunes. "Wow. I haven't seen one of those before. What kind is it?"

"A loggerhead. She's getting ready to lay her eggs. You don't actually catch them in the act very often. It's a rare sight."

"You mean that's what she's getting ready to do?" Gage sounded concerned.

Ruth laughed. "Yes, she is. Don't worry. You won't have to

help or anything."

He elbowed her gently. "Wisecracker."

Ruth's gaze was glued on the loggerhead as the turtle stopped at the top of the sand dune and swiped sand away with her fins, excavating an egg pit.

"What's she doing?" Gage whispered.

"She's digging a hole to lay her eggs in."

"Oh."

"Climb up here." Ruth tugged at Gage's hoodie sleeve, guiding him up to a better view. "You can see the whole operation better from here."

She leaned toward him explaining every step of what was happening, not realizing just how close she was.

~

Gage, on the other hand, knew exactly how close Ruth was. The vanilla and peach of whatever she'd used in her hair smelled terrific. He'd really like to tip her hat out of the way, because that's exactly what it was. In the way. But he couldn't do that.

He swallowed hard and tried concentrating on her words. Not on the sweet smell emanating from her hair. And the melodic sound of her voice? Yeah, that was always nice.

The turtle. Concentrate on the blasted turtle, you dope.

All of a sudden, the turtle was laying eggs. Round, white balls that looked like delicate soft pieces of white leather were collecting in the pit she'd dug. Amazing.

"Only the Creator God could perform such a miracle as that." Ruth's voice was filled with awe. "A long time ago He set in motion nature and how nature functions. I don't buy into the whole 'it just happened' theory. I believe in giving credit where credit is due, and I give all the credit to God who made all creation."

Gage turned to look at this woman who continually kept him guessing. "So, you're a Christian?"

"Yes, I am."

Gage nodded. He wasn't. He'd been told all about God years earlier when he'd made a mess of his life. He'd been told how he could and should give his life to Christ, but he hadn't. He'd chosen not to. He'd decided to clean up his life all by himself and go it alone. He didn't think he needed God, so he'd passed on that subject.

"And you?" Ruth asked.

Somehow, he'd known she'd ask. "Nope. Hey, I enjoyed the show. I've never seen anything like that before. How long before the eggs hatch?"

"About two months." Ruth jammed her hand on top of her hat as a gust of wind nearly unseated it.

"Well, thanks for explaining things. It was really interesting. But I need to finish my run. My shift starts in a while. Take care."

"No problem. Bye." Ruth raised a hand as Gage headed up the beach toward the parking lot.

The look in her eyes stayed with him the remainder of the day. He couldn't quite put his finger on what he'd seen there, but it almost looked like disappointment. Or sadness.

~

Antonio leaned back in the desk chair in his office on board his yacht, his feet propped on his desk. He was going through his Gramps Howard's journal to see if anything caught his eye.

The first entry was right after his great-uncle Big Tony Amato's rum-runner had been sunk by the feds.

"When the explosion had occurred, I wasn't really surprised. Uncle Tony always said he'd never let the feds take him. I saw it in my mind's eye. Uncle Tony probably threw a grenade in the boiler room furnace and blew up the boat himself. Did I feel remorse that he died? Not really. I never really felt much for the uncle that took me in. He was a cruel and vile man. Evil even. My mother never trusted her brother, but there hadn't been anyone else she'd have asked to raise her illegitimate son. She knew he could give me the best of everything. And now I'll go back and claim it all. Yes. That's what I'll do.

And the treasure? Was it still on the boat when it went down? Was it still in the cargo hold? Knowing Uncle Tony, he'd never leave it where he couldn't reach it. I'll return one day and search for it. I'll find it. Or die trying."

Antonio scanned further, then went back to the first entry. The treasure had to be on the rum-runner on the bottom of the Atlantic Ocean. But where? Howard had searched for years. He'd led many expeditions spending millions of dollars but hadn't found the rum-runner. How was he going to do any better?

He closed the journal and dropped it to the surface of his immaculate desk. Howard was sure it went down with the boat. Was that for certain? Could it have been left on the island instead? Could Big Tony have left it securely hidden somewhere? But then wouldn't he have told Howard? Howard was just a seventeen-year-old kid at the time and Big Tony hadn't planned to die.

Where was that treasure? And what was it? Had Howard known what it was? Maybe he'd known what it was, but he'd thought for sure it was on *The Satisfaction* because he'd dedicated his whole life to searching the Graveyard of the Atlantic for it.

~

"Hi, Mary." Maggie leaned against the counter in the Hatteras Village Library. "I'd like to introduce you to my father, Owen Lawrence. He's a professor at the University of North Carolina, at Chapel Hill."

Mary Kelly's eyes lifted from the computer screen and bounced from Maggie's face to that of her father's. A smile tilted her lips. She stood and offered her hand across the counter.

"It's a pleasure to meet you, Mr. Lawrence. Welcome to Cape Hatteras."

"Thank you, Mary. It's nice to meet you as well. Please call me Owen."

Mary retook her seat after Owen shook her hand and steepled her fingers beneath her chin. "Well, Maggie, how did your evening go with Ruth?"

"Ask me no questions, I'll tell you no lies," Maggie grinned.

"Owen, I suspect this daughter of yours was a troublemaker as a child." Mary chuckled and shook her head in resignation.

Owen released a chuckle of his own. "You have no idea what a troublemaker she was and still is."

"You two do know I'm standing right here, don't you?" Maggie swiped her hair behind her ear as she cast a dark glance on the pair.

"Of course, daughter." Owen patted her arm as it lay on the counter above Mary's computer monitor. Then he turned back to the grinning librarian.

"So, Mary, my niece, Ruthie, tells me you're the great-granddaughter of the famous local Bureau of Prohibition Agent Mike Kelly and his wife Ava Sinclair Kelly who put a quick stop to the dastardly mobster Big Tony Amato."

"That's correct, Owen. I am." Mary beamed proudly. "Ava Kelly was the first local librarian, and I'm happy to follow in her footsteps. It's been a family tradition for four generations."

"That's impressive. Something to be proud of." Owen nodded and leaned in slightly over the counter. "Mary, a while back, I had the distinct privilege of reading an article in a magazine that you had written about your illustrious great-grandparents and their exploits in halting the mobster. I thoroughly enjoyed it."

Maggie watched as the two older people chatted for a few minutes. Were Mary's cheeks flushed? She seemed a little twitterpated as her dad talked with her. Was there an attraction thing going on here? She suddenly felt like the proverbial third wheel.

"Well, Mary, I've been to Kingston, Jamaica, in search of the treasure *La Cruz de San Mateo*." Owen paused and Mary's eyes grew huge and round.

Maggie laughed inwardly. *Now that's a bombshell tossed into the conversation if there ever was one. Dad definitely got Mary's attention.*

Mary's mouth dropped open, her eyes pinned on Owen. He reached across the counter and lifted her chin, closing her mouth.

"It's okay, Mary. As you well know, I didn't find it, but I did discover that Big Tony Amato stole it from the museum in Kingston when he was there purchasing liquor to run illegally into the US of A, and brought it north on his rum-runner. It seems to have disappeared once it reached Cape Hatteras. No one has seen it since. The trail grows cold here, my dear. Can you tell me anything that will help in my search?"

"Oh...well...I...well...um...." Mary lifted her hands to her bright cheeks, eyes blinking as if she couldn't quite compute what he'd said.

"Are you okay, Mary?" Maggie looked closely at the older woman. "You don't look so good."

Mary released a huge sigh. "No, I'm...fine. I think. I just didn't know anyone was actively searching for..." she glanced around covertly then, leaning forward, whispered, "that item."

"Mary, why are you whispering?" Owen asked.

"Well, I don't know if you've found this information in your research, but supposedly there's a curse on...that item." Mary's brow furrowed and she looked flustered.

Owen's eyebrows shot up and he shook his head. "No, I hadn't discovered that tidbit of information. Interesting. However, I don't believe in such things, so it's of no consequence to me. My question for you, Mary, is do you know for sure if *La Cruz de San Mateo* went down with Big Tony Amato and *The Satisfaction* or is it possible that it's still here on Cape Hatteras somewhere?"

"Shhh," Mary held up a finger to her lips and hushed Owen. "Please stop saying that name. I do believe in curses. Look where it got Big Tony Amato. And yes, I believe it went down with Big Tony. His nephew Howard Amato, or Howie, as Tony referred to him, was very close to Big Tony, and I believe Howie would've known where the item was if Tony had told him. However, Howie spent millions of dollars and many years on expeditions searching out in the Graveyard of the Atlantic for *The Satisfaction*. He never really knew where it went down when the Coast Guard sank the rum-runner. In 1990 he funded his last expedition and it was rumored that he found a boat but an odd thing happened. The expedition boat sank and the whole crew of the expedition went down with the boat. Howie, who was age seventy-nine, and his son, Sebastian Amato, who was in his fifties at the time, were the only survivors."

"That's more than odd," Maggie said. "Big Tony never hid the fact he was a mob boss. Did Howard take over that part of his businesses too?"

Mary shrugged, giving them a knowing glance. "Very good question, Maggie. Even when prohibition ended and liquor was once again legal, the mob bosses still reigned. They eventually worked more quietly as they avoided the authorities, many of whom they bought off. Howard could very well have taken over Big Tony's businesses and kept things running. He likely passed it down to his son and his grandson, Antonio, too."

"Mary," Owen rubbed his chin in thought, "Ruthie said your great-grandmother wrote a book about the incident. Would you allow me to look through it? You know, to see if I can spot something useful in my research. I want to make sure there's no chance it's hidden here on the island somewhere."

Mary shoved her rolling desk chair back and stood. "Well, of course you can. But I've read through it several times. I don't think you'll find anything to support your theory that it's hidden on the island. Big Tony would've kept something like that close to him."

Maggie and Owen followed Mary to the Kelly display at the rear of the library. Withdrawing a small ring of keys from her slacks pocket, she unlocked the plexiglass case holding the handwritten book by Ava Sinclair Kelly.

"Here you go, Owen." Mary held out the delicate book, a smile on her face, her cheeks flushed. She tilted her head slightly with a "come-hither" look in her eyes. "Of course, I can't let the book out of the library, but you're welcome to come as often as you like to peruse it."

A smile tugged at the corners of Maggie's lips and she had to cover her mouth with her hand. Mary was practically flirting with her dad. Maggie's glance slid to him and spied a grin on his face.

"Thank you, Mary. I think I'll sit right over here now and glance through this very informative tome. Then of course, I'll be back. I'm sure I'll need to return for further information."

Oh, my. He's blathering. It was all Maggie could do not to roll her eyes.

"Dad, if you're going to be here a while, I think I'll leave you and come back later."

"Oh, that's alright, Maggie. We close at five." Mary glanced at her wristwatch. "I can always run him home, if necessary. I live in Buxton. I assume that's where you're staying?"

"That's right." Owen nodded eagerly. "I'll catch a ride with Mary, dear. You needn't worry about me."

Maggie's glance bounced between the two. Now she definitely was a third wheel. "Then I'll leave you to your research. Thanks, Mary. Have fun, Dad, but behave yourself."

Owen dropped a kiss on Maggie's forehead. "Always, sweetheart. Love you."

Maggie gave him a squeeze around his middle. "Love you, too, Dad. Bye."

Chapter Eight

R uth pulled the door of her office shut and hurried down the stairs. She had plenty of time before her evening program started but she always liked to be early. Visitors generally began arriving a half hour earlier than the scheduled time so she made it a habit of being there fifteen minutes earlier than that. She slipped her small, slim flashlight into her back pants pocket as she reached for the doorknob.

Just then the door swung in as someone turned the doorknob and shoved it open.

"Oohhh," Ruth groaned as the door nearly hit her in the face and slammed her hat down over her eyes. She quickly stepped back as the door banged into her toes and knuckles.

"Oh no, sorry, Ruth." Gage's voice was gruff with surprise as Ruth shifted her hat back into position and she met his horrified gaze. "Are you alright?"

Gage started to reach for Ruth's arm, but she pulled back before he could touch her.

"I'm fine, Gage. More startled than anything." She held her bruised knuckles behind her back. "What are you doing here anyway?"

"The medical examiner's report came in for the guy you found on the beach." Gage removed his hat and ran a hand through his hair, his voice a bit husky. He eyed her closely. "You sure you're okay?"

"I'm fine." Without thinking, she brought her hand from behind her back and waved his words away. "Really, I am."

His gaze zeroed in on the fresh red scrape on her knuckles and he nabbed her hand between gentle fingers. "It doesn't look like it."

Ruth swallowed hard and attempted to tug her hand away. Her breathing increased but she realized it wasn't from panic and that was genuinely surprising. Then there was the electric zing his gentle touch elicited.... No, this had to stop.

"It's really nothing, Gage. Just a scrape. I'll put something on it in a bit." She tugged hard and he let go, his gaze moving back to hers.

"Make sure you do. You don't want to get an infection."

Ruth nodded, her mind on anything but the scrape on her knuckles. "So, what were you saying about a medical examiner's report?"

Gage let his gaze rove over her features then he took a visible deep breath. "Um, yeah. The ME's report. It came in a little while ago. The man's name is Joe Pachino, a known criminal with a record as long as my arm. Apparently, he got on somebody's wrong side. His hands and legs were tied before he was killed. He was shot in the chest five times with a 9mm. A very heavy weight was attached to his feet, pulling joints out of position and breaking bones throughout his body. Then he was taken out to sea and tossed overboard. He was fortunate he was shot first. The medical examiner estimates the amount of weight that was used to inflict this damage would have been between three and four hundred pounds. There was no water in his lungs so more proof that he was dead before he was thrown overboard."

Ruth shook her head, her face wincing as he spoke. "How horrible. No one deserves to be treated like that. Not even a criminal."

"Perhaps not, but now we have to find out who did this to him."

"Do you have any leads?"

"Maybe." A grimace tilted Gage's lips. "Some things to check out at least. We'll see."

"Well, possible leads are good," Ruth said. "Have you located any family to claim the body?"

"Apparently Pachino had a sister out in the midwest. She'll see he's buried. Properly this time." Gage shifted his feet then crossed his arms over his chest. "Ruth, I know we haven't exactly got on so well since we met, but I'd really like to take you out for, oh say, coffee or dinner sometime. You know, just as friends, of course."

Ruth looked at him skeptically, but the panic still didn't overcome her like it usually did. What was with that anyway? She really needed to give it some thought, but if she did she might have to face some answers she wasn't ready to face.

"On one condition." She held up her index finger, half surprising herself that she was agreeing to go out with him at all.

Gage eyed it for a moment before returning his gaze to her face. "Oookay. What's the condition?"

"You go to church with me on Sunday."

Without any hesitation, Gage nodded, his gaze fixed on hers. "Deal. Do I pick you up or meet you there?"

Ruth's delicate brows rose as her eyes widened. "Really? Just that easy?"

"Sure." He shrugged, not even batting an eye.

Ruth licked her lips, a movement Gage's eyes followed closely. Heat flooded her cheeks as she lowered her gaze momentarily. Taking a deep breath, she finally spoke. "I'll meet you there. Maggie will want to come too."

Gage nodded and replaced his "Smokey-Bear" hat on his head.

"I believe you have visitors waiting for you, and I need to get back on patrol." His voice had a husky edge to it, and he cleared his throat. "I'll see you later, Ruth."

"See you."

Ruth stepped outside and pulled the door closed behind her, locking it. She watched as the tall, broad-shouldered park policeman strode toward the Cape Hatteras Lighthouse visitor entrance. She headed toward the lighthouse to meet her guests. Taking several deep breaths, she attempted to get her rapid breathing and accelerated heartbeat under control. Why did Gage Hampton have that effect on her? She knew why. Besides being the most handsome man she'd come across to date, he was always kind and acted like a true gentleman around her. But he'd admitted he wasn't a Christian. She was not now or anytime in the near future ready to begin a relationship with anyone, but a non-Christian? No. That wasn't going to happen. Not even with Gage Hampton. So how was she going to get her heart to stop beating in overdrive every time the man came into sight? *Lord, about that…*

~

Sunday morning, Ruth dressed in a chiffon navy floral dress with flowy cap sleeves, a V-neck, and a gathered waistline. She loved the way the hem rippled around her calves. She'd wrap a medium-weight cream shawl around her shoulders when it was time to head out. Pulling the sides of her honey-blond hair up, she fastened it with a clip and tugged tiny tendrils down to frame her face. Rarely did she wear makeup, but today she decided a little powder and lipstick might be in order.

When she walked into the kitchen with a pair of navy sandals dangling from her fingers, Maggie glanced up from making coffee.

"Wow, don't you look spiffy, cuz." Her eyebrows shot upward as her eyes grew round. "You clean up pretty good."

"Thanks." Ruth chuckled, dropping her sandals by a kitchen chair and padding in her hose-clad feet toward the fridge for creamer.

"You don't look so bad yourself." She elbowed Maggie as she reached for a mug from the cabinet above the coffee maker. "I love that skirt and blouse on you."

"These old things?" Maggie pinched the fabric of her blouse. "I've had these for ages, but thanks. Here, let me pour you a cup."

Ruth slipped her arm around Maggie's waist and leaned her head on her shoulder. "I'm so glad you're going with me this morning."

Maggie set the coffee pot back on the coffee maker and gave Ruth a squeeze. "Hey, I may not always be around for you, but when I can I will be. And don't worry, Gage Hampton doesn't look like the type to bite, sweetie. He strikes me as the trustworthy type."

Ruth raised her head. "How do you know for sure? I thought I did once. Boy was I wrong."

Maggie rubbed Ruth's arm. "I know, sweetie, but that was a long time ago. You have to stop looking back and look to the future."

Ruth poured creamer into her coffee, stirred it, then picked it up and stepped away from Maggie.

"That's harder to do than you can imagine, Mags. There's not a day goes by that something doesn't remind me of that day. I still have nightmares. And it wasn't as long ago as you make it seem. It was only seven years ago."

Ruth sat at the kitchen table and sipped her coffee. Maggie brought her cup and sat in the seat across from her.

"I'm sorry, Ruthie. I didn't mean to upset you or belittle your experience. I just wish and pray that one day you can move past it. I want you to find love one day, and I fear that you'll let your past prevent you from letting love in. You won't even entertain the idea of a date."

Ruth set her cup on the table and gave Maggie a look of exasperation. "Mags, Gage Hampton told me he wasn't a Christian. Point blank. He needs to hear the gospel. My main reason for asking him to come to church was first and foremost to hear the Word. His reason for coming was to ask me out. I told him if he came to church with me that I would go out with him. So I will, but only once. If he's not a Christian, I can't seriously date him. You know what the Bible says about being unequally yoked with unbelievers."

Maggie nodded then sipped her coffee. "I know, Ruthie. I know. It's a shame though. He seems like such a nice guy."

"Then pray for him. He needs the Lord, Mags."

~

Gage arrived at the church in Buxton just as they were closing the doors. He slipped in as the congregation was standing to sing. Drawing in a deep breath he told the usher who he was looking for and the white-haired gentleman led him halfway down the middle aisle to where Ruth sat on the end with Maggie beside her. Next to Maggie, an older man with salt and pepper hair, a mustache and tortoiseshell rimmed glasses slid down to make room when Gage stepped into the row. He grinned and tossed a wave in Gage's direction. Who could that be?

Gage nodded and turned his attention to Ruth who smelled faintly of vanilla and peaches. Mmmm. Boy, Ruth smelled nice. She lifted her gaze to meet his briefly then lowered it to the hymnbook she held out to share with him. He had a hard time concentrating on the words of the song, but he made a valiant effort.

"What can wash away my sins?
Nothing but the blood of Jesus."

He'd heard this song before. Years ago, when he was sixteen years old, Coach Watkins had taken him to youth camp. Mom and Dad had pretty much washed their hands of him that summer. He'd gotten into so much trouble with drugs and the cops, his parents had decided to go to Europe and leave him to deal with things himself. If it hadn't been for Coach Watkins stepping in and helping him, he'd probably be on the streets today. Or worse.

Wow, he'd tucked that horrible memory away so long ago and the words of one song had brought it rushing back like it had happened yesterday. Gage attempted to stuff the memory back where he'd tucked it so many years ago, but he couldn't. It hung around even as the song finished and the congregation took a seat.

He drew in a deep breath trying to clear his head and inhaled the fresh scent of the woman beside him. That was much more pleasant to dwell on.

"Welcome, friends," the pastor of the church greeted. "I hope you've come today to do business with the Lord. Whether you need to get things right with Him or whether you need to turn your sins over to Him and ask Him to come into your life today, let Christ work in your heart this morning."

Something teased at Gage's mind bringing with it a discomfort somewhere inside, but he shoved it away. It had nagged at him before but he'd always managed to ignore it. The pastor had to be talking to others. Gage had never been to this church before. The pastor didn't know him from a hole in the ground. Glancing at Ruth beside him, Gage tried to concentrate on her rather than the words of the man behind the pulpit.

The congregation stood again and sang another song before the pastor's message.

When the man finally stood to preach, Gage had grown rather uncomfortable and a bit fidgety. He noticed Ruth eyeing him. He planted his feet on the floor attempting to still their movement. This was ridiculous. What did he have to be jittery about? He glanced around the room, anywhere but at the preacher who seemed to have his eyes on Gage. Did he know Gage wasn't a Christian? How would he know? It wasn't like the man had a direct line to God or anything. Did he?

That niggle deep inside Gage drew him to the words of the

preacher even as he attempted to ignore him.

"For God's word says in Romans 3:23 'For all have sinned, and come short of the glory of God.' My friends, that means that not one of us has escaped sin. We're all sinners. We've missed the mark. We've come short of God's glory. His glory is perfect and pure and we've come short because of our sins. We can't reach that glory on our own, but God made a way.

"If you look in verse 24 it says, 'Being justified freely by his grace through the redemption that is in Christ Jesus.' That's the way. Do you know what justification is? My friends, justification means just as if I never sinned. We are justified freely by His grace through the redemption that is in Christ Jesus. And redemption means to deliver from. Jesus Christ has delivered us from sin.

"My friends, if you've accepted Christ as your personal Savior then you've been justified freely by His grace through the redemption that is in Christ Jesus. That should fill you with joy."

Gage felt something stirring but it wasn't joy. It was a hollow ache deep within him. He glanced at Ruth and Maggie beside her and saw pure joy on their faces. Even the man beside Maggie was smiling and nodding. What was *he* missing? Did that joy come from being a Christian? Coach Watkins had told him years ago that he needed to give his life to Christ, and He would fill him with a peace that would pass all understanding. Is that what this was all about?

"But friends, if you've never placed your faith in Christ," the preacher continued, "if you've never put your trust in Him as your personal Savior, it's time you do. You, too, can be justified freely by His grace through the redemption that is in Christ Jesus. Won't you come today?"

Gage swallowed hard and gripped his fingers together. This was something he'd have to think about. He hadn't remembered Coach's words in years. Perhaps it was time to give them some serious consideration as well as what he'd heard the preacher say today.

Gage had come to church to get a date with Ruth but somehow he thought this might have a far more life-impacting affect than that. He'd have to think about this. Later.

~

Antonio Amato leaned against the railing along the bow of

The Lucky Lady as she slipped from her berth and headed out to sea. Once they were clear of the harbor buoys, his new captain increased the twin caterpillar engines to 22 knots, and Antonio felt them purring beneath his feet. He'd hired Captain Warrick Carrington to pilot his yacht since he'd dismissed his last captain. The man had questioned Antonio's judgment concerning some…things. You don't question Antonio's judgement. Ever. And the former captain would never question him again. Or do anything else for that matter.

Today they were heading out for a simple little diving expedition to take a quick look-see just south of the lighthouse, a mile out from shore with sonar equipment. He'd hired a few divers who were trained on the equipment and who could dive if they found something.

Gramps Howie had paid millions to dive far out at sea and had no luck. Perhaps *The Satisfaction* was closer inland. It was worth a shot to take a look before he moved into deeper waters between the shallows and the much deeper waters where Gramps Howie searched.

Antonio straightened and headed to the bridge. Captain Carrington had been hired to do as he was told and to keep his mouth shut. Only time would tell if he could be trusted. The tall, spare, beady-eyed and balding man had put *The Lucky Lady* through the rigors, all the while treating her with care, and Antonio had been impressed. He'd see what the captain would do with his baby on the rough seas of the Graveyard of the Atlantic.

After checking in at the bridge, Antonio headed to the stern and found three divers preparing their gear. Lennie and Harland sat in chairs along the side of the deck watching.

Antonio eyed his underlings with a curled lip and a furrowed brow. "Don't you two have something you should be doing?"

"Nah, not really, boss." Lennie leaned forward in his chair. "Besides, these guys are really interestin' to watch."

Antonio crossed his arms over his chest. "Interesting, huh? Did you two follow up on the medical examiner's report on Joe? Have you gotten more information as to what the cops know? Can they link him to me?"

Harland eyed Antonio as the boss's voice raised a notch with each question. He punched Lennie on the arm to get his attention.

"What?" Lennie turned a glare in Harland's direction. Following Harland's gaze back to the boss's face, Lennie's expression instantly transformed to that of wariness and fear. His Adam's apple bobbed up and down as he swallowed. "Oh, boss. What's up? Ya need something?"

"Yeah, I need something. I need you two imbeciles to get off your duffs and get back to work. I want to know what's going on with the medical examiner's report on Joe, and I want to know now."

With every word his voice grew in volume, and the color drained from Lennie and Harland's faces. Both men stood from their chairs nearly at attention and in unison said,

"Yes, Boss."

They hightailed it off the lower stern deck and headed inside to the control center to do the boss's bidding.

Antonio turned around and observed the three divers setting up their sonar equipment. They were dressed in swim trunks and t-shirts and all wore sunglasses.

"Will this table be sufficient to meet your needs, gentlemen?" Antonio asked, tapping the long portable table that had been set up for this occasion. "If you need more space, I can have more tables set up. Just tell me what you need."

"This is plenty of space, Mr. Amato," one of the divers said as he reached for a pair of headphones. "There's not that much equipment. But thanks. We're good."

"No problem," Antonio nodded. "Just let me know if you need anything. Anything at all."

All the men nodded and continued to work.

Antonio pursed his lips and crossed his arms over his chest, slowly backing away. Electronics was not his thing. Running a business? He could do that. Keeping people in line. Yeah, he could do that too. Electronics? Not so much.

He took a deep breath and let it out in a rush. All at once he felt at loose ends. Until they reached the site where they would begin diving, he didn't really know what to do. He was excited about exploring, but he knew that it was a long shot that they'd find anything right off the bat. It would likely take a while and a lot of searching. Gramps Howie had searched his whole life and he'd never found anything. At least Antonio knew where not to look. Gramps had documented that well.

Antonio climbed up and through the yacht to the highest forward bow deck until he could see where the boat was headed. The wind was blowing his hair back, his light polo shirt billowing around his body.

Looking to his right, he spotted Cape Hatteras Lighthouse. It was just south of there that the female park ranger had found Joe's remains. Again, he reassured himself that no one could connect him to Joe. No one. Looking left, he remembered they'd taken Joe pretty far out and dumped him overboard. It had been rotten luck that he'd washed ashore. Now if they could just get their hands on that body again and make him disappear along with the report, he'd be a happy man.

Chapter Nine

Ruth noticed that Gage seemed rather quiet as he allowed her to step out of the row in front of him and into the aisle. He followed her quietly as they joined the congregation leaving the church. Maggie and Uncle Owen's quiet chatter were right behind them as they exited the building.

Pastor Goodman held out his hand as Ruth approached. "Hello, Ruthie. How're you doing this beautiful Sunday morning? It's good to see you."

"Good morning, Pastor Goodman. It's good to be here. Gage," Ruth turned to Gage and laid her hand lightly on his arm, "this is Pastor Goodman. Pastor, I'd like to introduce you to our newest park policeman out at the seashore. This is Gage Hampton."

Gage held out his hand to the older gentleman who grasped it firmly and gave him a welcome shake. "Good morning, sir. It's a pleasure to meet you."

"Oh, it's a pleasure to meet you, too, Gage. Welcome to the island. I hope you'll make yourself at home and come on back to join us again. We try to make our visitors welcome and feel more like family than visitors."

Ruth noticed Gage's hesitation before he nodded and said, "Thank you, sir."

"Ruthie, you bring this young man back. I suspect he needs a good home church." The older man patted Ruth's shoulder. "What do you think?"

"Yes, sir, I think you're probably right."

Ruth glanced in Gage's direction then slid her gaze away.

"Y'all take care and we'll see you later," the pastor said as he reached for Maggie's hand behind Ruth.

Ruth and Gage moved away, but before they'd walked more than a few feet, someone called Ruth's name.

"Hey, Ruth. How you been, sweetie?"

~

Gage turned to find a tall, blond and blue-eyed man strolling toward Ruth, his gaze fixed on her. His Hollywood-white smile lit up his face. When he reached her, he pulled her into a tight hug that left her breathless and cherry-cheeked. He planted a kiss on her flushed cheek that made Gage want to punch bunnies. Now why was that? He couldn't be jealous. He had no claim to the hazel-eyed, honey-haired beauty. Did this man? If so, she'd failed to mention him.

"Casey?" Ruth's voice squeaked the name with happiness. "When did you get back into town?"

"Yesterday. Glad to see me?" The Hollywood heartthrob waggled his eyebrows, but this time Gage noticed Ruth's cheeks had cooled and the red had faded not to return.

"Of course, I am." She punched him on the arm, giggling as she did. "But what about Bobbye? Where is she?"

"Ah she's here somewhere. Catching up with somebody or other."

Just then a beautiful, young blond woman slipped up beside Casey and wrapped her arm around his waist. "Who's catching up with who?"

"Bobbye!" Happiness oozed from Ruth as she reached for the woman and gave her a hug. "I'm so glad you're back."

Then holding her at arm's length, she added, "And look at you. You've got that glow everyone talks about."

Gage wasn't sure what that meant, but he did notice that although she had a slender build, the woman was very pregnant. She was indeed beautiful although in his opinion she didn't hold a candle to Ruth.

"And who's this?" Casey's voice held a touch of wariness as his eyes narrowed, raking Gage from head to toe.

If Gage didn't know better he'd think Casey was Ruth's older brother rather than a friend. The way he was eyeing him raised the hair on the back of Gage's neck. Heat rolled up from beneath his collar and he wasn't sure if it was from anger at the third-degree the man was laying on him or embarrassment from the same third-degree in front of Ruth.

"Casey, Bobbye, this is Gage Hampton, our newest park police officer out at the seashore." Ruth's soothing, musical voice drew Gage's gaze to her face and her gaze met his in a brief moment before returning to the couple. The look in her hazel eyes accompanied by a slight upward tilt of her sweet lips into a slight smile sent his heart soaring. It was only for a moment, but it reassured him nonetheless.

"Park police, huh?" Casey held out a hand. "Nice to meet you, Gage. Welcome to Cape Hatteras."

Gage eyed Casey's hand then shook it. He looked him in the eye, quirking a grin. "Not going to snap my head off after all?"

A flood of crimson rolled upward from Casey's shirt collar and tie right on up to his blond hairline. He swung his arm back around his wife. "Sorry about that, but I look after my friend, Ruthie. She's like my sister. What can I say?"

Bobbye reached across and shook Gage's hand. "It's nice to meet you, Gage. And don't mind this big guy. He sticks his foot in his mouth all the time. But he's really just a teddy bear."

"Shhhh, honey. Don't give away all my secrets." Casey gave his wife a squeeze.

They all chuckled then Casey looked at Gage and said, "Gage, we're having a beach party tonight after church. A bunch of us from our young adult Sunday School class are getting together on the beach and having a bonfire, food, singing and a great time. Sort of celebrating our return to the island. Why don't you join us?"

"Return from where?" Gage asked, his brow furrowing.

"Casey's a captain with the Coast Guard and they were temporarily stationed in Florida," Ruth explained. "They've just returned to the Coast Guard station here on Cape Hatteras."

"And I have to say it's so good to be home." Bobbye leaned her head against her husband's shoulder. "Florida was great, but it's just not our Cape Hatteras."

"Well the really nice thing is you're getting back just as the weather's turning warmer," Ruth said.

"Yep, should make for a nice night on the beach. So, what do you say, Gage? You coming?" Casey tilted his head in a challenge.

Gage thought he'd had enough of this church during the service and had hoped to find a way not to come back. He enjoyed

Ruth's company and he supposed that her company on the beach wouldn't really be the same as her company at church where there was preaching. Casey had said there would a bonfire, food, singing and a great time. Nothing about preaching. Maybe he'd be safe and not uncomfortable like he'd been during the service.

"Sure." He tilted his chin in an affirmative nod. "Sounds like it could be fun."

Ruth turned her gaze on him and gave him another slight smile. She had yet to turn a full-fledged smile on him but he'd take what he could get. At least she was looking in his direction.

"Great," Casey said. "We're meeting on the beach by the lighthouse. We'll see y'all there at six. Oh, and bring Maggie. I think I saw her talking with someone and she may not know about the get-together."

"I will," Ruth nodded. "See you later."

Casey and Bobbye left and Ruth turned to Gage.

"You know, Casey's just a little over-protective of me. Please don't take offense."

"You think?" Gage smiled broadly and waited for a return smile. Ruth's cheeks bloomed into color and her lips formed the smile he'd been waiting for but her gaze refused to meet his. Oh well, one step at a time.

"Don't worry, Ruth. I'm not offended. At least someone's looking out for you."

The smile disappeared as her gaze slid to his. Could he not have both? Then a thought struck him. Had something happened to her? Was that why Casey was so protective? Was that why she was so standoffish? The mystery of this woman was tugging at him and he was determined to get to the bottom of it.

~

Gage offered to pick Ruth and Maggie up at her house but she had declined and said they would meet him at the beach at six. The sun was already low in the west by the time they arrived and Casey and a couple of the guys had already built a bonfire. Although it was growing warmer in the daytime, as the sun disappeared, the bonfire felt amazing. Ruth pulled on her hoodie jacket, jammed her hands in the pockets and stood next to the glowing flames that leapt from the piled logs built far up on the sandy beach. The ocean waves wouldn't be able to reach the fire as the waves dashed across the shoreline.

A crowd of folks had gathered and placed their folding chairs around the bonfire. A couple of folding tables stood strategically where everyone could enjoy the food. As they arrived, the party goers deposited their contributions on the tables. A pile of wooden hotdog roasting sticks was laid nearby ready to use.

"Evening," a deep voice spoke from beside Ruth. She glanced up to find Gage, the bonfire's flames reflecting on his grinning face.

"Hi. Did you come with an appetite? There's usually lots of eats at these gatherings, you know."

"Really? That's good to know." Gage nodded, glancing around at the crowd. "Was I supposed to bring a chair?"

Ruth chuckled. "Yeah. Sorry. Maybe I should've mentioned that. But I have an extra one in my car. I always have a couple. I'll go get it."

"No worries, Ruthie." Maggie walked up, two folding chair bags over her shoulder. "I brought it. I had a feeling someone might need it."

"Mags, you're the best," Ruth said. "There you go, Gage. What can I say? I have an awesome cousin."

"I'd say so." Gage reached for the chair.

"Well, I guess we're even on one score, huh, copper." Maggie laughed. She pulled her chair from her bag and set it up. "Where's your chair, Ruth?"

"Over here." Ruth walked a few paces away and pulled her chair over.

They sat down and a few minutes later, Bobbye and Casey set their chairs up next to them.

"Hey guys, how're you doing?" Bobbye waved her hand at them and plopped into her chair.

"We're good. What about you, little mama?" Maggie pointed a finger at her. "You look exhausted."

"Oh, I am," Bobbye nodded. "And I just got up from a nap a little while ago."

"She needs to go have this baby." Casey dropped into his chair looking disgruntled. "I'm ready for this to be over with."

Bobbye cast an "I can't believe you just said that" look at him. "Really? Who's carrying this little bundle of joy, sweetheart?"

Casey looked sheepish. "Sorry, my love. I know you're even more ready."

"When are you due?" Gage asked.

"Next week." Bobbye smiled at him and shifted in her chair. "Not soon enough for me, umm, us. That's for sure."

A young man with a guitar stood and led the group in several hymns and choruses. Ruth noticed Gage didn't sing along much. He was fidgeting again like he'd done earlier in the morning service. He seemed uncomfortable with the gospel message. Was God working on his heart? Oh, please let it be so.

Lord, is that what You're doing? Is that why Gage is so fidgety? Please convict his heart and help him see his need for You.

~

Gage was relieved when the guitar guy stopped playing, prayed over the food and everyone headed for the food table and began roasting hotdogs. He'd been hungry earlier but now his appetite had left him. What was it about being amongst these Christians that made him so miserable? He knew exactly what it was. It brought back his ugly past that he'd tucked so neatly away and set it right back in front of his face. No, they couldn't see it. They didn't know. But he did. And God did, didn't He? Yeah, He did.

He glanced at Ruth who stood up with Maggie and Bobbye. They were heading up to the food line. He sucked in a deep breath and let it out in a rush. Maybe he should just slip away. He'd give an excuse later as to why he'd left. No one would really miss him. He'd see Ruth at work sometime this week, and it would be no big deal.

A heavy slap on his shoulder made him jump and he turned to find Casey beside him.

"Let's grab a hotdog stick before they're all gone, Gage." The other man led him over to the pile before he could make an excuse and leave. "So, do you like Cape Hatteras? As park police, you've got a lot of seashore to patrol."

Gage twirled the wooden stick between his fingers. Maybe he'd stick around for a little while. "Yeah, I like it here. I like it a lot. Patrolling the shoreline and Rt. 12 is part of what I like. There's miles and miles to patrol, plenty to see and lots of people to meet and interact with."

Casey stuck two hotdogs on his stick and waited as Gage did the same then they moved toward the bonfire.

"Yep, I can see how that would hold its appeal, but I'm a seaman myself. I love the ocean, but I get to interact with folks occasionally. Where are you from, Gage?"

"Denver, Colorado."

"Ah, so the ocean is new to you, huh?" Casey turned his hotdogs slowly. "I'm glad you like it here. It's nothing like Denver for sure. I'm from a little further north than Denver. I'm from Fairbanks, Alaska."

"A 'little further north'?" Gage chuckled. "I'd say so. The coldest city in the United States."

Casey joined with a deep laugh. "Yep. It sure is. Well, that's where I joined the Coast Guard. If you can make it in the Coast Guard in Alaska, you can make it anywhere."

Silence reigned for a few minutes as they finished their roasting, then as they headed back to load up their plates, Casey cleared his throat.

"So, I noticed how you look at my friend Ruthie. What are your intentions, Gage?"

Gage lifted an eyebrow and looked Casey in the eye before returning his gaze to filling his plate.

"I haven't known Ruth very long, Casey, but she seems like a wonderful woman that I'd like to get to know better." He shrugged his shoulders. "I can't say about the future because I don't know what the future holds, but if and when the time comes that's between Ruth and me."

Gage started to walk off but Casey stopped him with a hand on his upper bicep.

"Just a warning, my friend. Don't hurt her. She's been hurt enough."

Gage met Casey's stern expression with one of sincerity. "I would never dream of hurting her, Casey."

As the men moved back to their seats, a scream sounded above the hubbub of the chattering crowd. A hushed silence hung like a cloak in the air with only the sound of the ocean waves when a second scream rent the air. Gage and Casey dropped their plates onto their chairs and ran toward the sound of the scream.

A woman stood about thirty-five feet from the gathering just on the outer edge of the circle of light from the bonfire. A dark bundle lay at her feet, the ocean waves lapping at it.

"Susan, are you alright?" Casey laid an arm around the sobbing woman. "What in the world happened?"

"Th...tha...that!" The late twenties brunette sobbed and turned, burying her face in Casey's shoulder.

Gage glanced down and saw what he thought was a face in the dark bundle and from what he could see, it looked pretty messed up. Tugging his cellphone from his pocket, he turned on the flashlight app and, kneeling down, aimed it into the bundle. A man's face, or what was once a face, was framed in a burlap gunny sack. A yellow nylon rope was tied around where the chest area should be. The salt and pepper hair above the disfigured face was plastered to the scalp and forehead.

A couple other men had approached to see what was going on.

"Jake, can you take Susan back over by the fire and help her get warmed up please?" Casey asked one of the men.

"Sure thing." One glance at the body led the man to want to return to the fire himself.

"Actually, Casey, we need to keep her separate from the rest of the crowd until she's been questioned by park police," Gage said. "Jake, if you can grab a chair and a jacket and bring them back over this way for her to sit that would be better. And Jake, you can't say anything to anyone. Do you understand? They'll ask but you can't tell them."

Jake nodded. "Yes, sir. I understand."

Casey stayed with Susan until Jake returned with the chair and the jacket, then he made her as comfortable as possible under the circumstances. She was far enough away from the body not to see it but not close enough for the party crowd to question her.

"What do you make of that, Gage?" Casey knelt beside him.

"I'd say somebody broke him in half and stuffed him in a burlap sack. Look behind his head." Gage's voice was grim as he pointed. "Those are his feet. Then they pretty much ripped his face off. You can't see his fingers, but my guess would be, they've removed his fingerprints, too."

"Yep, looks like this guy got on someone's bad side."

Gage hit a speed dial number on his cellphone and put the

device to his ear.

"Hey Wayne. Yeah, I'm down here on the beach with some friends at a beach party. Unfortunately, there's been another body found. Totally different kind of death, but I'd bet a week's worth of paychecks it's the same killer."

Chapter Ten

S orry, Casey, but this area of the beach just became a crime scene." Gage clicked off his phone and slipped it into his shirt pocket. "Wayne Mitchell's headed over and we're going to have to move the body further up onto the beach. The tide's coming in and the medical examiner's flying over from Raleigh, but he won't get here for several hours. He's at another crime scene now."

"So, we have to shut down the party, huh?" Casey tossed a thumb over his shoulder toward the crowd at the bonfire. Murmurs could be heard as people talked. "You know they're wondering what all the hubbub is with the screaming and what we've found."

"Yeah, I should probably go have a talk with them." Gage straightened to his feet and strolled toward the circle of firelight, pulling out his credentials as he went. He felt more than heard Casey's presence behind him.

"Excuse me, folks. Can I have your attention please?" Gage raised his voice. Everyone swung their eyes in his direction as he held his park police credentials high. "I've met some of you but others I haven't. I'm Officer Gage Hampton, National Park Service Park Police. You're probably wondering what all the screaming was about. One of the ladies found a body washed ashore just over there at the edge of the water."

He pointed in the direction of the body. "I've already called it in, and we'll have more park police here soon. I'm closing off that section of the beach, and I have to ask you not to talk about this to anyone once you leave here tonight. It'll hit the news soon enough. The police will want to question everyone to see if anyone knows anything or has seen anything out of the ordinary. It's normal protocol, so don't worry. Just sit back and try to relax as best you can. It may be a long evening."

As a murmur spread through the crowd, Gage dropped his creds wallet back into his hip pocket. He turned to find Ruth walking toward him, her hands tucked into the pockets of her hoodie. The firelight played in her honey-colored hair as the gentle ocean breeze teased tendrils of it about her face. She was beautiful every time he saw her but there was something about the firelight that gave her a different kind of beauty. Was it the warmth of the fire that had burnished her cheeks to a gorgeous copper?

Gage swallowed hard as his pulse jackhammered in his chest. She stopped a couple of feet in front of him. He sucked in a deep breath as he tried to control his rapid breathing that her nearness instilled.

"So, is this one as bad as the last one?" A wry expression tilted Ruth's sweet lips.

"As bad as the last one?" Gage wracked his brain to figure out what she was talking about. Her nearness befuddled him. *Get it together, man.*

Ruth looked at him oddly, her head tilted a little sideways. She pointed out toward the darkness of the Atlantic Ocean. "The body?"

"Ah, yes, the body." Gage ran a hand around the back of his neck then jammed his hands into his jeans pockets and glanced around before meeting her gaze. He heaved another deep breath then released it. What was this woman doing to him?

"Well, it's pretty bad, but in a totally different way. I don't think you want to see it. The medical examiner's coming, but he won't be here for a while. He's on another case right now."

Ruth's gaze moved beyond Gage's left shoulder then returned to his face. "Wayne's here. I guess you'll be going on duty, huh? It'll probably be a long night for you."

Her normally hazel eyes were darkened pools of evergreen in this evening light, and Gage nearly fell in. He would've liked nothing more than to pull her close. He knew beyond a shadow of a doubt that wouldn't be appreciated and it would likely earn him a slap on the face or a punch on the jaw. And if Casey or Maggie were looking, it might elicit something worse. He'd best keep his distance and get down to police business.

"Yeah, I expect it will." He turned and watched as Wayne

approached across the stretch of sand then turned back to Ruth. "I'm sorry your Sunday School beach party was disrupted. This isn't how it should've ended."

"No, it isn't." Ruth shook her head, a sad smile on her lovely features. "I was hoping that since you went to church with me and you upheld your part of the bargain that perhaps I could still uphold mine."

Gage watched as her long golden lashes dropped over her cheeks and knew the color that flooded them wasn't from the warmth of the fire. Was she actually reaching out to him?

"So, you're still willing to go out to coffee or dinner with me?"

Ruth returned her gaze to his. She shrugged her shoulders. "I always keep my word."

"Then I'm going for the gusto. How about dinner Thursday evening? I have to work the weekend shift, and I know you have the program Friday night."

Ruth nodded. "I'm free Thursday."

"Great, it's a..." Gage paused, hesitant to use the word "date" in fear it would make her uncomfortable. "It's dinner then."

"Sounds good." Ruth smiled *and* looked at him. Wow. They were making headway. His heart soared. "Any suggestions about where to go? I'm still feeling my way around the island, you know."

"Actually, I don't go out much so I really wouldn't know what to suggest. Sorry."

Gage chuckled. "A homebody, huh?"

She nodded and laughed with him. "I really am. If I eat out it's usually something quick and simple, or I grab fresh fish at the fish market and take it home and cook it. I hear visitors talking about restaurants and how good they are, but I don't really pay much attention."

"It's okay. Leave it to me." Gage tilted his head in Wayne's direction. "I'd better get to work. Talk to you later?"

At Ruth's nod, he backed away, then turned and headed toward the crime scene.

~

Ruth poured a cup of coffee from the coffee maker and slipped onto the bar stool as Maggie walked into the kitchen the next morning, her mint-green fluffy bathrobe wrapped around her, matching fluffy slippers encasing her feet.

"Morning, Mags. You look like you could use some java. Not easy getting up this morning, huh?" Ruth sipped from her oversized coffee mug then cradled it between her hands. "Not the most fun way to end a beach party: having a body show up in the middle of cooking hotdogs then staying late to try and answer questions we couldn't answer."

Maggie poured a cup of coffee and joined Ruth on a matching bar stool. "No, not fun at all. From what I overheard Gage and Wayne Mitchell talking about, that poor man was pretty mangled. Who would do such a thing to someone?"

"Well, apparently someone's in the business of knocking off those he has no need of anymore. Or those who do him wrong." Ruth dropped off the stool and fetched her work oxfords from beside the backdoor. "I told you about the guy I found just south of the lighthouse, right?"

"Yeah." Maggie nodded. "Sounds like it could be the same killer."

"You never know." Ruth tied her shoes then straightened, returning to her stool and her coffee. "It's disturbing that there's a killer on the loose on our island and that his victims keep washing ashore."

"You've got that right." Maggie shuddered. "I hope the park police can figure it out soon."

"I'm sure they will. Just give them time. What are you doing today?" Ruth took a sip of her coffee.

"I'm going to take Dad around with me while I do errands. Then I'm supposed to meet Mr. Amato again. He wants to go back over some of the photos I took. Some he loved and some he thinks he may want to redo. They're opening the hotel in a couple of weeks, and they're planning a huge grand opening. He wants me to take care of the pictures for the website and some of the advertisements."

"Do you have to prepare the website?" Ruth asked.

"Oh, no, thank goodness." Maggie shook her head with vehemence. "I don't do that kind of thing. I can use them but I wouldn't know where to begin when it comes to building one. Oh no no no no no. I just take the photos and their people do the…whatever they do."

Maggie took another swig of coffee as Ruth chuckled.

Maggie set down her mug and smiled. "So, what were you and Gage chatting about last night? He looked pretty flustered, by the way. If he'd been wearing a hat, I'd say he looked like he'd swallowed it. What was going on?"

"Nothing." Ruth avoided Maggie's gaze. She didn't need to know just how happy it had made her that Gage had gone to church with them yesterday or that he'd come to the bonfire last night. But he was new to the community and she was under no illusions that it was her that brought him. He was likely looking for new people to hang out with, although he did want to take her out to dinner. That was no big deal but Maggie would try to make it one.

"Huh-un," Maggie shook her head. "You can't tell me it's nothing. What plans were you two making?"

"Just dinner." Ruth waved away the plan as if it were nothing at all.

"It's not 'just dinner,' Ruthie. That's a date. Where are you going?"

"I have no idea." Ruth reached for her shoulder bag that hung on a kitchen chair and the car keys that hung by the back door. "It doesn't really matter. Just two co-worker friends getting together to get to know each other a little better. Nothing more. It was a simple bargain. If he came to church with me I'd go out to dinner with him. Now I have to get to work. I'll see you later. Have a good day. Give Uncle Owen a hug for me. Tell him to come by tonight and we'll have supper. Love you, Mags."

Ruth hurried out the door and shut it as she heard her cousin trying to stop her. Her final words were. "Ruthie, one of these days…."

As Ruth unlocked her car and climbed in, she reminded herself how much she owed Maggie and Uncle Owen. They'd helped her through two of the worst times in her life. After her parents had died in a plane crash when she was in her early teens, Uncle Owen, Aunt Julie and Maggie had taken her in and treated her like their own family. Aunt Julie had passed away from a heart attack Maggie's sophomore year and Ruth's freshman year of college. That had left Uncle Owen, Maggie and Ruth. Unsure how they'd be able to go on and return to college, Uncle Owen had pushed them to go on. It was what Aunt Julie would've wanted.

Then when Ruth was a junior and Maggie a senior, they were fortunate enough to be roommates, Maggie studying photography and Ruth biology. That was the year the second worst thing had happened. *He* had nearly destroyed Ruth's life.

Frank's features flashed into Ruth's mind at the same time a chill ran through her body. As pleasant as it was outside, goose flesh flowed over Ruth, sending a shiver through her. She caught her breath at the memory of him. Shaking her head, she attempted to flush his face from her mind.

Turning the key in the ignition, she checked for traffic and pulled out, driving toward the lighthouse and work. Her heart hammered in her chest and her hands grew slippery against the steering wheel. She released one at a time, wiping them against her uniform slacks. She just needed to get to work and get busy. Reminiscing had been a bad idea. Look where it had led her.

She shook her head and shut her eyes, then opened them again. His face was still there, leering at her. Ruth's breathing accelerated. She needed to get it under control. If she didn't, she knew what could happen. *Breathe deeply, Ruth. Just breathe deeply. In. Out. In. Out.*

Ruth attempted to take her own advice and managed to get her breathing to slow down before the pinpricks of light started behind her eyes and the faintness she'd experienced in the past took over. She was behind the wheel of a car, for goodness sake, and even pulling over and passing out was something that she couldn't permit to happen.

She pulled into the first convenience store she reached and hurried inside to purchase a bottle of water. Returning to her car, Ruth sat with the windows open, allowing the morning sea breeze to blow across her face as she sipped the water.

"Hey, are you okay?"

Ruth glanced up to find Gage leaning down staring into her window, concern stamped on his features. He was in his uniform. His patrol car sat behind him, the car door wide open. He squatted beside her window. "You're not looking so good, Ruth. What's the matter?"

How could she tell him she'd just evaded a panic attack

brought on by a memory? She swallowed another swig of water, stalling for time. Then she took a deep breath and released it slowly.

"Ruth, you're pale. What's going on? Do you want me to call the EMTs?" Gage's voice had grown in concern.

"Oh, no, no, that's not necessary. Really. I'll be fine. I mean, I...I am fine." Oh boy. This was not going well.

"Ruth..."

"Gage, please, I'm fine. I'm on my way to work, and I just needed some water." She held up the half-empty plastic bottle then dropped it into the cup holder beside her seat. "I was just getting ready to leave when you startled me. I really need to get going."

Gage stood but leaned over still looking in the window. His gaze swept her features thoroughly. Would he believe her? "Alright, if you're sure. Call me if you have any problems, okay?"

"Okay. Thanks. And thanks for checking on me. That was so thoughtful of you."

"My pleasure." He winked at her before climbing back into his patrol car. He waited for her to start her car and drive away before he pulled out of the parking lot.

Ruth's stomach did a funny little flip as warmth invaded her cheeks at his wink. She couldn't ever remember a man winking at her before. She was a nerd and she knew it. Most guys couldn't get past that to see her as a woman so they just walked on past her to find someone...well...less nerdy. Then there was the fact that she didn't trust men so she didn't encourage them. The fact that she was a nerd really worked in her favor. But sometimes, just sometimes, it would be nice to think there would be someone for her someday too. If she could trust them.

~

Gage pulled his patrol car back onto Rt. 12 and followed Ruth north toward the lighthouse. He wouldn't pull into the visitor's center but he'd continue north on patrol. Following her to make sure she got to work safely was his main goal at the moment. She'd been so pale. A thought struck him and he picked up his cell phone speaking a name for voice call.

"Hey Maggie, it's Gage. How's it going? I didn't wake you, did I?"

"Oh hey, Gage. No, I'm up. Got up before Ruthie left for

work. What's up?"

"Well, I just saw Ruth and she didn't look so good. She was pulled over in a convenience store parking lot drinking a bottle of water. She was really pale and breathing more rapidly than normal. She had a sheen to her face and seemed a little disoriented as well. She told me she was fine. I don't buy it. How was she when she left home?"

There was a pregnant pause over the airwaves before Maggie spoke. "She was fine when she left, Gage. And, yes, this has happened before. I can't tell you why. It's not my story to tell. It's Ruth's."

"You mean you know why she has these symptoms?"

"Yes."

"Will you at least tell me this? Was it a panic attack?"

Another pause met his question. "Yes, and yes. And don't you dare say anything to her about it, do you understand me? She's been through enough. If she wants you to know, she'll tell you."

Gage felt as if someone stuck a knife in his gut for no reason. Something terrible had happened to Ruth and he wasn't allowed to ask why. "Maggie, that's not fair. As I suspect you know, I'm interested in your cousin. She's a sweet woman, and I'd like to get to know her better."

"I'm sorry, Gage, but it's not my story to tell. You're right. Ruth is as sweet as they come, and I'm going to be point blank here. She's a Christian, and if you're not, the Bible says, 'be not unequally yoked with unbelievers.' You don't have enough in common spiritually to start a relationship. If that's not what you're looking for, then great. Just be friends. But if you are, stop right there. It won't work. And I know my Ruthie well enough to know she won't go there."

A surge of emotions rippled through Gage as he drove up the highway: anger, disappointment, self-doubt, self-recrimination. The urge to lash out swept over him then immediately he knew that it was unwarranted. If it was anyone's fault, it was his own. He had his own issues to work through. He just wasn't sure if he was ready to pull them out, look them square in the face and deal with them. His pat response over the years had been to just keep shoving them back in his little secret place and slamming the lid shut then ignoring them until something else brought them to light.

"Gage, I know that probably makes you angry, but I'm not going to sugar-coat anything. That's not me."

Maggie's words yanked Gage's attention back to her. "No, I'm sure you're right, Maggie. I've never claimed to be a Christian, and I don't pretend to be something I'm not. I appreciate your candor and also for protecting Ruth. I know you love your cousin."

His heart lurched at the words. He suspected he was growing to as well although he couldn't understand how. He hadn't known Ruth but a few weeks and as Maggie had said, they didn't have a spiritual common ground to stand on.

"Maggie, do me a favor. I don't know what your schedule is, but check on Ruth sometime this morning if you can."

"Of course, I'll be happy to. I'm picking up my dad shortly to go run errands then I have a meeting with Mr. Amato. We'll stop in to see her before we start our errands."

"Thanks, Maggie."

"No problem, copper. You've got me concerned about her, and I want to see for myself that she's okay. Thanks for giving me a heads up."

"Sure. As you say, no problem."

When Gage clicked off the call, he gripped the steering wheel, his eyes on the road but Ruth's gorgeous face nestled before his mind's eye. Something terrible had happened in her life that only she could tell him and the chances of that were slim to none. She walked a different path in this life, a spiritual path that he wasn't sure he wanted to walk, and if he didn't there would be no relationship between them, at least nothing beyond a workday friendship. Did he want more than that? Of course, he did. In the worst way. Because Ruth Campbell was worth it. Was she worth him dealing with his past issues? That was the question, wasn't it? Maybe it was time he pulled them out and dealt with them once and for all. Dread filled him at the thought.

Chapter Eleven

R uth lowered her binoculars from the egret's nest, pleasure filling her. She turned and headed back toward the office. The young family was doing well. The eggs were laid two weeks earlier and should hatch any day. The world was watching them via the webcam and the internet. Comments were pouring in daily, especially from school children in classrooms across the country. Teachers loved this kind of thing. It was something they could use to teach in their classrooms, check on everyday and see progress. Yes, it had been worth her risk of life and limb to install the webcam, and it would help in one of her research papers for her PhD.

The only problem was, she was so busy she wasn't able to answer all the comments. She had enlisted help from the volunteers. Jodi Chandler and Erica Wilkerson were more than happy to spend time answering comments. The comments that were more biological in nature and needed Ruth's attention were compiled and given to her. Then when she answered them and returned the answers to the volunteers, they entered the information for her, saving her a lot of time.

Ruth stepped onto the porch of the office but before she could place her key in the lock, she heard her name called.

"Ruthie, wait up."

Turning, she spotted Maggie and Uncle Owen headed toward her.

"Hey. What are you two doing here?" Ruth stepped down from the porch and met them on the wide expanse of grass.

"We thought we'd come by to see you." Maggie halted in front of Ruth and reaching out, squeezed her shoulder. "We saw you were about to head up to your office. Can we come up for a few?"

Ruth gave her uncle a hug. "Morning, Uncle Owen. Have you had coffee yet?"

Her uncle rolled his eyes and shook his head. "If you can call the swill that we picked up at the convenience store coffee."

Ruth laughed. "Well, come on up. I have a fresh brewed pot in my office. I just put it on before I checked on the egrets."

"Oh, and how are they doing?" Maggie asked.

"They're amazing," Ruth said, turning her key in the outer door lock. Opening the door, she led them upstairs. "I have them up on one of the computer monitors in my office. You can see them. I could watch them all day long, and some days I'm tempted to."

"There's such enthusiasm in your voice, niece. You love this job, don't you?"

Ruth turned a smile on her uncle as she led them to the back of the upstairs hallway. "Yes, I do, and I love Cape Hatteras. It's an amazing ecosystem to study for my PhD, but not just for that. I love sharing it with my visitors."

As they entered Ruth's office, she arranged chairs for her uncle and cousin to sit on while she grabbed coffee for them. Then before they sat down, she showed them the computer monitor with the live feed of the egret family.

"Oh, Ruthie, that's awesome." Maggie watched transfixed as one egret parent flew away and the other settled onto the eggs. "Look at that. It's so clear. You did a great job getting a close-up view of the action."

"Thanks. They keep me company. Sometimes it's hard to get work done, and I have to turn off the monitor."

Uncle Owen chuckled. "I imagine so. You think it's hard to work now? Just wait till the little one's hatch."

Ruth let out a heavy sigh. "Don't I know it."

She took her seat behind her desk. "Now, to what do I owe the pleasure of this visit? I don't believe this was on your agenda for the day."

Maggie and Uncle Owen took their seats and exchanged brief glances, not missed by Ruth.

"When you left me this morning, Ruthie, you were fine, but I got a call from Gage a short while later." Ruth saw Maggie draw in a deep breath before she continued. "He saw you at the convenience store and said you weren't fine. He thought you were close to having a panic attack. He wanted to know what was going on and he wanted to know why."

A chill raced through Ruth at her cousin's words. "You didn't tell him anything, did you?"

"Of course not, sweetie. It's not my story to tell. But he was beyond worried about you and asked that I check up on you. If you hadn't noticed, the man's quite taken with you, to put it mildly."

Ruth shook her head. "No, I think you're wrong about that. But back to this morning, yes, I almost had a panic attack."

"What happened, Ruthie?" Uncle Owen's voice was gentle and soft. "What brought it on?"

Ruth sucked in a shuddering breath and released it. "I had a few minutes of reminiscing when I went out to the car, and a memory of...of that...time flashed into my mind. His face..."

Maggie jumped up and came around the desk. She squatted down beside Ruth, wrapping her arms around her. "Shhh. Don't go there, Ruthie. It's okay. We're not trying to dredge up memories. We only wanted to make sure you're okay."

"I am, really I am. One memory just sort of led to another then another, and I panicked. I guess I gave Gage something to be concerned about, although by that time I was on the back end of it."

"Ruthie," Uncle Owen stood and reached his hands out to the two women, "come here. You, too, Maggie. Now is a good time to talk to the Lord, don't you think?"

There in the middle of Ruth's office the three linked hands in a tiny circle and Owen lifted his voice to heaven.

"Lord God, our sweet Ruthie had a bad time of it this morning. Bad memories haunting her again. We know that You don't plague her with these, but the evil one who would make her stumble and become ineffective for You is doing this. Lord, put a hedge around our Ruthie and give her strength to stand tall and strong. To put the past in the past and leave it there. We know You have great and wonderful things for her future. Help her to lean on You and trust You and You alone. Fill her with Your Holy Spirit and give her grace to face what lies ahead. We love You, Lord. Amen.

Peace filled Ruth's heart like she hadn't felt in a long while. Had she allowed the evil one to oppress and cause her to become ineffective for the Lord? It would sure seem so. *Oh, forgive me Lord!*

Ruth gave first Maggie then Uncle Owen a hug.

"Thanks for stopping by. I love you both. I guess I needed this visit in more ways than one."

"Hey, what's family for, cuz?" Maggie wiped the moisture from her eyes before it could leak out. "Are we still on for supper with Dad?"

"Of course we are."

"Then we need to get on with our errands and my appointment with Mr. Amato."

Ruth squeezed Maggie's arm. "Yeah, I want to hear how that goes."

Maggie winked. "I'll tell all over supper tonight."

~

After their errands, Maggie dropped her dad at his RV and hurried home to dress for her appointment with Mr. Amato, then she drove to The Brigand's Cove Hotel for her appointment. She was excited to go over the photographs she had taken with the businessman. When she'd gotten the call from his secretary, Jane Williams, the woman had indicated that he was pleased with the majority of the photographs. There were just a few that he wanted re-done. Her camera bag sat on the backseat ready for business.

As she once again entered the brass-trimmed glass revolving door, Maggie felt a thrill run through her. Things were different this time. There was more activity as staff rushed around preparing for the grand opening. It was brighter in the lobby, the brass trimming everything from the elevators to the wall sconces gleamed in the light from the high ceiling art deco chandeliers.

Maggie would be present for the grand opening. Mr. Amato had hired her to take pictures of the event so she would see everything in all its glory. It should be quite thrilling. Guests were encouraged to wear costumes from the 1920's era. How fun would that be? But it was a few weeks away. From the activity going on around her, they weren't letting the grass grow under their feet.

She approached the reception desk where a young woman in a business suit worked at a computer. Her dark hair was pulled back in a severe chignon and her makeup was meticulously applied

"Excuse me," Maggie said. "My name is Maggie Lawrence. I have an appointment with Mr. Amato."

The young woman's eyes raked over the part of Maggie she could see above the Italian marble counter then settled on Maggie's face. A thin smile barely lifted the corners of her bright red lips even as her eyes remained cool and detached.

"If you'll have a seat, I'll let him know you've arrived." She indicated the Italian leather couches and chairs grouped in front of the large Italian marble fireplace.

"Thank you." Maggie strolled over to the fireplace. It would be so warm and welcoming once the gas logs were lit, enticing visitors to sit and relax. Rather than sit now, she pulled out her camera and snapped a few pictures of the chair grouping and the fireplace with its art deco picture hanging above. She played with different angles until she heard soft footfalls crossing the thick art deco carpet and approach her.

"Miss. Lawrence, how are you? Do you ever not have a camera attached to the end of your arm?" Mr. Amato chuckled as he reached out his hand toward her.

Maggie placed her camera in her left hand and shook his hand, a grin on her lips. "Well, when a subject looks good enough to photograph, why pass it up? I thought it might look good in some of your advertising. If not, it can always be deleted."

"An opportunist." His cool eyes surveyed her face. "Nothing wrong with that. I'm one myself."

He stuffed one hand into his pants pocket and indicated for her to precede him with the other. "Please. This way. We'll go over the photos in my office with my assistant."

~

Antonio Amato watched Maggie closely as she gave suggestions concerning the photos she'd taken the last time she was at the hotel. She was a talented photographer with an eye for light and depth and she'd taken some amazing shots. He was looking forward to seeing what she would come up with the night of the grand opening. But these photos were for the hotel's advertisements. He needed to get these to his advertisers right away. He'd told her a few needed tweaking, but in reality, they were all perfect. There was nothing wrong with them. He'd only wanted her to come back so he could see her again. Was she younger than him? Of course, she was. By at least twenty-seven or so years. Who cared? Certainly not him. He'd dated younger woman before.

"Well what do you think, Mr. Amato? Do you think the advertisers will go for that?" Maggie asked, a furrow on her brow.

Antonio had no idea what she'd asked but he had no doubt whatever it was, the advertisers would love her work. He would make sure they did. "Of course, they will."

A smile lifted those luscious lips of hers and he wondered if she would accept an invitation to dinner on his yacht. He'd have to move carefully. She'd always been discreet around him, never throwing herself at him like so many women did when they found out how much he was worth.

Maggie Lawrence may be harder to pursue than most women, but so what? A little challenge every now and again was worth it. Besides, he was used to getting what he wanted and he wanted Maggie Lawrence.

~

"I'm giving a little dinner party on my yacht Saturday night, Miss. Lawrence," Mr. Amato said as he accompanied Maggie across the lobby to the revolving door. "Just a few friends, you know. I'd like to invite you to come as well."

Maggie stopped in her tracks and turned to look at the man beside her. She certainly didn't fit in with the millionaire crowd so why was she being invited to dinner?

"Well, I appreciate the invitation, Mr. Amato, but I don't...know...about..."

"Oh, don't worry, Miss. Lawrence. It's all quite respectable. There will be quite a few people there, I assure you."

Maggie searched the man's features for...for what? He was a businessman, for goodness sake. His eyes were cool and unreadable.

"I just want to introduce you to some business friends of mine. Perhaps they'll be able to use you in their own advertising. I'll be sure to put in a good word for you, Miss. Lawrence. You know, drum up some business for you. You've done well for me, that's for sure."

Maggie drew in a deep breath and released it. "Thank you, sir.

I appreciate that. What time and where?"

Antonio Amato nodded, pleased at her answer. "I'll send around a car for you about five-thirty. We dress in evening attire."

Maggie tilted her head slightly. "Of course. Thank you for the invitation."

He nodded again. "My secretary will be in touch"

"I look forward to it, Mr. Amato."

"Till Saturday then." He bowed grandly and turning, walked way, his footfalls sinking into the thick carpet.

Maggie stepped into the revolving door and gave it a push then stepped out into the warm air. What had she just agreed to?

~

Ruth pulled the pan of homemade mac-n-cheese from the oven and set it on the counter while Maggie set the table. "Uncle Owen, can you grab the tea from the fridge, please? I think that's everything. We're ready to eat."

"My, my, that striped bass looks and smells delicious, Ruthie." Owen set the pitcher of tea on the table. "One thing's for sure. They don't fall short of variety when it comes to fish around here, do they?"

"Not at all. I love having fresh fish all the time, and as you say, a variety." Ruth set the mac-n-cheese on a trivet on the table.

They took their chairs, said grace and began eating.

"So how did your appointment with Mr. Amato go, Mags," Ruth asked. "Did you get the photos straightened out."

Maggie pushed her food around on her plate without taking a bite. "It turned out there wasn't anything wrong with any of them."

"What do you mean?" Ruth picked up her glass of tea.

Maggie shook her head. "I mean there was nothing wrong with any of the pictures. He was happy with all of them. He wanted every one of them sent to the advertisers."

"Then why the second appointment?" Owen asked as he reached for a roll from the bread basket.

Maggie sucked in a deep breath and laid down her fork. "I'm not sure. Afterward as he walked me out, he invited me to a dinner party onboard his yacht Saturday evening. He said it's to introduce me to other businessmen for advertising purposes, but I'm not so sure."

"What do you mean, you're not sure?" Owen eyed her over

the rim of his glasses. "That sounds ominous."

Maggie shook her head. "Maybe not ominous, but something feels off, and I can't put my finger on it."

"Then we'll have to pray about it, Mags." Ruth placed a hand on her cousin's arm. "The Lord knows what it's all about."

"Yeah, He does, doesn't He?" Maggie picked up her fork but still didn't take a bite.

"What is it? Is there something else, Maggie?" her dad asked.

Maggie looked from one to the other. "He kept watching me. You don't think somehow he found out we snuck into The Rusty Hook, do you?"

"I doubt he'd be giving you all his advertising business if he did, Mags," Ruth said. "Besides, there were no signs of cameras and there wasn't anything there to protect. Just an old rotting, dilapidated building that'll fall into the ocean if something's not done to prevent it before long."

"Yeah, I suppose you're right. I just find it odd that he would watch me the way he was."

"You're a beautiful woman, daughter. Why wouldn't he watch you?"

"Dad, that's kind of creepy, you know."

"Why, because you think an older man can't find a younger woman attractive? Please." Owen waved a hand. "Older men have just as much going as younger men…"

"Okay, Dad, I am not having this conversation with you. Not now, not ever."

Ruth laughed, then Owen joined in. Maggie glared at both of them. "I have to go to this dinner party, not because I want to, but for business. Maybe I'll drum up some for photography's sake. If not, then I'll chalk it up to experience."

She shoved her plate away. "I've had enough."

"But you didn't eat anything," Ruth said.

"It's not the cooking. I'm sure it's delicious, Ruthie, I just don't have an appetite right now."

"Well, there's plenty of left-overs. Help yourself when your appetite comes back."

Owen reached for a second helping and chuckled. "If there's anything left."

~

Gage pulled the cold-water mask down over his eyes and slipped the regulator into his mouth, taking a deep breath of the compressed air from the tanks on his back. The rolling waves rocked the boat as he glanced around at his fellow scuba diving students. There were three others but they were all at least twenty years older than he was. Oh, well. What was that saying? Life begins at forty? Or was it fifty? Either way, he wasn't there yet, and he was already enjoying life.

He was taking this scuba class because a certification could come in handy with his job. Gage had talked it over with Wayne and he'd thought it was a great idea. There was diving equipment in the park police office, and sometimes it was needed. A couple of the other guys were certified, and Gage didn't want to remain on the sidelines if he could jump into the fray.

As the instructor reminded them how to properly hold onto their masks as they fall backward into the water then swim away, excitement filled Gage. This was going to be amazing. He would eventually purchase his own equipment and team up with someone to go diving. The Graveyard of the Atlantic was a mecca for divers what with all the sunken ships from the 1700's right up to the late 1900's. There was an arsenal of WWII ships down there just waiting to be explored.

When the instructor pointed at him to enter the water, Gage held firmly to his mask and fell backward, the ocean water closing around him as he sank below its depths. Kicking his fins, he swam away from the boat. He breathed deeply of the compressed air, filling his lungs, the rhythmic sound strange to his ears. Out of the way, he watched as his fellow students entered the water along with the instructor.

They followed the instructor as he led them to a nearby ship, a WWII merchant supply with a gaping hole in the side. It had obviously been sunk by a torpedo during the war, most likely a German U-boat that had patrolled off the coast of North Carolina. They were much closer than people realized. A thrill ran through Gage. The history that sat on the ocean floor before him was amazing, and this training opened up a whole new world for him.

The instructor gave the signal for the students to gather around him. Then he wrote on his little magnetic slate: remove your masks, replace, reseal and clear the water.

This was the test they'd all been waiting for. The procedure for clearing their masks was a simple one. They had to breath in air, remove their masks completely, then put it back on and reseal it. Then vent air out through the top of their masks pushing the water back out so they had nothing but air left in the mask. If they couldn't do this operation, then no certification.

Breathing deeply and holding his breath, Gage slipped off his mask. The salt water instantly stung his eyes, but he managed to do what was necessary to replace and clear his mask. The instructor gave him a reassuring thumbs up. Each student in turn received one after performing the task as required. The instructor wiped his magnetic slate clean and wrote: Great job everyone. Let's explore.

Gage and the others followed as they swam around the old wreck both inside and out, the reward for learning well. He hadn't told Ruth he was taking the class, but it would be fun to share. Eventually.

Chapter Twelve

Gage was thankful for the warmer day but at the moment his unsteady nerves were making him warmer still and rather uncomfortable. What did he have to be unsteady about? Wasn't he a man of strength? Not much shook him, right? So why did standing in front of Ruth Campbell's door waiting for her to answer his ring have him shaking in his size ten and a half's? She was just a slip of a thing, and a gorgeous one at that. No threat at all, right? He could drown in her hazel eyes, listen to her musical voice forever and he longed to touch what promised to be silky honey-blond hair. And *that's* why he was shaking in his shoes. He was already under her spell and she hadn't even tried.

He heaved a heavy sigh and released it just as the door opened to…Maggie. Hmmm. Disappointment swirled in his midsection, but it was okay. Just a little longer. Ruth was still here. Then a thought struck him. Had she backed out? Changed her mind? Decided not to uphold her end of the bargain? Was Maggie here to tell him that? No, no, no. Not happening.

"Hi, Gage." Maggie stepped back. "Come on in. Ruth's almost ready. She got in from work a little late, but she'll be out in a few minutes. Come on back to the kitchen. Want some coffee?"

Relief shoved the disappointment away. "No thanks. I'll pass."

Gage dropped onto the stool at the counter. "How's your week going?"

"Pretty good. Yours?"

"Okay. Still trying to figure out who killed the guy we found Sunday night on the beach as well as the guy Ruth found."

"Oh yeah." Maggie folded her arms over her midriff and leaned back against the kitchen counter facing Gage. "Any leads at all?"

"Not much to go on, but we have one lead that may pan out. The guy from Sunday night has a tattoo. Starting tomorrow we'll put a picture of it out on the local news and see if anyone recognizes it. If he's local, surely someone will."

"Will that cover Ocracoke and up to Kitty Hawk and Manteo? There's a lot of real-estate in the area to cover."

Gage leaned his elbows on the edge of the bar. "Tell me about it. Yeah, it'll reach all of Dare County, over to the mainland and north."

Maggie's eyes shifted past Gage and he turned to see what she was staring at. His heart tripped over itself as he stood and turned to face Ruth. She stood in the doorway to one of the bedrooms looking utterly stunning. Dressed in a bottle green dress of something light and frilly, it seemed to pull the green from her hazel eyes, and wow, he couldn't put the effect into words, but he liked it. No, he loved it.

The hem of her dress danced around her shapely calves as she walked toward him or was that his fanciful imagination? Yanking his attention back to her face where it belonged he took in her hair. He'd never seen it up before except in a ponytail, but this evening she'd fashioned it into a twist of some kind and it, too, was beautiful, the highlights shimmering in the overhead light.

"Hi." Was that his voice? He swallowed and tried again. "You look...amazing."

Wonderful color flooded Ruth's cheeks, but for once she didn't drop her gaze. "Thanks. You look pretty sharp yourself in that tie and jacket. I wasn't sure what to wear, so I decided to err on the side of caution and wear a dress."

She glanced down at it. "I...I hope it's okay."

"It's...um...it's beautiful."

"So where are you two kids heading?" Maggie tossed into the awkward conversation, an amused note in her voice.

Gage turned, remembering they weren't alone. "Oh, yeah. I called Casey and he recommended The Captain's Table. He said it's one of the best restaurants around here."

"That's what I've heard." Maggie nodded. "You'll have to tell me what you think."

"We will, but we'd better get going. We have reservations shortly." Gage turned to Ruth. "Ready?"

He watched as she took a deep breath then nodded. He knew this was an effort for her, and although he didn't understand why it was, he'd do everything he could to make it an enjoyable evening for her.

Maggie reached for Ruth and gave her a hug. She whispered something in her ear then stepped back, a huge smile on her face. Ruth nodded again and smiled, hers a little more forced. Gage fought an inner battle with frustration and tamped down a touch of anger. Not at these women but at the situation. Would he ever learn what had happened to this woman and would she ever come to trust him fully?

Since he'd met her, she'd made steps forward in their friendship, but he was eager to move even further. Then he remembered Maggie's talk with him. The one where she'd told him there would be no serious relationship with Ruth if he didn't make a life change and commit his life to Christ. Shoving that thought aside, he followed Ruth out the front door. There was time to think about that later. Yes, he had a decision to make, but not tonight. Tonight, he would just revel in Ruth's company and the fulfillment of her promise. Besides, she might not ever go out with him again. He'd enjoy her leisurely company while he could.

~

The Captain's Table sat on a slight rise above Pamlico Sound. A wide wooden deck at the rear of the building had tables and chairs overlooking the water. The wind whipped the sound into choppy little whitecaps and sent the restaurant patrons inside this evening. Preferring to sit inside along the glass wall, they were rewarded with a gorgeous sunset over the sound.

Across the room a bright and cheery fire danced in the large stone fireplace, it's light welcoming patrons to sit and enjoy the cozy atmosphere. Fine bone china, crystal and silver flatware as well as cloth tablecloths and napkins adorned the antique tables scattered around the elongated room. A few nice paintings of sailing ships and lighthouses decorated the walls. Small brass lanterns lit each table while brass wall sconces and brass chandeliers lit the room.

Gage held Ruth's chair as she took her seat.

"Thank you." She glanced first at him, around the room, then out the window. "This is amazing. And look at that view. The sunset is going to be spectacular, I think."

Gage sat down, his gaze following hers out the window. "I think you're right. I've seen a lot of nice sunsets since I've been here."

"How about at the Grand Canyon? I'd think you would see some pretty ones there too."

"Oh, yeah. We have some beautiful sunsets at the Grand Canyon. They're just different there. Here, they're over water. The sun reflects across the sound, which is really spectacular. At the canyon, they're over rocks but the rocks reflect the color and sort of blend with them then fade into darkness. I don't know. I guess it's all in the perspective."

"It's all in the hand of the Creator." Ruth smiled. What would he think of that? She watched for a reaction and didn't have long to wait. His gaze dropped to his hands folded on the edge of the table.

"You're so certain there is one."

"A Creator? Beyond the shadow of a doubt."

Gage looked uncomfortable and glanced away. They'd just gotten here and hadn't even ordered yet. Ruth didn't want him feeling that way.

"So, did Casey make any suggestions about what would be good to order?" Ruth opened her menu.

Gage reached for his and flipped to the first page. "He mentioned the mahi-mahi here is delicious. He also suggested the red drum and flounder."

"I've never had mahi-mahi before. I think I'll give it a try." Ruth glanced through the sides and when the waiter came they were ready to place their orders.

Ruth watched as one of the waiters walked out to the deck and lit the gaslights that bordered its railings. One by one they gave the deck a pleasing glow, their globes protecting the flames from the wind.

"What a beautiful effect," she said. "I bet it's nice out there in the summertime. It's probably popular with tourists."

"Maybe we'll have to come back and give it a try," Gage said, his eyes on her features.

Ruth's heart stumbled as she returned her gaze out the window. This was going to be harder than she'd expected. She should never have agreed to come to dinner with him. He would want to further their relationship and that was something she just could not do. At least not until he made some changes in his life.

"We could always bring Maggie and your uncle. They'd probably like it here."

Ruth returned her gaze to his and found him grinning. She relaxed and smiled. "Yeah, they probably would."

They chatted until the waiter brought their food, then Ruth asked, "Perhaps this isn't the greatest dinner conversation, but what have you learned about the two men who were found on the beach?"

"Hmmm. You want to know now? You? The one with the weak stomach?" Gage chuckled, slicing off a bite of his red drum and eating it.

Ruth rolled her eyes. "Well, you don't have to go into great detail, and you don't have to tell me anything you don't think I won't want to know. 'All we want are the facts, ma'am.'."

Gage eyed her with one brow raised in question.

Ruth shrugged. "What? Didn't you ever watch the old Dragnet reruns when you were a kid?"

Gage snapped his fingers. "Oh, yeah. Actually, I did. I forgot about that. Cute."

"Well?" Ruth stabbed a bite of her mahi-mahi. "Tell me what you've found out. That is if you can. I know it's an ongoing investigation. But I do work for the park service, and I did find one of the bodies."

"Oh, I haven't forgotten." Gage laid down his fork and sipped his iced tea. "Well, we know who the first body is. He was a low-life criminal with a record as long as my arm. He has connections to the Chicago mafia."

"The mafia?" The whispered word slipped from Ruth as she laid down her fork. "I thought they were put out of business decades ago."

"Oh, no." Gage shook his head. "Just because they aren't shooting up the streets and working in the open doesn't mean they're just...operating more subtly these days. They still have their hands into money laundering, racketeering, drug dealing and human trafficking, to name a few."

"Wow, I didn't realize."

"Not too many people do."

"Have you connected him to any particular mob boss? Isn't that what you call them? Are you going after them? What's next?" Ruth lifted a hand, palm up in query, excitement filling her voice.

Gage chuckled at the sparkle in her eye and reached across to take her hand, laying it on the table. "Ok, Sherlock. Calm your jets. First off, we're still trying to make connections, and that's all I can tell you. It's not that I don't trust you, but there's always that inadvertent chance something will slip out."

He was right and Ruth certainly didn't have a need to know. She couldn't help the disappointment that swept through her, but when the case came to its conclusion, she would certainly be able to find out more. She'd just have to bide her time.

"I understand. How about the second man? Anything you can tell me there?"

"Well, he's a little more interesting. He was disposed of only the day before he washed ashore. Once again, I don't think he was meant to be found. Whoever is disposing of these bodies has the worst luck and it's only a matter of time before we find out who that is." Gage looked up as the waiter approached. "Would you like dessert?"

"What?" Ruth tried to refocus from murdered victims to dessert and it was a stretch. "Oh, um, do you have cheesecake?"

"Yes, ma'am," the waiter said. "Carmel or raspberry sauce?"

"Definitely caramel."

"And you, sir?"

Gage winked at his dinner companion and grinned. "Make that two."

As the waiter gathered their plates and departed, Ruth returned to the subject, her voice barely more than a whisper, "So he was disposed of the day before he washed ashore. What else?"

Gage leaned forward with his elbows on the edge of the table and shook his head, laughing. "Are you some kind of amateur detective or something?"

"No, but I've never had two murdered bodies show up in my own backyard before. I may not want to look them in the face, but I am interested in how the case is going."

"Well, one of the interesting things is someone removed this man's face and broke him in half before stuffing him in a burlap gunny sack."

Ruth gasped as her fingers covered her mouth in horror. "That's...that's awful. The things that humans do to one another."

"Yeah, it's pretty messed up." Gage nodded. "The ME said he was alive when his face was removed and died instantly when they broke him in half. That's a given, I would imagine. Whoever did this also removed his fingerprints and his teeth. I guess they weren't taking many chances since the last body washed ashore. I guess they somehow got word about it. So, the ME can't identify him from dental records or by the Integrated Automated Fingerprint Identification System or IAFIS. However, they missed something."

Ruth watched as a sly smile lifted one corner of his lips and he waggled his eyebrows. A thrill ran through her unbidden. Swallowing hard, she attempted to tamp it down but failed miserably. He winked again and her pulse fluttered, sending butterflies dancing in her mid-region. That was not good. *Lord, help me. I can't let this attraction build. I need Your strength because I'm weak.* And where was the panic she usually felt at the attention of a young man? There certainly hadn't been many, thank goodness, but now? It wasn't here.

Swallowing again, she focused on his last statement. "What was missing?"

The waiter took that moment to arrive with their cheesecake and a carafe of coffee. He placed their plates in front of them then offered the coffee. Both accepted and he hurried away to allow them to enjoy their desserts.

Gage picked up the conversation. "It's not what was missing. It's what they missed. What they failed to removed. The ME found a tattoo on the man's forearm."

He slipped his cellphone out of his pocket and pulled up a picture. It was a tattoo of a colorful mermaid entwined with an anchor and holding a trident. Beneath was the word, Celia. The whole tattoo was very clear.

"Have you been able to find out anything about him from his tattoo?" Ruth laid down her dessert fork and took the phone.

"We're still broadcasting the picture on the local news." Gage took a bite of his cheesecake and swallowed it before continuing. "Unfortunately, we haven't gotten a response from anyone yet."

"Is there anything I can do to help?" Ruth handed the phone

back to Gage and finished off her cheesecake.

"As much as I appreciate your offer, I don't want you anywhere near this case, Ruth."

"Why? I'm sure I could help with something."

Gage's mouth formed a wry smile. "I'm sure you could, but we're talking the mafia here. It's far too dangerous. I don't want you involved. It's bad enough you found the first body."

Ruth hesitated a moment then let out a heavy sigh. "I suppose. But if you change your mind, let me know."

He reached across and laid gentle fingers on hers as they rested on the table cloth. "Thanks, Ruth. I appreciate the offer. Should I change my mind, I'll let you know, but don't expect that to happen."

Ruth's heart bumped erratically as the warmth of his fingers seeped into hers. They felt nice. Ever so nice. Her first instinct was to yank hers away, but that would be rude, wouldn't it? Of course, it would. He'd been nothing but a gentleman to her and still he wasn't demanding. *Chill, Ruth. He's just a friend.*

~

The zing that charged up Gage's arm almost caused him to yank his hand away, but the warmth of Ruth's fingers felt oh so pleasant, and Gage let his lay where they were. He wasn't going to demand anything of her. *She can only be a friend, remember, you idiot? No matter how much you might want more.* The fact that they were sitting here enjoying time together and she was opening up to him was a miracle in itself. Was there truly a God, and had He orchestrated this? Ruth certainly believed there was.

The waiter brought the check and they prepared to leave. As they pushed back from the table, the thought of Ruth tangling with the mob chilled Gage's blood. No way would he allow that. He'd tried to keep his information vague. Not that he had a whole lot more. They knew who the first guy was, just not the scum mafia boss he belonged to. But they would find out eventually. Perhaps finding who the second body was would lead them to the boss of both men. Gage believed that both bodies were connected to one boss. It was too coincidental. Hopefully that tattoo was the evidence that would crack the case. And Celia? Who in the world was that?

All at once Gage wished he had a relationship with God so he could pray for the case. Was that a good reason to have a relationship with Him? He wasn't sure. All he knew was that they needed a break. He had a feeling if asked, Ruth would pray about it. She had a relationship with God.

As they walked out the door and to the car, Gage heaved a heavy sigh. When was he going to quit shoving God in a box in the corner and deal with this? Perhaps one day....

Chapter Thirteen

Antonio watched as the dive team prepared to drop off the stern of the yacht. Two of the divers were suited in neoprene cold water dive suits with air tanks attached to their backs. Their suits fit like second skins, and they wore full-face cold-water scuba masks. Although the air temperature was in the upper seventies today, the Atlantic Ocean along the coastline was only in the lower fifties. Antonio was happy they were going down and not him.

The third diver sat at a table on the stern deck with the sonar equipment and would monitor the sonar and the diver's progress. He would be in communication with them during the dive.

Antonio pulled up a chair near the diver.

"Mind if I watch?" he asked.

The well-built blond man turned to look at Antonio and removed his headset. "Pardon?"

"Mind if I watch?"

"Oh, not at all, Mr. Amato. It's your expedition, after all." The young man replaced the headset and turned back to his equipment.

Antonio leaned forward, elbows on his knees and his hands clasped between his knees as he tried to figure out what the equipment was for.

The divers at the back platform gave a thumbs up and when they received one back from the man at the table, they dropped into the water.

The last two dives these guys had done had yielded nothing. Antonio hadn't been surprised. If they yielded nothing today, he still wouldn't be surprised. He expected to have to run up most of the Hatteras seashore before they found something, but it still didn't prevent the excitement and the frustration every time they went out and came back with nothing.

Antonio would do nothing less than Gramps Howie had done. He'd spend the rest of his life searching if he had to. Gramps had searched further out and deeper but since he hadn't found anything there, Antonio figured *The Satisfaction* went down closer inland. If only he had coordinates for 'x marks the spot' but that was a pipe dream. Gramps had even tried getting the information from various Coast Guardsmen, even killing several to get the information, but none had anything to spill. According to Gramps journal, he'd killed fourteen Coasties through the years to try and get the information. Nothing. At least if they did, they took it with them to their graves.

Gramps Howie had talked about how he'd looked through binoculars while he'd watched from the pier behind The Rusty Hook restaurant but who knew what angle he was looking from and how far out Big Tony's rum-runner had been. There were just too many variables. Then there was the fact the ship could've gone down in pieces and floated down in different directions. There had been an explosion, after all, and Gramps had only been seventeen. His memory could've been flawed.

Tony got up and strolled to his office, retrieving Howie's journal. Rather than return to sit next to the diver, he went to the upper stern skydeck where comfortable chairs stood near a hot tub and a wet bar. He dropped into one of the cushioned chairs beneath the canvas awning and was approached by a uniformed staff member.

"Can I get you anything, Mr. Amato? A drink perhaps or something to eat?" The tall, slender man bowed slightly, his longish hair ruffling in the sea breeze. A pair of sunglasses covered his eyes.

Antonio glanced at him as he opened the journal. "Yeah, yeah, Miguel. A bottle of Pellegrino water."

The man bowed and slipped away, returning within minutes with an ice-cold green bottle of natural sparkling mineral water and a glass of ice on a tray and set them on the table beside Antonio's chair.

"Will there be anything else, sir?"

Antonio was reading through the journal and without looking up, waved the man away. "Nah, nothing else, for now, Miguel."

The man faded away to the shaded entrance to the deck and stood out of sight waiting in case the boss might have a need later.

Antonio thumbed through the first pages until he found what he was looking for. He'd read these paragraphs over and over until the words were almost imprinted onto his brain.

"When the explosion had occurred, I wasn't really surprised. Uncle Tony always said he'd never let the feds take him. I saw it in my mind's eye. Uncle Tony probably threw a grenade in the boiler room furnace and blew up the boat himself. Did I feel remorse that he died? Not really. I never really felt much for the uncle that took me in. He was a cruel and vile man. Evil even. My mother never trusted her brother, but there hadn't been anyone else she'd have asked to raise her illegitimate son. She knew he could give me the best of everything. And now I'll go back and claim it all. Yes. That's what I'll do.

And the treasure? Was it still on the boat when it went down? Was it still in the cargo hold? Knowing Uncle Tony, he'd never leave it where he couldn't reach it. I'll return one day and search for it. I'll find it. Or die trying."

The questions that had plagued Gramps Howie, plagued Antonio even now. Was that treasure on the boat? If Big Tony had kept the treasure in a safe, had it survived the explosion? Could it possibly be sitting on the ocean floor where it could be found? Surely it would be a lot harder to find than the *The Satisfaction*.

Footsteps approached through the lounge and Antonio glanced up to see Lennie step out onto the skydeck, a worried expression marking his features.

Antonio eyed the man as he halted in front of him. "What? You're not looking so good, Lennie. What's the matter now?"

Lennie swallowed hard as he wrung his hands. "Well, boss, that's cuz I got some not so good news to tell ya."

Antonio closed the journal and laid it on the table beside his chair. He dropped his leg from where it had rested on his knee, and leaned forward, elbows on his knees, hands clasped loosely between them.

"So, tell me."

"I was just down in the communications room, and…and I got a call from our contact in Manteo. He, um…well, he got news that the cops found another body washed up on shore a few days ago."

Antonio narrowed his eyes. "Yeah? And? Who was it? Tell me it was some poor schmuck who'd committed suicide or drowned by accident. DON'T tell me it was Capt. Ed Garcia."

The color drained from Lennie's face. "I didn't have nothin' to do with that, Boss. I was with you when he was taken care of, remember? It wasn't me, I'm tellin' ya."

Antonio stood from his chair and walked to the rear railing of the sky deck and looked over, watching the diver at the equipment table below.

"No, Lennie. I know it wasn't you. You're a very faithful guy." Antonio turned around and leaned against the railing, crossing his arms over his chest and looking Lennie in the eye. "Who did the job?"

Lennie swallowed. "Boss, please don't ask me to squeal."

"Do you want to take their place, Lennie? Somebody's got to pay for messing up. I can't run a shoddy business, my friend. I have to set an example or everybody will grow lax. That's two bodies that have washed ashore, and I can't afford for this to happen again."

"But, Boss, they'll never lead back to you. They removed Capt. Ed's face, his teeth and his fingerprints. What more could they have done?"

Antonio straightened from the railing and strolled slowly over to Lennie and when he stood next to him, he placed a hand on his shoulder and leaned close, speaking softly in his ear. "Did they remove his tattoo?"

If it was possible, Lennie grew paler than before.

Antonio gently clapped his shoulder and spoke softly again. "Now who did the job, Lennie? Give me his name or you take his place."

Lennie hesitated for a moment then in a voice that was little more than a whisper, he said. "Harland."

"Now that wasn't so hard, was it, Lennie?" Antonio's smile was cheerful as he patted Lennie's shoulder. "I want you to take care of this one. And I don't want him showing up on the beach or anywhere else. Is that understood? If he does, I'll take care of you myself. And if you show up, it'll be in one-inch pieces they'll never be able to put back together."

Antonio moved toward the entrance to the lounge then turned halfway around. "Oh, and we're getting a little short on staff. Send for a couple of the boys from Chicago. I think we might be needing them."

~

"Hi, Mary." Owen Lawrence greeted the librarian as he leaned against the counter and smiled. "My but don't you look lovely today."

Mary Kelly reached up a hand and patted her gray-streaked brunette hair. "Why thank you, Owen. It's kind of you to say so. What can I help you with today? Are you here for more research?"

"I sure am. I'd like to take another look at your dear great-grandmother's book, if you don't mind."

"Why I don't mind at all, Owen." Mary stood from her desk chair and waved for him to follow her. "Come along."

She unlocked the display case at the rear of the library and handed Owen a pair of cotton gloves for him to put on, then she allowed him to carefully remove the antique book from the case and take it to a table. "If you need anything, don't hesitate to ask. I'll be right over there."

Owen grinned at the flirtatious smile she cast in his direction before she sauntered back to her desk. He shook his head. Mary was quite a woman. He suspected she was a lonely one, to be sure. It was sad really, and he chided himself for encouraging her. He really wasn't interested in a relationship with any woman at this point in his life although Maggie had mentioned that she thought he should be or he might die a lonely old man.

How could he when he had Maggie and Ruth to keep him company? It was true that both of them would likely one day land husbands and go off to begin lives of their own. Should that happen, then perhaps he'd rethink his own relationship status. But until then, he was fine.

With painstaking care, he turned the pages in Ava Sinclair Kelly's journal. She had beautiful penmanship and he scanned the words once more looking for clues that might help him discover what could've become of *La Cruz de San Mateo*. Of course, there was no mention of the treasure itself because it was doubtful Ava would've known of its existence. Perhaps she could help pinpoint were the rum-runner went down when it sank.

Owen flipped a few more pages reading as he went, then he found a passage and read:

My heart pounded with anticipation as five men stood on deck amidst the crates of liquor, their eyes shifting uncertainly. Was this the whole crew?

A gunshot rang out moments before an explosion rocked *The Satisfaction*, sending a fireball skyward. Billows of flame and smoke spread out in every direction. The men on the deck screamed in agony as they were engulfed in the inferno. The ones closest to the railing attempted to leap over the edge, but it happened so quickly it was doubtful they made it over.

"Nooo!" I screamed. Martin had been on board that boat. He'd never made it to the deck. I felt the band of Mike's arms supporting me. All I wanted was to curl into a ball and sob. How was I ever going to break this news to Mother?

The bonfire which was *The Satisfaction* reflected on the ocean waves as we watched in horror. Captain Spinner ordered *The Sea Dog* to be moved back to a distance as the trailing fuel from *The Satisfaction* caught fire.

Much to our surprise, before the boat could completely burn, it listed then sank.

"The explosion must have blown a hole in the bottom of the boat," I remember Captain Naka saying.

Captain Spinner directed a crewman to mark the location of the sinking and to record it in the log.

Tears streamed down my cheeks as Mike held me.

"There are no words I can give you, sweetheart," he said. "None that are adequate anyway."

"I don't need words. Just hold me."

"That I can do." And he held me.

"What's that?" Captain Naka asked. "Do you hear something? I mean something above the sound of the engines?"

We all listened.

"Help! Help me! Help me!"

I jerked my head from Mike's shoulder and ran to the railing. "It sounds like Martin. It is Martin! Look!"

I pointed down into the water.

There in the ever-brightening morning light, Martin's wet head bobbed in the waves. The others joined me at the railing, he waved.

"Someone help him aboard," I demanded.

"Lower the cargo net," Captain Spinner commanded.

"How in the world did he survive that?" Mike asked.

"I'd say the good Lord was looking after that boy," Captain Naka said.

Owen re-read the passage. The group onboard the Coast Guard cutter, *The Sea Dog,* had surmised *The Satisfaction* had sunk quickly thinking the bottom of the boat had been blown out due to the explosion. If *La Cruz de San Mateo* had been on board before the explosion, it likely went down with the scattered remnants of the boat, whether in a safe or not, and settled somewhere on the ocean floor.

Owen removed his glasses and scrubbed a hand down his face, frustration roiling through him. Would Big Tony Amato have placed the golden cross in a safe? Surely, he kept his money from his rum-running transactions in one. It would've been foolhardy not to. He ran with criminals after all, and criminals didn't trust one another. It was doubtful Big Tony would've trusted his compatriots with the knowledge of *La Cruz de San Mateo* so keeping it hidden in a safe would've been a prudent measure.

Finding a safe on the floor of the Atlantic Ocean would be a daunting task, especially amongst the many terrible currents and tides that tore through the shifting sandbars of the Diamond Shoals. Who knew but it could be completely covered over by now by nearly a century of those same shifting sands?

Something niggled at the edge of Owen's mind. He spent another hour searching through Ava's journal but found nothing more that would help him so he closed the delicate pages and returned it to its case. He told Mary he was ready for her to lock it.

"Thank you, Mary. I appreciate you allowing me to peruse Ava's words. She had quite a way with them, you know."

"Oh yes, I do," Mary said, turning her key in the lock. "My great-grandmother was an extraordinary woman. Did you know my great-grandfather bought her an old school bus and had it converted into the first book mobile on the island? She didn't even know how to drive, but he taught her so she could take books to the children in the various villages."

Owen heard the pride radiating through Mary's voice as he slipped his notebook under his arm. "She was quite remarkable. You have a heritage to be proud of, Mary. Well, I must be going. Maggie will be waiting for me. You take care."

"You, too, Owen. Come on back anytime."

~

Antonio leaned back in his desk chair and held his cell phone to his ear, the ringing indicating his call was attempting to go through. His fingers drummed on the smooth glass-like mahogany surface of his desk as he waited.

"Hello?" a note of dread in Lennie's voice lifting a corner of Antonio's lips.

"Well?" Antonio asked. "Is it done?"

"Yeah. Yeah, it's done, Mr. Amato." Lennie let out a heavy sigh. "And you won't have no trouble out o' this one. Harland ain't comin' back."

"Good, good, Lennie. Glad to hear it."

"It was hard, Mr. Amato. Real hard. Harland was my friend."

"I understand, Lennie, but sometimes we have to make sacrifices in this business. You understand, right? Tell me you understand, Lennie. Sacrifices have to be made."

"Yes, sir. Sacrifices have to be made in this business."

"Right. You do understand, Lennie. That's good. Just don't ever forget. You got that, Lennie?"

"Yes, sir, Mr. Amato." A pause then Lennie continued. "I got it."

Chapter Fourteen

Well, what do you think?" Maggie stepped out of her bedroom and into the kitchen Saturday evening. She did a slow twirl for Ruth's perusal.

She wore a silky black sheath dress with a scoop neckline in both front and back. Loose sleeves draped to her elbows while the fabric gathered on one hip draped to the calf-length hemline. A large, loose bow draped elegantly down her side. A long, slim gold chain encircled her neck and hung perfectly down her front. She wore medium sized gold hoop earrings. She'd arranged her auburn hair in a twisted chignon with loose curled tendrils framing her face and a few pulled free against her neck. Black high-heeled strappy sandals encased her feet giving a good view of burgundy painted toenails.

"Well?" Maggie turned back to face her cousin.

Ruth propped the spoon she'd been stirring a pot of potato corn chowder with on the spoon rest and leaned against the counter.

"Well, if you're going for high-society glamour and want to impress, you're going to. You're gorgeous, Mags. Simply gorgeous. You'll have every male eye on that yacht centered on you."

"Oh, I doubt that." Maggie grabbed a black clutch and wrap from just inside her bedroom door and turned back to Ruth. "There's bound to be far more sophisticated women onboard that yacht than me."

"Are you taking your camera?"

"Not the big one. I have a smaller DSL I can use if I need one." She patted her clutch. "I never go anywhere without a camera."

Ruth chuckled. "A true photographer if there ever was one."

The front doorbell rang and Maggie glanced at her gold bracelet wristwatch. "Oh, I'm sure that's the car they sent for me."

"The car they sent for you?" Ruth looked impressed and, reaching over, tapped Maggie's shoulder. "Wow, touch you. There'll be no living with you now. Chauffeurs, no less."

Maggie rolled her eyes and gave her cousin a hug. "Bye, cuz. Don't wait up. Love you."

"Love you, Mags. Have fun." Ruthie gave Maggie a return hug. "Remember us lowly loved ones on your way to the top."

"Bye, Ruthie." Maggie waved over her shoulder as her high-heels tapped down the hallway to the front door.

A chauffeur in a black jacket, slacks, white shirt, black tie and cap bowed slightly then led the way to a black stretch limousine where he helped Maggie into the backseat. He climbed into the driver's seat then pulled out onto Rt. 12 and headed north.

Maggie had had a few rides in limos in her years since she'd been in business as a freelance photographer, but she'd never been to a dinner party onboard a yacht before. Butterflies were performing a tap-dance in her stomach. Mr. Amato had implied he would be introducing her to a group of businessmen at this dinner party with the purpose of drumming up business for her. Whether that was what was truly going to happen or not, she had yet to find out.

She watched as familiar landmarks passed by then the lighthouse came into view. It always reminded her of Ruthie. Her cousin loved Cape Hatteras, and she suspected she'd stay here forever if she could arrange it with the park service.

On her left was The Brigand's Cove Hotel and there on the right was the time-worn and battered old Rusty Hook restaurant. What an interesting landmark. It still brought chills to her remembering the night she and Ruthie snuck in. Thank goodness it had been Gage who had chanced upon them leaving and not a local policeman. Still, she was glad they'd gone inside. She just regretted they hadn't found anything. Did she have the nerve to ask Mr. Amato about his plans for the old restaurant? Would it be too forward, or would it just be a business-like question? After all, it was he who had told her he was planning to renovate it.

The limo continued north on Rt. 12 until it came into one of the little towns Maggie wasn't familiar with. The driver turned the car to the right down a road that led to a security gate. A sign read: Diamond Sands Yacht Club. The security guard waved them right through.

As they drove past slips where yachts were moored, Maggie noticed these were not just your average fishing boat or pleasure cruiser. These boats were worth millions of dollars at a minimum. This was an exclusive yacht club. Membership alone would cost millions. The butterflies in her stomach weren't dancing anymore. They were performing kamikaze dive-bombing exercises. *Lord, help me. What am I doing here?*

The chauffeur parked the limo beside the gangway to a yacht with the name *The Luck Lady* emblazoned across the stern then assisted Maggie out of the backseat. A tall, blond-haired young man from the yacht descended the gangway and welcomed her.

"Good evening. Miss Lawrence, I believe?" he bowed slightly, his accent British.

"Yes, that's right." Maggie grasped her wrap around her shoulders and held her clutch beneath her arm.

He held out an arm toward the gangway. "If you'll follow me, I'll take you aboard. Mr. Amato would like for me to show you where you can stow your wrap, then I'll take you to him. He's amongst his other guests."

"Thank you."

"Most certainly. Welcome aboard." He bowed again.

He led her to a cloak room where she checked her wrap then he led her to the lounge where Mr. Amato was already entertaining his guests. Several businessmen and their female companions were in attendance. As Ruth glanced around at her female counterparts, she noticed most were her age or younger, however, most of the men in the room were the same age as Mr. Amato or older. What did that say for the kind of party this was going to be? Maggie would bet her most expensive camera that most of these men left their wives at home and brought their girlfriends to this party. Great.

Antonio spotted her the moment she walked into the room. "Miss Lawrence, please come over here. I want to introduce you to some folks. Come, please."

Maggie sucked in a deep cleansing breath and walked over to

her host, pasting on as sincere a smile as she could muster. All at once she wanted to be home with Ruthie eating homemade potato corn chowder. *Help me, Lord.*

"Good evening, Mr. Amato."

"Why, don't you look stunning, Miss Lawrence." Her host's eyes raked down her and back up again, eliciting a feeling of discomfort. Fortunately, he didn't dwell on her but moved back to his other guests. "Gentlemen, ladies, may I introduce Miss Maggie Lawrence, the photographer I've been telling you about. She does amazing work. But we'll get to that. Maggie these are…." and he introduced each one by name.

There was no way Maggie would ever remember every name although she tried to come up with something to associate them with, but he was going too fast and she finally had to give up.

"It's a real pleasure to meet you all," she said, not sure if that was a lie or not.

They chatted for several minutes before Mr. Amato took her arm and pulled her away to introduce her to someone else. For the next half hour it was one introduction after another with several businessmen and a couple businesswomen asking for her business card. If she got some photography business from this dinner party, then she hoped it would be worth it.

When all guests were on board, the yacht pulled away from the slip and moved out of the harbor and beyond the rolling waves. It was a calm sea this evening and the captain kept the yacht steady and pleasant for the guests.

Somewhere a dinner gong sounded, and Mr. Amato led the group into the dining salon. A huge round table was set with china, crystal, silver and linen. He took Maggie's arm and led her to a chair next to his own.

"You're right here next to me, my dear."

The look in his eye gave Maggie an uneasy feeling, but what could she do? For the time being he was her boss. At least until this job was finished. And what about The Rusty Hook? She wanted that job. That is if he was ever going to get to it.

Waiters brought out the first course and began serving as conversation hummed around the table. The man on her right chatted with her occasionally as did Mr. Amato. With the large round table, it was easy for everyone to chat with everyone else so conversation flowed freely. Several of the others asked about her photography freelancing and about the places she'd traveled.

During a lull in the conversation, Maggie decided there was no time like the present to ask Mr. Amato about his plans for The Rusty Hook.

"Mr. Amato, now that you've completed The Brigand's Cove Hotel, will you be starting on The Rusty Hook? Do you plan to bring it back to its original glory or will you tear it down and start over?" Maggie's heart beat a little faster at her temerity.

Her host turned a thoughtful gaze on her without immediately answering. He propped his elbows on the table and held one fist inside the other.

"Well, Maggie, I've been so caught up with The Brigand's Cove that I haven't spent a lot of time thinking about it. Do you think I should?"

Maggie blinked a couple of times. Was he sincerely asking *her*?

"You really want me to tell you what I think, sir?"

"Whoa, whoa, whoa. What's this sir stuff? You know, you're always calling me Mr. Amato this and Mr. Amato that. Why don't you just call me Antonio?"

Maggie shook her head slowly. "Oh, well, I don't think I...."

"Just say it. Antonio." He waved a hand as if directing a choir.

Feeling worse than uncomfortable, Maggie nodded. "Well, okay. Ummm, Antonio."

"See that wasn't so bad, huh? Now, back to your question. Maybe it's time for me to think about The Rusty Hook. Yeah, I'd planned to bring it back to its original glory. Back to the way it was in its heyday. It was a speakeasy, you know. Of course, liquor's legal these days, so that's not a problem."

He nodded and looked at Maggie. "Good idea, Maggie. Thanks for bringing it up. I don't suppose you might want the photography job on this one, too, do you?"

He laughed and picked up his glass to take a drink.

Maggie felt her cheeks grow warm. "Well, you know my work, Mr. Ama...uh...Antonio. If you decide to hire me, I'll do as good a job on that one as I did on The Brigand's Cove."

He leaned back in his chair and draped his arm casually over the back of hers. "I'm sure you will, Maggie. I'm sure you will."

~

After dessert was served, the guests gathered once again in the lounge and on the stern skydeck where the canvas awning was rolled back to reveal the night sky. Music was played by a D.J. and some of the guests swayed to the tunes on the wooden deck beneath the stars.

Maggie strolled down a companionway and to a lower deck to get away from the crowd for a bit and to find a lady's room. She hoped she wouldn't be missed. Unsure exactly were the bathroom was she tried several doors and opening one, flipped on a light and found a beautiful office with a couch and chairs. Would they miss her if she sat in here for a while? The portholes were open and there was a nice breeze. She started to sit down when she noticed the smooth mahogany desk on the right. Then a very old leatherbound journal-looking book caught her eye. How could it not? It was the only thing on the desktop and its age made it interesting.

She reached for it and thumbed through, certain words catching her attention: Howard Amato. Big Tony Amato. *The Satisfaction*. Could it be that this was a journal from someone in the Amato family? Was there information in here about the original Rusty Hook? And how about the treasure that Dad was looking for?

Without a second's hesitation, Maggie grabbed the camera from her clutch and, laying the journal open on the desk, snapped pictures of the pages, one after the other. Not even looking to see what they were, she just snapped away.

Maggie was only nineteen pages into the journal when she heard male voices approaching from down the companionway. Would they come in here or carry on past the door? She couldn't take that chance. Closing the journal, she returned it to its original position, then dropping her camera back into her clutch, looked around the room for a place to hide. The wet bar wouldn't do. They may decide to use it.

The only place was behind the couch. It was just far enough from the wall that she could slip behind it, but barely. Just in time she remembered to turn off the overhead light, then dashed to the couch and slipped behind it before she heard the doorknob turn and the overhead light came on. Maggie's heart raced like a freight train. Could they hear it? Breathing deeply, she released the air slowly, attempting to regain control of her breathing.

"Well, what do you have, Lennie? It better be important. You know I don't like interruptions during my dinner parties."

The couch shifted slightly as if someone sat on it. Maggie caught her breath, then closing her eyes, let it out slowly. *Lord, please get me out of this. Alive.*

"Yeah, I know, Mr. Amato, but this is important. The coppers, they're askin' all over the place about the body what washed up on shore. And it's all over the local news."

The couch creaked as the person sitting on it shifted again. It had to be Mr. Amato. "What do you mean, they're asking all over the place about it?"

"They're askin' around about the tattoo they found on his arm?"

"The tattoo?" The word was almost yelled as Mr. Amato leapt off the couch, shoving it back against Maggie. She stifled a groan. "I knew that would come back to haunt us when Harland didn't remove it before he disposed of the body."

Maggie held her breath. Disposed of the body? Was Mr. Amato responsible for the death of the man that washed up on shore? Could he be responsible for both bodies?

"Yeah, I guess you were right, Mr. Amato.". Lennie's voice shook as he spoke.

"You guess?" Rage filled Antonio's voice. "I already told you I want you to find those bodies. I want them to disappear. Do you understand me? Take a couple of the new guys and get on it."

"Ye...yeah, Boss. But the coppers already have the reports written up on 'em by now."

"Then find those reports and make them disappear too. Just as soon as we get back to shore, get on it."

"Yeah, but, boss. We found out about Joe Pachino. Ya don't have ta worry none about him. His body was claimed by his sister. She took him home ta some place out in the midwest and buried him. He ain't gonna bother ya no more."

Silence filled the office and Maggie could hear her heartbeat in her ears.

"Then take the boys and get the other body. I don't want it left around. Got it?"

"Got it, Boss."

"Get out of here."

Maggie heard the door close softly but the light was still on. She heard footfalls cross the carpet and then the sound of ice in glass. The sound of liquid pouring, someone gulping the liquid then glass smashing against a wall. Maggie jumped and stifled the cry that threatened to emerge from her throat.

How in the world was she going to act normally around Mr. Amato for the rest of the evening knowing he'd had those men killed? She needed to get off this boat, but they were out to sea. Could she plead a headache and stay in the lady's room? *I need Your help, Lord. What am I going to do?*

First things first, she couldn't go anywhere until he left. This was obviously his office and she was trapped in it until he decided to leave and that could be a while considering his current frame of mind.

Maggie lay behind the couch praying for wisdom and guidance, when all of a sudden, the door opened, the lights went out and the door slammed shut. Maggie jumped then waited. Silence filled the void except for the beating of her own heart in her eardrums. Was he gone? She waited a few more minutes then started to crawl out. Considering the couch had been shoved against her when Antonio stood up, Maggie had some difficulty pushing it away enough to crawl forward. When she reached the edge of the couch, she peeked around. Yes, he was gone. She crawled the rest of the way out, then climbing to her feet, she hurried from the office. As much as she wanted to photograph more of the journal, she wasn't about to risk it.

Looking left, she longed to go out to the lower stern deck and sit alone but thought she'd better go mingle with the other guests instead. Hurrying up the inside stairs to the lounge, she slipped in amongst the guests, easily jumping into a conversation with a businessman and his female companion.

To Maggie's relief, Antonio remained absent for much of the remainder of the evening until the yacht returned to the harbor and slipped into its berth at the yacht club. He made an appearance a few minutes before everyone disembarked and played the gracious host, thanking everyone for coming.

Distracted, he gave Maggie's hand a squeeze and thanked her for coming. "I'll be in touch about The Rusty Hook. I'll let you know what I'm going to do about that, okay?"

"Certainly, Mr. Amato. Thank you for a pleasant evening. Goodnight." He hadn't even noticed her return to the more formal use of his name. That's the way she'd prefer it, especially after what she'd overheard tonight.

Maggie tugged her wrap around her shoulders and walked down the gangway to the waiting limo. The chauffeur held the door for her as she climbed in. Settling back against the butter-soft leather cushions, all at once she felt weary. Her experience tonight had drained her. The knowledge she held was horrible and dangerous. She had a phone call to make when she got home.

Was there anything in the photos from the journal that might help in Gage's investigation? Would it help her Dad in his search for *La Cruz de San Mateo*? All she knew was that they were up against some very dangerous people. Not only was Antonio Amato a savvy businessman, but he was in the killing business. Just like his grandfather and his mobster great-uncle Big Tony Amato. He was carrying on his family business in every way.

Chapter Fifteen

Gage knocked on Ruth's front door and waited for an answer. Glancing at his watch in the porch light, he saw it was one in the morning. He'd gotten off duty at midnight, gone home and changed out of his uniform when he received the call from Ruth saying Maggie had returned home from a yacht party excited about something. She had news for him that might help with his investigation and could he please come over. ASAP.

Footfalls padded down the hallway toward the front door, then the door opened a sliver. Ruth's sweet face appeared in the narrow space.

"Oh, good. It's you."

She shut the door and Gage heard the bolt slide before she swung the door wide.

"Hi. Come on in."

Ruth wore an oversized coral t-shirt with the words "Prayer is the Answer" emblazoned across the front and a pair of gray sweat pants. Her feet were encased in fluffy white bunny slippers. He couldn't stop the grin that lifted his lips but he managed to stifle the chuckle that threated to burst out. Ruth's honey-blond hair was pulled up in a clip, tendrils having escaped and framed her face. He had the desire to reach out and twist one around his finger and tug her close. *Nope. Just shove that thought away. It will get you nowhere.*

As he stepped inside, she closed the door behind him and relocked it.

"Come on into the kitchen." Ruth led the way toward the back of the house. "Maggie's pretty worked up about her evening, but I think I've got her settled down enough that she can explain what happened."

"Okay." Gage had no idea what was going on or where Maggie had been. Something about a yacht party?

As they entered the softly lit kitchen, Maggie stepped from her bedroom. She was no longer dressed in evening wear but had changed into sweats and a t-shirt. She was brushing out her hair.

Tossing her brush back into her room, she turned back to Gage. "Hey copper. How's it going?"

"Well, that's what I'm here to find out. Ruth said you wanted to talk to me. What's up?"

Maggie drew in a deep breath and dropped onto one of the kitchen stools while Ruth grabbed the coffee carafe. She clasped her hands tightly together beneath her chin.

"Coffee, Gage, or would you prefer something less caffeinated this time of night?" Ruth asked.

"I'll just have water, thanks." Gage pulled out a chair from the kitchen table and turned it to face Maggie. He straddled it and rested his arms along the top of the back.

"How about you, Mags? Coffee?"

"Yes, please." Maggie jumped up from the stool and gathered a mug along with honey and creamer to doctor her coffee. When she sat back at the counter, she prepared it and took a sip.

Ruth handed Gage a glass of water then sat at the kitchen table near him but out of the way. He waited, not rushing Maggie. He wanted to allow her to begin in her own time. He could tell she was wired and anxious. She sipped her coffee, which at one-fifteen in the morning wasn't going to help her get any sleep, even if she could relax after sharing with him whatever it was she'd called him over for.

Finally, Maggie set her mug down and turned toward Gage and Ruth. Twisting her fingers together, she drew in a deep breath and let it out in a rush.

"Alright, I know you're wondering why I had Ruth call you over here in the middle of the night. Actually, I was hoping you were still on duty, so I'm sorry I caught you after hours."

Gage waved away her words. "It's not a problem, Maggie. It sounds like this is really important, and I'm glad to help in any way I can. If it helps in our investigation, then that's even better. I can tell you're pretty upset, so take your time and don't rush. Think it through. It's far more important for you to be accurate than for me to get home, so don't worry."

Maggie nodded and took another swig of her coffee. She cradled the warm mug between her hands and began.

"Okay. So, Antonio Amato invited me to a yacht party this evening to introduce me to some of his business acquaintances in order to possibly drum up some photography business for me." Maggie told him about the events from the time the chauffeur picked her up until he dropped her back at Ruth's door. Of particular interest was the time she spent in Antonio's office taking pictures and hiding behind his couch eavesdropping on Antonio and Lennie's conversation concerning disposal of the bodies and the medical examiner's reports.

Gage sat listening, his heart hammering with excitement. They finally had a lead.

When Maggie was finished, Ruth leaned forward and looked at Gage. "So, you have him dead to rights. Go get him."

Gage turned his gaze on her, shaking his head. "It's not that easy, Ruth. We have no evidence. All we have is hear-say. Maggie's hear-say. It would never stand up in court. Antonio's lawyer would shoot it down in less than a minute. We need evidence. Hard, factual evidence."

Maggie stood and went back into her room, returning almost immediately. She held out a micro-SD chip toward Gage. "Here are the digital pics I got from his grandfather's journal. I already removed my own pictures. I doubt it'll have anything to do with Antonio's activities. It's more likely to help my dad with his research."

"We'll still go through it." Gage shrugged, accepting the chip. "You never know."

"But what about Antonio's orders for guys to go steal the bodies and the records?" Maggie asked.

"I wouldn't worry too much about it. I'll give the ME a heads-up about their plan though. They need to know what the gangsters are up to. The first body has already been released to his sister and has most likely been buried by now. The ME can make sure that information is secure. The second body can be moved to another secure facility just in case they actually do get through to the morgue. As for the ME's reports, those records are on a secure server run by the state of North Carolina. I don't think they're going to hack that. Thanks, Maggie. I appreciate this information. At least we know who the boss is now."

Ruth stood and walked over to her cousin, wrapping her arms around her. "Your guardian angels were sure looking after you this evening, Mags. To think you were in the room hiding while those gangsters were there talking…. It sends chills down my spine just thinking about it."

Maggie returned Ruth's hug. "Yeah, I know. Once when Antonio moved, maybe to stand suddenly? I don't know…it shoved the couch back against me and I stifled a groan. What if I hadn't stifled it? I might've been swimming with the fishes too."

"I don't like you working for that man now, Mags. Is there any way you can stop?" Ruth hugged her tighter.

Maggie shook her head. "I don't think so. He wants me to work on The Rusty Hook when that project begins, and to be honest, I still want to work it."

Ruth held Maggie. "I don't know what I'm going to do with you, Mags."

Not having close relatives or siblings, Gage envied the relationship between these cousins who had become more like sisters due to life's circumstances. He stood and cleared his throat.

"I think I'd better be going." He shifted his weight from one foot to the other. At the moment he felt more like a third wheel.

The women released each other and Maggie stood. They accompanied Gage to the front door.

"Thanks for coming, Gage," Maggie said. "I can't tell you how relieved I feel for getting that off my chest."

"I'm glad you told me. I'll make a few calls tonight before I hit the sack and get the ball rolling. Antonio Amato is a business man with a mobster family history. The apple doesn't fall far from the tree, as they say. Perhaps we'll find he's actually still attached to his family tree."

Ruth shivered. "How terrible to think he could be. And that he's operating right here in our Cape Hatteras."

Gage winked at her, delighting at the red surge that swept up from the rounded neck of her t-shirt. "Well, we'll have to put a stop to his business, like Mary Kelly's great-grandparents did to his great-great uncle, huh?

~

"Please come," Bobbye Buchanan's voice held a wheedling note. "Casey is dying to have a cookout now that warm weather is in full swing."

"Well," Ruth hesitated, "I don't know...."

"Bring Mags and her dad, Ruthie. And that new guy that came to church and to the beach party. What was his name?"

"His name's Gage, but..."

"That's right, Gage. He seems like a really nice guy, but I get the impression he might not be a believer. We need to encourage him to keep coming, don't you think?"

Ruth sighed and squeezed the cell phone in her fingers. Yes, she wanted to encourage Gage to become a believer, but in doing so, did that encourage him in thinking she wanted more in a relationship? She couldn't do that until he became a believer. What a catch-22. And did she even want a relationship at all? Was she ready for one? Considering her past and how she generally responded to men, she didn't think so. She was genuinely surprised, though, how Gage seemed to get a different response from her.

"Ruthie, are you there?"

"Yes, I'm here."

"So, you'll come? Saturday night?"

"I can't speak for the others but I'll ask. And as for Gage, I don't know his duty schedule, but I'll...I'll ask him."

"Awesome. Sounds like a plan. Let me know as soon as you can, okay?"

"I sure will. Thanks for the invitation, Bobbye. I'll talk to you soon."

When she hung up, Ruth dropped her cell phone onto her desk and leaned her head back against her desk chair, closing her eyes. Maybe she could ask Maggie to ask Gage to join them. That was the coward's way out, wasn't it? Yeah, it was.

Ruth sat up and continued working on the paper she'd been writing when Bobbye called. She hadn't been working long when a knock sounded at her office door.

Without looking up from her computer, she called, "Come in."

The door opened and Gage stuck his head in, a grin on his face. "You look busy. I can come back later."

As impossible as it was, how did just thinking of Gage

Hampton always seem to conjure him up? Of course, that was ridiculous.

Ruth waved him in. "No, it's okay. Come on in. It's nothing I can't work on later. What's up?"

Gage swung the door open, leaving it ajar and took the chair in front of her desk. "What are you working on? Friday's program?"

Ruth shook her head, wiping her palms on her pant legs. "No. It's my paper I'm writing for my PhD. One of them, that is. It's on the egrets and their progress."

"When's it due?" Gage crossed his ankle over his knee and laid his hat on them.

"In three weeks. I'm almost done, though. I'll be glad to get it off my plate. It's a lot more fun watching their progress than writing about it."

Gage chuckled. "I'm sure it is."

"So, what brings you up to my office. It's not like this is on your way to someplace else. You have to come up here specifically."

"Well, I wanted to give you an update on the case. Something interesting has happened"

Ruth clasped her hands in her lap. "Oh really? What?"

Gage shifted in his seat. "I just talked to the medical examiner a few minutes ago. It seems there was an attempted robbery made on his office and the morgue last night. Apparently, the thieves attempted to steal a body. However, the body in question, namely the one in our investigation had already been moved to another undisclosed location per my phone call two nights ago, thanks to Maggie's undercover information."

A grin lifted the corners of Gage's lips, sending warmth through Ruth. How could something so small and simple as a grin cause her to react in such a way? This conversation didn't warrant a physical reaction. It wasn't the conversation, she reminded herself. It was the grin he cast her way, and the gorgeous steel-blue of his eyes that shone when he gazed at her.

No, no, no, she chastised herself. She couldn't afford to allow him into her heart. Not now. Not without changes. And even then, she didn't think *she* was ready to let a man get close, not with her past still looming like a dark cloud over her.

"Ruth? Are you alright?"

She glanced back at Gage. His demeanor had changed. He was leaning forward, elbows on his knees, full attention on her. That gorgeous grin had vanished and a pair of pensive grooves drew down between his brows. His gaze was filled with concern.

She swallowed and attempted to plaster on a smile. "I'm fine."

Gage shook his head. "I lost you. What happened? Where did you go?"

His gaze was so direct and questioning and held hers for several moments before she managed to look away.

"Ruth, I know that something happened in the past. I have no idea what it was, but I can surmise that you were injured somehow, emotionally at least." Gage drew in a heavy breath and released it in a rush. "I hope that you consider me your friend, and I'd like to help you if you'll allow me to. I think you're hurting. Is there anything I can do?"

A gasp slipped from Ruth before she could prevent it. Had he read her thoughts? How uncanny. No, that was impossible. Gage Hampton was not a mind reader. He was an investigator who read the signals, taken notice and put two and two together. It was no secret she'd been stand-offish and held him at arms-length from day one.

When she could no longer stand his direct scrutiny, Ruth stood from her chair and strolled to the window that overlooked the lighthouse. Crossing her arms over her midriff, she stared at the black and white spiral-painted beacon, not actually seeing it. A night seven years earlier threatened to parade before her vision. She snapped her eyes shut then quickly opened them, attempting to focus on the lighthouse and prevent the memories from flooding back.

"Yes, something did happen, Gage, but I'd rather not discuss it. It's hard to talk about." Ruth's voice sounded raspy even to her own ears. She cleared her throat. "It was a...." she paused. "It was a difficult time for me."

Hearing the creak of Gage's chair and his footsteps on the old wooden floorboards, Ruth turned to find him closer than she'd anticipated. The light from the window made the irises in his eyes brighter than ever as his gaze roamed tenderly over her features. He shook his head ever so slightly.

"I'll never push you to tell me what you don't want to, Ruth."

He reached up a gentle finger and stroked her face from her brow down her cheek to the side of her chin. "But know this, if you ever need me for anything, or if you just want to talk, all you have to do is call. I'll be there for you. Do you understand?"

Ruth's pulse raced as her breathing accelerated. Swallowing hard, she attempted to get both under control.

"Thanks." Her voice came out more like a squeak. *Great. Way to sound normal, Ruth.*

Gage's Adam's apple bobbed as he swallowed. He stepped back and placed his hat on his head, attempting a grin.

"I'd better get going." His voice was husky as he turned toward the door.

Ruth drew in a deep breath as she sagged against the window sill. "Thanks for bringing the info about the near-robbery. I'm glad the ME and his staff we on their toes and foiled the gangsters."

Gage turned back, his hand on the doorknob. "Yeah, me too. But the question is, for how long?"

Ruth nodded as he headed out. Bobbye's invitation popped into her mind. She may as well ask Gage since he was here rather than expect Maggie to ask him. He'd certainly shown himself to be a friend. She could do no less.

"Oh, Gage, hold up," Ruth called just before he closed the door.

He stuck his head back around, a question on his handsome features.

"Sorry, I just remembered something. Bobbye and Casey Buchanan have invited you to a cookout at their house Saturday evening. Maggie, Uncle Owen and I will be going. I hope you aren't working and will be able to go too."

Gage opened the door wider and leaned against the door jam. "Really? You really mean that?"

Heat rolled over Ruth as she looked anywhere except at Gage. "Well, yeah, of course. Why not? Bobbye and Casey are good friends, and we'll have a great time."

Gage strolled back into the room, stopped right in front of her, and with a single gentle finger, tipped Ruth's chin up. Her gaze slowly came up to meet his. He winked.

"Yep, we'll have a great time."

Chapter Sixteen

"So how do you like your burgers, Gage?" Casey asked, dropping raw patties onto the grill.

"Medium rare, of course. Is there any other way?" Gage pulled a bottle of cream soda from a cooler near the back door to the screened-in porch.

"Well, not in my opinion, but I think the ladies wouldn't necessarily agree." Casey chuckled as he seasoned the already-sizzling and flaming burgers.

"Each to their own." Gage twisted off the cap of his soda and took a swallow. Glancing across the patio, his gaze landed on Ruth who was never far from his thoughts these days.

"You know, unless you turn your life over to Christ, she's as far away as the moon no matter how close you think she may be." Casey had leaned in and lowered his voice. "But don't do it for her. You need Christ for your own sake, man, not for hers."

Gage nodded involuntarily before he could stop himself. Casey's words were true and he couldn't deny them. Coach Watkins had pointed that out to him long ago, but he'd turned his back on God. He'd been running from Him, and he'd been miserable ever since. It was so simple, even a child could put their trust in Him, so Coach had told him. Gage knew what to do. *Am I really that stubborn and self-willed? Yeah, I guess I am.*

Gage took another drink of his soda as conviction weighed heavy on his heart. He shook his head and glanced over at the women and Uncle Owen seated in patio chairs beside a large metal fire pit, their melodic laughter and Owen's deep chuckle drifting his way and drawing his attention. Anything to break the heaviness that hung over him like a storm cloud.

"Hey, ladies and Owen," Casey raised his voice. "Burgers are almost ready. Grab a plate and let's say grace."

They all gathered near as Casey lifted words of gratitude and praise to the heavenly Father for the food, friends and fellowship, then he placed the sizzling burgers on a platter that Bobbye held for him.

Light chatter and banter surrounded the food table as burgers were prepared and chips and potato salad were dished out.

"Is this Watergate salad, Bobbye?" Maggie pointed to a bowl of green fluff.

"It sure is. My mother's recipe. She used to make it and freeze it when we were kids." Bobbye dropped a spoonful of potato salad on her plate. "Then she'd scoop it out like ice cream. We kids loved it."

"Now that sounds amazing." Ruth reached for the spoon that Maggie returned to the Watergate salad bowl. "Ice cream is my all-time favorite dessert. There aren't too many flavors I won't eat, and I love Watergate salad, too, so it sounds like a match made in heaven."

Gage tucked that tidbit of information away. He was an ice cream kind of guy too. Year around. "Can I get you something to drink?"

Ruth's gaze lifted to his and a smile tugged at her lips. "That would be nice. Thanks. I'll take a lemonade, please."

"Grab a seat and I'll bring it to you."

The color that suffused her features was delightful. Ducking her head, she gave a quick nod and turned away, heading back to the patio chairs around the firepit. When Gage followed with his plate in one hand and their drinks in the other, he noticed she sat next to an empty chair. Was it for him?

"Here you go." He handed her the bottle of lemonade.

"Thank you." She didn't quite meet his gaze but her hand touched the arm of the empty seat. "This one's for you."

Gage moved around the patio chair and lowered himself into it. "Thanks. That was thoughtful."

Ruth shrugged her shoulders and opened her lemonade, taking a swallow. Then she picked up her burger and began eating, the subject closed. Gage was just happy to be sitting beside her, and that she'd saved the seat for him. There was a time not so long ago that would not have happened.

~

Not so long ago, Ruth wouldn't have had the nerve to save a guy a seat. She wouldn't have been comfortable being near a guy. What had happened to her? Was it Gage? Or was it her? Had she changed? She'd been alone with Gage on several occasions and had come to realize she could trust him. She felt more comfortable in his presence now and never threatened. But there was still the fact that he hadn't placed his trust in the Lord, and that was a big deal. He stirred her heart, but until he put his trust in Christ, she'd have to fight against it. She'd never just been friends with a guy, except for her co-workers, at least not since before.... *Lord, I need Your help. I need Your strength. And please work in Gage's heart. Please help him to turn his heart and life over to You. He needs You so much.*

"Bobbye, I thought you were supposed to have that baby by now." Maggie's voice interrupted Ruth's prayer.

"So did I." Bobbye grimaced. "I'm a week overdue and this baby's still not showing signs of making an appearance."

"What does the doctor say?" Ruth asked.

Bobbye leaned forward and stretched her back. "I see him again on Monday. If the baby hasn't made an appearance before then, he'll induce me. Believe me, I'm ready."

"You and me both, honey." Casey reached his arm around her shoulders and gave her a squeeze. Everyone ate quietly for a few minutes then Casey broke the silence.

He lifted his voice to reach Gage across the firepit. "Hey, Gage, I saw on the evening news they were asking for anyone having information about an unknown man sporting a tattoo with the name Celia. Isn't that the guy Susan found the night of the church bonfire? Have you had any response from it yet?"

"Nothing so far, but they're going to continue running the spot every night for the next week. We also have a lead, thanks to Maggie." Gage's head tilted toward Ruth's cousin sitting beside her. "There was an attempted robbery at the ME's office a few nights ago."

"Really?" Casey's eyebrows shot up. "What'd they try to steal?"

"The body. The one from the beach the night of the church bonfire. The one Ruth found several weeks ago was released to a relative. We believe both men were connected to Antonio Amato."

"Amato." Casey drew his eyebrows back down in thought and placed his paper plate on his knee, crossing his arms over his chest. "Now why does that name sound familiar?"

"He's the big-wig that runs The Brigand's Cove Hotel that was just remodeled across the road from The Rusty Hook restaurant which also belongs to his family," Maggie said. "I did the photo shoot for his advertising promo."

"Hmmmmm." Casey shook his head. "No, I don't think that's it."

"Mary Kelly, the librarian in Hatteras Village, is the great-granddaughter of the infamous Mike and Ava Kelly who put the rum-runner Big Tony Amato out of business back in 1928," Ruth said. "That account is known by everyone on the island."

Casey zeroed in on Ruth and nodded. "Yeah, I think it had something to do with that, but something more specific than that general knowledge."

He scrubbed his hand down his face and glanced at his wife. "Honey?"

"Don't look at me, sweetheart. I have no idea what you're talking about." Bobbye swished her blond ponytail and grinned at him. "Could it be something from work that you ran across? Some old logs you read at some point that may have had to do with the rum-runner case?"

Casey's brows furrowed further. He said nothing more while the chatter around him continued. Ruth noticed he chowed down on his burger and chips but contributed nothing more to the conversation.

"Do you think he'll remember it?" Gage leaned toward Ruth and asked in a low voice.

She nodded. "Eventually. Once he's got something between his teeth, he won't give up until he sees it through."

Sure enough, a few minutes later, Casey snapped his fingers and proclaimed, "Got it."

"Got what, Casey?" Bobbye turned a surprised look on her husband.

"I remember where I heard the name Amato." Casey tossed his empty paper plate into the firepit and watched as the flames enveloped it. "Actually, I didn't hear it. I read it. And thanks to you, honey, for your nudge in the right direction. It was something I came across at work that had to do with the 1928 rum-runner case."

"Oh, well, glad that I could help." The extremely pregnant Bobbye struggled up from her chair and waddled toward the drink cooler.

"Well, don't keep us in suspense, Casey." Ruth set her plate down beside her chair and leaned forward, elbows on her knees. "Tell us what you know."

Casey leaned forward as well propping his own elbows on his knees.

"It was a ship's log I found in some of the old records at the station a while back. The log was recorded by a Captain...Captain," he paused for a moment and closed his eyes in thought. He opened them and snapped his fingers again. "Captain Joseph Spinner who was commander of the Coast Guard Cutter *The Sea Dog*. Most of the entries I found in the log were the usual stuff. You know, storm rescues, ships going down, illegal fishing. That sort of thing. I'd already heard about the infamous Mike and Ava Kelly and Big Tony Amato, but this entry stood out to me because Captain Spinner had marked the exact location with coordinates where Big Tony's rum-runner, *The Satisfaction,* went down."

A chorus of "What?" rang out around the firepit with Uncle Owen's being the loudest.

Casey blinked several times as chatter grew louder and questions bombarded him. He waved his hands in the air. "Hold up. Wait, everybody. Hold on."

When that didn't work he gave a shrill whistle that silenced them all.

"Wow, folks. I had no idea my find would elicit a firestorm of excitement like this."

Uncle Owen jumped to his feet, snapping his fingers at the same time. "That's it. That's what she said in her book. It makes sense to me now."

"What makes sense, Uncle Owen?" Ruth asked.

He turned to her and grinned. "I was reading Ava Sinclair Kelly's journal. She mentioned something about the captain of the Coast Guard cutter, *The Sea Dog,* having logged the coordinates where Big Tony Amato's rum-runner went down. I missed it until Casey just said he read that in Captain Spinner's log. It makes perfect sense now."

"Did she have the coordinates in her journal?" Gage asked.

"Oh no," Uncle Owen said. "Just that he had logged it."

"Her journal is like an arrow pointing to the captain's log book," Gage said. "And now Casey has read the log stating the coordinates of where *The Satisfaction* went down."

"It would seem so," Casey grinned. "This is getting exciting, don't you think?"

"Are you kidding me?" Maggie jumped up from her seat. "If Antonio Amato finds out you have this information, your life is forfeit, Casey. No way can you let this get out of this circle."

She turned to Gage and pointed at Casey. "Tell him, Gage. His life and Bobbye's both are at risk if this gets out. As a matter of fact, all of our lives are at risk. Every single one of us, and that's no exaggeration."

Maggie moved just behind her chair and began to pace, worry inscribed on her features. Ruth watched her. After Maggie's incident at the dinner party onboard Antonio Amato's yacht, she'd been nervous and experiencing difficulty sleeping. She was having second thoughts in wanting to take the ad job for The Rusty Hook restaurant renovation. Mr. Amato had even called Friday morning saying they would begin work on the old building first thing Monday morning. He wanted Maggie to photograph before, during and after renovation shots. If she was going to work with them, she would need to be on-site a few days a week. That made her nervous.

Gage leaned forward, elbows on his knees, hands clasped loosely together. "Maggie's right, Casey. Maggie was onboard Antonio Amato's yacht and hid in his office while he and one of his lackey's planned the robbery of the aforementioned body. Had they found her, she'd likely have been a third body. These guys don't mess around. When you hear that the mafia is no more, don't believe it. They're alive and thriving, and Antonio Amato is carrying on his family's name. He may have some legit businesses as fronts, but that's all they are. Fronts. They're covering for some pretty shady things. Money laundering, racketeering, extortion and credit card fraud, to name a few. We haven't found all the proof yet, but we think he may even be involved in human trafficking. He's got his fingers in a lot of pies."

"Are you serious?" Bobbye stood beside her husband then lowered herself awkwardly onto his lap. Casey wrapped his arms around her. "We're in danger?"

"We all are, if this information gets out to the wrong people." Gage nodded but kept his voice soft. "There are only six of us. We just have to make sure it doesn't get out."

"And here I thought the information I found would be helpful." Casey's lips turned down in a grimace.

Owen stood and strolled over to Casey's side, slapping him on the shoulder. "This information is more than helpful, my young friend. Have you ever heard of *La Cruz de San Mateo*?"

Casey gazed at Owen with a skeptical eye. "Uh, no, I haven't. What is *La Cruz...de...*whatever you said?"

Owen chuckled. "*La Cruz de San Mateo*. It translates Saint Matthew's Cross. It's a gold cross with a ruby heart. Big Tony Amato stole it from the museum in Kingston, Jamaica sometime in 1928. I'm searching for it as I'm more than certain Antonio Amato is. Should I find it, I intend to return it to the museum. I doubt Mr. Amato's intentions are as reputable."

"Wow," Casey and Gage said at the same time.

"And this *La Cruz de San Mateo* supposedly went down with *The Satisfaction*?" Gage asked, rubbing his chin as he gazed at Owen.

"That's the general thought," Owen said, "but there's speculation that it could also be on the cape somewhere. No one really knows what Big Tony did with it."

Gage grinned as he turned toward Casey. "Do you dive? As a Coastie I assume you do?"

"I do. Why?"

"Because you and I are going to those coordinates and we're going to look for *La Cruz de San Mateo*." He turned to Uncle Owen. "Do you dive, Owen?"

Owen shook his head. "Sadly, it's one thing I never took the time to learn. I was too busy studying world history and traveling to take the time."

"Well, perhaps you'll still come along. Think we can find someone with a boat?" He turned his attention back to Casey.

"Yeah, I know someone with a boat. Friend from church. Just have to tell him we want to do some wreck diving, and he'll be happy to take us out. Don't have to tell him anything else."

"Sweetheart," Bobbye turned Casey's face toward her with her slender fingers. "I don't know about this. What if those mafia guys are out there while you're out there? What if they try to stop you?"

"How are they going to know what we're doing, honey?" Casey planted a gentle kiss on the tip of her nose. "We could just be any old divers out there diving for the fun of it. But Owen will be in the boat, and we'll make sure we have some fire power. Don't worry."

"I would say let me come along, too, but they know me for sure," Maggie plopped back into her patio chair.

Gage shook his head adamantly. "Nope. There's no way you're coming. Sure dead giveaway. They don't know us and we can pull it off."

Maggie heaved a sigh. Ruth knew her cousin well enough to know that she wanted to do something to help, but also knew that she needed to stay far away from that expedition. Maggie was a go-getter. She always had been. It was hard for her to stay on the sidelines. When Ruth had been through her...well, her ordeal, Maggie had wanted to take things into her own hands and meet out retribution, but she hadn't been allowed to. Justice had prevailed in the end without her help.

"I'm off again next weekend." Gage returned his attention to Casey. "Think we can set up something for Saturday?"

"I'm sure of it. I'll call my buddy and set it up. He'll have no idea we're looking for anything specific."

"None of this goes any further, right?" Maggie asked, worry still etching her features. "As much as I love each of you, I'm not in a hurry to die for any of you. Got it?"

Owen wrapped his arms around her. "It'll be fine, Maggie girl. We're all secure in the Father's arms. Just trust in Him. Remember, we're the good guys."

Ruth turned and looked at Gage. His chin rested on steepled fingers, his elbows on his knees. His gaze was fixed on the flames in the firepit, and his forehead was furrowed. Was he thinking how he wasn't secure in the Father's arms? She certainly was.

~

Gage shut the door of his beachside townhouse behind him and tossed his car keys on the kitchen counter. Crossing over to the sliding glass door, he unlocked it, slid it open, stepped out and closed it behind him.

He liked being on the bottom floor so he could just walk out to the beach anytime he liked. Now Gage dropped onto the lounge chair that sat in the corner of the patio and pulled out his phone. Gazing at it for a moment, he hesitated, then pulled up his contact list, scrolling through until he found Coach Watkins's phone number. His thumb hovered over the call button for a second as he again hesitated. Gage swallowed. Hard. Drawing in a deep breath, he released it all at once. What was he doing? This was ridiculous. He didn't need Coach to tell him what to do. He already knew.

Dropping the phone on the table beside the lounge chair, Gage scooted to the edge of the seat and dropped to his knees, his heart pounding.

Oh God, are You there? Do You hear me? I don't deserve for You to. I deserve for You to turn Your back on me like I turned mine on You so long ago. I didn't want You in my life then, but I need You. I really need You. I was wrong. I can't make it on my own. I'm not secure in You should something go wrong. Either with the mob or if I'm just doing my job and somebody else takes me out. But it's more than that, isn't it? I need You because I'm a sinner. Oh God, please, save me.

Gage felt such agony in his spirit and longed for peace to ease it. Coach Watkins had told him a long time ago that only God could bring him peace. As he called out to the God that he'd denied, he released the grip that he'd had over his life and in return received the peace that passed all understanding.

With his head bowed on his arms there on the lounge chair, the sound of the ocean waves softly crashing in the distance, Gage felt God's peace envelop him as the Holy Spirit took up residence within him.

Thank You, Lord. Thank You. After a time, Gage stood and shoved his hands into his pockets as he turned and looked out toward the ocean. It was a bright night with a sky full of stars and a three-quarter moon that reflected on the white-capped breakers that washed onto the shore. Somehow it seemed to make the Lord a little closer.

Welcome home, son. No, Gage realized, he hadn't heard those words. He'd felt them in his very being. He couldn't explain it, even to himself. But…gazing up at the inky sky…he loved the peace that filled him.

A smile lifted the corners of his lips. There was someone he needed to tell about this. Someone who had been waiting for years to hear this news. He picked up his cell phone from the table where he'd dropped it and hit speed dial for Coach Watkins.

After a couple of rings, a gruff elderly voice enquired, "Hello?"

"Hey Coach, it's Gage. I've got something to tell you. Some good news actually."

Chapter Seventeen

These are the books that arrived this morning, Ruthie," Naysa Withem dropped a cardboard box onto the counter in the visitor center gift shop. "Some of them are kid's books and some are adult. You'll be happy to know that some are about biological topics and are new to us. Any ideas about how we should display them for their best sales potential?"

"Well, let's see what you have there." Ruth waited while Naysa made stacks of the books, then she glanced through them.

"Wow, these are great. Especially the kid's books. They're very interactive and should draw some interest from the kids and their parents."

They spent the next forty-five minutes arranging the new books in the gift shop and had just finished the last display when a guy in a hoodie walked in, his hands in his jacket pockets, the hood drawn low over his eyes.

"Sir, I'm sorry, but we're closed," Naysa called to him. She lowered her voice so only Ruthie could hear. "Oh, shoot. I forgot to lock the door when I turned the Closed sign."

Ruthie's heart began to hammer as she eyed the stranger. This was not good. She pulled her cell phone from her pocket and immediately dialed Gage's number.

"Hello?"

"Gage, there's a stranger…"

"Hang up," the man said.

Ruth looked up to see the hooded man pointing a gun at her. Gasping, she simply stared for a moment.

"I said hang up." Without raising his voice, he moved the gun toward Naysa.

"Ruth?" Naysa whispered.

147

"Gage, help." Ruth whispered into the phone just before she hung up. Had he heard her? Would he be able to have the call traced to the gift shop? Would it have made a difference? *Please, God, Help us!*

"Slide the phone away." The man's voice was deep and soft. "You, old woman, open the cash register and get the money out."

Naysa jerked her head back and forth. "I...I can't. There's none in there."

"Where is it?" The words came through gritted teeth.

Naysa glanced at Ruth. Ruth nodded. "Tell him, Naysa. It's not worth your life."

"In the...um..." Naysa swallowed hard, "in the safe."

"Then open the safe." The stranger walked closer, the gun still pointed at Naysa.

Naysa closed her eyes, brow scrunched tight, shaking her head. "Please don't make me do this. Please, sir."

"I said open the safe, old woman. I ain't waitin' here all night."

Naysa's eyes opened, and she glanced at Ruth then at the hooded man. "And if I refuse? I'm the only one here who can open it."

A smirk crossed the man's wide mouth as the gun moved to cover Ruth. "Then I'll kill her. Now open it."

Naysa heaved a heavy sigh and stood up, moving slowly toward the office behind the checkout counter. Pulling her keys from her slacks pocket, she unlocked the door and started to open it.

"Hold up, old woman. You," he motioned toward Ruth, "you come along too."

Ruth didn't want to be anywhere near this man. Panic raised its ugly head as she edged closer. He grabbed her arm, and she jerked it away. Grateful that he didn't grab it again, she hurried to follow Naysa as she entered the office and stayed as close to her as she could. Ruth took deep breaths in an attempt to control her breathing. *In, out, in, out. Slowly.*

Naysa flipped on the overhead lights and they all went inside the office. The safe was inside a cabinet behind the desk. Ruth pressed herself into the corner nearest the door and as far away from the man as she could get while Naysa opened the cabinet with the safe inside.

Ruth watched as Naysa turned the dial on the safe. Her fingers were trembling. Would she get the combination right?

All of a sudden, she spun the dial hard and started all over again.

"What's the matter, old woman?"

"You're making me nervous. It's hard to remember the combination when you're breathing down my neck, mister."

"Well, ya better hurry up. Your little friend's life here depends on it."

Ruth heard the click of the hammer on the gun as it was cocked back. She closed her eyes. *Oh, Lord. Please send help!*

Naysa's fingers fumbled again, but she slowed down her movements, and finally got the safe open.

The man stepped forward and shoved her aside, making her fall and hit her head on the corner of the cabinet. Ruth hurried over and pulled Naysa to her feet, wrapping an arm around her trembling friend.

Glancing around the room, Ruth looked for something to disable the man. In his rush to grab the money he'd forgotten about them. He should've told them to take it out, but he'd gotten greedy.

There was nothing in the room she could hit him with, but there was a Billy club under the counter in the gift shop for just this purpose. If she could just sneak out and get it....

Ruth put a finger over her lips and motioned for Naysa to stay put, then she edged toward the door one step at a time. The man was busy shoving cash into the bank bags that stayed in the safe for bank deposits.

Step by step she moved until she was in the doorway. Just a couple more feet. If he turned and saw her, he'd likely fire on her. At least Naysa was out of the way as she remained on the far side of the room.

Ruth glanced below the counter where the Billy club was stored. Yes. The sliding cabinet door was open. Just as her fingers reached for it, she glanced out the front door and her gaze collided with the most beautiful pair of steel-blue eyes she'd ever seen. Her mouth dropped open and Gage put his finger to his lips then indicated she should step aside.

Joy filled her heart as Ruth was glad to hand over the capture of the criminal to the experts. She would have done what she needed to do, but since help had arrived, she'd gladly step aside.

Quietly Gage opened the front door and, followed by Wayne Mitchell and two other officers, stepped inside. On silent feet they made their way into the office just as the hooded man finished filling his last bag and stood. He turned to find he was surrounded by four park police officers, all aiming their weapons at him.

"You're under arrest," Wayne Mitchell said, a grin splitting his features. "And you can just leave those bags on the floor. We'll take care of them."

~

"I didn't want to open the safe," Naysa said, "but what could I do? He was going to shoot Ruthie. I wasn't about to let that happen."

"You did the right thing, Naysa," Wayne jotted in his notebook. "When it comes to someone's life, you give up the money. We can always get that back, or at least attempt to. You can't get a life back."

Ruth slipped her arm through Naysa's. "This was one brave woman, Wayne. She was stalling to try to give you guys time to get here."

Naysa cast her a questioning glance over her glasses. "Stalling? I wasn't stalling. I was just so nervous, I kept fumbling the dial. Just like I told the guy."

"Well, thank goodness it's over." Wayne flipped his notebook shut. "That fella's been robbing businesses up and down the Outer Banks for a while now, but he's going away where he can't bother anybody for a long time."

Gage picked up his hat from the sales counter and twirled it in his hand. "Well, thanks to Ruth calling me and giving me a heads up, I was able to find out where she was. I gave Maggie a call, and she said you were working late with Naysa this evening in the gift shop. Then I called in the troops. That's all it took."

Naysa walked over and wrapped her arms around him. "Boy am I glad she did. Thank you for heading up that posse, young man. I'm not sure we would've walked away from this little adventure had you not. It was mighty scary, I don't mind saying."

She pulled away and stepped back, but didn't release his arms. "If there's anything I can do for you," then she looked at the rest of the officers, "for any of you fellas, please don't hesitate to ask. You saved our lives, you know. And that's not an exaggeration."

Naysa released him and wrapped her arm around Ruth's waist. "Love you, Ruthie. No one I'd rather have gone through that experience with, but I don't want to ever go through it again. Agreed?"

Ruth hugged Naysa's shoulder and nodded. "Agreed. Now why don't you go home? I'll get these gentlemen to help me box the rest of these books up and put them in the office. We're done with the displays, thank goodness."

"I'm going to take you up on that, Ruthie." Naysa nodded and walked into the office, returning with her purse. "Would one of you fine gentlemen walk me out to my car, please? I know he's gone, but I'd just feel a little better."

Wayne stuck his arm out. "I'd be happy to walk you to your car, Naysa. I'll leave the heavy lifting to the younger fellas."

"Don't blame you, Wayne. Let's go."

When all the boxes were neatly stacked back in the office and the gift shop was back in order, the other officers said goodnight and took their leave. Ruth left on the security lighting and headed for the door. Gage held it open for her then closed it for her to lock up.

"I'm sorry you had such a stressful evening. It can't have been easy for you." He stepped out from under the covered porch in front of the gift shop and stopped on the sidewalk leading to the parking lot.

Ruth didn't bother to put on her uniform hat, but held it in her hand. She looked out past the parking lot toward the ocean before speaking then she nodded. "Yes, there were some moments where I started to panic, but I talked myself down with breathing exercises I've learned over the years. Most of the time they work. It depends on how far along I get in the panic attack before I begin the breathing exercise."

"Do the same things always cause you to panic?"

Ruth dropped her eyes and chewed on the corner of her lip. She had hoped he wouldn't ask that. "It just depends."

Would he press for more? He knew she didn't want to talk about it, but she knew at some point she should tell him. They were friends after all. But did she owe it to him to tell him? She didn't think so.

"Look, Gage, I should be going. As you said, it's been a stressful evening."

"You don't have an interpretive program tonight?"

Did he look disappointed? Perhaps that she still wasn't willing to share her past with him?

"Oh no. That's tomorrow night. I couldn't have stayed and helped Naysa this late then had a program to boot."

"I see, well, I better get back on patrol. I'm on until midnight, then I'm on again tomorrow afternoon. You have a good evening and get some rest." He moved toward his patrol car parked at the end of the sidewalk, the blue lights still flashing.

Ruth glanced back at the gift shop then at the patrol car. She was impressed. No way could the perpetrator have seen these lights and the officers had all approached silently. They had done a wonderful job in saving Naysa and her.

"Thanks again for rescuing us. It was done flawlessly, you know. He didn't see it coming. You got the drop on him, and it went down without a hitch. You guys were amazing."

Gage tipped his hat and attempted a John Wayne imitation. "It's our job, little lady. Glad to help."

"Hey not bad. If you ever get tired of the park police, perhaps Hollywood?"

He shook his head. "Not a chance. Besides, I'd miss your smile.

Warmth surged past Ruth's collar filling her face. Was there enough light from the lighthouse welcome sign for him to see?

"Oh, Hollywood's full of smiles, Gage. Goodnight." She turned and fled to her car. This conversation needed to end. Now.

~

Antonio reclined on the leather sofa in the dimly lit lounge on board the yacht. A pile of sofa pillows propped him at just the right angle to enjoy the baseball game on his 86-inch flat screen TV. A bowl of popcorn and a couple of beers sat on the coffee table within reach. Lennie sat in an armchair, his own popcorn and beer nearby.

"Woohoo," Antonio cheered and clapped his hands together at the conclusion of the game as his favorite team won. "Way to go, team. I knew they'd win, Lennie."

"Yeah, Boss. They did good. Real good."

"You betcha." Antonio switched channels with the remote. "Can't wait till the next game. This is promising to be a good season."

He scrolled through until he found the local news. "Let's find out what's happening around here. Need to stay up on the news, you know."

"Yeah, Boss."

"...Local park police have found an unidentified body and the only identifying mark is a tattoo. If you know anything about this tattoo or the man with this tattoo please call this number."

A picture of the tattoo and a phone number below it appeared on the TV screen causing Antonio to instantly come up off the couch to his feet. His face turned an angry red as a string of expletives spewed from his mouth, his fists clenching at his sides. "Just because Harland is dead, doesn't mean our problems are over. Did Garcia have a family, Lennie?"

"I don't know, Boss. He never talked about 'em if he did." Lennie shrugged his shoulders.

Antonio turned his angry gaze on his underling. "Then find out."

~

Saturday morning Gage picked up Uncle Owen at the RV park and they drove north to the marina in Avon where Casey's friend kept his boat docked. After parking in the marina parking lot, they searched for the slip where Casey had instructed them to meet him.

Sure enough, as they approached down the boardwalk, they spotted Casey waving.

"Morning, fellas. Over here."

"Good morning," Gage dropped his gear bag on the sun-faded boards. "That's quite a boat."

"Yep, it is. Morning, Owen," Casey shook the older man's hand. "Ready for a voyage on board *The Sand Piper*?"

Owen pulled down his prescription sunglasses and gazed at the boat over their upper rims. A whistle eased from his lips. "That's a beauty, Casey. Where's the captain?"

"Right here, sir." A young man in his mid-thirties appeared from the cabin area and walked across the rear dive deck, jumping to the boardwalk. He extended his hand. "It's a pleasure to meet you, gentlemen. Casey says you're in need of a charter boat for diving."

Casey stepped slightly behind the young man and nodded emphatically.

Gage eyed Casey then nodded slowly. "Um yeah, that's right. A charter boat for diving."

"Gage, Owen, this is Coy Nelson, a friend of mine from church. He runs a charter boat diving service. The best in the business in these parts."

"It's a pleasure to meet you, Coy," Gage shook the young man's hand. "You come highly recommended. I've no doubt you can take us right where we need to dive."

"You bet I can. Casey's already given me several coordinates to check out."

Gage and Uncle Owen exchanged quizzical glances then looked at Casey.

"Really? That's a great way to be thorough, Casey." Gage grabbed his gear bag. "What do you say we get this expedition under way?"

"I'm ready," Uncle Owen agreed.

"There's a little bit of paperwork to fill out as we leave the harbor." Coy walked over to release one of the lines securing the boat to the dock. "Come on inside and have a seat at the table. You can take care of that while I get us underway."

~

"A charter, Casey?" Gage's voice was barely above a low whisper once they were settled inside the cabin. "How are we supposed to pay for this? It can't be inexpensive, and I can't expense it to the park service."

Casey waved his words away. "Not to worry. I've got it covered. He gave me a great friends and family deal, so you let me worry about the cost. You and Owen fill out your paperwork. It's just a release form."

Owen sat at the table and perused one of the forms laying there. "Looks pretty straight forward to me, Gage. It's just protecting Coy from libel or lawsuits."

Gage sat across from Owen and picked up the second form. After reading it, he picked up one of the pens and signed it, then standing, he clapped Casey on the shoulder.

"Thanks for arranging all this, Casey. And Coy knows nothing of our mission, right?"

"Right. He thinks we're just out diving for fun. I gave him a couple of coordinates for us to go to. The first one is the correct one so we can spend the longest time there."

"Let's just hope and pray we have success," Gage said as Owen stood to join them.

"Oh, I've been praying, brother," Casey grinned. "Come on fellas. Let's go find *La Cruz de San Mateo*."

~

"You just can't leave your work alone, can you, Ruth?" Maggie shoved away a wisp of hair that the wind whipped across her face. "Not even on the weekend."

"I want to check on the turtle eggs and then the piping plovers, Mags." Ruth dug her toes into the warm sand as they strode along the beach southward. "I'm especially concerned about the eggs. There are so many predators and careless humans around."

"How much longer before the turtle eggs hatch?"

The wind whipped Ruth's ponytail but she didn't care. She loved the ocean breeze and stared off to her left at the Atlantic Ocean. "Likely several more weeks at least, is my guess. When Gage and I saw the mama turtle lay her eggs, it was so amazing. It's not something you see every day. Then off she went, never to see them again. Once they hatch, they'll have to make their way to the water and very few of them will survive. Most will be eaten by predators. Seagulls and other birds mostly. If I knew when they would hatch, I'd be there to ward them off, but there's just no knowing."

"Yeah, that's kind of sad," Maggie said. "Too bad we can't stage a "hatch watch" with a rotating group of people watching for them to hatch."

"Yeah, but who would you enlist to watch? They hatch at night and there aren't too many people who are going to sit up at night waiting for turtles to hatch."

"That's true." Maggie shoved a hank of hair from her eyes as she turned to look out at the ocean. "I wonder if the guys are having any success."

"I'm praying they do." Ruth gazed out at the white-capped rolling breakers. "You know, God is the only one who knows where that gold cross is. What if He just doesn't want it found?"

"Then there will probably be a lot more people to lose their lives." Maggie turned to look at her cousin, her eyes squinting in the sunlight. She pulled her sunglasses from her shirt pocket and settled them on her nose.

"What do you mean?" Ruth shaded her eyes with her hand.

"Think about it. As long as Antonio Amato is looking for that treasure, he'll do anything to find it. Including taking out anyone in his way."

"Then we need to pray the guys find it and get it into the proper hands before Antonio Amato does."

"Yep." Maggie stopped walking and looked out past the waves. "I don't see any boats from here. Do you?"

"No, but I think...wait. Is that a boat? There. Look." Ruth pointed northeast of their position. "We're right beside the lighthouse. The Rusty Hook is about three-quarter of a mile up the main road from the lighthouse. It looks to me like that boat might be about a mile out and just northeast of The Rusty Hook. Could that be the guys out there? Do you think that could be where *The Satisfaction* went down?"

Maggie heaved a heavy sigh. "I sure wish I had a pair of strong binoculars right about now."

"Wouldn't that be nice." Ruth propped her hands on her hips. "Want to jump in the car and ride up the road to the beach perpendicular to their position? Just to see if we can see any better? We can stop by my office and grab my binoculars."

"Why not? It can't hurt."

The women took off at a jog back to the car.

Chapter Eighteen

When Gage had taken diving lessons, he'd learned with a face mask that covered his eyes and nose and a regulator that fit into his mouth for breathing. However Coy had provided him and Casey with a full-face mask and a microphone that allowed him to talk to Casey as well as Coy and Owen. Gage and Casey had agreed to use hand signals and their magnetic writing boards to communicate in order to prevent Coy from catching on to their mission.

Once they arrived at the first coordinates, Casey and Gage donned their diving gear and descended down a rope to the bottom of the ocean, a mere thirty-three feet below Coy's dive boat. Was it possible that *The Satisfaction* landed that shallow or had nearly a century of sands and tides shifted it elsewhere? It was a vast ocean and nearly a century had passed since it's sinking.

Gage felt the weight of their task settle on him as they descended to the ocean floor. It was soon replaced with a thrill of excitement, however. At this shallow depth, the bright morning sunlight filtered through the water and allowed him his first glimpse of what was scattered across the seaweed and sandy ocean bottom.

To his right lay what looked like a World War II submarine laying on its side, a large torpedo hole blown into the bulkhead. It was covered in barnacles, seaweed, anemones and other undersea growth. Right next to it lay the remains of an old wooden ship from a century or two past. Who knew how old it could be? Ribs and side planking were about all that remained of it along with the sea creatures that had claimed it for their home.

"So, what's the weather like down there, fellas?" Coy's chuckle came through the speaker in Gage's ear.

"Very nice," Casey's voice responded. "The water's pretty clear and the sun's filtering through nicely. The current isn't too strong at the moment and the ocean floor is littered with wrecks. So far, we've spotted a WWII submarine that looks like a U-boat, an old wooden hull that's a couple centuries old, I'd say, and I see what looks like pieces and parts of something scattered around the ocean floor. Some of it are pretty big pieces and some is just scattered. I think we'll just have to explore then get back to you, Coy."

"Sure thing, Casey. Have fun." Coy signed off.

Casey waved Gage over and wrote on his magnetic board. "Let's check out the debris field."

Gage gave him a thumbs up and began inspecting the scattered items. With *The Satisfaction* having been sunk in an explosion, it stood to reason that this could possibly be it. There were ripped wooden boards that looked like parts of a boat, and what looked like pieces of crates and broken glass bottles scattered everywhere. He even found a few intact bottles of rum. Gage's heart rate accelerated. Looking around, he searched for Casey. Should he call this one over the radio? No, he couldn't allow this over the radio waves. If somehow it got out that a rum-runner had been found, Antonio Amato would be all over it.

With one of the bottles in his hand he swam the ten yards to where Casey searched. He tapped him on the shoulder, and when he turned, Gage held up the antique bottle of rum. Casey's grin lit up his face inside the dive mask as he gave a thumbs up.

Picking up his magnetic board he wrote, "We must be on the right track."

Gage nodded and pulled out his board. "There must've been a safe. We must find it."

Casey eyed his diving gauges. "Coy, we're going to need new air bottles in about twenty minutes."

"Sure thing. I'll lower them down the rope. You can change when you're ready. Give a tug and we'll bring the used ones up."

"Sounds like a plan, my friend."

Gage set the vibration alarm on his dive watch for fifteen minutes then swam back through the debris field continuing his search for the safe. He picked up a few non-relevant items, discarding them until he found an old black leather oxford. As he held it in his hand an odd sensation swept over him. If this had been *The Satisfaction*, someone had been wearing this shoe when the boat was blown up. They died that day, possibly in the explosion. Just how many had died? He didn't know anything about the boat, but maybe Casey did.

His wristwatch vibrated indicating it was time to head back to the rope and change out his compressed air tank. He glanced at his air gauge. Yep. It was almost empty. He started to drop the shoe, but instead took it with him. He wasn't sure why, but he might keep this item. At least long enough to show it to Casey.

Gage and Casey changed out their air tanks then Gage showed Casey the leather shoe. His friend held it in his hand, turning it over and examining it. He shook his head then handed it back to Gage. Picking up his writing board, he wrote, "How sad. I wonder how many died on that boat."

Gage shook his head and wrote on his own writing board, "My thoughts exactly."

Casey didn't have that information. Swimming back to the debris field, Gage returned the oxford to where he'd found it. It belonged here where its owner had rested, whoever he'd been. Was he one of the rum-runners on Big Tony Amato's boat? Was he Big Tony Amato himself? It was a stark reminder of man's mortality. A piece of humanity laying here on the bottom of the ocean floor.

Gage shook his head and got back to work searching. He only had so much time before his new bottle of air ran out. They still had two more dives today. Best get to it.

~

Owen was busy going through his research papers at the table in the cabin when he heard the sound of voices greeting Coy. What in the world? He stuffed his papers back into his briefcase and tucked it in the storage compartment underneath the dining seat where he'd been sitting. Then he went out to see who Coy was talking to.

A large yacht had pulled near Coy's dive boat and a gentleman in casual slacks and a polo was leaning over the lower stern deck railing talking to him.

"Oh, hello there," the gentleman said as Owen stepped out. "I was just talking to the dive master here. He was telling me you folks are chartering his dive boat."

"Hello," Owen greeted him. "Yes, that's right. He's a very knowledgeable young man."

"Is that so? Who do you have down there?" the gentleman asked, a toothpick rolling between his lips.

Owen answered before Coy could get a word in. "A couple of friends. It's such a beautiful day and they've been wanting to get out for a dive, so we said let's go."

Owen noticed the man watched him with cold eyes despite the warm smile on his face.

"Really? Why here in particular?" the man asked.

"We used sonar," Owen said. "Looked like a wealth of ships to dive on. There's a U-boat down there as well as a two-century old wooden hull. After this we're going to drop anchor in a couple other places. Right, Coy?"

Owen dropped a hand on Coy's shoulder, and although the younger man looked slightly confused, he instantly agreed. "Yeah, you bet. You can't go wrong in the Graveyard of the Atlantic. You're bound to find something of interest to dive on wherever you go."

"I see." The man on the yacht straightened from the railing and gave them a partial salute. "Well, I wish you happy diving, gentlemen."

Owen waved. "Thanks."

The man disappeared inside the yacht and within minutes it pulled away. The name *The Lucky Lady* was painted on her stern.

"Ever seen that boat around?" Owen asked as casually as he could.

"Sure, I have," Coy nodded, hands on his hips, his gaze following the departing yacht. "I see it all over the place. It berths at the Diamond Sands Yacht Club. Too rich for my blood. But I see it all around these waters."

"Hmm. Interesting. Know who that man was?"

"Oh yeah. Anyone with a boat around these parts knows him. That's Antonio Amato. He just remodeled that hotel in Buxton north of the lighthouse. He's a real estate developer. Word is he's getting ready to develop The Rusty Hook, that old restaurant across the road from that hotel. His family owns it and the hotel."

"Yeah, I've heard that." Owen scratched his chin. "What were you all talking about before I came out here?"

"He just asked how many divers we had in the water."

The hair on the back of Owen's neck stood up. "Anything else?"

"He asked if we were looking for treasure."

Owen felt like someone punched him in the stomach. "And what did you say?"

"I said 'isn't everyone?'."

~

Gage swam over to where a large wooden structure lay in a patch of seaweed. It looked like it could've at one time been a part of a boat cabin. It still had part of the wall and roof connected together. A window pane was still intact minus the glass. Sea life had claimed it but unfortunately for them, he was going to have to disturb them. He attempted to lift it, and at first it wouldn't budge. However, after planting his finned feet on the ocean floor and digging in his heels, he lifted with all his might and it began to shift. All of a sudden, Casey was at his side, and the two of them were able to shove the structure up and over, revealing a clear area of debris where no seaweed had grown beneath it.

Gage scanned the debris and found a collection of various items: a mangled piece of stove pipe, what looked like a rusted door to a wood stove, broken pieces of wood that could've been boards to a boat, bits of broken glass. The list went on. He picked up each board in the hope there would be a name on it.

He checked his air gauge. Fifteen minutes until they needed to climb the rope for their decompression stop. Flipping over more scattered boards, his heart banged in his chest when letters appeared on one. They were faint but definitely letters. He wiped a layer of silt away and took a closer look. The board was approximately four feet long and six inches wide and broken on both ends. Only the letters TISFACTI were visible, but it was enough for Gage to believe it was likely *The Satisfaction*. How could it not be? What other boat would have a name with that many letters that close? Unfortunately, none of the other boards that he'd found so far had turned up any more letters, but he hadn't checked all of them.

Gage glanced around for Casey's location and spotted him about twenty feet away. With board in hand, he swam over to his friend, excitement filling him. This had to be the wreckage of *The*

Satisfaction. Now if they could just find that safe. The only problem was, they were running out of air, and their time was almost up.

Once he reached Casey's side, he tapped him on the shoulder. When he had the other man's attention, he pointed at the board. Casey's eyes lit up once again inside his helmet. He nodded then pointed at his air gauge.

"Time's up, buddy. Air's almost out. We still have two more dives to make." Casey pulled out his writing board and scribbled before handing it to Gage. "This has to be the resting place of *The Satisfaction*. We'll return another day to search for the safe."

Gage dropped the board with the partial name of *The Satisfaction* and nodded. Aloud he said, "Yeah, let's get up top and move on."

With reluctance, they both swam upward alongside the anchor rope until they reached the fifteen-foot mark where they waited to decompress for five minutes before heading slowly to the surface.

Removing their tanks, both Owen and Coy were there to collect them and help them aboard. As Gage and Casey climbed the ladder and stepped onto the stern deck, they removed their helmets and the rest of their diving gear.

"So, how was it down there?" A broad grin lit Coy's carefree face.

"Really cool," Casey said. "Downright amazing actually. A diver's dream come true. If I had to guess, I really believe that WWII sub is a U-boat. And the hull of that other ship has to be a couple hundred years old. There's pieces and parts of another boat but I'm not sure about it. It looked like a couple more in the distance. No wonder they call it the Graveyard of the Atlantic."

"Have you ever done any diving around here, Coy?" Gage unzipped his diving suit but left it on.

"Oh sure. I don't just charter people out. I teach scuba lessons. We obviously don't go out this far for lessons, but I've been out this far many times."

"Why don't we head to the next coordinates?" Casey unzipped his dive suit then dropped onto a bench. "We may not get two more dives in, but we can at least attempt another one."

"Yeah, those coordinates are closer in to shore and a little further north. Coy moved toward the steps leading to the bridge.

"A lot of ships went down in that area. Should make for some great diving."

As they neared the second coordinates, Gage stepped into the cabin to grab something to drink from the small fridge in the galley. He heard his phone ringing and grabbed it from his jeans pocket.

"Hello?"

"Hi Gage. It's Liz at dispatch."

"Oh, hi, Liz. What's up?"

"I have a lady on the phone that wants to speak with you. She says it's pretty urgent."

"Did she leave a name?"

"No, she wouldn't give me her name, but she said you'd know when she talked with you."

Odd. Gage couldn't think why there would be a woman calling him. "Ok. Can you patch her through to my cell phone?"

"Sure thing. Hold on a sec."

There was a click on the line then a woman's voice. "Hello?"

"This is Park Police Officer Gage Hampton, ma'am. Can I help you?"

"Well, I'm not sure." Her voice was breathy and timid. "I believe y'all are looking for a woman by the name of Celia."

Gage set down the bottle of ice tea he'd been drinking and stood a little straighter. "Yes, that's right ma'am. Did you see our bulletin on the news channel?"

"Yes, I did and that's why I'm calling." Her voice shook. Was she afraid?

"Ma'am, can you tell us anything about Celia?"

A pregnant pause followed Gage's question before she answered. "Y…yes."

"Well, first, can you tell me your name?"

In a voice barely above a whisper, she said, "I'm Celia."

~

Antonio Amato turned from the rear deck railing and spoke to Lennie. "Tell the captain to head back to the club."

Lennie nodded and spun on his heel. "You betcha, Boss."

Antonio climbed the outer steps to the upper deck and took a seat under the awning. He leaned back and crossed one ankle over his knee, his eyes on the charter boat they'd just left behind. It grew smaller and smaller as they headed inland.

"Can I get you something cool to drink, Mr. Amato?"

Antonio glanced up at the crewman who was never far from him when he was on the yacht. Miguel was silent and stayed out of the way until he thought he might be needed then he stepped forward. A good employee, he'd been with Antonio for several years.

"Yeah, I'll take my usual, Miguel. On the rocks. You know how I like it."

"Yes sir." And the man slipped away.

Within minutes he returned with the drink and set it on the table at Antonio's elbow then he retreated into the near shadows, waiting to be needed again. Just like Antonio liked him to be.

By this time Antonio could no longer see the charter boat. It was as if the ocean had swallowed it up. But he knew it was still there. But why? What were they doing there? The older man on the boat said they were just diving because it was a beautiful day. He'd also said they were going to dive on two other locations.

Antonio scrubbed his hand across his face in thought. He wasn't stupid enough to think that there weren't lots of charter boats out here all the time with people diving on shipwrecks. It was a popular pastime and sport. He shook his head and reached for his drink.

He should follow them to the other two dive sites. He took another drink. That was ridiculous. He couldn't follow every dive boat to every dive site. That was just plain impractical.

But what was it that the charter guy had said when he'd asked if they were looking for treasure? "Isn't everyone?"

How serious should he take that? Treasure could be interpreted in a lot of ways. He was looking for treasure, but he didn't even know what he was looking for, so how could he know what anyone else on this stupid ocean was looking for?

The more he thought about it the more agitated he grew. He had no idea who those people where on that charter boat or who was under the water, but he wanted to know what they were looking for. He wasn't around for every charter boat, but he was for this one.

"Lennie," he called, raising his voice. "Lennie."

When his underling didn't appear immediately, Miguel

approached. "Would you like for me to fetch him for you, Mr. Amato? He may still be on the bridge with the captain."

"Yeah. Thanks, Miguel." Antonio's eyes never left the ocean behind the yacht. He wanted to see that charter boat again.

Within minutes Lennie was at his side. "You called, boss."

"Yeah, I did. Tell the captain to turn around. Find that charter boat, but don't get too close. I just want it within sight. Then mark the coordinates of where it's anchored. If it moves and anchors again, mark the coordinates." Antonio lifted his drink and took a swallow.

"Sure thing, boss, but why are we marking their location? Who are they?"

"I don't know. Just do it."

Chapter Nineteen

As Coy brought *The Sand Piper* into its berth, Casey and Gage both jumped to the weathered planks of the dock and secured the ropes then climbed back aboard to retrieve their gear. The engine fell silent as Coy stepped from the bridge

"I hope you guys had a great day of diving. It's my goal to ensure that you did."

Gage nodded and hiked his gear bag over one shoulder. "I know I did, but I'd like to go back out again soon."

"Yeah, maybe back to the first coordinates." Casey scratched his cheek. "There were some great wrecks there. Think we could set something up for next weekend? Would that work for you, Gage?"

"Sure. I'm off again on the weekend."

"Owen?" Casey looked at the older man.

"I'm in."

"Then it's a plan." Coy opened an app on his cell phone. "I'll put it on my schedule. If anything changes, let me know."

"You bet." Casey gathered his gear. "See you at church tomorrow."

"See ya." Coy waved and headed into the cabin.

The three men jumped to the weathered dock and headed toward the parking lot.

"Seeing as how we were never alone long enough for you two to give me a report on any findings," Owen said, "how about we head to my RV and you can fill me in on what you found? I'll rustle us up something to eat while you talk."

Gage shook his head. "Sorry, I need to meet…"

Just then Casey's cell phone rang. He pulled it from his shirt pocket. "Hmmm. It's Ruthie."

"Ruthie?" Gage's heart bumped at the mention of her name. Why would she be calling Casey? Something must have happened.

"What's up, Ruthie?" Casey answered the call. He stopped in the middle of the parking lot and listened, the color in his face draining, leaving it blanched white.

"What? Now?" His voice was husky and strained. "Yeah. I'll be right there. What? Yes, I promise to be careful."

He punched the button ending the call.

"What's wrong, Case?" Gage asked.

"Bobbye's on her way to the hospital in Nags Head with Maggie and Ruthie. She's in labor."

Gage watched as Casey just stood for several seconds as the information sank in, then all of a sudden he said, "I've gotta go, guys. My wife's having our baby. I've gotta go now."

Gage grabbed one arm just as Owen grabbed the other. "Now wait a minute, Case. You can't just go off half-cocked like that. You'll get yourself in an accident. I may have only heard one side of the conversation, but I'm pretty sure you just promised Ruth you'd be careful because she asked you not to drive too fast. Am I right?"

Casey tugged his arms, but the two men held on tight. "Yeah, she did, but I need to get to my wife."

"Casey, my friend, if there's one thing I learned as a father," Owen said, "first babies are notoriously famous for taking a long time to arrive. Not always, but as a general rule. There's time to get there and drive safely."

"Look," Gage said. "One of the things I was going to tell you guys about when we talked, was I got a call from Celia."

"Celia?" Casey's expression was blank. "Who's Celia?"

Gage chuckled. "Figures that right now you can't put two and two together. Celia from the tattoo on the second dead man's arm. After the first dive, as we were heading toward the second, I got a call from Liz, the park dispatcher. She patched in a call to me from a lady named Celia. She'd seen our news report on TV asking for information about the tattoo. She's scared but agreed to talk to me. So just before Ruth called, I was getting ready to tell you I couldn't go to the RV with you. I need to meet with Celia before she gets cold feet and changes her mind. Owen, can you drive Casey to the hospital and make sure he gets there safely?"

Owen nodded, a grin lighting his face. "I'd be happy to. Besides, my girls are there. We'll catch up on the details of your dive after this little one is born. You go get your information from Celia. Maybe she can shed some light on the unfortunate dead man."

Casey opened his car and started to climb into the driver's seat.

"Casey, my friend." Owen held out his hand. "Please give me the keys. I think you know it will be much safer if I drive, and we both know you don't need a ticket or us involved in an accident. Where would your wife and child be then?"

Casey weighed the car keys in his hand, one foot inside the car, his arm draped over the door, a wry expression marring his features. After a few seconds, he dropped them into Owen's hand and walked around to the passenger side.

"Fine, but promise you'll at least do the speed limit."

Owen chuckled. "Oh, I promise. I've even been known to do a few over when the occasion calls for it."

"Well, this occasion calls for it." Casey slammed the door.

Owen winked at Gage as he climbed into his truck.

"Keep me posted." Gage shut his door, started his engine and rolled his window down. "I want all the details when you have them. I have a feeling whatever that baby is, it's going to take after it's dad."

Owen laughed. "We certainly will."

"Come on, Owen. Let's get these wheels rolling." Casey said.

"Hey, Casey, give mama a hug from me."

Casey grinned. "Will do, man. Will do."

Gage watched as Owen turned the car out of the parking lot and headed north on RT 12. *Lord, I know I'm new to praying, but would You please keep them safe and help Bobbye to deliver that baby without any problems? And help me get the information from Celia that will lead us to the killer.*

~

Gage headed north on RT 12 as well but only as far as Avon. Celia had given him an address to a little house on a back street near Pamlico Sound. His GPS told him to turn left onto a street that wound along a canal then turned to the left and back south. By the time he arrived it was dark and hard to see the house. The reflective house number, although a bit faded, was on the mailbox. The house was set back from the street, and one dimly lit yellow bulb burned beside the front door. The houses in this neighborhood were old and not in the best of care, and he didn't have a pulse on what kind of neighborhood it truly was.

Reaching into his glove box he retrieved his waistband holster and Smith and Wesson 9mm and slipped them inside his waistband then tugged his t-shirt over them. Now he felt better prepared.

Climbing out of the truck, he locked it then strolled down the cracked and broken cement sidewalk to a set of three wobbly wooden steps. Gage climbed them with caution then gingerly stepped across the old wooden porch. After knocking on the broken screen door, he waited, all the while glancing around the neighborhood. He didn't like leaving his back vulnerable to whatever might be out there.

The door opened a few inches revealing the shadowy, partial face of a woman looking past a safety chain. One eye looked him over before she spoke.

"Can I help you?" Her voice was soft and reserved.

Gage pulled out his credentials. "Celia? I'm Gage Hampton. You called me earlier today?"

The woman eyed his credentials, looking at them closely then back at him. "Yes, that's right. Are you alone?"

"Yes, I am." Gage tossed a thumb over his shoulder at his pickup. "There's no one in my truck. It's just me."

The woman nodded. "Very well then."

She closed the door and Gage heard the chain slide before the door opened wide enough for him to slip through, then she immediately closed it behind him. As he stepped further into a dimly lit hallway, Gage heard the lock click and the chain slide back into place.

He turned around, a question in his gaze.

Celia caught it and waved a hand toward the door. "I'm sorry, but I don't take chances. Ever."

She must trust him if she was willing to lock herself in with a complete stranger.

"I know who you are, Mr. Hampton." Celia led him into the living room. "Please, won't you have a seat?"

Gage glanced around the room. It was clean and neat even

though the furnishings were old and sparse.

"What do you mean, you know who I am?" He sat on the couch while she took an old armchair. He took stock of his hostess. Celia was in her late fifties with graying brunette hair arranged in a neat twist at the back of her head. What once would have been a beautiful complexion now displayed wrinkles and age spots but her makeup was applied delicately. Her brown eyes watched him with a keen interest and a touch of wariness. She still maintained a graceful posture when she walked and sat.

"I've seen you around the Cape. You help people out. I've heard people talking about what a nice man you are and how helpful you are. I'm generally a good judge of character, Mr. Hampton, and I believe I can trust you. That's why when I saw the report on the news and it stated that if anyone had any information that we should call you, I didn't hesitate for a moment."

"Well, I'm glad you did, Celia." Gage pulled a notepad and pen from his pocket. "What can you tell me about the tattoo on the man's arm? I take it you've seen the tattoo before?"

Celia nodded and lowered her gaze to her clasped hands in her lap. "Yes, I have. You see, the man was my husband."

Whatever Gage had been expecting, this wasn't it. "Your husband?"

"Yes, that's right. We were married for over thirty-five years and he captained boats of all kinds. I stayed home and raised our family. We have four children. We lived in Maine for most of our marriage until the last job he was hired for. The children are all grown and have families of their own now. This job he found through a hiring agency, and we thought it would be a good one. He'd only been with them for a few months when...when..."

Closing her eyes, she covered her mouth with her hand as tears rolled down her cheeks.

Gage leaned forward. "I'm sorry, Celia. We can stop for a few minutes if you need to."

She shook her head slowly, then opened her eyes. "No, I need to finish this so you can stop these people. My husband is dead because of them."

"Okay," Gage nodded. "When you're ready."

Celia placed a hand on her chest and took several deep breaths, releasing them slowly, then she clasped her hands in her lap and when once again composed she spoke. "My husband's name was Edward Garcia. He was a wonderful husband and father. He loved being the captain of boats, and he captained various sizes, but usually yachts. He was good at it and was usually well paid. I don't know what happened or why he was killed on this last job, but I know they killed him. Can you tell me how?"

Gage swallowed and shifted uncomfortably on the couch. "Celia, your husband was tortured, and I don't think it's a good idea to tell you how or to what extreme. That's why we needed to use the tattoo to identify him. It would be better if you just remember him as you do. Whole and well."

Celia's face crumpled as she shook her head. "How horrible. My sweet Edward. He was such a gentle man. I can't imagine what he must've done to illicit torture."

"Nor can I, but we'll do everything we can to capture those who did it."

She nodded as she reached for a tissue from a box on a side table and wiped her eyes. "Thank you. I hope you can put every single one of them behind bars."

"Can you tell me who he was working for?"

"Yes. Antonio Amato, the real estate developer. He has a huge yacht, and he needed a captain for it. The last job Edward had, the owner of the yacht passed away and he was out of a job. He did an online search and found a listing for this job. He applied and was hired immediately. Edward hadn't been with them long before he went missing. I didn't know where he was. One day he just didn't come home. Then a few days ago I saw your news clip. I knew he had to have been murdered, and I didn't know what to do at first. I almost didn't call, but after talking it over with my kids, they told me I should."

"I see." Gage jotted in his notepad. "Do you think Mr. Amato was capable of doing this? Do you think he would have a reason to?"

"I have no idea. I've never met the man. I've never even seen him. As I told you, Edward didn't work for him very long before he was killed."

"You mentioned your husband was paid well for captaining yachts yet you're living here where I'd say...well...this isn't a high-end neighborhood."

Celia glanced down at her fingers that she was twisting together in her lap. "No, you're right, Mr. Hampton. We were used to living in better places than this."

She brought her gaze back to his as warmth flooded her pale cheeks. "When I learned that my husband had been killed, I went into hiding. I left my home in Manteo and closed out my bank account and I came here. I wanted to stay close to try and find out what had happened to him. I have a couple of loyal friends who are trying to help me, but not even my children know where I am."

"Celia, it would be much safer if you went into police protection and you allowed us to find out what happened to your husband. You're not safe here. There's no protection for you. Especially now that the news report has been on TV for a while. The bad guys that killed your husband will be looking for you."

Celia's hands gripped tighter together until her knuckles were white. "Oh my. I…I hadn't thought of that."

Gage stood. "Pack a bag with only what you need for a couple of days. You're coming with me. I'm going to get you into protective custody tonight. That news report has been running for a week. Who knows if Amato has seen it or not."

"You're sure it's him?"

"Not a hundred percent, but even if it's not, we still need to get you into protective custody."

Celia stood and hurried into another room. She was back within minutes with a small overnight bag and a purse. "Can I send someone back here if I need something?"

"I don't see why not." Gage grinned and hurried her toward the door. All of a sudden he was filled with an urgency that he hadn't felt when he'd first arrived. "Let's lock up and get out of here. You can tell me more when we get you safely settled."

Celia nodded as she glanced around on her way to the door. "Do you know if I'll ever come back?"

"I don't know, Celia, but I'll do my best to take care of you, okay?"

She nodded again. "I believe you, Mr. Hampton."

They locked the door behind them and hurried down the sidewalk. "Well, I believe it's time you call me Gage."

He unlocked the truck and helped her into the passenger seat.

"Thank you, Gage."

He shut the door and hurried around to climb in.

As he started the truck, she said. "I suppose calling you Mr. Hampton is a bit silly. I'm old enough to be your mother."

They both chuckled just as a loud pop sounded and the rear window shattered. Celia squealed and ducked, getting as low as she could.

"What was that?" she cried from her bent over position as Gage jammed the truck into first gear and took off down the street.

"Somebody's shooting at us. Stay down just like you are. You aren't hurt, are you?"

"No, I…I don't think so."

"Good then hang on."

In his rearview mirror, Gage spotted a dark SUV following them, its headlights flipping on as it pursued. Ahead he saw the right turn at the canal coming up and knew he'd have to slow down or he wouldn't make it. They'd roll right into the canal. If he played his cards right, maybe he could get the SUV to go into the canal. *Lord, I could use Your intervention here. And if not here, somewhere.*

The SUV was right on his tail. It rammed Gage's rear bumper eliciting another squeal from Celia. Gage gunned his engine putting a little distance between them. Another shot was fired taking out his rearview mirror. Too close for comfort, that was for sure.

"It's ok, Celia. Hang on and if you're a praying woman, pray."

"Oh, I am." Her muffled words barely reached his ears.

In his side-view mirror Gage spotted the headlights of the SUV gaining on them again and gauged the distance to the canal and the right turn. Apparently, he blocked the SUV driver's view of the turn ahead. Good. That was to his advantage.

At the edge of the right turn, Gage shifted into second gear, turned his steering wheel into the turn and gave it some gas. The truck drifted around the corner. In his sideview mirror he saw the SUV go straight…right into the canal, with a huge splash as it landed in the water. Gage shifted into third and away he and Celia went. He wasn't going to wait around to see if there was another vehicle following him, but he didn't see any other headlights. When he got to RT 12, he headed south as fast as he could. *Thank You, Lord.*

"Are you okay, Celia?" Gage reached across and patted her arm.

She straightened up and settled back in her seat, her overnight bag clutched tightly to her chest. Glancing out the back window, she nodded. "I'm okay, but I'm afraid they ruined the back window of your pickup truck."

Wind whizzed loudly around the cab through the broken back window.

Gage waved away her words. "That's what insurance is for. As long as you're okay, that's the important thing."

"You came just in time, Gage. And what if you hadn't? I would be dead just like my husband."

"Celia, your children will need protective custody as well until this is settled. They aren't safe either."

"No, they aren't. And Mr. Amato won't stop until he's killed us all."

~

"Report." Antonio sipped his drink as he watched the ballgame. He was stretched out on his couch in the lounge and never even looked up as Lennie stepped into the darkened room onboard the yacht.

"They got away, Boss." Lennie stepped back, unsure how the boss was going to explode this time. "The guys drove into the canal while the park cop drove away with the captain's wife. I'm thinkin' by now she's probably in protective custody."

Just as Lennie expected, Antonio threw his tumbler at the TV and, striking the top edge, shards of glass streaked across the surface of the screen instantly followed by the amber liquid of his drink spewing everywhere. Droplets shot across the room along with glass pieces, making a huge mess.

Antonio jumped up, grasping his head and shouting through clenched teeth. "I'm surrounded by idiots that can't do what I ask them to. Four men can't even bring in one woman? How hard can it be?"

"Well, I don't know, Boss. I wasn't there."

"Of course, you weren't, Lennie." Antonio rounded on him. "You never are. That's because you're the faithful one, aren't you?"

Lennie didn't like the look in the boss's eye. He needed to get out. Soon. "I try very hard, Boss."

"Sure, you do, Lennie." Antonio staggered over to within inches of Lennie's face. The underling smelled alcohol on his boss's breath but he dared not step away. "But everyone else? They're all against me, aren't they? They don't have your dedication. I want everyone's dedication. Everyone's!"

Antonio blinked and turned away. "What about the dead man's family? Did you find them? Because I want them dead too. I don't want anybody pointing a finger back at me."

Lennie swallowed. "Yeah, Boss. We know where they are and some o' the guys are on their way ta get 'em. But if the feds already got his wife, they're probably on their way ta get 'em too."

"Yeah, yeah, I know." Antonio waved a drunken hand. "It'll be a race to see who gets there first. Well, it better be us."

Lennie sucked in a deep breath and blew it out slowly. This was getting hard. Really hard. He watched as the boss dropped back onto the couch and called for Miguel to bring him another drink.

Chapter Twenty

She's the prettiest baby I've ever seen, Bobbye and Casey." Ruth cuddled the tiny newborn close against her shoulder and loved the feel of her soft silky warm skin against her cheek. Her downy hair felt like peach fuzz against her hand as she supported the tiny head. What a precious bundle of joy. "I'm honored you would use my name in hers. Meredith Ruth. And you're going to call her Merry. I love it."

Bobbye shifted on the hospital bed. "I hope she'll be Merry because she sure was slow. I thought she'd never get here. It was terrific of all of you to hang around all night and all morning but you really didn't have to do that. Besides, you all missed church for her arrival."

Owen chuckled from a chair across the room as he stretched his arms above his head. "See, Papa Casey. I told you there was no reason to rush."

Casey grimaced. "Yeah, yeah, I know."

"Now, with the next one, you might want to move a little faster," Owen said, holding his index finger and thumb slightly apart indicating a small amount. "Or so I've been told. I only had Maggie, so I couldn't really tell you."

"Why bother when you have perfection?" Maggie held her arms aloft and gave a big smile.

"Oh yes, no humility there." Owen chuckled then turned his attention back to Bobbye. "And as for why we all stayed, we wanted to be here when your little princess was born. It's much too far to drive home and then have to drive back up here again. So, we all just slept in the waiting room."

A knock sounded on the door and Gage stuck his head in. "I heard there's a new member of the population in here."

"Hi, Gage." "Hey, Buddy." "Well, look who's late to the party."

Everyone greeted him as he came into the room, except Ruth who remained silent. She sat along the wall, and was it her imagination or did his gaze seek her out as the greetings faded away? Her breath caught as his gaze met hers, her heart beat tripping up then speeding on like a jackhammer. Both had been perfectly normal a few seconds earlier. Why had seeing him walk through that door send them into a tizzy? A grin lifted a corner of his lips at the sight of her. He started her way just as Casey asked him a question.

"Gage, so how did your investigation with the mysterious Celia go?"

He paused and turned to answer. "Oh, um, she's not as mysterious as we thought. She's a very nice lady and our evening turned out a whole lot different than I anticipated. I went to question her and we ended up running for our lives."

A round of "whats" followed by questions filled the room.

"Okay, hang on everybody. I'll tell you. I started asking Celia questions and found that she's wife of Edward Garcia, a yacht captain. He was last employed by none other than...drum roll...Antonio Amato."

"Shocker," Maggie said, a wry expression covering her face.

"You got it," Gage nodded. "He hadn't been working for him long when he went missing. Then she saw our news clip about the tattoo. That's when she found out he was dead. After a couple of days and at the advice of her adult kids, she decided to call. He was well paid as a yacht captain, but when he was killed, she left her home, closed her bank account and hid in an old house on a back street in Avon. I told her she needed to go into police protective custody. So, she packed a bag, locked the house and we climbed into my truck to leave when someone started shooting at us. I drove away as fast as I could and they chased us.

"There was a canal at the end of the street she lived on. I made the turn and they didn't. Celia's in protective custody and her adult children and their families are being contacted now. They'll be brought into protective custody as soon as possible. If Antonio Amato's goons found Celia, they'll find her family as well."

The room broke into a quite hubbub of discussion, peppering

Gage with questions. After a while, he slipped over to where Ruth sat in a chair along the wall. She still held the sleeping baby against her shoulder.

"You look like a natural holding that baby." Gage's voice was husky. He ran his fingers through his hair then cleared his throat. "She seems very comfortable on your shoulder."

Ruth's heart hammered. Was he feeling awkward for some reason? He was sure making her feel that way.

"I don't mind holding her. She smells so sweet and she's cuddly. And Bobbye definitely needs the rest. She had a long delivery last night and this morning. But you had quite a night last night too." Her voice was quiet as she gently stroked the baby's downy soft head. "I'm so thankful you're alright.

"Yeah, me too." Gage stuck his hands into his jeans pockets and leaned against the wall by her chair. "It got a bit dicey. I really felt for Celia though. She wasn't expecting her evening to turn topsy-turvy like that, but at least now she's safe."

Ruth turned her gaze up to his. "What will happen now?"

"We continue to look for evidence linking Antonio Amato to the two deaths. It's not going to be easy, but it's what we have to do."

"Uncle Owen said you and Casey found some things on your dive, but Casey wouldn't talk until you came."

Gage grinned. "I appreciate that. I need to talk to him before we release any of that information though. We've scheduled another dive as well, but keep that under your hat. We can't have that getting out to the wrong people."

"No problem." Ruth nodded.

~

Gage glanced at the others in the room then knelt casually beside Ruth's chair. It was difficult to carry on a conversation standing above her.

"So, I have it on good authority that you like ice cream." He propped an arm over one knee and grinned. "Is that true?"

Ruth looked at him seriously and shook her head. "Nope. Sorry."

Gage's forehead furrowed and he cocked his head. "Really? But I thought you said…."

Ruth's serious expression gave way to a smile and she quietly laughed her sweet musical laughter. "I don't like ice cream. I love it. It's my downfall. I can be bribed with ice cream. Just ask Maggie."

Gage's face cleared and he grinned. "Oh, really? That's good information that I'll tuck away for later. You never know when it may come in handy."

"Hmm. Maybe I shouldn't have shared that." She giggled.

Gage's heart tripped over itself at the musical sound. There was a time when she would barely look at him much less laugh with him. So much progress had been made between them, and now that he'd put his faith in Jesus Christ, was there hope for a future between them? Dared he hope she would ever be ready for that? *Oh Lord, You worked a miracle in my heart. I pray you'll work a miracle in Ruth's because I can't help myself. I'm in love with her.*

Ruth looked at him with an expectant expression. "I guess you like ice cream too?"

"What? Oh, yeah. I love it. I, um…was wondering if you'd like to maybe go with me after work tomorrow to The Dairy Barn for a scoop or two. I'm on dayshift this week so it works out."

Ruth nodded. "That's great. Yeah, sure. I'd like that."

She reached up a finger and touched his cheek, sending his pulse into overdrive. She'd never had the boldness to do anything like that before and it took him by surprise. Then as if she realized what she'd done, she yanked her hand back, color rolling upward from her t-shirt neckline all the way to the top of her forehead.

"What happened there?" Her gaze scooted away from him. How had she dared touch his face? What was she thinking?

"I don't know. I haven't looked in a mirror. What is it?"

Ruth swung her gaze back but just to his face, refusing to meet his gaze.

"You have several small cuts on your face. One not so small. What happened?"

Gage shrugged his shoulders. "Must have happened when the bad guys shot out my rear-view mirror."

Ruth's gaze instantly sought his. "What? Are you serious? They came that close to shooting you?"

A sheepish expression shaped Gage's features and he shrugged again. "Yeah, but we outsmarted them and high-tailed it out of there. What's more, Celia is safe in police protection."

All of a sudden Gage realized the room was quiet. He turned to find the other occupants silent and listening to their conversation. As he turned, they all pretended to talk.

He turned back to Ruth. "I have a feeling we have a room full of eavesdroppers."

Ruth glanced around the room. "I think you might be right."

He lowered his voice to a whisper. "I'll pick you up at your office after work."

The baby in Ruth's arms began to stir and whimper. Within seconds she was crying.

"Well, I'm pretty sure Merry's problem is something that only Mama is going to be able to handle." Ruth stood and Gage stood beside her.

"Oh? What's wrong with her?" He gazed over her shoulder at the disgruntled infant. "Should her face be that red?"

"She's probably hungry." Ruth smiled and headed toward Bobbye.

Gage scratched his chin and sighed. It was certainly not something he knew anything about.

~

"Boss, I found out about that dive boat for ya." Lennie approached Antonio as he sat bubbling in the jacuzzi on the skydeck, his arms stretched along the sides of the tub. A TV had been set up on a table near the jacuzzi and the boss was watching another ballgame.

Antonio tore his gaze from the game. "Yeah? And?"

"It belongs to a Coy Nelson. Nothing unusual about him. He does charter runs for folks just like he said, and he teaches diving."

Antonio moved across the jacuzzi to be nearer to Lennie. "Okay, so what about the other man that was on the boat? And the two divers? What did you find out about them?"

"Couldn't find out nothing about 'em, Boss. He ain't got no office that he works out of, so I couldn't find nothing."

"Lennie, if he has a business and it's legit, he's got to have records of some kind. If he works out of his home or out of a box, he has to have records. Keep looking."

Lennie released a heavy sigh. "Yes, Boss."

Antonio returned to reclining on the back side of the jacuzzi and watched his ballgame. Lennie turned and left the skydeck, shaking his head as he went. Sometimes, just sometimes....

~

Ruth strolled across the green expanse of grass from the primary lighthouse keeper's home where her office was housed toward the ticket booth. She glanced up at the lighthouse on her right. It never failed to stir her imaginative juices and send a thrill through her. Thanks to modern technology onboard ships, its job was mostly symbolic these days. However, it stands as a historic landmark to the heroes who kept her light burning so ships could avoid the shoreline. Unfortunately, the shoals further out claimed hundreds of ships throughout the centuries, hence the name Graveyard of the Atlantic.

She stopped outside the ticket booth and bent to speak into the hole at the bottom of the ticket window.

"Hi, Beth. Want to open the door for me?"

"Hi Ruth. Sure, come on around," came Beth's reply.

Ruth rounded the tiny building to the door at the rear and waited for Bethany to open it. When it swung open, she stepped inside.

"Hey Ruth, what's up?" the perky teen swung her dark ponytail over her shoulder and sat back on her high stool at the ticket window.

"Not much. I just came to get the cash bag to take to Naysa. It's about time for you to close up." Ruth leaned back against the counter.

"Yep." Beth closed the ticket window and pulled out the cash drawer. "So how are things going with you and Gage?"

"What do you mean? There is no Gage and me, Beth. We just work together."

Beth gave her a skeptical glance as she counted her money and checked her records for the day. She handed Ruth the clipboard for her to double check.

"Right. That's not what everybody's saying."

Ruth's gaze lifted from the clipboard. "What? What's everybody saying?"

"That you two are an item."

Ruth sighed. "Beth, let me straighten you out. First, Gage and I are simply co-workers, and second, you shouldn't listen to gossip. Furthermore, you shouldn't repeat it."

"But didn't you go out with him?" Beth's brow furrowed.

"We went out to eat while discussing a case. Nothing more. Sometimes people read too much into things without knowing the whole story then they make up the rest to make it interesting. They pass their version around and before you know it, it's blown all out of proportion."

"So, you're not dating him?" Beth's shoulders sagged.

Ruth thought about her ice cream "date" this afternoon. She hesitated then said, "Not officially. He hasn't asked me to."

"But if he did, would you?"

"You know, this is not a conversation I'm having with you today." Ruth lifted the clipboard and perused the columns.

"This looks great. I'll take the cash up to Naysa." She straightened from the counter and reached for the cash bag.

Beth handed it to her.

Ruth saw concern written on Beth's face and, pulling up another high stool, took a seat.

"What's up, Beth? You look like you have something on your mind other than my relationship status."

The younger woman turned on her stool so that she faced Ruth better. "Well, I was in here this morning just after opening and these two guys came past my booth. You know I sit in here and most people don't even see me because with the sun so bright out there it seems dark in here. Unless they plan to get tickets for the museum or to climb the lighthouse, they don't take a second look this way. Well, these two men stopped just past the ticket booth and stood looking over toward your office. They never once looked at the lighthouse."

"How do you know, Beth?"

Her young friend took a deep breath and let it out with a rush. "Because I went out the back door and watched them from behind the building. They walked over to the primary lightkeeper's house and tried the door but they couldn't get in. Thank goodness you lock it when you go inside. They hung around the door for a few minutes looking around until some other people, visitors I guess, came along and they took off. I came around and waited on the other side of the building to see which way they'd go. They walked past here again then headed back out toward the parking lot."

Fear froze Ruth's heart. Who had attempted to enter her office door this morning? She'd been there early working on her interpretive program so she'd been there when they'd tried. With her office in the back on the second floor, she'd never heard them. Nausea roiled within her.

She placed a gentle hand on Beth's arm and tried to keep any reproach from her voice. "The best thing to do in a suspicious situation like that is to immediately call park police, Beth. There's no time to waste. As it is now, the best they can do is probably get a police artist and hopefully you can get a description to them. Think you can do that?"

Beth shook her head. "I'm so sorry, Ruth. They're long gone now."

"Yeah, but can you give a description?"

"Oh, yeah. I got a great look at both of them."

Ruth smiled and squeezed her arm. She pulled out her cell phone. "Then that's a start."

~

It was six forty-five by the time Gage and Ruth parked at The Dairy Barn. Gage seated his uniform hat on his head and climbed out of the truck, walking around to open Ruth's door.

A smile lifted the corners of Ruth's lips as well as filled her heart. *You have to love a man with good manners.* The smile froze on her lips. *Love? Where had that come from?* Ruth sucked in a deep breath and released it slowly as Gage opened her door. *Food for thought. Some other time.*

"My lady." He bowed grandly as she climbed out.

"Why thank you, kind sir." Ruth curtseyed then put on her hat. "I'm not sure why the royal treatment, but hey, I'll take it."

Gage's gaze swept over her features, a flame igniting there. His Adam's apple bobbed as he swallowed. Hard. "I'm pretty sure you deserve it."

His voice was husky. He cleared it then turning took her arm, leading her into The Dairy Barn. He seemed to be as disturbed as she was. His gaze had turned her limbs to Jell-O and as usual all he had to do was look at her to get her pulse hammering like a triphammer.

"It's a good thing they have more than ice cream in here." He quickly changed the subject. "We're a lot later getting here than I anticipated. I'm hungry for more than just ice cream. How about you?"

"I know, but Beth's report was better late than never, I suppose."

"As law enforcement, it's just frustrating because if we'd gotten the call immediately while the men had been there, we might have at least stopped them for questioning. They didn't actually break and enter, but from her description, it almost sounds like they were planning to."

They placed their orders for hamburgers and fries then stood waiting in the pick-up line.

"Gage, do you think they'll be back?" Ruth asked. "I mean, if they didn't get in today, what's going to stop them from getting in later?"

Gage's brow furrowed as he reached for her hand and twined his fingers with hers. "Maybe. We'll have to do something to protect you and the other staff in that office."

"Do you think they were targeting m…me?" A gasp slipped from Ruth as she put her other hand over her mouth. She was fully aware of her hand in his and it fit nicely within his warm one. Should she pull hers away? Probably, but it felt so nice.

"Is there anything of importance in those offices that anyone would want?"

Ruth thought for a moment then shook her head. "Not that I'm aware of. The superintendent's office is there, but I don't know of anything he's working on that's that important."

"Then they may be after you, Ruth. You're the one that found the first body. They must think you know more than you do."

Ruth closed her eyes for a brief moment and sighed heavily, shaking her head. "Gage, what are we going to do?"

He squeezed her fingers. "Don't worry, we'll come up with a way to keep you safe."

"Order's up." The short order cook placed their food on the counter and headed back into the kitchen.

"Thanks." Gage collected both of their trays and found a table while Ruth went to fill their cups.

When they were settled at a table, hats stacked on the side, Ruth started to bow her head in silent prayer as was her usual custom in Gage's presence, but Gage reached across and clasped her fingers.

"May I?" His gaze searched hers.

Confusion filled Ruth and she knew it was there plain for him to see in her gaze, but she had to discover what he wanted to share. "Okay."

Still holding Ruth's hand, Gage closed his eyes and began to pray.

"Father, God. Thank You for this time of fellowship with Ruth. It's precious to me, Lord, but You know that. We don't understand everything that's happening around us with the search for the murderers, the search for the missing gold cross, for Celia Garcia and her family and now with these men who may be attempting to get to Ruth. Lord, You see it all. Guide us and direct our paths. Please protect us from the evil ones who would harm us as we seek the truth and lead us to that truth in Your time. Thank You for this food. We love You. Amen.

~

When Gage opened his eyes and lifted his head, Ruth was staring at him with those sweet lips gaping apart. He felt a grin lift the corners of his mouth.

"What?" he asked.

She shook her head slowly, her delicate eyebrows lifting in question. "Is there something you forgot to tell me?"

With a sheepish grin, Gage ducked his head as he opened his burger wrapper. "No, not really. That's sort of why I invited you out for ice cream."

Ruth leaned slightly forward, her musical voice soft as she spoke, a smile beginning to light her face. "Then tell me. Don't leave out any of the details."

"You're happy about it?" Gage asked with uncertainty, his burger sitting before him untouched.

"Happy?" Ruth reached across and squeezed his hand. "I've been praying for you like you have no idea, Gage. I know you've been struggling for a long time. I don't know what your struggle has been only that you weren't a Christian."

Gage looked down at Ruth's hand on his. He turned his over to twine his fingers with hers then lifted his gaze. It thrilled him to see her smile and the trust she placed in him. Should he share his past with her? If there was ever to be a future for them, the past had to be cleared away. Would she share her past with him? That was the big question.

Perhaps if he shared, she would see that it was a two-way street. But what if she didn't want a relationship with him once she heard about his past? Would she still trust him then? *Lord, You're in control of all this, aren't You? I could worry myself to death over all these questions and get nowhere, but I need to leave it all in Your hands. Right?*

"Yeah, that's right. I've struggled for a long time," he said, their food forgotten. "I made a lot of mistakes in high school, Ruth. I didn't grow up in a Christian home. I came from a very wealthy family where my parents were rarely at home. As a child I had a housekeeper and a nanny who took care of me, then as I got older, I was left on my own a lot except for the housekeeper. I went out for football in high school, and I had a great football coach, but I got into drugs. I ended up in jail a few times. The coach threatened to cut me from the team if I didn't get clean and straighten up. My parents washed their hands of me. They were out of the country on business most of the time anyway. Coach Watkins made me his personal project. He spent time with me and helped me get clean. I stayed on the team and graduated. I even won a college football scholarship."

Gage couldn't bring himself to meet Ruth's gaze as he told his story, but she didn't pull her hand away. Her fingers felt warm within his grasp. She even squeezed his from time to time.

"In college I studied Parks and Recreation and after college I went to the police academy. What I didn't mention was Coach Watkins was a believer. Throughout high school he talked to me about God and my need for Christ, but I was a pretty headstrong teenager. I decided I had recovered on my own. I didn't need Him, and I could continue to make it on my own. So, I set out to face my future without Him. Coach stayed in touch with me all through college and throughout the academy. I still stay in touch with him. The night I accepted Christ I called him and he was over the moon about it. He'd been praying for me since I was a teenager. He'd never given up on me."

Ruth placed her other hand over their twined fingers. "When did you accept Him, Gage?"

He risked a glance at her to see what her expression might

reveal and was thrilled to see a smile on her lips. "It was a few days before the incident with you and Naysa and the same night after the cookout at Casey and Bobbye's. Things have just been so crazy, I haven't had a chance to get you alone to tell you. I didn't really want to tell you over the phone, or…"

"Gage, it's not a problem." Ruth shrugged her shoulders. "The important thing is you did. Thank you for sharing your past with me. That can't have been easy. Kids and drugs and a bad family life happen a lot. Our church has a ministry to teens that I bet you'd be great serving in."

"Really?" Gage's interest was piqued. Someone had helped him, and if he could pass that on, then what he'd been through would make it all worth it.

"Sure. If you're interested you can talk to the pastor about it."

"Maybe after this case is solved I'll look into it." A wave of relief flowed through Gage. Ruth didn't hold his past against him. *Thank You, Lord.*

Ruth withdrew her hand and reached for her burger. A grimace marred her face. "Oh no. I wonder if they'll microwave these."

Gage chuckled. "I can ask, but if not, I'll place another order. It's a good thing we didn't start with the ice cream."

Chapter Twenty-One

With the superintendent's approval, an alarm system was installed in the primary lightkeeper's house first thing the next morning. Gage stood watch inside the ticket booth, much to Beth's pleasure, while the alarm company worked. He and Beth watched in the hopes that the two men would show up again but they didn't.

"Do you think they got tipped off somehow, Gage?" Beth asked.

"Doubtful. There would be no way they'd know ahead of time. We only called it in as an emergency installation late last evening."

"Hmm. Then I wonder why they didn't come back." The teen swung around on her high stool.

"I don't know."

"Gage, are you and Ruthie an item?"

Gage crossed his arms over his chest and eyed her from under lowered brows. "Why would you think that, Beth?"

"Because that's what everybody's saying."

"You mean gossip."

"Well, yeah."

"Don't listen to gossip, Beth."

"Yeah, that's what Ruthie said too."

"You asked Ruth if we were an item?"

"Yep."

"And she said?"

"Don't listen to gossip, only with a whole lot more words.

Gage chuckled. "Yeah, I bet she did."

"So, do you like her?"

"We're not having this conversation, Beth.

"She said that too.

Gage chuckled again. "Beth, I'm going to check on the alarm guys. If those men show up, call my cell phone immediately. *Don't wait.* Understood?"

"Yes, sir. Understood." She gave him a woefully sorry imitation of a military salute.

Gage headed for the door.

"And I know you like her." Beth's sing-song voice followed him out the door. That wasn't the question. He'd bared his past to her and she'd accepted it, but it still remained to be seen if she'd share with him her painful past. If she couldn't, then what? *Lord, help her to know that no matter what secrets her past held, nothing would prevent him from loving her.*

"Well, how's it going?" He asked the guys installing the alarms.

"Great. Is there anyone inside? We need to install the window alarms."

"I'm not sure. Let me check." He opened the door and hurried through the offices. A few secretaries were in the lower offices as well as a couple of the rangers. Ruth was also in her office in the upstairs back. He informed all of them that the alarm company needed to work in their offices.

He knocked on Ruth's door then stuck his head in. "Hi, Ruth."

"Oh, good morning." She glanced up from her computer. "What are you doing up here?"

"The alarm company's downstairs. They've installed the alarm at all the entrances, but they need access to the windows. I imagine it'll be awhile before they make it up here, but I just wanted to let you know."

"Oh, okay. Thanks."

Ruth wore her honey-colored hair long today, a departure from her usual ponytail.

"Wow. Your hair looks nice. I like it down like that." Gage shoved his hands into his uniform slacks. "It's, uh, it's very nice actually."

"Oh, thank you." Ruth licked her lips awkwardly. "I was in a hurry this morning and just left it down."

"Well, I'm glad you did." Gage's Adam's apple bobbed as he swallowed. He should get out of here and back to work. He sounded like a love-sick seventh grader. "Well, I'd better go and let you return to whatever you were doing. Have a great day, Ruthie."

"You too, Gage."

He charged down the staircase and out the door. "Yeah, there's a lot of people in their offices, guys, but they know you need to work, so go on in."

Gage hurried across the expansive yard to the ticket booth and beyond. He didn't feel like being questioned by Beth. He'd hang out in the gift shop for a while and watch for the goons. He'd seen the drawings and he had the sketches on his cell phone. Naysa wouldn't bother him.

One thing was for sure. He was in love with Ruth and he needed a resolution with her soon. He didn't know how much more of not knowing he could take.

~

"Hey, cuz, Dad is cooking tonight and he'd like to invite Gage to supper. Think you can ask him to come?" Maggie spoke across the airwaves.

Ruth stopped typing and pulled the phone receiver away her shoulder. "If the invitation is coming from Uncle Owen, why doesn't he call him?"

"You know Dad, he's not much for phones."

"I know." Ruth sighed. "Yeah, alright. I'll call him. Too bad you didn't call a little sooner. He was in here about fifteen minutes ago."

"Oh, yeah? Anything good?" Maggie's question dripped with intrigue.

"No. We have a company installing alarms on the doors and windows here at the office." Ruth slid the receiver back onto her shoulder and started typing again.

"Why? That doesn't usually happen unless there's an incident."

"Well, there was. Sort of."

"What do you mean, 'sort of'?"

Ruth immediately wished she hadn't headed down that road. She attempted to make light of the situation. "Nothing really. Just a couple visitors tried to walk into our offices. That's all."

"And why would they do that, Ruth?"

"People do it all the time, Mags. They think if they can go into the museum then they should be able to come into our building."

There was a pause on the phone line. "Mags? You still there?"

"Ruth, your voice is too cheery and I know you too well. You're covering something up. What is it?"

Ruth huffed out a breath. "Really, Maggie? You don't trust me?"

"Fine, I'll get it out of Gage. See you tonight." Click. The line went dead.

Ruth held the receiver away from her ear before dropping it back onto the cradle. Sometimes her cousin knew her too well.

~

"What do you think of the pages I photographed from Howard Amato's journal, Gage?" Maggie set plates on the table and directed her questions at the man seated at the kitchen counter. "You did get a chance to look at them, didn't you?"

Gage nodded, his arms folded along the counter. "Sure did. I'm not certain what to make of them though. He rambled a lot. Did a lot of surmising as to the location of *La Cruz de San Mateo*. At one point he determined that it went down with his Uncle Big Tony Amato and *The Satisfaction*. He talks about how it must be lying on the ocean floor and where it went down. Then further on there are entries as to *why* he thinks his uncle would have it on the rum runner with him."

"Why did he think it was on the rum-runner?" Uncle Owen asked from in front of the stove as he stirred a pot of clam chowder.

"He thought that as a treasure his uncle would never leave it behind. He was sure he would've taken it with him."

"Did he actually mention there being a safe on board?" Ruth asked as she sliced homemade cornbread right in front of Gage.

He reached across and nabbed a small sliver that fell from a piece as she placed the squares on a plate. He popped it into his mouth and chewed it up.

"Mmm. Did you make that?"

"Yes." She nodded, glancing at him.

He winked at her. "Very tasty."

Uncle Owen cleared his throat. "Excuse me. Are you flirting with my niece?"

"Um, no not at all." Gage grinned. "Just complimenting her delicious cornbread."

"Well, that's okay then." Uncle Owen lifted the pot of soup and carried it to the table. "Soup's on."

They sat around the table and held hands during prayer. Gage grasped Ruth's hand giving it a squeeze. When the prayer was finished, he reluctantly released it, eliciting color in her cheeks and knowing smiles from her uncle and cousin.

"No one answered my question," Ruth quickly attempted to draw attention away from her and Gage and back to the topic of the journal pages.

"What question was that, dear?" Uncle Owen filled bowls with the chowder and passed them around.

"Did Howard actually mention there being a safe on board *The Satisfaction*?"

Gage accepted a bowl of chowder and set it in front of him then reached for a square of cornbread. "Actually, he did. He thought it was possible his uncle had the cross on board keeping it close to him."

"But what if he didn't?" Maggie suggested. "Was there anything in the journal that would suggest he thought his uncle might've kept it somewhere other than on the rum-runner?"

Gage swallowed a spoonful of the creamy soup. "Sure. The pages you photographed were full of doubt as to where the cross was kept. It's really something how Big Tony Amato never shared that information with his nephew. Howard even thought it was possible he kept it at The Rusty Hook."

"Really?" Maggie dropped her spoon to the table. "Did he say where he thought he might have kept it there?"

"No, and if he had any idea, he would've found it a long time ago himself and saved millions of dollars on dives," Gage pointed out. "The cross eluded Howard his whole life as well as his son and grandson. Whatever is in that journal is only Howard's thoughts and impressions. Nothing concrete. And to make another point, he never even mentioned what the treasure was. It's doubtful Howard knew. Perhaps his uncle never got around to telling him."

"Interesting. Then it's quite possible that Antonio Amato doesn't know what the treasure is either." Maggie leaned her elbow on the table and rested her chin in her palm. "Howard ran out of time, but Antonio Amato will carry on his grandfather's search. I doubt he'll give up any time soon. There has to be a clue that Howard missed somewhere."

"We still have the advantage of the coordinates where the rum-runner sank," Gage reminded her.

"Yeah, you never did tell us what you found," Uncle Owen said. "I'm still waiting to find out. The arrival of Casey's princess interrupted that as did your call to interview Celia."

Gage slathered butter on his steaming cornbread. "I know. At this point it would be best to wait until after our next dive on Saturday. My hopes are we'll find even more."

"It sounds exciting," Ruth said.

"I will say this," Gage leaned his forearms on the edge of the table. "We saw a WWII U-boat as well as the hull of another ship that must have been at least a couple of centuries old. Then the boat we were diving on, well, I can't tell you more now, but it was good."

Maggie slapped his arm. "That's not fair."

Gage laughed. "I guess not. Sorry."

Uncle Owen laughed. "The suspense is a killer, Gage."

"Yeah, well, let's hope not."

"By the way, my niece says there's good news you have to tell. Something about turning your life over to Christ?" Owen clapped Gage's shoulder. "That's wonderful news, son."

"Yes, it is, Gage," Maggie said. "We've been praying for you."

Gage ducked his head. "Thank you. I appreciate it. It's a case of why did I wait so long when I could've had this peace and joy much sooner? You know what I mean?"

"Oh yes, my boy." Uncle Owen reached for the ladle and refilled his empty bowl. "Why do any of us wait so long? Because the evil one blinds us to our sins and makes us think we're just fine. He wants us under his thumb and he doesn't want to lose us to Christ. I'm so thankful Christ continued to convict you until you realized you needed Him. I believe it's the prayers of saints who continue to storm heaven for souls that eventually breaches that barrier that Satan puts up. Nothing can stop the power of God. Those strongholds that Satan erects will fall when God steps in."

"Well, thank you for your prayers. All of you." Gage's voice grew gruff as he spoke. He cleared his throat. There was silence for a few moments then Ruth stood.

"Anyone ready for dessert?"

~

Antonio Amato sat at the mahogany desk in his office onboard *The Lucky Lady* reading through his great-great uncle's journal. It was frustrating because Howard wasn't settled on what he believed Big Tony had done with the treasure. Antonio scrubbed his hand down his face then reached for the glass of scotch on his desk.

One minute Howard was determined that the treasure had gone down with *The Satisfaction* to the bottom of the Graveyard of the Atlantic and he'd spent millions on dives searching for it. He'd seen the explosion and knew in his heart that his uncle had that treasure onboard. He'd never leave it behind. Then the next thing he indicated in his journal was that Big Tony had most likely left it at The Rusty Hook. But Howard had torn the old restaurant apart looking for it decades ago. It just wasn't there.

A thought struck Antonio all of a sudden causing him to sit straight up in his chair. Was it possible it was in the old home place in Chicago where his dad lived? Had Howard torn that place apart years ago looking for the treasure? No one had ever really talked about that possibility.

He picked up his cell phone and dialed his father, Sebastiano's, number.

"Hullo?" An elderly gruff voice answered.

"Hey, Pops. How are you doing?"

"Antonio? That you?"

"Yeah, Pops. It's me."

The old man chuckled. "Oh, Antonio. Ya only call me when ya need somethin'. Ya never come ta see me anymore. What do ya need this time?"

"Oh, Pops, that's not true and you know it. Remember I'm trying to get the new hotel up and running and now I've started renovating The Rusty Hook. Do you remember The Rusty Hook, Pops?"

"Sure, I do, son. I heard it was a peach in its hay day. Wish I coulda seen it."

"Yeah, Grandpa Howard used to talk a lot about it, huh?"

"Yeah, he did. He said Big Tony ran a tight ship at The Rusty

Hook and onboard *The Satisfaction* too."

"Hey, Pops, is there any chance Big Tony could've hidden that treasure at your house?" Antonio leaned forward, elbows on the desk.

"Here? At this house? Why would you think that, Antonio?"

"Because I've searched through Howard's journal, Pops, and he mentions the treasure possibly going down with the rum-runner, and then later on he mentions that maybe it was at The Rusty Hook. You know how many dives Grandpa Howard made searching for that treasure. And he tore The Rusty Hook apart looking for it."

"Oh, yeah. He looked here. A long time ago, Antonio. It's not here. Besides, after he started rum-running, Big Tony never came here. He lived in Buxton at The Rusty Hook and onboard *The Satisfaction*. Nowhere else. If he had business in Chicago, he sent someone. He didn't come here. There were too many mob competitors that woulda took him out."

"Really? Hmm. Who knew?" Antonio slid the journal in front of him and thumbed through the pages. "Okay Pops. Well, I feel like I'm still at square one. I don't have any leads on that treasure. I don't even know what I'm looking for."

"No? Still don't know, huh?"

"No, Pops, I don't have any idea. Are you sure Grandpa Howard never told you what the treasure was?"

"Nope. He never told me because I don't think he ever knew, Antonio."

"Pops, why would Big Tony keep that from Howard?"

"Because he wasn't expecting ta die, so why would he tell a seventeen-year old."

"True, I suppose."

"Antonio."

"Yeah, Pops?"

"Don't give up. You keep lookin'. That treasure, whatever it is, is out there somewhere. Big Tony kept it safe. It's up to you to find it."

Chapter Twenty-Two

Maggie parked in front of The Rusty Hook and, grabbing her camera case, slid out from behind the steering wheel and closed the car door behind her. There was only one other car here. Could it be that Mr. Amato hadn't arrived yet? Or was he the only other occupant? She hoped not. Surely his secretary would be coming as well. They'd never met alone before. Her gut clenched with dread. Perhaps Miss Williams was running late.

Glancing around, she waited for a few minutes hoping another car would drive up. With their two previous meetings here, a contractor and Miss Williams had always been present. This was just plain awkward.

As she glanced around, her gaze landed on the locked chain-link gate that led to the walkway along the side of the old building to the back. She was reminded of the night she and Ruth broke in and how Gage caught them locking the gate as they were leaving. What luck that it had been him to catch them rather than the local police. No. There was no such thing as luck. It was providence. It was the good Lord looking after them in spite of themselves.

Maggie checked her watch. It was two minutes till her appointment time. She had to get inside whether anyone else was here or not. *Oh Lord. Please look after me. I don't like going in here if it's just Mr. Amato.*

Drawing in a deep breath, she released it slowly as she headed for the front door. Stopping just inside, she let her eyes adjust to the darkened interior from the bright sunlight outside. She scanned the huge room. The contractors had been busy since the last time she was here. The old peeling wallpaper had not only been torn down, but the outer walls themselves had been removed. The floor had been stripped of the old worn and moldy carpet and the rotting flooring was left exposed. The antique seashore décor that had once decorated the restaurant walls had been piled in wooden crates with packing confetti in a corner of the room, a few pieces lay on the floor next to the crates. They would be refurbished and reused in the new remodeled restaurant.

A few bare lit light bulbs were strung around the large dining room where the workmen had been working, but no one was here.

Pulling out her camera, Maggie adjusted her settings and snapped some pictures. The ones of the seashore antiques would be especially nice shots.

She remembered the first time Mr. Amato brought her into the restaurant dining room. It looked like the owners had walked out nearly a century before and left it as it was. Fishing nets hung from the ceiling and walls with stuffed fish of all varieties attached. A few lobster pots sporting stuffed lobsters added to the décor as well as lobster trap buoys. She could see those peeking from the crates now. What once would have been white tablecloths covered tables but were now dingy with layers of dust and time. Burned down candles covered with cobwebs sat in the middle of each table. A few oil wall sconces would have once helped light the room, but now they gave spiders a place to call home. These had all been taken down and crated.

She walked around snapping pictures, stepping gingerly as the rotting floor creaked.

"There you are, Maggie. I wondered what was taking you so long."

Maggie lowered her camera and turned toward the man who had hired her for this job. So, he was the only one here. Her stomach clenched. Did he look displeased? Or was he preoccupied? With him you could never tell. *Lord, please look after me.*

"I'm sorry, Mr. Amato. I saw the changes the workmen have made, and I started snapping away. Is there somewhere else you need me to photograph?"

"Yeah, actually. Come on back. They've started tearing out the kitchen too." He turned and headed back through the swinging door he had entered from.

Maggie snagged her camera bag and hurried after him.

"See?" He waved an arm indicating the old kitchen. "They've already taken out those old ice boxes and the stoves they used to use wood to cook in. Wow. Can you imagine cooking like that?"

Maggie shook her head. "No, I, uh, I sure can't, Mr. Amato."

"You know I told you to call me Antonio. Why are you still calling me Mr. Amato?" He propped his hands on his hips and turned to look at her, a slight smile lifting the corners of his lips.

Maggie held her camera in front of her, almost like a shield. "It's very hard for me to be so familiar with someone that I'm working for. I…it's easier for me to keep a distance that way."

His eyebrows rose then he chuckled as he stepped nearer. "But you see, Maggie. I like you. I like you a lot. I don't want there to be a distance between us."

He reached out a hand and with one finger stroked her forearm as he stepped even nearer. "I don't want there to be any distance at all."

Maggie's heart plummeted into her stomach. This just could not be happening. *Lord, I need Your help. Now. Please.*

His hand reached behind her hair to the nape of her neck and tugged her closer. Panic filled Maggie as she realized he was going to kiss her. Here and now. Then what? *Lord, Please!*

"Hey, Mr. Amato, the trucks are here with the delivery of pilings," a deep voice called before the person appeared in the kitchen doorway.

Antonio stepped back releasing Maggie before a tall man with a bald head and a wrestler's physique spotted them close together.

Maggie dragged in a deep breath as she sagged against an old wooden table. *Thank you, Lord. That was all You.*

Antonio cursed under his breath. Aloud he said, "What do you mean the pilings are here? They weren't supposed to arrive for three more days."

"Yeah, Boss. I'd say it's a miracle. There's three semi-trucks out there piled with 'em. The crew to install 'em is here too."

Antonio's mouth dropped open. "Are you serious?"

"As a heart attack, Boss."

"Tell 'em I'll be out in a minute." Antonio turned to Maggie, a look of contemplation on his handsome face. "I'm rushing you, aren't I, baby?"

Maggie swallowed and took a deep breath. "I…I wasn't

expecting this. To say I'm surprised is...is an understatement."

Antonio cupped her cheek and rubbed it gently with the pad of his thumb. It was all she could do not to yank her face away.

"I understand, baby. I'll go slow and give you time." He turned to leave the room then turned back at the door. He pointed a finger at her and his gaze was no longer warm. It was ice cold. "But not too much time."

~

Maggie and Ruth settled in the living room on the couch that evening with large mugs of hot tea.

Ruth tucked her feet beneath her and took a sip of her tea then eyed her cousin. "You were awfully quiet during supper, Mags. Unusually so. What's up? I can tell you have something weighing on your mind. So, spill."

Maggie's gaze swung from the inside of her mug to meet her cousin's then moved to the dusky evening view out the front window. A heavy sigh escaped her. "Yeah, I suppose so."

"Did something happen today when you met Mr. Amato at The Rusty Hook? Did things not go as you had hoped?"

Maggie turned her gaze back to Ruth. "Well, you could say that."

"Mags, would you stop with the evasive comments and just tell me what happened?"

Maggie reached across and squeezed Ruth's arm. "I'm sorry, Ruthie. It's just that, well, I'm just afraid, really afraid for the first time in a long time that I may be into something deeper than I know how to get out of, and I did nothing intentionally to get there."

"Okay, so now you've got me worried." Ruth turned her body to face Maggie.

A wry expression settled on Maggie's face. "Yeah, me too. Okay, so somewhere along the way Mr. Amato fell for me. I don't know how or why, because I treated him like a boss and nothing more. I've never, well, you know, done anything to try to get his attention in a personal way. But today he tried to...to...to kiss me."

She covered her face with her hand and shook her head.

"How could this have happened to me?" Her muffled voice came from behind her hand.

There was silence for several minutes, and when she finally looked up to see Ruth's reaction, she found a shocked and horrified look on her cousin's face.

Maggie reached for Ruth's mug and set it on the coffee table before she spilled it.

"Oh, Mags. That's not good at all," Ruth finally spoke, her voice filled with horror. "What happened after he…did you say he tried? What happened to stop him?"

Maggie sipped her tea. "Well, in my honest opinion, I'd say God intervened. Three semi-truck loads of pilings to replace the underpinning pilings below the restaurant arrived along with a crew to begin the process of replacing them. We were the only ones in the restaurant and that was the first time that had ever happened. When he started to kiss me, I prayed for God to do something and He did. In a huge way."

Ruth started laughing, her hands over her mouth. "Oh, what a mighty God we serve, Mags. That's amazing."

Maggie nodded. "Yeah, it is, but before he left the room, Mr. Amato told me he understood my surprise at his interest in me and that he'd give me time. But very coldly he said, not too much time."

"Ugh." Ruth's features twisted into a scowl. "Nope, that's not good. Let's hope and pray Gage and Wayne pin him to those murders and soon."

"Well," Maggie sipped her tea and set the mug on the coffee table. She turned to face Ruth better. "I wanted to talk to you about something."

Ruth's brows lowered and she eyed Maggie through narrowed lids. "I have a funny feeling I'm not going to like what you're going to say."

"Probably not, but if it helps move things along for Dad, would you be willing to go back to The Rusty Hook with me and look for *La Cruz de San Mateo*?"

Ruth jumped up from the couch and paced across the room. "I knew it. Absolutely not. There is no way I'm going to help you break into that place again. Not even for Uncle Owen. No way. No how. Uh un."

She sliced the air with both hands in a definitive no.

Maggie stood and pulled something from her pocket. She held

it dangling in the air and smiled. "Not even if I have the key to open the front door?"

~

The crew worked diligently to replace the pilings under The Rusty Hook and it only took three days for them to do it. With the right equipment it was a cinch. And of course, when you paid them the right amount of money you could get anything done. Antonio had watched the process from the deck of his yacht behind the ancient building and had been impressed with the work they'd gotten accomplished.

Now the contractors were back to work inside the building and he was taking time to look around Big Tony Amato's old office. He had half an hour before he had a meeting over in the hotel with possible investors for the restaurant. He needed to convince them this enterprise was worth investing in. With a restaurant in the front and the bar in the back reminiscent of the old speakeasy that Big Tony had run in 1928, it should be a hit.

He stepped into the mahogany-walled room and flipped on the flashlight he'd brought with him. There had been no electricity run to this part of the building yet. He flicked the LED light around the room. What once must have been Chinese red carpet covering the floor was now faded with dust and time. The same with the chairs and couch that were arranged on either side of the room. The mahogany desk that stood at the far end could be refurbished and reused. It was a solid piece of furniture.

The Chinese paintings covering the walls were a mess. He doubted they were worth much, especially in their present condition. He'd start there. He yanked them away from the old paneling to see if there was a wall safe behind them. Nothing. He tapped on the walls with his knuckles and listened for a solid sound. Nothing except the normal two-by fours every eighteen inches. He pulled the furniture away from the walls and did the same behind them. Still nothing.

Antonio pulled out a crisp white linen handkerchief from his hip pocket and wiped off the old wooden desk chair that sat behind the mahogany desk. Taking a seat, he was thankful for his Cordovan leather desk chair onboard *The Lucky Lady*. This thing was atrocious.

Pulling each drawer out, he aimed his flashlight into the

drawers and riffled through old receipts and papers. Hey, these were old purchase receipts from Jamaica for rum and other liquors. Big Tony must've tossed 'em in here when he came through after a run from Jamaica. But that was all he found. No treasure. No nothing even hinting at a treasure. No keys to a treasure. Nothing but liquor receipts.

Antonio slammed the last drawer shut and leaned back in the old squeaky wooden chair. His anger rose and he felt defeat stirring within him, feeding his anger. Gazing at the desk, he let his eyes roam over the drawers wondering what he'd missed, if anything. Then another thought hit him. Yanking out each drawer one at a time, he dumped the contents on the floor and searched each one for a possible hidden compartment. Would Big Tony have had one built into the desk somewhere?

When he'd searched each drawer, he made a pile of them on the floor then got down on his hands and knees and beneath the desk looked for…for what? He had no idea. A trigger or a button that would reveal a hidden compartment? Anything. He flipped the desk on it's back looking beneath. He found nothing. Frustration gnawed at his gut.

Antonio jammed a hand through his hair and glanced at his watch. He had five minutes to make it across the road to the hotel for his meeting. He'd have to look further another day. Maybe there was a safe in another room. He slammed his fist onto the desk. Where had Big Tony put that treasure? And what was it? He had to find it. Something somewhere had to give.

Maybe when the workmen got to this section of the restaurant and started tearing out the walls, they'd find something. When they started working in here, he'd be here to watch.

~

"Ok, so the guys are diving again tomorrow, Ruth." Maggie poured herself a cup of coffee. "We can go to the restaurant tomorrow morning and take a look around. Since I have the key Mr. Amato gave me, we aren't breaking and entering. I'll take my camera, and if anyone comes in, I'll just tell them I'm snapping pictures. And I'll do that while we're there too. It'll be a safe cover story."

Ruth reached for her uniform shoes and, slipping her feet in, tied them. She shook her head. "I don't know. I guess I feel a little better about it this time, but what if they ask why I'm there?"

"No problem. I'll just tell them I brought my cousin along to keep me company."

"You always make it sound so easy." Ruth straightened and reached for her "Smokey-Bear" hat and purse then heaved a heavy sigh. "Alright. I'll go. For Uncle Owen. I sure hope the cross is there and we end at least this part of the mystery. Then Gage and the park police can take care of Antonio Amato."

"I know that since you have your program this evening you won't have time to go see Mary at the library." Maggie sat at the kitchen counter and stirred her coffee. "I want to find out if Ava Kelly's journal had any information about Big Tony's office that might help in our search. I'll run by there this morning and see what I can find out."

Hand on the doorknob, Ruth nodded. "That's a good idea. If anyone had that information, it would be Ava Kelly. And Mary will be glad to help you. Just be careful how you tell her you're going to use that information."

"Why? We're not breaking and entering, Ruth. It's all above board."

"Yeah? Bet you wouldn't tell that to Mr. Amato, now would you?"

~

"Hi Mary." Maggie greeted the librarian as she stepped inside the library. "How's it going today?"

Mary's mouth hung open and she eyed Maggie over her wire-framed glasses.

"Oh my. Mary, you look harassed. What happened?" Maggie set her shoulder bag on the high counter in front of Mary's computer and leaned forward. "Are you okay?"

Mary's shoulders sagged. "I will be. In time. It's the last day of school and the third-grade class just came in for a field trip to see our collection of seashells and driftwood. Unfortunately, it didn't hold their interest, and they did everything but swing from the ceiling lights. They were even punching buttons on the xerox machine and paper was popping out sheet after sheet. I have books strewn all over my floors."

Maggie looked around the library and was horrified to see it was a mess. A potted plant lay in a pile of dirt, the shards of the pot broken around it. Torn magazines lay scattered around the room along with books all over the floor. Mary's book displays were a shamble.

"Oh, my goodness. Mary, I'm so sorry. What were the teachers doing?"

"Oh, they were attempting to maintain control, but there was none." Mary rested her forehead in her hands. "You just missed it, Maggie. Aren't you fortunate?"

Maggie shook her head. "Is there anything I can do to help you?"

Mary lifted her head and heaved a sigh. "No, thank you, dear. I appreciate your offer, but I'm just going to close the library and do what I can this afternoon, then I'll finish up in the morning before we open. I'll probably have to put a sign on the door in the morning stating that we'll be opening late due to...oh, I don't know. Due to unforeseen circumstances. I think this qualifies, don't you?"

Maggie smiled. "I'd say so."

"Re-stacking the books alone will take hours." The shake of Mary's head was rather forlorn. "Well, dear, what can I help you with? I'm pretty sure you didn't come in here to hear about my woes."

"Perhaps, not, but you do have a pretty big woe, Mary."

Mary smiled and started chuckling. "If you could've only seen it, Maggie. It was something to behold."

"I bet it was."

"Anyway, what did you need, dear?"

"Mary, do you know if Ava wrote anything in her journal about details concerning Big Tony Amato's office? Possibly anything concerning a safe there?"

Mary's brow furrowed in thought. "Hmm. Not that I can recall. It certainly doesn't ring a bell. You should've asked your father. He's read that journal almost as many times as I have."

"Um, yeah," Maggie evaded, her eyes moving to the Ava Kelly display at the rear of the room. "Think I could take a look?"

"Why certainly, dear. You know you're welcome to look at it anytime you'd like to."

"Thanks, Mary."

Within minutes, Maggie was sitting at a table in the back of the room thumbing carefully through Ava's journal. Unfortunately, she could find nothing about Big Tony's office other than the description of the furniture and the décor. Her tale was specific to her kidnapping by the mobster and their attempt to spirit her away to Chicago. Disappointed, Maggie returned the journal to the librarian.

"Thanks, Mary. I didn't find what I was looking for."

"Well, I am sorry, Maggie." Mary eyed the younger woman over the rim of her glasses again. "You aren't thinking of dragging Ruth back to that place and breaking in again, are you?"

Maggie chuckled. "I'm working for Mr. Amato as his photographer while they're renovating it. I actually have a key to the front door now, so I don't have to break in anymore."

Mary looked only slightly less concerned.

"But you're still looking for..." she lowered her voice and looked around the room to make sure she wouldn't be overheard, "that item?"

"Ask me no questions, I'll tell you no lies." Maggie draped the handle of her shoulder bag over her shoulder and winked at Mary. "Bye, Mary."

"At least tell me when your 'not doing this thing' so when you get in trouble someone knows where you are."

"We're not going to get into trouble, Mary."

"Maggie. Please. When are you going? If not for your sake, then for Ruth's."

Maggie spotted the concern in the older woman's gaze and thought of her cousin. "Alright. You've been wonderful in helping us get information from Ava's journal. Tomorrow morning."

"Thank you, Maggie." Mary breathed a sigh of relief. "I wish you wouldn't go, but I'll be praying for you two. Will you call me at noon to let me know things are going okay?"

"Sure. We can do that. Take care, Mary. We'll talk to you soon, and you'll see. Everything will be just fine."

Chapter Twenty-Three

I'm not happy that the Garcia family was found by the feds before our guys got there." Antonio watched as Miguel dropped ice cubes into a tumbler then poured amber liquid from a bottle over the ice cubes. The waiter handed the glass to Antonio who walked to a chair on the skydeck and took a seat.

Lennie followed him. "I know, Boss. It's tough luck all around, but the guys weren't that far behind."

"Maybe. Maybe not." Antonio slipped on a pair of sunglasses and waved a hand at the waiter. "Hey, Miguel. Bring me some aspirin. My head's pounding"

He rubbed his forehead and looked out to sea. "And what about those divers that were on that dive boat last weekend? Did you ever find out who they were?"

Lennie watched as Miguel placed two aspirin in the boss's hand then the boss swallowed them with his glass of scotch. "No records, Boss. The boys searched that dive boat. Nothing. Coy Nelson doesn't leave records anywhere."

"I'm telling you, he has to. If he runs a business, he has to have insurance records, liability waivers, all kinds of things. It just depends on where he keeps them."

Antonio closed his eyes and rested his head against the back of the chair.

"Tell the captain to take us into harbor. I have some business to attend to."

Lennie furrowed his brow. "Anything I can help ya with, Boss?"

"We'll see. Right now, I just want to be left alone for a while. I need to get rid of this pounding headache. I guess it'll teach me to go on a drinking binge, huh?"

Lennie turned and walked off the skydeck and took the stairs down to the control center. Yeah, you'd think it would, but it seemed the boss was drinkin' a lot these days. Frustration cuz things weren't going his way or cuz he couldn't find that treasure? Or a lot a both? Yeah, most likely. But Antonio Amato had chosen to walk the road of life he was headin' down just like he, Lennie, had done. But Lennie was thinkin' about makin' some changes. Did he dare? What would Mr. Amato do if he caught him? Lennie knew exactly what he'd do. He'd kill him.

~

The Sand Piper anchored at the original coordinates from the week before and Gage and Casey prepared for their dive. Coy and Uncle Owen helped them check their equipment. Once they were suited up, had their tanks, masks and other equipment on, they dropped over the rear deck and descended the anchor rope. Once on the bottom, Gage heard Casey report the visibility.

"It's not as clear as last week, Coy, but not terrible either. The current is a little rougher. We'll see how searching around down here goes. I don't think it'll be too bad"

"Roger," Coy sounded in Gage's headgear speakers. "Just keep us informed and let us know if and when you're ready for more air."

"Roger," Casey responded.

Gage didn't wait around for more chit chat. He only had so much air and he wanted to spend every second searching for that elusive safe or anything else that might hold the treasure. Avoiding the areas he had already explored, he struck out for unsearched territory.

More broken boards and cases of broken and unbroken bottles of rum and other liquors lay around. It was encouraging to find these. It meant they were likely on the right track. He'd already spotted the board with the letters TISFACTI from last week's search. Great. Now to find that safe. He kept moving and spread out further.

The plan was to stay here all day if they had to, and that's what they'd do.

He pulled back a pile of broken boards and found clothing laid out as if someone had lain there then vanished. A chill ran up his spine. They most likely had. He swam further on and found a few more piles of clothing laid out in various ways. He supposed they wouldn't all have landed on their backs. He shook his head, realizing this was a graveyard for those who died onboard *The Satisfaction*. And what of Big Tony Amato? Where was he? Had he been one of those he'd found?

After a while he felt a tap on his shoulder and looked up to see Casey waggling a finger indicating he should follow him. He swam after Casey as he led him about seventy-five yards away near the two-hundred-year-old wooden ship remains. He stopped about half-way down and pointed at a dark object laying on the sandy bottom half covered over with sand and silt.

Gage swam to it and determined it was an old pin-striped suit. Some of it had been eaten away by the scrubbing of the sand and the current. Casey's finger pointed at something that lay amongst the fabric and Gage moved in closer. It was a diamond tie tack attached to what remained of a piece of fabric. An old tie perhaps? Most likely.

Casey wrote on his magnetic board. "Big Tony's signature diamond and his pin striped suit."

He held up a finger then dug beneath the sand down below where a pant leg would have been. He pulled up an old, black patent leather shoe, the spit-shine long eaten away.

Gage shook his head and wrote on his board. "A sad end for a big, rich man."

"Look where it got him." Casey wrote.

Gage watched as Casey pulled out an underwater digital camera and took a couple of photos. He then jotted on his board, "Remembered to bring my camera this time."

Gage gave a thumbs up.

He started to swim back to where he had been searching but something caught his eye as he turned from Big Tony's resting place. It was hard to tell in the cloudier water, but there was something next to the WWII sub that didn't seem like it should be there. Had it been there the week before? Or was it that he just hadn't seen it from this angle?

He swam toward the sub and the object. It wasn't very big in comparison, and it certainly wasn't part of the sub. The closer he got, he realized it wasn't even that close to the sub. It was actually about twenty yards from it. Amazing how underwater items could seem so out of proportion.

Was it a box of some sort? It seemed to be partially covered over with silt and sand. He swam over to it, his heart nearly stopped then ran on like a freight train. It was made of heavy metal with a rounded corner. Just like a safe. But the three exposed sides were flat and smooth except for the barnacles that encrusted the surfaces. If it was a safe, the door side was buried.

Gage grasped the object and heaved with all his might but it barely moved. Not good. He dug around the sides with his fingers hoping to reach another edge that he could grasp and lift out of the ocean floor, but he couldn't seem to find one.

"Hey Casey. Come over here for a minute. I'm by the sub's bow end." That shouldn't give anything away to Coy.

"On my way." Casey's reply sounded through his speakers.

He prepared his comments on his writing board and had it ready when Casey arrived.

"No idea how big this is but I think it's a safe."

Casey's hands surveilled the surface of the object and he nodded in agreement. He wrote. "We'll have to dig it out."

He glanced at his air gauge and showed it to Gage who checked his own.

"Hey Coy," Casey said. "We've got 30 minutes of air. Can you send down two bottles please?"

"You've got it," came Coy's response.

"Thanks, bud."

"No problem. How's visibility?" Coy asked.

"It's worsened a bit, but we're still able to work."

"And the currents?"

"Maybe a little stronger but we're doing okay."

"Roger. I'll send the bottles down with weights on them so the currents don't carry them away."

"Roger." Casey said. "Let me know when you start them down and I'll retrieve them."

"Roger."

"Oh, and Coy? Can you send down a couple of hand shovels?"

"Sure thing."

"Thanks."

Gage found a broken bottle and held the neck while digging with the broken part of it. It would suffice until the shovels arrived.

He couldn't sit around on his thumbs wasting air. They'd already proven to themselves that this was the wreck of *The Satisfaction* and he wasn't wasting anymore time. This had to be the safe. Even if they could get it onboard, they still had to unbury it first.

Casey brought back the bottles of air and they switched them out then started digging with better results once they started using the hand shovels. Before long they found the buried edge of what was a safe. Gage's heart beat with excitement, and he had to talk himself down. He'd use more air if his heart beat faster and he breathed faster. *Get it under control, buddy.*

There was no proof this safe was onboard *The Satisfaction*. So far there were no scorch marks or burned edges or anything to indicate it had been in a fire or an explosion, but then they hadn't seen the whole thing either.

Together he and Casey got their fingers beneath that newfound edge and they pulled until the safe began to move. They wiggled and tugged it until it finally gave way. A cloud of silt surrounded them making it hard to see as they settled the safe onto the ocean floor a few feet away.

They swam out of the silty cloud, and Gage held up his hand and Casey high-fived it.

"Now to get it onboard." Gage wrote on his magnetic writing board.

Casey swam against the current for a few seconds as he nodded and stared at the safe, the silt cloud clearing away quickly with the current. He jotted on his writing board.

"We state truth. Found safe on ocean floor. Want to open & see what's inside."

Gage wrote. "Not on *Sand Piper*. Must be @ Park Police HQ."

He wiped off the words to write more. "If cross inside, Owen must have 1st look then Jamaican museum gets back."

Casey nodded.

"Hey Coy. We need to bring something up that's heavy. Got a way to do that?" Casey asked.

"Sure thing." Coy's reply sounded in their ears. "I've got a boom with a wench. How heavy?"

"No idea. It's hard to judge underwater, but I'd say at least a couple hundred pounds. It's an old safe.""

"No problem. I'll send it down."

~

Maggie unlocked the front door of The Rusty Hook and she and Ruth stepped inside. She'd parked across the street at the hotel amongst the hotel guest's cars to discourage anyone from thinking there might be someone at the restaurant on a Saturday morning. Locking the door behind her, Maggie led Ruth through the building to the rear.

"I haven't seen these rooms before." Ruth glanced around as they made their way through the dining room and kitchen.

"Even if you had, you wouldn't recognize them. They've torn everything out and are starting the remodel phase." Maggie led her into the back rooms. "I think you'll recognize the rooms back here. These are phase II. They'll begin tearing out this part next week."

"Oh, I definitely remember this." A chill ran down Ruth's back. "How could I forget? At least the floor feels sturdy now. I hear the waves crashing outside, but I don't feel them in my feet."

"That's because they replaced all the old rotten pilings beneath the building as well as the joists they were attached to. You'd be amazed at how they did all that work. Anyway, as you say, it's a pretty sturdy building now."

"Thank goodness for that." Ruth said under her breath. Maggie may have a key to this place but it didn't make it any easier being here.

They slipped down a hallway and Ruth followed Maggie into Big Tony Amato's office. They had both brought flashlights and flipped them on as they stepped through the door.

"Oh, my goodness," Ruth gasped. "What happened in here?"

"I have no idea." Maggie gaped at the whirlwind of destruction that covered the floor. Chinese paintings had been ripped from the walls, the desk had been tipped over and the drawers had been emptied and stacked.

"Isn't it weird that someone came through and wrecked such havoc then stacked the drawers?" Maggie asked.

"Someone was looking for something, Mags. Look. Remember how the Chinese paintings hung on the walls? They tore them down hoping to find a safe behind one of them. Then they likely were looking in the drawers to find a false bottom or a hidden compartment."

"You're right, cuz." Maggie's gaze searched the room. "My

guess is it was Mr. Amato. Who else would have the access or the all-encompassing desire to search for it? We know he wants that treasure."

"Yep. So, if he looked behind the Chinese paintings, that must mean he checked all the walls. It's doubtful it's behind the paneling. It would be too hard to access."

"Agreed." Maggie moved further into the room, stepping over and around items in her way.

Ruth moved to the tumbled-over desk. "It looks like he checked this out extensively."

"Yeah. I doubt Big Tony kept it in his desk." She shuffled through the papers on the floor. "We've already been through all these papers. There was never any hint about a treasure."

"I remember. So, if there's nothing in the walls or the desk," she glanced at the only other furniture in the room, "and putting it in a chair or the couch would just be impractical, where else might he put it in this room?"

Maggie looked up at the ceiling and shone her flashlight around. "Look at that, Ruthie. Big Tony may not have had electricity available, but he sure knew how to make a kerosene lantern look fancy."

The plaster ceiling was flat like a normal ceiling except for a dome shaped area that was recessed. In the middle of the dome, a crystal kerosene lantern was hung, its chimney extended into an opening to release the smoke from the lantern's chimney into the attic. The light from the lantern, however would've been reflected from the dome, giving the room more light.

"Help me set the desk back up," Maggie reached for one side of the overturned piece of furniture.

Ruth helped her right the desk then moved it beneath the lantern. With great care, she removed the lantern and handed it to Ruth.

On tiptoes, Maggie strained to reach into the hole in the ceiling and felt around. She made a face. "I don't think I want to know what I just put my hand in, but I definitely feel spiderwebs, and I don't want to get bitten. Besides, I don't feel anything up here."

"It seems like a lot of trouble for Big Tony to go through if he wanted to get to his treasure."

"Doesn't it." Maggie pulled her hand down and scowled. Her hand was covered in dust and...who knew what else. She brushed her hands together. "Okay, hand me the lantern. What's next?"

Ruth glanced around the room with her flashlight. The carpet in this room was old and faded. At one time it might have been bright Chinese red but now was faded to a murky rust color. As the bright white beam of her LED flashlight swept across the floor between the papers it landed on a slightly brighter area that caught her eye. She realized this was where the desk had sat. If the desk hadn't been moved out of its position it would've likely gone unnoticed.

Ruth moved over to that spot and swept away the few papers and receipts that covered the edges. When she looked closer, she realized there was a separation between the pieces of carpet. It was about two feet by three feet and looked like it was pieced to match the rest of the floor. Was it a carpet-covered panel that could be removed?

"Well, that's that." Maggie climbed down from the desk. "Here, Ruthie. Help me move the desk back."

"Wait a sec, Mags. Take a look at this." Her voice was soft and she was kneeling by the spot now. She lifted her gaze to Maggie's, her eyes aglow. "I think we might be onto something."

~

Wayne folded his arms across his chest and listened as Gage told his story. He nodded occasionally and swiped his hand across his face and chin as he leaned back in his chair.

Casey, Coy and Uncle Owen sat around the unopened safe which rested on a wooden dolly next to Wayne's desk.

"And there you have it, Coy. Now you know what we were diving for." Gage held up his hands.

Coy shook his head, his brow furrowed. "That's quite a tale, man. I'm kind of glad I didn't know anything about any of this while you guys were out diving. Especially when Mr. Amato came by last week on *The Lucky Lady*."

Casey clapped him on the shoulder. "You can't let this information leave this room, Coy. Your life is at risk if you do. All our lives are at risk."

"If *La Cruz de San Mateo* is in that safe," Gage said, "then it's the property of the museum in Jamaica. Big Tony Amato stole it and it has to be returned. We have to keep it out of the hands of Antonio Amato."

Wayne once again swiped his hand down his face and stood from his chair. "That's a heck of a story, fellas. And it seems the Amato family's in the middle of everything around here. When Jack Brewster gets here, we'll find out if that *La Cruz* is in there or not."

"I'm here, Wayne. I'm here. Quit ye're worrying. Whatever's in that thing, I'll have it open in no time."

A fellow in his late sixties walked into the room dressed in a t-shirt and cargo shorts and carrying a small canvas bag. He sported a short salt and pepper goatee that matched the hair peeking from beneath his ballcap.

"Come on in, Jack. The quicker you get this thing open, the quicker we can get some answers." Wayne stood and shook Jack's hand then introduced the men in the room.

"No problem, Wayne. Let me at that thing."

Jack pulled a chair over and sat in front of the safe then pulled out a pair of wire framed glasses, settling them on his wrinkled, tanned face.

"Where'd you fellas find this safe? It's interesting." His hands roved over the barnacle encrusted and salt water damaged surface.

"On the ocean floor," Casey said. "Can you give us an age or time frame when this safe might've been in use?"

"Oh, that's kind of difficult to determine because they can be used for a long time, but I can tell you this particular safe was produced in the early 1920's in Chicago." Jack pulled out some instruments from his canvas bag. "I have no idea how long it's been on the ocean floor, so I couldn't tell you how long it was in use. Sorry. Perhaps something inside will help out with that."

"We're hoping," Gage said.

All eyes on the safe, silence fell over the group as Jack worked. After about fifteen minutes of whirring the dial with various clicks of the tumblers, and with Jack listening closely, he finally sat back and looked around at his audience.

"Too much silt and sand has gotten down in the mechanism and has damaged things in there. I can hear it scraping. Kind of a locksmith's worse nightmare, you know. Anyway, I'm not going to be able to open it the conventional way, so I'm going to have to break into it. This is going to render the safe unusable. Is that going to be a problem?"

"Friend, that's not a problem," Gage said. "It's far more important that we find out what's inside."

"Very well." Jack pulled out his tools and proceeded to break into the safe. He cut the hinges with an electric grinder then used the same tool on the dial. Then he went to work on the mechanism inside and within a few minutes he was able to get the door open.

Gage dragged in a lung full of air then released it. He hadn't realized he'd been holding his breath. This was ridiculous. Either the cross was in the safe or it wasn't. It just meant they'd have to keep searching if it wasn't. Oh, but he'd sure love to stop searching. He glanced over at Owen. If anyone was ready for the search to be over, it was him.

The poor man's eyes were glued to the safe. He longed to lay eyes on that cross like none other. *Thy will be done, Lord. For Owen's sake and Your glory.*

"Well, fellas, here goes nothin'." Jack lifted the heavy door of the safe and slide it to the side, leaving a gaping hole before them. He grunted as Wayne helped him steady it and lean it against Wayne's desk.

They all stood around staring into the mouth of the safe, but no one moved.

Jack stood back and looked from one man to the next. "You know, fellas, I didn't open that daggone thing for everybody to just stand around staring at it. Somebody get in there and check it out."

Casey slapped Gage's shoulder. "Gage, go for it."

Gage shook his head and turned to Owen. "Nope, it's not my place. Owen, you've been looking for *La Cruz de San Mateo* for a long time. Have at it, my friend."

Owen swallowed hard and rubbed suddenly sweaty palms together, stepping closer to the safe. He knelt in front of it and rubbed his palms on his cargo shorts.

"Here you go, buddy." Wayne handed him a small flashlight. "Maybe that'll help."

Owen nodded and accepted it, turning on the LED beam. Aiming it inside the safe, he illuminated three shelves. "Amazingly enough, everything seems to be dry. This was one very well made safe.

"I'm not surprised," Jack said. "It's from an era when things were well made. Not like today when they make things cheap so you have to throw 'em away and go buy 'em again."

"That's very true." Owen reached into the top shelf, pulled out the contents and examined them.

"These are definitely papers belonging to Big Tony Amato. This one is dated 1927 and this one 1928." Owen looked up at the group, a grin lighting his features. "This is proof that this safe belonged to Big Tony Amato."

The group around him whooped and cheered, even giving a couple high-fives.

Owen wasted no more time. He pulled everything out of the safe until there was nothing left, then he proceeded to go through things methodically. A wooden box about eight inches by ten inches had been stored on the bottom shelf of the safe. The room grew quiet again as Owen reached for it. His hand hesitated before opening the lid.

"Go for it, Owen," Gage said. "It's either there or it isn't but you have to open it to find out."

Owen blew out a breath and pulled off the lid.

"Are those what I think they are?" Casey asked. "Are those gold Spanish doubloons?"

Owen nodded, his shoulders sagging. "Yep. That's exactly what they are. But they aren't *La Cruz de San Mateo*."

Chapter Twenty-Four

Ruth ran her finger around the edge of the rectangle where the carpet edges met. "We need something to pry this up with, Mags. I'd bet my job on this thing coming up somehow."

Maggie snapped her fingers. "Hang on, Ruthie. There are workman's tools back in the kitchen. Let me go see what I can find."

"Ok, but hurry. We need to do this fast and get out of here. The hair keeps standing up on my neck."

"You think old Big Tony Amato knows you're getting close to his treasure and he's not happy?" Maggie giggled.

Ruth rolled her eyes. "Would you go find that tool, please, before someone comes in and finds us?"

"Right." Maggie climbed to her feet and left the room. Within minutes she returned with a small crowbar.

"This should do it, don't you think?" A broad smile lifted her lips.

"Oh yeah." Ruth accepted the thick, curved bar. She wedged the flat end between the edges of the carpet and put her weight on the curved end. She repeated this action all the way around the rectangle until she had the panel removed.

"Wow, Ruthie. That's amazing that you saw that. Now what's inside?" Maggie's voice was barely above a whisper.

Ruth set the panel aside and picked up her flashlight. Beneath where the panel had been someone had reinforced a section of the subfloor with a wooden box and a wooden lid. Ruth removed the lid, and inside was old yellowed tissue paper. She carefully folded this back to reveal a faded red velvet bag and a smaller wooden box. With great care, she removed the velvet bag and opened the draw string, pouring its contents into her palm.

Out poured a colorful array of cut gems of all sizes.

"Mags, do you think those are genuine gemstones?"

"I have no idea. What I know about gemstones you could put on the point of a pencil."

"Yeah, me too." Ruth returned them to the bag and set it aside then reached for the wooden box.

When she lifted the lid of the wooden box, a gasp slipped from her lips at the same time one escaped from Maggie. There, lying on a bed of yellowed white satin, lay a golden embossed cross with a faceted ruby heart.

Ruth's hand shook and she swallowed as she turned to her cousin. "Maggie, it's…it's the…"

"I know, Ruthie. We found it." Maggie's fingers squeezed Ruth's shoulder gently. "Quickly, cover it up. Bring it and the velvet bag. We need to get out of here."

"Not so fast, ladies. I'd like to show my appreciation first," a familiar voice spoke from the doorway as the room lit up.

Ruth's heart froze and panic began to rise. No, no, no. *Oh Lord. Please not this.* She felt Maggie's arms slip around her as her cousin moved to her side.

"It was very nice of you to search out and find my treasure for me." Antonio Amato strolled further into the room, a flashlight in his hand. "You know, my family's been looking for that for a long, long time."

Three of Mr. Amato's lackies stood just inside the doorway and in the hall, flashlights in their hands as well, all aimed at Ruth and Maggie. There would be no escaping.

Ruth kept her gaze on the floor, willing it to open up and swallow her and Maggie. *Lord, would You do a miracle like that for us? You held back the sun for Joshua, and you dropped the walls of Jericho for the children of Israel. What miracle will you do for Maggie and me?*

Panic threatened to swallow her before the floor did as she felt her breathing increase. *No, slow it down. In, out. In, out. Slow it down.* Maggie's arms tightened ever so slightly indicating she was there for her. *Lord, help me. I need to keep my head. Please don't let me panic.*

Antonio stepped closer holding out his hand. "So, what did

you ladies find for me?" His voice was so congenial, but there was an underlying threat that Ruth picked up on. *In, out. In, out.*

"It's a cross of some kind, Mr. Amato." Maggie said, handing him the box. "It's quite lovely."

He opened the box and whistled. "It certainly is. I have to say my great-great uncle had good taste, don't you think? You know he never told anyone in the family what the treasure was? I'm the first one to see it. It's gorgeous. And I have you ladies to thank for finding it for me."

He slipped the box into his slacks pocket. "What other goodies did you ladies find?"

Maggie took a deep breath, releasing it slowly then she handed him the bag of jewels.

"What do we have here?" He dumped the contents of the bag into his hand and nodded. "Well, well, well. That's a dandy haul, I must say. It'll make a nice addition to my coffers. Anything else?"

Maggie poked around in the wooden box in the floor then shook her head. "No sir. Nothing else."

Antonio stepped closer to the woman and lifted Maggie's chin, running his thumb over her lips. "It's a real shame you decided to do this, you know. Now I'm going to have to do something with you two. But thanks for finding my treasure."

Then as if seeing her for the first time, he stepped in front of Ruth and tipped her chin up. "Who is this lovely creature?"

Maggie's arms tightened around Ruth. "She's my cousin. Please leave her alone."

Antonio grinned. "Your cousin, you say? She's kinda cute. What's your name, sweetheart?"

Ruth's heart hammered. *Help me, Lord. Just breath. In, out. In, out.* "Ruth."

"Well, Ruth. Maybe you'd like to stay on with me for a while. What do you say?"

His thumb brushed Ruth's cheek and panic welled inside her. She yanked her face away and buried it on Maggie's shoulder.

"Please, Mr. Amato. Please leave her be. Take me wherever and kill me if you must, but please leave Ruthie alone."

Antonio's cold gaze swept them both and he considered for a moment before turning toward the door. "Bring them both to my yacht."

~

"Excuse me," Lennie Campo knocked on the open door to Wayne Mitchell's office. "The officer at the front desk told me I should come on in."

Wayne, who sat behind his desk, waved Lennie forward. "Then come on in, sir. What can I do for you?"

Lennie glanced at the young man seated in front of Wayne's desk and he walked toward them. "I'm here to give you the information you need to take down Antonio Amato."

Wayne stood and stared at Lennie. "Excuse me? And who are you?"

"I'm the man that can take down Antonio Amato. I'll testify in court as a witness against him. But before I say anything else, I want ta see a lawyer."

Wayne nodded and picked up his phone. "You got it buddy. We'll get you a lawyer right away. Gage, escort him to an interrogation room."

Gage waved Lennie to follow him. "Right this way, sir."

He opened the door to the interrogation room and allowed Lennie to precede him. "Have a seat at the table, sir. Someone will be with you shortly."

"Thanks," Lennie glanced around the room and took a seat.

"Can I get you a bottle of water?" Gage asked before leaving.

"Yeah, that'd be nice, thanks."

Gage brought the water then took up a post in the observation room where Wayne soon joined him.

"Hank Smyth is on his way." Wayne nodded at the man through the two-way glass. "What do you think?"

"I have no idea."

"Want to take first crack at him?"

"Sure. I've got some questions."

"Then go for it."

The court appointed lawyer Hank Smyth showed up within a few minutes and Gage joined him and Lennie in the interrogation room.

"For the record, what is your name sir?" Gage asked.

"Lennie Campo."

"And who is your employer?"

Lennie sighed heavily. "Well, I did work for Mr. Amato but I quit today. I just couldn't do it no more."

"Do what, Mr. Campo?" Gage leaned his forearms on the edge of the table.

"Mr. Amato runs a lot of dirty businesses, ya know. Mafia businesses. Money laundering, human trafficking, drug running, other stuff. He kills people, and he expects his people to kill people."

"Have you killed people, Mr. Campo?"

Hank held up a hand. "You don't have to answer that question, Mr. Campo. You're not required to answer anything that will incriminate you."

Lennie turned to look at his lawyer. "I know, but I've done some things I'm not real proud of, but Mr. Amato has got to be stopped. I want to make a deal. I want to turn states evidence. I may not be a smart man but I know what states evidence is. I'll testify against him in court, and I'll even do time in prison but you give me a lighter sentence. You stop him and stop all o' his dirty businesses.

Gage glanced at Hank then back at Lennie. "You seem like you've thought this out, Lennie."

"Oh, I have, sir."

"Let me ask you a couple more questions. Who killed Joe Pachino and Capt. Ed Garcia?"

Without hesitation Lennie said, "Harland killed Capt. Ed and when he was found that was why Mr. Amato wanted Harland killed. Because Capt. Ed was found. He wasn't supposed to be found. Ever. Same with Joe. He wasn't supposed to be found either."

"Who killed Joe, Lennie?"

Lennie's gaze slid away and he swallowed. "Harland and me. And then he made me kill my best friend, Harland. He threatened that if I didn't kill him, he'd kill me and spread me in one-inch pieces all over the place. That was the last person I ever killed. I just can't do this no more. And I gotta put a stop to him."

Gage sat back in his chair and crossed his arms over his chest.

"So when one of Antonio's underlings fails him, he disposes of them and replaces them?"

"Yeah, pretty much."

"How long have you been with Mr. Amato?"

"About twenty years. I was his father's chauffeur when Antonio was young. He was a nice man, but he was just as much into the dirty businesses. He didn't kill off his people like Antonio does though."

"Do you know the ins and outs of Mr. Amato's businesses, Lennie? Do the people in those businesses trust you?"

"Yeah, I guess so. I went with him to most of the meetings. They all know me. The one that I didn't like going to the most is the one where they sell the women. You know, human trafficking. That's a tough one."

Gage saw opportunities here and hoped that Lennie would help them shut the businesses down. But first they'd have to find Amato and shut him down.

"Lennie, do you know where Amato is now?"

"Yeah. He was heading to The Rusty Hook."

"You know that I have to arrest you and read you your rights, don't you, Lennie? You've committed crimes that you have to pay for. But with your lawyer's help, you should be able to turn state's evidence and get your sentence reduced."

Lennie heaved a sigh and held out his wrists. "Yeah, I know. I didn't expect no less."

Gage stood and tugged a set of handcuffs from his cargo shorts pocket that he'd dropped in earlier.

"So, what's Lennie short for? Leonard?"

"Yes, sir."

Gage nodded. "Would you stand please. We'll cuff you in front. You're not resisting. Leonard Campo, you have the right to remain silent. Anything you say can and will be used against you in a court of law. You...."

The desk sergeant stuck his head in the door.

"Hey Gage. There's a Mary Kelly on the phone. She says it's urgent and it can't wait."

What in the world was she calling for? It had to have something to do with Ruth or Maggie. His pulse skipped a beat, his gaze bouncing between the lawyer and Lennie.

"I have to take this. I'll be right back."

Stepping out of the room, he hurried to a desk with a phone and clicked the answer call button.

"This is officer Gage Hampton. Mary? What's up?"

"Oh, Gage. Thank goodness. Maggie talked Ruth into going back to The Rusty Hook this morning. Maggie now has a key to the front door but that still doesn't make me feel any better about the whole thing. I made her promise they'd call me at noon just to check in with me. That was twenty minutes ago. I gave them a few minutes just in case they got caught up in something, but I just couldn't wait any longer. Gage, I'm worried."

"You did the right thing, Mary. I'll check it out."

"Thank you. I feel better knowing you will."

"If you hear anything let me know immediately."

"Yes, I certainly will, and thanks again, Gage."

"No problem, Mary. Thanks for calling."

Gage hurried to Wayne's office and explained the situation, then both hurried to the interrogation room. Gage quickly read Lennie his rights and Wayne called for police protection for the erstwhile gangster while Gage left for the The Rusty Hook.

~

Maggie and Ruth held tightly to one another as they were roughly pulled from the trunk of Antonio's limo. The women blinked in the bright sunlight as their eyes attempted to adjust from the darkness of the trunk. Two of Antonio's lackeys grasped them by the arms and walked them toward *The Lucky Lady*.

Dread filled Maggie's gut as they neared Antonio's yacht. What in the world did he have in store for them? Was he going to take them out, tie cinderblocks to their legs and drop them overboard as he'd had done with Joe Pachino? Or was he going to keep them for himself? He'd already told her he wanted a relationship with her. But now with this turn of events, what would happen? And what of Ruthie? That wouldn't go well at all. She was already traumatized in his presence.

She glanced at her cousin walking beside her. Ruth's body was stiff, her gaze straight ahead, her jaw clenched, her nose flared, and her face was pale. In spite of all that, her chin was up. Maggie knew her well enough to know she was fighting panic. She wanted to reach over and put her arm around her but knew the men with them wouldn't allow it. It was better for both their sakes if she left well enough alone. *Lord, please be with Ruth. Help her fight the panic that I know is threatening to overwhelm her.*

As they reached the gangway that led to Antonio's yacht,

Maggie's steps slowed as did Ruth's.

The men behind them shoved them forward and one spoke. "What are you waitin' on. Get aboard."

Maggie stepped onto the metal bridge-like structure first, Ruth following close behind. When they reached the deck, Maggie took Ruth's hand and held on tightly, tugging her to her side.

The men pushed them forward. "Head up those stairs."

They did as they were told and together climbed to the upper skydeck. As they moved forward, they found Antonio Amato sitting in a deck chair, one leg crossed over the other in a relaxed manner. He spread his arms wide.

"Welcome aboard, ladies. Please, have a seat." With a smile on his face, he indicated two other deck chairs. "Miguel, please, bring refreshments for our guests."

Miguel, who was never far, nodded and went to do his boss's bidding.

Maggie and Ruth stood where they were, not moving a muscle.

Antonio's relaxed manner stiffened as the smile on his face faded. He planted his elbows on the arms of his chairs and clasped his fingers together. "I said, have a seat."

"We'd rather stand, thank you." Ruth's voice came out raspy.

Maggie squeezed her hand.

Antonio stood and walked over to the cousins. Ice glittered in his dark eyes. "Fine. Then stand. You can stand all day for all I care."

Miguel approached with a tray of drinks. Antonio waved him away. "Our guests have decided they aren't interested in hospitality, Miguel. Take it away."

He eyed Maggie. "It's too bad, you know. We could've been good together, you and me. But now you're going to find yourself in a real pickle."

Maggie glared at him and clamped her lips together. She wouldn't give him the satisfaction of a reply.

"Don't you even want to know what I'm going to do with you two?"

Maggie remained silent.

"So that's how it's going be?"

His gaze returned to Ruth. "You know, your little cousin here is quite a looker. Perhaps I'll let the boys get to know her a little while you and I have a talk."

Maggie felt the tension in Ruth's hand as she squeezed Maggie's. No, she couldn't allow Ruth out of her sight. "What do you want me to say, Mr. Amato?"

"Well, now that wasn't so hard, was it?"

"I suppose not."

"Then why don't you ladies have a seat." His voice sounded congenial but a thread of steel ran through it.

Ruth dropped Maggie's hand and took a deck chair before Maggie could.

Antonio sat across from them. "Well, isn't your curiosity piqued even a little bit? Don't you want to know what I'm going to do with you?"

"I suppose you're going to kill us, aren't you?" Ruth shoved a tendril of hair behind her ear and sucked in a deep breath, attempting to release it slowly.

A cruel laugh rang across the deck as Antonio slapped his knee. "That's probably what you'll want me to do when you find out my plan, but no. I can make too much money by not killing you."

Maggie's heart dropped into the pit of her stomach. If he wasn't going to kill them, then he was going to sell them. How else was he going to make money off of them?

"You're into human trafficking, aren't you?" Her voice was barely above a whisper. "You're going to sell us."

Antonio pointed a finger at her as he chuckled. "Give the woman a gold star. I always took you for a smart woman, Maggie. And now, I have two of you to sell."

The engines of the yacht turned over and purred to life sending panic into every corner of Maggie's being. How in the world would she and Ruth get out of this one?

Chapter Twenty-Five

Casey, I've just checked The Rusty Hook, and they're not here." Gage had just explained everything that Mary had told him up to this point. "Big Tony Amato's office is torn apart, and it looks like they dug up the floor and found something under the floorboards. There was a compartment and I suspect it had something in it, but there's no way of knowing what it was. There's yellowed tissue paper left behind and it has reddish-pink on it like it was wrapped around something that faded on it."

"Well, the girl's found something, but you can't say it was the gold cross." Casey's words sounded in his ear.

"Of course not, but whatever it was, was taken."

"Is one of their cars parked there?"

"Not here at The Rusty Hook, but they've been known to park across the street at the hotel. I'll check over there and call you back."

Within minutes Gage had located Maggie's car and called Casey back.

"Maggie's car is still here. The fact it is and they aren't has me totally concerned."

"Do you think someone came in while they were searching for the cross?"

"Yeah, I think it's a real possibility, and I think that someone was Antonio Amato. It's his building. He would be the most likely person."

"Yeah, and if nothing else, it's the best place to start."

"Casey, if they did find the cross and he walked in on them, he's going to be really glad they found it for him, but I'll bet he's going to dispose of them in some way."

Gage ran a hand through his hair and closed his eyes. The

thought of Ruth and her cousin in that gangster's hands drove his heart right down into the pit of stomach. They would have to move fast to try and find them.

"Yeah, I agree. So, what are you thinking, buddy?"

"I'm going to call the Diamond Sands Yacht Club and find out if his yacht is still there. Can you launch the Coast Guard Cutter? I have a feeling we may be looking at two possible situations."

"And what are those?"

"He's either going to kill them, or he's going to make a profit off of them."

"A profit? How's that?"

"Think about some of the businesses he's involved in. Human trafficking to name one. Why kill them when he can make a profit from them."

A pregnant silence crossed the line. "Gage, we have to stop him. This will…"

Gage waited a moment before prompting Casey. "Will what, Casey? It has something to do with Ruth, doesn't it?"

A heavy sigh vibrated in his ear. "Yeah. I'll get the crew onboard the cutter. Let me know as soon as you know something about Amato's yacht. I'll send a helicopter for you to board the cutter. I doubt you'll want to be left behind."

"Thanks, Casey, but I have another idea. I'll let you know if it won't work then I'll take you up on it."

When Gage hung up with Casey, he immediately called the Diamond Sands Yacht Club and pretended to be an insurance salesman. He told them he had lost Mr. Amato's business card and asked if they could go and tell him he would be late for his appointment with him that afternoon.

"Well, sir. I hate to break it to you, but *The Lucky Lady* just pulled away from her slip about five minutes ago heading out to sea."

"Really? And I had an appointment too." Gage put as much disappointment into his voice as he could muster.

"I'm really sorry, sir. I guess you'll have to reschedule. I'd call Mr. Amato on Monday if I were you."

"Oh, why is that?"

"It sort of looked like maybe he was going to have a party or something. He took a couple of girls onboard."

"Hmmm. Lucky him, huh?" Gage forced the cheery tone he was far from feeling.

"Yes, sir. He has lots of parties on that yacht."

"Thanks. I'll get with him soon."

"Hey, man. No problem."

Gage clicked off then called Coy Nelson. "Hey, Coy. You up for another job? There could be some danger involved this time. I need to tell you that upfront, but you could help put some criminals away for a long, long time."

~

Gage pulled his diving gear from the jump seat behind the driver's side of his pick-up as Uncle Owen climbed out of the passenger seat.

"I'm glad you called, Gage. There's no way I could've sat at the RV and not been a part of this rescue, but you knew that, huh?"

"Yep. I knew once you got word, you'd worry." Gage tossed the gear bag strap over his shoulder and hurried toward the marina. "Besides, we're going to need all hands-on-deck for this one."

"That scum has my girls and there's no way I'd sit on the sidelines. I'm all in. Just tell me what you need me to do."

When they reached Coy's boat, Gage tossed his gear on the deck, then he and Owen climbed aboard. The engines were already purring and all but one mooring line had been released.

"Coy?"

The young boat captain stuck his head out. "Get that line and we're ready to cast off."

Gage released the line, and Coy moved the boat away from the slip. He and Owen joined the young man on the bridge.

"So, you want to tell me why were heading out like this and chasing criminals? You do know there's a storm coming, right?" Coy steered the boat out of the harbor and into open water, gunning the engines. "What's our heading?"

Gage gave him coordinates for the Coast Guard Cutter then explained what had happened to Ruth and Maggie. They were to meet up unless the cutter spotted the yacht first. The cutter had the equipment to find the yacht, but they would likely have to eliminate a few others in the process.

"The fact there's a storm coming may help us out. Other

yachts and boats are going to be heading in. Amato's boat won't."

He pulled his phone from his pocket and hit speed dial. "I need to make a call before we get too far out. Hey Wayne. I need you to ask Lennie something. Ask him how they arrange the sale of the women for trafficking and where they get shipped to. Yeah, I'll wait. But hurry. We're already heading out to sea."

Within minutes, Wayne was back and Gage nodded. "Thanks, that's what I needed to know."

He clicked the end button, and turned to the other two men. "According to our informant, Antonio arranges to meet another boat that picks up the girls and takes them to Norfolk, Virginia. There they are transferred to a shipping container along with other women and girls who have been abducted from all over the country. When they have their quota, the container is stacked onboard a cargo ship bound for Hong Kong or Thailand. Antonio Amato is but one seller in the grand scheme of things, but if we can put him out of business, then it's one step toward putting them all out of business."

"Did your informant say what kind of boat it is?"

"It's a fishing boat called *My Pleasure*."

"You're kidding. He actually gave you a name?"

Gage shrugged. "Our informant seems to mean business."

"Isn't this a job for the FBI?" Coy asked.

"Technically yes." Gage grabbed a bottle of water from the small fridge Coy kept handy. "but when you consider we just found out about this, we didn't have time to call them in. The bad guys are getting away with the girls and we need to rescue them. Don't worry. We'll gladly hand them over once we have them in custody."

Owen stood looking out the front window overlooking the bow. He hadn't said much since they'd come aboard. Coy laid a hand on his shoulder.

"We'll do everything we can to find them, Owen."

Owen nodded but didn't speak. Gage had a feeling the man was praying with everything he had in him.

The radio crackled then Casey's voice came in loud and clear.

"Coast Guard Cutter C-107 to *The Sand Piper*, come in"

Coy reached for the hand mic and holding it to his mouth, pressed the call button. "This is *The Sand Piper*. Come in Coast

Guard Cutter C-107."

"We have you on radar and on visual. We're at .75 miles off your starboard stern. Cut engines and wait to be boarded."

"What the heck?" Coy turned to Gage. "They want to board us?"

"Yeah. I suspect he doesn't want to use the radio much in case Antonio's listening in. Do as he says and wait here."

Coy cut the engines to idle and waited for the Coast Guard Cutter to pull alongside. The much larger boat dwarfed them. The three men stepped out onto the aft deck and waited for a coast guard crewman to toss a rope over to steady the smaller boat against the side of the larger one.

The same crewman dropped a set of steps to the deck of *The Sand Piper* and Casey, dressed in his Coast Guard whites, stepped gingerly onto the smaller boat.

"Hey Case," Gage slapped the officer on the shoulder. "imagine meeting you out here."

"Yeah, just imagine." Casey held up a handheld radio. "This is set to a Coast Guard frequency that we can pick up, but Amato can't. Use it to communicate with us. They'll be able to monitor the regular radio waves and hear us coming."

He handed the radio to Gage and pointed at it. "It's pretty expensive so do me a favor and don't drop it overboard, okay?"

Gage chuckled. "I'll do my best."

"What's your plan?" Casey planted his hands on his hips.

"One of Amato's underlings turned himself in this morning. Said he'd turn state's evidence against Amato. He said there's a fishing boat named *My Pleasure* out of Norfolk that Antonio meets up with to transfer the women and get his money. You've got the equipment to find Amato and the fishing boat. Let's get to it. We'll follow you."

Gage waved the radio. "Stay in touch."

Casey headed for the steps back to the cutter. "You've got it."

Within minutes the two boats parted and the cutter took the lead. Gage and Owen each took binoculars and scanned the darkening ocean for signs of the two boats. At Casey's recommendation, they stayed about a half mile off the port stern from the cutter.

"Coy, do you have air tanks ready to go?" Gage asked as he

scanned off the port side.

"Sure I do. I keep them ready to go all the time. Why?"

"Because if we spot them and can stay hidden behind the cutter, I'm going to dive and make a run for *The Lucky Lady*. I may be able to sneak onboard and rescue the girls."

Owen spun around. "Are you nuts? You'll be on that yacht all by yourself amongst those gangsters, and you won't be able to save them by yourself. No telling how many thugs are onboard that yacht."

"But I'll have the element of surprise on my side." Gage opened his gear bag and pulled out his mask and regulator.

"That isn't going to help you much against armed thugs. You won't be able to take a gun with you." Owen crossed his arms over his chest and raised an eyebrow.

"Now that's where you're wrong." Gage pulled out a waterproof dive bag, and pulling his handgun from his holster, slipped it into the small bag and sealed it. He held it up for Owen's inspection.

Owen deflated a bit. "Oh, I didn't know they had such things. Nice."

Gage chuckled and reopened the bag, returning the weapon to his holster. "It's okay."

"I'd still feel better if Casey went with you, Gage. Two would work better in a rescue than one."

Gage eyed the older man. Owen wanted them back but he didn't want to risk the girls in any way, and he felt a one-man rescue was a risk.

Gage nodded. "Okay. I'll run it past him and see what he says. The whole thing is iffy anyway. We have no idea how this thing is going to go down, Owen. I'm just trying to plan ahead in case the opportunity avails itself."

Owen nodded and swallowed, his head hanging. "I know. I've been praying since the moment I heard that man took my girls. I don't know what else to do. I feel so helpless, but I know God sees them where they are. I just keep praying God will keep them safe and somehow bring them back to me alive."

"I know," Gage's voice was husky. He coughed to clear it.

"I know you do, Gage, because you're in love with my niece, aren't you?" Owen placed a hand on Gage's shoulder. "I see it in your eyes when you look at her and hear it in your voice when you speak to her."

The radio crackled to life just then saving Gage from having to answer. He picked it up and pressed the call button.

"What's up, Case?"

"We have two boat's in our sights and on radar, Gage. We're cutting engines. Suggest you do the same."

"Casey, I have an idea."

Gage told him of his plan to dive and swim over to *The Lucky Lady* and of Owen's request that the two of them rescue the girls together.

Gage pressed the call button. "How close are the two boats?"

"We have a visual on *The Lucky Lady* and she's approximately a mile ahead. The second boat is approaching from the north and is about five miles out."

Gage exhaled a heavy breath. "And you're sure it's *The Lucky Lady*?"

"Positive visual identification."

"Then that doesn't give us long. Want to join me?" Gage slipped into his wet suit as he talked and Coy helped him gear up.

"Are you kidding me? I wouldn't miss taking down a huge crime syndicate boss for the world. Let's do it. Bring your boat alongside and drop anchor then we'll swim the rest of the way."

"Roger that. I'll meet you on deck in five minutes."

~

Maggie and Ruth sat in deck chairs side by side holding hands and praying. Antonio Amato had left a guard to keep watch over them and had gone up to the salon to watch a baseball game. Every now and then his voice was raised in cheering as his team made a good play or he cursed when something didn't go well.

"Miguel, bring me another drink," he shouted several times. "And make it a double."

Ruth squeezed Maggie's fingers and when her cousin barely turned her head and met her gaze, Ruth gave a faint smile and dropped a wink. From the furrowed brow that Maggie cast her way, Ruth knew she didn't understand. Ruth tried to convey beneath the watchful gaze of their captor that she would be fine. She had been praying, and still was, that God would send someone to rescue them. She had asked for peace and wisdom, for strength and grace. That peace that passed all understanding that comes only from knowing God had filled her. Never in her life had she felt it like this. She wanted so much for Maggie to know that she had that peace flowing through her right now, and that for the first time in many years, she wasn't afraid.

Lord, in Your word you gave David peace, didn't You? He put his trust in You and wasn't afraid of what man could do to him, so why should I be afraid of what man can do to me. Yes, someone tried to hurt me, but You sent Maggie to rescue me, didn't You? Will You send someone to rescue us today? And even if You don't, You'll go with us because You told us You would never leave us nor forsake us. Oh Lord, You promised.

Curses from the deck above filled her ears and she cringed. She just had to hang onto the Lord's promises and that peace that filled her. She squeezed Maggie's fingers again and her cousin turned to look a little more fully toward her, a question in her gaze.

The guard had been standing near the bar where Miguel prepared a drink for Antonio, but when the waiter headed up the stairs to deliver it, the guard moved across the skydeck to stand at the railing, his back to them. When he did, Ruth took the opportunity to lean across and whisper to Maggie.

"Don't worry. Everything will be fine."

Maggie whispered back in Ruth's ear. "How can you be sure? Do you know something I don't know?"

Ruth shook her head. "No. Just that God has given me peace that He'll work it out. Don't worry. He will."

Maggie leaned back and stared at her for several moments. Then she nodded slowly, her brow still furrowed. One corner of her mouth lifted, but a smile never quite covered her lips. She turned to look straight ahead.

Ruth watched her cousin. She didn't think Maggie was as convinced as she was.

The guard walked along the railing before he made his way back through the skydeck. Ruth had spotted the handgun in the holster on his right hip. He was average height but looked like he worked out. A lot. There was no way they could take him down, could they? She closed her eyes and took a deep breath. What in the world was she thinking? Of course, they couldn't take him down. Where had that thought come from?

A crack of thunder made Ruth jump and she opened her eyes. Her gaze roved over the distant sky beyond the railing at the stern. Wow! The sky had grown dark to the south. Had there been lightening while her eyes had been closed?

A thin streak of jagged light danced across the sky to the south confirming what she'd suspected. A minute later, thunder followed. A storm was definitely brewing.

Maggie's gaze flashed to Ruth's, despair in its depths.

Ruth swallowed hard. *Oh Lord, You once calmed the seas. But if this is part of Your plan to rescue us, then so be it.*

Chapter Twenty-Six

Gage swam swiftly through the water at Casey's side, sticking close to him. They swam in a zig-zag pattern toward *The Lucky Lady*. Should they get picked up on any sonar equipment that the yacht might have, then the hope would be that they appear as one large fish swimming in the yacht's general direction. They maintained radio silence as they swam.

Once they reached the yacht, they surfaced and tied their tanks, fins, and other equipment to the bottom of the ladder on the lower stern deck. Gage climbed up first, searching the deck for occupants. He also scanned the upper decks to see if anyone was at any of the railings. With no one in sight, he and Casey slipped silently onboard.

A flash of lightning lit the southern sky and was soon followed by a crack of thunder reverberating across the heavens.

"Great." Casey whispered, a grimace marring his features. He eyed the darkening sky. The wind was picking up too "It's going to be a rough one."

"Yep." Gage removed his waterproof bag from his dive suit and slipped out his handgun. "With this storm bearing down and that other boat heading our way, we need to move fast."

Casey followed suit, removing his own handgun, and they moved silently down a corridor toward the bow of the yacht. They cleared the rooms as they passed them. One was an engine room and another was storage. At the bow, a sign on the last door said Control Room.

Gage quietly attempted to turn the knob and the door opened silently. Not even a squeak. This door was well maintained, something he was thankful for. Opening it further, he held his handgun in an offensive position. Casey did likewise, keeping an eye behind them as well as on the room.

Three men sat before a long console, their backs to the door. Several computer monitors and telephones filled the console and the three men were busy, never having heard the door open.

"Hands up, gentlemen, and turn around slowly," Gage commanded in a stern but quiet voice.

The three men froze and two did as they were told instantly. One took a couple seconds longer to react.

"Do as I said." Gage poked his shoulder. "And don't push that button I know you have under the console. I can't have you notifying anyone. Just raise your hands and turn around. Now!"

Gage pulled a flattened roll of duct tape from a zippered pocket in his dive suit and proceeded to cover the men's mouths then tape their hands behind their backs.

"There you go, fellas. Now you're going for a little swim. I hope you can at least tread water without your hands.

One of the men's eyes grew large and frightened and he shook his head emphatically.

Gage slapped his shoulder. "Sorry, buddy. You should've chosen a more...shall we say honorable desk job? Hopefully your buddies here will help you out.

"Cover me, Casey. I'm going to walk them out."

Gage walked the three men at gunpoint to the stern deck and helped them into the water. One started kicking water hard to try and draw attention.

Gage pointed his firearm at him and spoke quietly. "I don't have a problem with bringing you back onboard and strapping your legs with tape, buddy. Besides, your ride is on the way. You won't have to tread for long."

The man stopped his kicking and treaded water along with his fellow criminals.

Lightning flashed, followed by rumbles of thunder. Three pair of frightened eyes turned to Gage.

"You'll be safe onboard before it gets here. Now sink or swim."

Gage hurried back to where Casey waited. "I hate to split up, but the captain needs to be taken down so this boat is dead in the water. Can you take care of that while I find the girls? They most likely have a guard on them."

"You're the boss." Casey grinned and gave a quick salute. "Let's do this."

They found a set of service stairs that took them to the bow and the next deck up. They heard what sounded like a baseball game on the third deck. Was that Antonio Amato cheering it on? They parted ways here, each to accomplish their own mission.

With handgun drawn and in position, Gage proceeded down a short corridor until he saw an opening and there were the girls, sitting on chairs out on the deck. Surely they weren't alone. His visibility was limited here. Then he noticed another set of stairs on the right. Perhaps if he came up those he could see better.

Before he could move, a man of average height but bulky muscles walked across the deck toward the railing.

No, he had to stop him from seeing the men in the water. He slapped the wall beside him and dove back out of sight.

"What was that?" A man's voice asked

"I have no idea. It didn't sound like the boss." A second man responded.

So, there were two out there. Could there be more?

"Go look, Paulo."

"Why me, Miguel?"

"Because you're the one with a gun, stupid."

"Whatever."

Gage risked a quick peek. Great. Paulo was the average height bulky muscle guy. He'd have to take him down. Then he'd deal with whoever was still on deck with the girls.

Gage slipped back and waited for muscleman to search for the noisemaker. The man stood in the corridor and looked around, checked a closet then shrugged his shoulders and with no concern turned to head back. Gage struck him on the head with the butt of his gun and the man went down.

That was a lot easier than he'd expected. Bending, he checked his pulse. Good. It was strong and steady. He'd have a headache when he woke up as well as a goose egg. He taped his mouth then his hands behind him and his feet together then dragged him down the back stairs to the lower deck and put him in the engine compartment. If he woke up and tried to make noise, no one would hear him over the sound of the engines.

He decided to go up the stern staircase this time to see who the other man on the deck with the girls was, but before he could head up, Casey arrived with a man in his fifties duct tape over his mouth, hands taped behind his back.

"Who's your friend?" Gage tipped his chin toward the man.

"This is the captain of the yacht. I cleared the bridge deck too. You?"

"There's one asleep in the engine room. I still have one with the girls. Not sure if there are any others besides Amato." Gage shook his head. "Heading back up now."

"Let me drop him over and call Coy to pick these guys up. His boat is smaller and less likely to be seen. I'll also check on the status of *My Pleasure* to see how far out it is. I want that boat stopped too."

"You bet." Gage turned toward the staircase that led to the skydeck, his tread soft as he neared the top. Staying low, he looked toward the back of the deck, the area he couldn't see before from the corridor. A man in a waiter's uniform stood wiping crystal with a white cloth and holding it up to the light to inspect it.

All of a sudden Gage's gut tightened. Something didn't feel right. The baseball game still played on the deck above, but....

"Whoever you are on the stairs, please join us. I enjoy it when guests come to my yacht."

Gage's eyes met the cold eyes of the waiter. The man set the glass on the shelf along with all the others and folded the cloth, stowing it beneath the bar. Then he folded his hands and stood to the side.

"Please, don't keep me waiting." The voice that spoke held a touch of anger. If it was his yacht, it had to be Antonio Amato himself.

Gage moved on up the stairs and onto the deck. As the rest of the deck and its occupants came into view, his heart surged into his throat. *Oh, Lord, please no.* Antonio held Ruth against him, a gun to her temple. His arm wrapped around her middle.

Gage sought Ruth's gaze and found terror there, but her chin was up. Her lips trembled but she cast him the faintest smile.

Was she trying to reassure him? Of what? She was terrified, of that he had no doubt, but what did the smile mean? There it was again. And she held her chin up. She was a child of God. Was she trusting? Did she trust him? Gage? No way. He was just a man. No, she was trusting God. One thing he had picked up on in his short Christian journey was that God looked after his kids in life and in death. Perhaps that's what she was trying to tell him. She was terrified but also at peace with God.

Maggie sat in a chair in front of them looking just as terrified.

"I suggest you drop your gun, Mr. ...whoever you are. You know you aren't really a guest on my yacht. I didn't invite you." Antonio shoved the gun against Ruth's head a little harder, ripping at Gage's heart.

Ruth eyes squeezed shut and tears slipped down her cheeks, but she didn't make a sound.

Gage leaned down and placed his gun on the floor.

"Now kick it away." Antonio's voice raised. "I don't want to damage the goods here. I know you took my men, and I'm not happy with that. But I'll get them back, sell these girls, retrieve my money, then be on my way."

"I don't think so, Amato. The Coast Guard is out there to stop you. You have to know that."

Antonio lifted his chin. "Nobody stops an Amato."

"You mean like they didn't stop Big Tony Amato back in 1928?"

Antonio's features morphed into hatred. "The feds have always been after my family. Big Tony made mistakes. But I won't."

"Are you sure about that? Or are you just as arrogant as he was?"

Antonio kicked Maggie's chair. "Stand up."

Maggie jumped when he kicked the chair and she quickly got to her feet.

"You, uninvited man, move across to the railing over there. I'm taking these women down those steps and getting my men back on board."

With hands up, Gage slowly stepped to the other side of the deck.

"You'll never make it, you know. The Coast Guard will never allow it. They'll take you down, Amato."

"Yeah, yeah. You're starting to sound a bit redundant. What happened? Did that coward Lennie betray? Did he make the feds a deal of some kind? I haven't seen him around since this morning. I tried calling him and he hasn't answered. It's ok. My reach is far and wide. I'll find him. Even in prison.

"Move it." He shoved Ruth in front of him but never took his arm from around her nor the gun from her head. "You, too, Maggie. Head for the stairs and go down slow like."

~

Ever since Antonio had come back onto the skydeck, Ruth's heart had plummeted. She'd prayed and prayed that somehow she and Maggie would be rescued. When their guard had disappeared down the corridor to follow up on that strange sound they'd heard, he hadn't made a reappearance. She'd gotten her hopes up that maybe a rescue was underway. Then Antonio had come down from his baseball game. She could still hear the game playing on the upper deck and wished with everything in her that he'd return to it. But he wouldn't.

Instead, Antonio jerked Ruth from her seat and pulled a gun from his waistband beneath his shirttail and shoved it against her head.

A gasp of surprise had escaped her but she determined she wouldn't utter another sound if she could help it. *Lord, help me to be strong. I need some more of that peace that passeth all understanding.*

The pressure of the cold steel against the flesh of her temple made her insides quake. Ruth drew in a slow lung full of air and released it just as slowly then repeated the movement. She swallowed and continued to slow her breathing. Now was not the time for a panic attack. She had to keep her wits about her. For Antonio to be holding her in this position, he must know something she didn't.

Then he uttered the words she'd been hoping for.

"Whoever you are on the stairs, please join us. I enjoy it when guests come to my yacht."

Someone was here to rescue them or he wouldn't have her in this position. She watched the top of the stairs until Gage made his appearance. Her heart leapt with joy. As his gaze met hers, she tried to put her emotions on her face, but although Antonio couldn't see her expression, Miguel stood across the room and could see everything. She had to be careful

Gage's lips formed a slight grin before he and Antonio began sparing words. When Antonio jammed the cold steel of his handgun further against her temple, she closed her eyes against the pain and bit her tongue. No. She wouldn't utter a sound.

Lord, help us. Help us all to get out of this alive.

~

Gage watched as Antonio gave Maggie a shove to the head of the staircase, then pushed her. She tripped and fell down the first few steps. Anger ripped through him. He couldn't see her but from the sounds he could tell she hadn't fallen all the way down. Antonio had released Ruth but still held the handgun to her temple.

Just before they moved out of sight Antonio turned and his gaze met Gage's. He swung the gun in Gage's direction and fired. Gage dove behind a couch but even as he did, he felt a blaze of fire streak through his right side. Not good. He grabbed his side with his left hand and felt dampness. Glancing at his hand, his fingers were covered with blood.

Sucking in a deep breath, he looked around the side of the couch then over to the waiter standing by the bar.

"So, you're left here to guard me?"

The man lifted a hand and waved it toward the staircase. "Be my guest. I owe that man no allegiance. He has killed too many of my friends and holds me captive here when I only want to be with my family. Do what you must do. I won't stop you."

Gage eyed him for a split second then he took off, grabbing his gun from the floor as he went. The man tossed him a towel as he left the skydeck. Pain surged through his side, but he clamped his teeth together and moved on, cleaning his hand on the towel, he pressed it to his side. Rather than go down behind Antonio, he ran through the corridor and down the back stairs to the bottom deck. He'd left Casey there minutes before. Would he stop Antonio?

In the moments since he'd left Casey, the storm had moved in. It was raining now, the water had grown choppy, tossing the yacht about. Lightning flashed in the dark sky above them as thunder crashed and rumbled.

Gage cautiously stepped to the edge of the corridor where it opened out to the stern deck and saw Antonio standing with Ruth pulled against his rigid frame. He had his feet planted wide to steady himself on the rain-soaked heaving deck, his left hand around Ruth's throat, his right with the handgun to her head. Maggie stood two feet in front of them and between them and Casey. Casey's handgun was drawn and aimed in their direction, but from the looks of things, he had no clear shot with Maggie and Ruth as shields for Antonio.

"Where are my men?" Antonio shouted over the rumble of thunder.

"They're all gone, Amato," Casey's voice raised as rain dripped down his face. "They've all been picked up and are now in Coast Guard custody. It's just you now. Let these women go. You've already got enough murders and felonies to answer for. Don't add two more."

"I don't want to kill these fine ladies, officer. I only want to send them on their way where they'll bring happiness to others."

"And line your pockets with money. They can bring plenty of happiness right here with their own family. Drop the gun. Now."

The sound of a boat engine approached the starboard side of the yacht. Gage's heart plummeted. It had to be *My Pleasure* arriving to make the pickup for the girls. Why hadn't the cutter intercepted it?

"I don't think so." Antonio started to back toward the far deck railing just as a speed boat pulled alongside. He dragged Ruth with him.

Oh, no. He couldn't let her get off this boat.

"Maggie, come along now." Antonio's voice was a loud command. "I won't tell you a second time. You're not going to let your cousin go alone, now are ya?"

Maggie stood shaking her head as she stared at Casey.

"Stay put, Maggie," Casey ordered. "Don't move."

Gage had lost sight of Ruth and Antonio. His heart hammered in his chest. He took a quick peek around the corner of the opening of the corridor then stepped back. Antonio was moving closer to the railing, taking Ruth with him. *My Pleasure* was a good fifteen feet from *The Lucky Lady*. They had to do something and fast. Ruth was either going to be spirited away or die if they didn't.

Could he use the element of surprise and catch Antonio off guard giving Casey a clean shot, or would Antonio fire on Ruth anyway?

Dear Lord, this seems impossible. We need your intervention here.

At the same time a flash of lightning ripped across the sky and a crack of thunder boomed, a huge wave hit the side of the boat knocking everyone to the deck. Casey lost his grip on his handgun and it skittered away, landing in front of Maggie. Gage regained his footing and dove across the deck in time to see Antonio reach for Ruth but she had fallen to the deck and was scrambling away from her captor.

Maggie grabbed Casey's gun and whirled around on her knees to face Antonio just as he aimed his gun at Gage and fired. She fired at the same time, triple tapping at her erstwhile boss.

Antonio Amato fell backwards to the deck, his gun slipping from his fingers as crimson circles formed on his white polo shirt. The rain blended with the crimson, forming rivulets on the deck and washing them over the edge into the choppy ocean waters.

My Pleasure gunned her engines and took off but the Coast Guard cutter out matched her engines and blocked her way. Coy pulled up behind her blocking her from the rear with *The Sand Piper*. She was boarded and her occupants led away in handcuffs.

Thunder rumbled and cracked as Gage got to his feet and hurried to Ruth's side and, helping her up, he pulled her into his arms. "Are you alright, swee…um…Ruth?" To his delight she didn't struggle or pull away, but nestled against his chest. Oh, to hold her here forever. However, he didn't want to frighten her by holding her too long. Grasping her upper arms, he held her back so he could look into her dear features. As many times as he'd wanted to hold her in his arms, he'd never done so. He had to tread lightly until they talked. Oh yes, they *had* to talk. And still she might reject him. *Oh Lord, please don't let that happen. I love her.*

Ruth nodded, her teeth chattering. Rain dripped from her soaked hair over her face and down her chin. Even as warm as the day was, she had been through so much.

"Casey, we need to get these girls onboard the cutter and get them warmed up."

"Sure thing. Coy and Owen are helping transfer Amato's men to the cutter and Owen will be waiting onboard for them." Casey tipped his head in the direction of the coast guard ship that was anchored alongside the yacht. "I'll get someone over here to take this yacht in at the same time *My Pleasure* is towed in."

"Oh yeah," Gage snapped his fingers. "I almost forgot. There's a guy tied up in the engine room and a waiter is on the skydeck. I don't think you'll have any problem with him cooperating."

"Good to know."

Gage hurried over to help Ruth and Maggie as they prepared to board the Coast Guard Cutter. He dropped an arm around both Ruth's and Maggie's shoulders. "I owe you one, Maggie. You saved my life. He fired on me, but you got him first. Thanks for that, by the way."

Maggie patted his hand on her shoulder. "Nope, I think we're even now, copper. Remember? I told you I always pay back what I owe."

"Well, thank you." He looked down at Ruth. "I'm alive to…to pursue…well, to pursue what I hope will be a happy future."

Maggie cast a watery smile at him. "I'm sure you will, Gage. And for what it's worth, you've got my support. Come on Ruthie. I'm freezing in these wet duds. Let's go get warm."

Ruth nodded, her chin shivering as rain poured over her face. "Sounds like a wo…wonderful idea."

Gage handed them off to a Coast Guard officer then returned to where Casey was bent over Antonio Amato's prone body. Casey tugged something from Antonio's pants pocket.

"What do you have there?" Gage asked as thunder rumbled around them.

"Give this to Owen, okay? I think he might be happy to get it."

Casey handed him a wooden box and a velvet bag which Gage tucked into his wetsuit before they got too wet with the rain. "Will do. I'm sure he'll be thrilled to see these."

Gage put out his hand and shook Casey's. "Thanks for all your help, buddy. Couldn't have done all this without it. You know without the force of the Coast Guard behind me, I mean."

He chuckled and gave Casey a light punch on the shoulder.

Casey laughed. "Right, gotcha. Just the Coast Guard. Not me or anything like that."

Gage sobered. "Yeah, it was great having the Coast Guard behind me, but I'm thankful I had you as a friend at my back, Casey. Thanks."

Casey's face reddened as rain ran down his features and

plastered his hair to his head. "Hey, don't get all slobbery on me, okay?"

"Right, no slobber. Want to help me retrieve our gear from the ladder beneath this boat so we can get out of this storm?"

"You got it, buddy. Then I think you need to have that side looked at. Amato got you after all, huh?"

Gage ran a hand over his side and came away with blood on his fingers. "Just a graze. Nothing a large band-aid won't fix."

"Yeah, well, we'll see about that." Casey climbed down the ladder to retrieve the diving gear. "I have a great doc onboard who can take a look-see."

Chapter Twenty-Seven

Ruth and Maggie were checked out in the cutter's infirmary by the Coast Guard doctor, given a clean bill of health, dry surgical scrubs to wear and sent to the galley to be fed. Then he took a look at Gage's side, confirmed that it was a graze, cleaned it, bandaged it and sent him to join the others. Owen and Casey joined them in the galley.

"What are you eating?" Gage pulled out a chair next to Ruth at the table where she and Maggie sat devouring bowls of a tempting substance. "It smells amazing."

"Oh, it is." Ruth broke off a chunk of French bread and held it up. "It's beef vegetable soup. Sounds pretty commonplace, but I'm starving, and it's delicious."

Maggie nodded, swallowing a spoonful. "Yes, it is. And the bread tastes like homemade."

Casey grabbed a chair, turned it around backward and placed his arms along the top of the back. "That's because we have a great cook on this ship. I'm glad you're enjoying his fare. Gage, Owen. Help yourselves."

He lifted a hand and waved to a young man near the door to the kitchen and within minutes, bowls of the thick savory soup were placed in front of them as well as another basket of bread and butter.

"Thanks, Casey," Gage said, digging in.

After a few minutes of eating, Gage set his spoon down. "Thanks for grabbing my clothes from Coy's boat before he took off. I'd hate to have had to stay in my wetsuit the rest of the day."

"No problem." Casey waved his words away. "And I made sure he knew how much we appreciated his help in capturing the bad guys. He'll be compensated for his gas as well as given a civilian award for heroism in a time of great risk to himself and his property to rescue these ladies."

"That's great," Ruth said. "You all did a wonderful job of coming to our rescue. It was an all-around effort on everyone's part."

She reached for Maggie's hand and squeezed it. Maggie smiled at her.

"You were right, Cuz. You knew the Lord had something planned for our rescue. Who knew he'd send in the Coast Guard?"

Everyone chuckled.

"Since your brig is full of bad guys and you're hauling two boats into the Coast Guard Station, think it's time to call the FBI?" Gage asked. "They might want in on this, you know."

"Oh, I'm pretty sure they will," Casey said. "Now that we've done all the dirty work. They can breeze in, take over and claim the fame. I'll give them a call shortly."

"Right, but first things first. Owen," Gage pulled the box and the velvet bag from his cargo shorts pocket and laid them in front of Owen. "I believe you've been looking for these for a long time."

Maggie gasped, then she and Ruth exchanged a smile. Ruth turned her gaze on Gage. His pulse hammered as her smile spread her sweet lips. No inhibitions there at all. Could it be? She was smiling at him. At *him*. He felt his own lips tilt in a grin. He wanted so much to reach over and twine her fingers with his own, but would she withdraw? This was agony not knowing how to approach her. There had to be a reckoning time with her. And if she wouldn't have him, he would have to leave. There would be no way he could stay and see her day in and day out if she wouldn't.

Gage turned to watch Owen's response. He opened the box and exposed *La Cruz de San Mateo*. Owen's mouth hung open and he simply stared for a full minute.

"Dad?" Maggie shook his arm. "Dad, are you okay?"

Own nodded ever so slightly. "Yeah. I'm fine. I…I just…I never thought I'd ever lay eyes on it. Not really. It's…it's…well, it's simply amazing. It's beautiful."

"What are you going to do with it, Owen?" Casey asked.

Owen turned his gaze to Casey. "Why return it, of course. It belongs to the museum in Jamaica. Big Tony Amato stole it. It was never his to take. I'll return it to its rightful owners."

"Open the bag, Dad." Maggie pointed to the velvet bag.

Owen slipped the strings back on the velvet bag and dumped its contents into his palm. An array of precious colored gems sparkled in the galley lights.

"Wow, aren't those spectacular." He shoved them around with the tip of his finger. "I don't remember these being from Jamaica. They were never listed as stolen from the museum anyway."

"You mean you don't know where these came from?" Maggie asked.

Owen shook his head. "Not a clue. Big Tony could have picked these up anywhere."

"Then I'd say they're yours," Casey grinned. "A finder's fee, perhaps, for returning the cross to the Jamaican museum? What do you all say?"

Gage shrugged. "Sounds good to me. He's done all the work over the years trying to track that thing down."

"I think so," Ruth said.

Maggie patted her dad's shoulder. "Couldn't go to a better researcher."

Owen shook his head in awe. "I don't know what to say."

"How about, 'I'm going to open up a safe deposit box first thing Monday morning'?" Gage chuckled.

"You know, for nearly a century everyone thought the cross was at the bottom of the ocean," Ruth said. "They thought it went down with Big Tony Amato and *The Satisfaction*. Why do you think Big Tony buried the cross in the floor in his office instead of taking it with him on the boat?"

"In retrospect it's simple," Uncle Owen said. "He didn't plan to die. He wouldn't have taken it to sea with him. It would have been too risky to have it on the rum-runner. He was in a risky business and at any time, that boat could've been sunk."

"Why do you think he never confided in his nephew Howard?" Maggie leaned her elbows on the table.

"Again, he didn't plan to die. Howard was but seventeen when Big Tony died. He probably planned to tell him, but just hadn't gotten around to it. Mobsters were notorious for being arrogant and self-absorbed. Things were done on their time. Big Tony stayed away from Chicago and probably felt pretty safe down here."

"Makes sense," Gage nodded. "I'm just glad it's been found

and the mystery's been solved. Antonio Amato has been stopped along with some of his henchmen. With Lennie Campo's help we have names and addresses to put a lot of people out of business."

"I wonder what will become of his dynasty." Sadness filled Maggie's voice. "You know, the grand opening of The Brigand's Cove Hotel. Will they continue with it or cancel? And The Rusty Hook. I wonder if the renovations will just stop and the building once again rot away."

"Those are very good questions, daughter." Owen covered her hand and gave it a squeeze. "It would be a shame if it did."

"You know," Gage said, "it seems that Antonio Amato, the arrogant rich mobster, has come to an end just like his great-great uncle and name-sake, Big Tony Amato did. He said onboard the yacht this afternoon that no one can stop an Amato."

"Boy, was he wrong." Owen shook his head. "Casey, you and Gage have yet to tell me what you found on your dives. I know you found *The Satisfaction* because you found Big Tony's safe, but what else did you find?"

Casey and Gage exchanged grins. "Some pretty interesting stuff, actually. Want to share, Gage? You found most of it."

"Well, I found lots of broken and unbroken rum and liquor bottles as well as part of a board with the letters TISFACTI written on it. No doubt it's part of the name *The Satisfaction.* I also found a lot of clothing and shoes. Most likely where the bodies of crew members came to rest."

"Oh, how sad," Ruth said.

Gage nodded. "Yeah, it is. But ask Casey about the one he found."

"Well, Casey?" Ruth turned to him. "Tell us."

"Yeah, the one I found was especially interesting. I took a picture. Here, I had it transferred to my phone." He laid the phone on the table so they could take a look. "We believe this was the final resting place of Big Tony himself. It was a pinstriped suit and see the diamond tie tack? That was what he was known for. He never dressed without it."

"Wow." Maggie shook her head, tapping the table with her fingernail. "So that's the end of the great man himself. Just goes to show, you can't take it with you."

"You've got that right, daughter," Owen said. "These rich men have stocked up earthly riches and have left it all behind. He couldn't even sneak a little diamond into eternity."

"Nor Antonio a gold cross," Ruth said. "But they will answer for what they've done. I wouldn't want to be in their shoes on judgement day."

~

Monday morning found Ruth climbing the lighthouse. The storm had surged through the rest of Saturday evening and most of the day Sunday, but Monday had dawned beautiful and clear. Leaving her uniform hat on the old oil reservoir on the landing below the lantern room, Ruth stepped out on the black iron balcony. Immediately the ocean breeze whipped her ponytail around her neck and tendrils around her face. She folded her arms along the smooth rounded railing that was already absorbing the warmth from the sun. It was going to be a beautiful, warm day.

Ruth's gaze roamed over the horizon as she watched the waves roll in and morph into breakers as they prepared to hit the shore. Even way up here she could hear the crash as they broke along the sandy beach then pulled back out to sea, one after another. There should be lots of interesting things on the beach that the storm washed ashore. Beach combers would be showing up soon. Perhaps she'd take a walk later and see what she could find.

She closed her eyes and felt the warmth of the sun caress her skin. Drawing in a cleansing breath, she released it slowly. What a weekend it had been. This. This moment felt amazing. Up here far above everything. *Thank you, Father. Thank You again for bringing us through the storm. Both the weather storm and the one with the criminals. You saw us safely through them both.*

"Good morning," Gage's voice sent her pulse into overdrive. What was *he* doing up here? Her eyes popped open and she jerked her head to the left to find the object of most of her thoughts lately standing beside her, his arms folded on the railing next to hers.

"Oh, good morning." Did her voice sound too breathy? Uh yeah, it did. Was there a squeak at the end? She cleared her throat. "Um, what are you doing way up here?"

"I could ask you the same thing?"

Ruth glanced down to see he wasn't in uniform. "You're off today?"

"Yep." He nodded. "I decided since I've been working at the

seashore a few months now, maybe it was high time I finally climbed the lighthouse."

Ruth nodded. "Well, that makes sense, I suppose. I come up a couple times a week. Keeps me in shape, you know."

"I can see how that would be the case." Gage pointed out toward the ocean. "And the view? It's quite something."

"Yes, it is."

Ruth had the feeling they were just passing words back and forth and there was something beneath, another reason Gage was here.

Silence followed for several minutes.

Then Gage finally turned to her, jamming his hands into jeans pockets. "Ruth, we need to talk."

Ruth tugged her gaze from the view before her and turned to face the man who had come to mean so much to her. Far more than she'd wanted to admit, even to herself. Lifting her gaze to his, she nodded.

"I know. I owe you an explanation of...of some things."

His blue eyes held something in their depths that snagged her breath and held on. Her heart hammered in her chest and she swallowed hard. Her lips felt really dry. She licked them and his eyes followed the movement.

Gage took a deep breath and exhaled, ramming his fingers through his hair. He scratched his chin. Somehow, she suspected her presence affected him as much as his did her.

"Think we could take a walk along the beach and maybe have that talk now?" he asked. "You could always check your plover nests if you think you need to."

Ruth laughed as she turned back into the lighthouse. She grabbed her hat and headed down the spiral staircase, her steps ringing on the iron stairs. Gage was close behind, his rubber soles silent as they descended.

Once they were out of the lighthouse and walking across the grass toward the entrance Gage matched his longer stride to her shorter one.

"Want to drive down to the beach parking lot?" he asked.

Ruth shook her head. "No. It's far too beautiful a morning. Why don't we just walk?"

"Great." Gage gazed up at the clear blue sky then back at his companion. "You'd never know we had such a bad storm the last two days, would you?"

"Not really. But the shoreline is where you'll see the big difference. Storms have a tendency to wash up some interesting things as well as wreak havoc with wildlife nests and shift the sand dunes to name a couple of things."

Gage tossed his thumb over his shoulder at the lighthouse. "It would be interesting to know exactly how many storms that thing has seen and withstood."

"Wouldn't it though? Are you aware that it used to stand right over there?"

Gage turned a shocked look on Ruth. "Are you serious?"

"As a heart attack. See how much closer that circled area is to the water's edge? The beach was eroding and it was feared that the lighthouse was in grave danger of toppling, so in 1999, it, along with the lighthouse keeper's quarters were moved back to where they are today."

Gage looked at the empty, sandy beach area where the lighthouse and buildings once stood and where they now rested. "Wow that must've been a marvel feat of engineering."

"I imagine so. It was before my time, but I've studied the pictures and read how they did it. It was quite amazing. I'll be happy to loan you what I have on it."

They stopped on the wide entrance to the beach and Gage turned to Ruth. "Sure. I'd appreciate that."

Ruth met his gaze. Gage had something other than the lighthouse on his mind. He wanted to talk. About them. Her pulse rate picked up. It was time to tell him everything. *Lord, help me. Don't let the panic attack start. I have to get this out for Gage's sake.*

Ruth turned and started walking along the beach. It would be easier if they kept walking.

"Gage, this isn't going to be easy. Only a few people have known about this like Maggie, Uncle Owen, Casey and Bobbye, and of course a few others at the time it happened."

She took off her hat and held it in her hands, allowing the breeze to whip her ponytail wherever it would. Gage remained silent.

Ruth drew in a deep breath, released it all at once then

launched into her tale. "This happened just over seven years ago. Maggie and I were in college. She was a senior and I was a junior. We were roommates along with another young woman named Kelly. I was dating a guy named Frank."

Waiting for panic to ensue, she was thankful that the name didn't invoke the dreaded emotion.

"We had dated for over a year, almost since the beginning of my sophomore year. Nearing the middle of my junior year, he...he...um...."

"Ruth." Gage took her hand within his own large, warm one and it felt so good. She didn't want to pull away. She wanted to leave it right where it was within his reassuring touch. "You don't have to go on if you don't want to. We'll do this a little at a time."

With an adamant shake of her head, Ruth continued. "No, I'm...I'm going to get this out. We're clearing the air today. Right now."

She squeezed his hand but didn't let go. Ruth took another cleansing breath and released it. "I went out with him to a movie that evening. It was Saturday night. We'd gone out like that dozens of times. But when we came back to my room, instead of him leaving me at the door as he usually did, he wanted to come inside. I told him, no, that was out of the question. We never did that. We were dating steady, but nothing more. Ever.

"I said goodnight, unlocked my door and went inside but before I could shut the door, he put his foot in and blocked it. He...he, um, he forced his way in, and when he saw Maggie and Kelly weren't there, he," Ruth swallowed, her voice low and shaking as she spoke, "he forced himself on me."

~

Gage had entwined his fingers with hers while she spoke and gave them a gentle squeeze. He wanted to pull her into his arms and hold her, comfort her and protect her. But the damage had been done long ago. As gentle as he wanted to be with her, he wanted to find that guy and throttle the life out of him. Wisdom dictated that he remain quiet and let her talk. Let her continue her story until she'd told him all she wanted to tell him. He needed to be her sounding board at the moment. If she was ever to allow him to love her, she had to purge this demon that stood between them, and he had to be patient until she had.

Ruth responded to his gentle squeeze, then continued with her story. With her face straight ahead, she spoke in almost a whisper. He had to strain to hear her words over the growl and crash of the ocean waves.

"He forced himself on me, pushing me onto one of the bunks and trying to strip me and himself. I fought with everything that was in me to keep him from succeeding, but he was much stronger than I was."

Gage could tell that Ruth was seeing that moment in her mind's eye. Her features were screwed up with horror, and he wanted to stop her from reliving it, but if he did, it would always be there between them. He had to let her go on.

"I knew that he was going to rape me, and there wasn't anything I could do to stop him. I cried out to God to please put a stop to it. Somehow, someway."

Tears ran down Ruth's face now and she wasn't even aware of them, but as much as Gage wanted to draw her close and wipe them away, he let her continue. His heart ached for this woman who held it in her hands. Did she even know it?

"One thing I know beyond a shadow of a doubt," Ruth said, her voice growing stronger, "is that God heard my cry. Maggie and Kelly came into the room just then and stopped him. Maggie had pepper spray in her shoulder bag."

A corner of Ruth's mouth lifted at a memory. "She got him good, too. He couldn't find his way to the door. Couldn't even get his pants back up. He fell to the floor. She threw a blanket over him and called security. She may or may not have double sprayed him. None of us will ever swear to that in a court of law."

Gage stopped strolling and pulled Ruth into his arms. "Oh sweetheart. I don't have the right words for this because saying I'm sorry is more than inadequate. And saying I'd like to throttle him doesn't cut it either."

Ruth stiffened in his arms at first, but Gage just held her there as she didn't pull away. After several seconds, she began to relax and lean into him. His heart did a flip-flop then sang praise to God. *Thank you, Lord.*

After several minutes, Ruth stepped back, but Gage didn't release her completely.

"You don't have to worry about throttling him, Gage."

"Why is that?"

"Frank was the son of one of the university deans. When it came out what he'd done, because you can bet Maggie made sure it did, his father nearly lost his job. His father was going to send him away and he wasn't allowed to finish his college education. A month and a half after he…well, after the incident, he committed suicide. He hung himself in his father's home. But before that, he tried contacting me several times. At first, he tried blaming it on me and so did his father. They said I lured him into my room, but Maggie's and Kelly's testimonies at what they saw made short work of that. Then he tried contacting me to apologize and say that he loved me and wanted my forgiveness. Wanted to know if we could get back together."

"That took a lot of nerve."

Ruth shook her head. "I'm not sure what it was, but I'd dated this guy for over a year. How had I not seen something to indicate what his true colors were? How could I ever trust another man? For that matter, how could I ever trust my own judgement again?"

"And that's why you've always held men away, right?"

Ruth lifted her gaze to meet his. "Yes, it is. I'm terrified, Gage. I thought I knew him so well. He even told me he was a Christian, or I wouldn't have invested so much time with him. He went to church with me every Sunday. His parents went to a different church, but they went. He was raised in church."

"I don't know what to say about that guy, Ruth, except that it's possible he didn't truly know Christ. That's between him and his Maker. He'll answer for his actions and may already be doing so." Gage slipped a warm hand along Ruth's cheek. "All I know is that I love you with all my heart and I always will."

Ruth's features held awe intermixed with love and a newfound peace that hadn't been there before. "You mean that knowing what nearly happened to me doesn't bother you?"

Gage pressed a gentle kiss on her forehead. "Sweetheart, of course not. Had he succeeded in his endeavor, it still wouldn't have mattered, except that the selfish part of me would still have wanted to meet out justice. It would have been hard for me not to. But in my love for you? Never."

He tugged her closer and wrapped his arms tenderly around her waist. Just holding her there where she fit so well sent his pulse into overdrive.

Ruth dropped her forehead against his chest. With a finger beneath her chin he lifted her face.

"Look up, gorgeous. I've waited a long time to kiss those sweet lips, and I can't hold out much longer."

The color that flooded Ruth's features pleased Gage. If she did that for the rest of their lives, it would make him happy. He'd look for opportunities to make it happen.

Ever so slowly and gently Gage lowered his head, claiming her lips. He enjoyed the sweetness he tasted there and the softness beneath his own. It was heaven on earth as his lungs seized up. Oh, how he loved this woman.

With reluctance, he pulled away and opened his eyes. Ruth's eyes remained closed for a few seconds, and as they opened ever so reluctantly, she looked dazed.

"Wow," was the only whispered word that escaped her soft, reddened lips. Then she sighed with contentment. "I love you, Gage Hampton."

Gage hugged her to him where she rested her ear against his heartbeat. "Ruth, I can promise you that I'll always love you and care for you. I'll do everything in my power to protect you. Am I a perfect man? Not by a long shot. I'm bound to disappoint you sometimes. I'm human. But I'm a believer, and I've given my life to Christ. I'm learning what that means. It means to be Christ-like. That's my goal, so as a Christian, my goal is to be Christ-like. Are you willing to see where this goes? Think you can trust me?"

Ruth lifted her head from his chest and placed her hand on his cheek. "I'm not perfect either, my love. But did you notice when I was telling you my story that I didn't go into a panic attack? I'm growing and changing, and with God's grace and strength, we'll both become more Christ-like. And, yes, I can certainly trust you. You rescued me and time and again you've shown how trustworthy you are."

Gage lowered his head, aiming for her lips. "Well, I think we might need a little more practice on the kissing. We're a little behind on that part. What do you say?"

Epilogue

It was killing Gage to have the little velvet box in his pocket every night this week and not give it to Ruth, but he was determined to give it to her when the turtles hatched from the egg pit. It would be a lot more special to her. She'd told him that according to her calculations this was the week when the turtles would most likely be hatching and making their way to the ocean. He'd arranged with Wayne to work the afternoon shifts so he could be off every night to help her turtle watch. They'd taken the opportunity of their nightly watches to get to know each other better. If it didn't happen this week then Wayne said he'd work with him next week as well.

Since their walk on the beach several weeks ago he'd taken every opportunity to spend as much time with the woman he loved as possible. He intended to spend a lifetime with her, but he wanted her to grow more comfortable being with him.

"Any thoughts on whether you think this will be the night?" he asked as they climbed the dune hand in hand.

"I have no idea," Ruth shook her head. "The moon's pretty bright and it's over the ocean, so that's a good draw for once they're hatched, but who knows if they…"

Her words trailed off as they stopped near the top of the dune. There at the top, a few tiny turtles were working their flippers, trying to make their way through the sand. A couple more topped the dune and tumbled forward. Another one breached the top, then another.

"It's happening." Ruth's excited voice was little more than a whisper. "It's happening now."

She released Gage's hand and climbed the rest of the way to the top of the dune, Gage on her heels.

There they found a fountain of tiny turtles erupting from the sand and making their way to the edge of the dune.

"It's happening, Gage. It's happening." Ruth flung her arms around Gage's neck. "I've never seen this miracle before, but God's allowing us to see it."

Gage swung her around, his pleasure stemming from hers. Setting her back on her feet, he gave her a kiss square on the mouth.

"So, now what?"

"We keep the predators away. Seagulls and other birds will try and eat them, but we need to give these little guys a fighting chance. We can't do anything about the ones in the water, but we can between here and the water's edge. Let's go. And don't get between them and the moonlight. That's what draws them toward the ocean."

"Gotcha." Gage headed back down the dune and waved his arms as a bird flew up. He waved his arms to frighten the bird away. "Can't we just pick them up and put them in the water?"

"Oh, no, they need to build strength in their flippers between the egg pit and the water."

A steady stream of tiny turtles made their way across the sand toward the ocean, their flippers leaving imprints in the wet sand near the surf. Seagulls and birds congregated making it hard for Ruth and Gage to prevent any from getting to the tiny babies. A few were snatched, but with the two running back and forth waving their arms on either side of the turtle trail far fewer were taken.

This phenomenon took several hours before the last of the tiny creatures slipped beneath the waves. Gage and Ruth finally fell exhausted on the dry sand above the shoreline and leaned against each other.

"Wow, that was amazing." Ruth snuggled against Gage's side, his arm wrapped around her.

"Yeah, it was, but I'm glad it happened in the middle of the night."

"Why?"

"Because if anyone saw that, I'm sure they would've called a paddy wagon and hauled us off for having lost our freaking minds. They'd say the full moon had worked it's magic on us." Gage laughed. "We must've looked pretty idiotic running around out here all over the beach waving our arms and yelling at the birds."

Ruth laughed that musical laugh Gage loved so much, and when she was done, he tilted her face up for a kiss.

"I have something for you." He slipped his hand into his cargo shorts pocket and pulled out the ring box. With the full moon it was easy to see and when he opened it and gave it to her, the solitaire diamond sparkled in the moon's light. "Make me complete, Ruth Campbell, and please marry me. Will you?"

~

Ruth looked from the sparkling diamond to the man who held her in his arms. She loved this man with all her heart. In the many weeks since they'd declared their love for one another, they'd spent a lot of time getting to know each other and spent time growing in their relationship with Christ. There wasn't a doubt in her mind that a lifetime with Gage Hampton was where she wanted to be and where she felt the Lord was leading her.

"Oh yes. With everything that's in me, my answer is yes. Because I love…"

Gage's lips covered hers before she could finish her sentence. But that was okay. Because as they say, actions speak louder than words. And this was one action she hoped Gage spent a lot of time doing.

The End

Dear Reader,

If you enjoyed reading this book and want to help me to continue writing and publishing more books for your enjoyment, please take a moment to leave a review. They are very important to authors. We depend on them to let other readers know what they think about our books so they in turn will know whether or not to purchase and read them. Should you not care for it, I would appreciate an email to me rather than a negative review. And remember, the author has no control over prices, so please keep that in mind if you're not happy with the cost.

You can find me at Amazon, Goodreads and BookBub should you choose to leave a review.

Thank you again for reading my story. I hope you enjoyed it.

For His glory,

J. Carol Nemeth

A native North Carolinian, J. Carol Nemeth has always loved reading since childhood and enjoyed making up stories ever since junior high school, most based in the places she has lived or traveled to. She worked in the National Park Service as a Park Aid and served in the US Army where she was stationed in Italy, traveling to over thirteen countries while there. She met the love of her life, Mark Nemeth, also an Army veteran, while stationed in Italy. After they married, they lived in various locations, including North Yorkshire, England. They now live in West Virginia, where, in their spare time, Carol and Mark enjoy RVing, sightseeing and are active in their church. They have a son, Matt, who is Army 82nd Airborne and a daughter, Jennifer, her husband Flint, who serves in the Air Force Reserve, and three grandchildren, Martin, Ava and Gage. Their two four-footed kids are pretty special too: Haley, a white German Shepherd, and Holly, a black Lab. They love traveling in their RV, and when they pack up to go, the pups are waiting inside for them to head out.

Mountain of Peril, Faith in the Parks Book 1 - Buy Link
goo.gl/XMM32A
Canyon of Death, Faith in the Parks Book 2 Buy Link
goo.gl/1B8bSY
Yorkshire Lass- Buy Link goo.gl/uodShD
Dedication to Love - Buy Link goo.gl/WU9L22
Wilderness Weddings National Park Historical Collection - Buy
Link goo.gl/3SC8XZ
Prohibition Hearts – goo.gl/audwwC
A Beacon of Love – Buy Link goo.gl/vqTR7Q
A Soldier's Heart – Buy Link goo.gl/ZRD9Yf
A Soldier's Hope – Buy Link goo.gl/QvzkmG
A Soldier's Healing – Buy Link goo.gl/3czJun
Amazon Author Central – goo.gl/SHnk5H
www.JCarolNemeth.com
www.facebook.com/J.CarolNemeth
https://twitter.com/nemeth_jcarol
https://www.goodreads.com/author/dashboard
https://www.pinterest.com/WingedPublications/j-carol-nemeth/
https://www.youtube.com/channel/UCnUhQR2avhaC3Pb-
2nbozZg/videos
https://www.bookbub.com/authors/j-carol-nemeth

Monthly newsletter signup through my webpage or my Facebook
Author page